# RIGHT ON CUE

Tom McGonagle

ISBN: 1-4392-0387-3
ISBN-13: 9781439203873

I would like to dedicate this story to my wife Barbara, my two sons John and Ryan, my mom and dad, my brothers and sister and all my family members. I would also like to thank many of the great players and room owners that helped make up part of the story. Especially Boston Shorty, Ingy, Nick Vhalos, George Rippe, Gene Tivnan, Sy and Dolly and if I fail to mention your name it's because I could write another story thanking all of you. One last thank you goes to Peter Griffin his inspiration led to me writing this story.

# CHAPTER I

August 1998. A few months after the completion of the United States Open Nine-ball Tournament, ESPN televises the rerun of the last six matches. While one of the matches is being aired, twenty-three-year-old Johnny Jordan sits in his southern California home watching. He's a few weeks away from returning to college for his final year and has become very interested in the game of pool. He sits perched in front of the television with his elbows on his knees watching the match. One of the men involved in the match is Billy Bates; Johnny has fallen in love with the way Billy plays the game. Johnny is in such awe of the way Billy shoots that he calls for his mother as she comes up the stairs leading to the family room. He says, "Mom, you gotta come over and watch this guy playing pool. He's by far the best player I've ever watched play."

Elaine, Johnny's mom, has been going all day, and she is looking forward to watching something *she* might enjoy. But she humors her son and watches the pool match, which has him glued to the television. When she sits down in her usual seat, the younger man is at the table, not the player Johnny wants her to watch. Elaine starts to walk away, but the younger player misses a shot, and Billy comes to the table. She has a hard time believing her eyes. The older man looks familiar. She sits there thinking, *Can this really be him?* She goes as far as telling her son that the television needs to be dusted, and she gets her rag and cleans off the TV. She takes her time and gets a good look at the man. He's twenty-four years older than the last time she had seen him, but after one long last stare at him, Elaine knows that she knows this man. She refrains from blurting out the fact to her son. As she sits down, Johnny focuses on the pool match. She slips into the past and begins to recall the details of the first time they met. She falls into a trance as she starts to remember the vivid details of their brief affair in northern California.

In fact, as Elaine begins to recall, a game of pool was involved with their first encounter...

I was at a nightclub, minding my own business, when a loud, boisterous drunk began trying to make advances. The drunk was getting rude and obnoxious when Johnny, as he was known then, came to my rescue. Johnny told the drunk, "Set any shot on the pool table, within reason. If I make it, you will leave the lady alone." By the time Johnny and the drunk agreed on the shot, Johnny had the man settled down and a shot set up for himself, which he had made many times before. Without making a big deal, Johnny quietly made the shot, sending the drunk on his way with the impression that Johnny had done him a favor.

Johnny then turned his attention to me. I was impressed with the way he had turned a potentially ugly scene into a quiet departure. As he introduced himself, I thanked him for such a valiant and gracious rescue. Johnny said to me, "I was hoping to find a way to introduce myself to you. That guy did me a big favor." I sensed a big come on from Johnny, but it never happened. He was nervous and unsure of himself, a total change from the man who had just handled a tense situation with great ease. To say the least, I was confused; I was also interested in finding out more about my savior. I introduced myself to Johnny as Katie Starr. Billy Bates introduced himself as Johnny Ames. The fantasy of Katie Starr and Johnny Ames was ready to begin.

I told Johnny I thought he had made a pretty bold statement to the drunk about how he could make any shot the man set up on the table. Johnny explained to me how he manipulated the drunk into a shot he knew he could make without the drunk knowing his intentions. "It's the secret of being a hustler," said Johnny. "I make my living off people like him. I better be able to handle them."

I asked, "Are you hustling me?"

"I wasn't trying to. I learned the pool game real well. When I get to women, I'm usually behind the eight-ball, as they say. Besides, you usually don't tell the person what's going on. The only time you might let on that you're a hustler is if the person becomes offensive. Some people don't take too kindly to being hustled. I stick mainly to loudmouths and drunks. My favorites are the loud, obnoxious drunks who really think they're good pool players. I usually let them get to a point where everybody in the bar is sick of listening to them. Bragging about how good they are—that's when I step in. It usually doesn't take long for me to shut the guy up and take his money. Everyone in the place is on my side if any trouble starts. The last thing I want to do is start a fight. That's the problem with pool and alcohol; you never know who is just looking for someone to fight or someone to lose to."

"What do you mean 'someone to lose to'?" I asked.

"There are people who want to play, just so they can lose to you. I used to call these people my 'steady customers.' If you set up in one poolroom for a while, you'll probably find two or three of them around. They play knowing they are not going to win. The secret to playing these people is never embarrassing them in front of anybody. Accept the money they give you graciously. Tell them they could have won if they had gotten a few breaks. They not only go away feeling better, but usually come back again for more of the same treatment. I had one guy who came to play me twice a week for two years and never beat me. I made a big mistake one day—I let the guy beat me. We never played again. I found out later the guy just wanted to be able to say he had beaten me. The last thing you should do in a poolroom is try to figure people out. Most of them have logic only *they* can understand. A psychiatrist would have a field day in a poolroom." Johnny excused himself for rambling on so much. He said, "I didn't mean to carry on like that. I hope I didn't bore you. When someone asks me questions about hustling pool, I have a tendency to get carried away. It's the thing I know the most about, so I like to talk about it."

"I wasn't bored at all," I answered. "I find the whole thing rather interesting."

There is a lull in the conversation before Johnny asked me, "What do you do to keep busy?"

"I'm a junior at UCLA—my major is psychology."

"So you've been sitting there analyzing me the whole time. Am I going to be the subject of a research paper?"

"A psychologist is supposed to be able to get people to open up and talk to them. I'm glad that you told me so much about yourself and what you do. I was only trying to get to know you better. I didn't mean to let my job get in the way. Wasn't it you who used what you do best to meet me? Isn't turnabout fair play in your business?"

"I guess you're right. Maybe I'm a little too sensitive. I would hate to think I'm being hustled."

"Maybe you should consider what it feels like the next time you hustle someone."

"I don't hustle because I like to, I do it because it's what I do best and it puts money in my pockets."

It was getting late in the evening and a band started to play. The music was loud, and carrying on a conversation was difficult. Johnny asked me if I would like to dance. I accepted, and we went onto the dance floor. When a slow song played, I felt warm and secure in Johnny's arms. The mood of the evening began to swing. After a few glasses of wine, a few more dances, and some polite conversation, when the band takes a break, we relaxed and got to know each other a little more. Johnny was smart and witty and got me doing something I hadn't done much in years: laugh. When I decided it was time to leave, I asked Johnny if he would walk me home. Johnny paid our tab, and we walked across the crowded club towards the exit.

The evening air was chilly. Being in the mountains of northern California, the stars seemed touchable. The mountain background and a full moon created the perfect setting for a passionate evening. During the walk, we paused for a short time and shared our first kiss. The kiss was not long or overbearing. It set the tone for what we both knew we wanted from each other.

We started walking again, in the direction of my bungalow. The walk didn't take long enough to warrant any more conversation. When we reached the door, I asked Johnny to come in for another glass of wine. He accepted the invitation. "There's two beds here. I thought you were here alone?"

"I have a friend who I go away with every so often. We spend the days together, but, at night, we each go our own way. My friend is in search of any man she can find. She has managed to keep a perfect record of the last three trips we have taken together. She has yet to sleep alone. I don't think she'll come back here tonight either."

"We could go to my place."

"I'd rather stay here. Why don't you open the wine in the cooler and pour us a glass? I'll turn on the radio."

As we sipped the wine, the song, "Smoke Gets in Your Eyes" by the Platters began to play. Johnny said, "I used to love playing pool while listening to the Platters and other groups of the late fifties and early sixties. Their music contains a certain serenity. It has a way of alerting your senses." He took my hand, and we stood and began to dance. As our eyes met and our lips parted, the sensitivity of the moment began to overtake us.

I had never experienced a man such as Johnny before. I hadn't been with many men, but I knew this man holding me wasn't what I was accustomed to; he was taking his time. I felt my partners of the past had completed sexual acts before they started. This was the feeling I had hoped to experience with men before. As Johnny kissed my neck, I felt an aching and desire for him. When he started making further advances, I didn't discourage him. I began to unbutton my blouse and welcomed his warm, moist mouth onto the top of my breasts. When he unsnapped my bra, he slowly removed it and dropped it on the floor. I stood before him; my nipples were aroused as never before. Johnny saw this as an open invitation to pleasure them. Using his tongue and the tips of his fingers, he was able to keep both nipples fully aroused. I was filled with sexual desires I had never experienced before. All that remained was for each one of us to remove the rest of our clothing. With our clothing removed, we began to kiss each other passionately. I can still remember the words of the song, "When your heart's on fire, you must realize smoke gets in your eyes." After that line, he lowered me onto the bed. He continued to explore my body, caressing the tender areas until I could stand no more. Finally, I whispered to him, "Please, Johnny, please. Take me now." Any inhibitions I might have felt before were now lost in a sea of love. Johnny penetrated my body, and we became totally consumed in each other's sensuality. The love making lasted long enough for us to change positions more than once. I found myself on top of him, and I began to rub myself against his long, hard penis. At this time, I knew what people had talked about when they mentioned the word lover—Johnny brought me to an orgasm I didn't know existed. Earthquakes have smaller tremors than the one my body felt. The juices were flowing in me as never before. I expressed the way I felt to him openly and honestly. Then I collapsed on his chest.

Knowing he had satisfied my needs, Johnny flipped me over and slowly built his body to where he wanted to be. The fluids my body had produced made it easy for him to move in and out of me at a faster pace, and he responded to the pleasure he was feeling. His body reached the point of no return, and he sent a warm injection deep into my body. The love making continued until both of our bodies were spent, then we collapsed into each other's arms. I lay back wishing I had been honest from the beginning. How was I to know this might have been that special someone?

After a shower, he convinced me to try some Vietnamese marijuana. After smoking, Johnny began to touch me and aroused my interest once again by massaging my body; this eventually led to another round of making love. When we finished, we collapsed into each other's arms; the alcohol and grass helped us fall into a deep sleep until morning.

We woke to the sound of birds chirping. Words weren't as easy to find as the previous night. We stumbled in an attempt to break the ice and begin a new day. The conversation was light and polite through breakfast. I went to take a shower after breakfast. I wanted to invite Johnny to come along, but I decided to use the time to be alone. Maybe I could figure out a way to explain why I lied about my name.

While Johnny sat waiting for me to finish my shower, the front door suddenly turned into total mayhem. From outside, Johnny heard someone trying desperately to open the door. All he could hear was a young girl cursing the lock and banging on the door. She was also talking aloud. "I have to piss so bad I can taste it!" The rest of the talk was basic cursing. While the girl was still trying to get the door to open, Johnny unlocked the door from the inside. As he did this, Cindy flew halfway into the room and landed flat on her ass. The crash caused her pocketbook to fly open and its belongings to empty all over her. Without missing a beat, Cindy jumped to her feet and yelled at Johnny, "Who the fuck are you? Where the fuck is my roommate? Am I in the right bungalow?" she asked.

"Your roommate is in taking a shower. Maybe it's best if she explains."

Cindy walked to the bathroom saying, "I've gotta take a wicked piss anyway."

As she opened the bathroom door, I was stepping out from the shower in deep thought. As I turned my head, I saw Cindy standing in the bathroom with me. Totally not expecting anyone to be in the bathroom, I let out a small scream and grabbed a towel to cover myself up. After a few seconds, I realized who it was and we burst into laughter about the situation.

"Cindy," I said, "I didn't think you would be back so early."

"I did it again, Elaine; I went to bed with another of my long list of fucking assholes. This guy was enough to turn any woman against men. He came on like he was some kind of Superman. The only thing that he and Superman had in common is they both were faster than a speeding bullet. I don't know why I bother with people at these places anyway. All they're after is a quick hop in the sack. I'm the idiot because I provide it for them. It looks like you had some fun last night. Maybe I should come back early more often. All this time I thought you were being faithful to Cliff—"

"—Believe it or not, this is the first time I've slept with anyone but Cliff for over two years. By the way, my name is Katie Starr."

"The same Katie Starr you hated in high school, and the one that followed you to UCLA and flunked out last semester?" said Cindy.

"It was the only name I could think of at the time. I wasn't sure I was going to like this guy. I'll explain later. Now get the hell out of here and let me get dressed. Entertain Johnny for me for a while." As Cindy opened the door, I whispered, "I feel like a little girl again, Cindy. I think I found what you came to look for."

I hurried to get ready. *There are two more days in which to explain why I lied about my name. Surely the right time will come.* I put on jeans and a red blouse. I left the bathroom and came into the kitchenette where Cindy and Johnny were making small talk. As I entered the kitchen, Cindy turned away from Johnny and winked at me saying, "Katie, are you two spending the day together?"

"I hadn't thought about it, Cindy. What do you think, Johnny?"

"I have been thinking about going on a picnic in the mountains. I know a nice place about an hour from here. If you're interested, I could go to my place and shower and shave while you pack a lunch for us."

I told Johnny, "Sounds like fun, but I'll have to go to the store for some things. Why don't we meet back here in two hours?"

As Johnny started out the door, he turned and kissed me, then he said, "You might want to bring a bathing suit. There's a nice place to swim where we're going." With that, Johnny walked back through the woods to his own bungalow.

When Johnny returned, Cindy and I were sitting outside the bungalow. Lunch was packed, and we were taking pictures. Cindy told Johnny to come and pose with me in front of the bungalow. After the picture was snapped, Johnny and I headed for the parking lot with our lunch packed in my cooler. When I got to Johnny's car, I liked what I saw. A mint, 1965 GTO, metallic blue with mag wheels, and a four speed; I always liked fast cars.

I said, "A friend of mine back home has a GTO. He races his at Pomona. Do you race, Johnny?"

"I won this car in a pool game. The guy I was playing wanted a chance to get even with me. I made him put up the car as collateral."

"You won a car in a pool game? I didn't realize people would bet so much on a game of pool."

"It took me two days of playing before I broke this guy, and the only thing left for him to bet was the car. When people reach the point of desperation, it's amazing the things they will bet. The thing to know is how much you can win before you play someone. You don't want to lose your money to someone who's only taking a shot at you."

"A shot at you?"

"A guy who's willing to lose only a hundred dollars if you're willing to lose a thousand. The odds are too big in his favor. You have to be very careful who you play in this business." We were now in the car. The engine started with a mighty roar. "I'll explain more about the game of pool to you some other time. Why don't you sit back and enjoy the ride?" Without another word, Johnny accelerated from the parking lot. The power of the car snapped me back in my seat each time Johnny shifted gears. I enjoyed the power and speed of the car. As we headed up into the mountains, I put my hand over Johnny's while it rested on the shift. We looked look into each other's eyes as the wind blew through our hair. All that mattered was the spirit of this moment.

The ride on the highway lasted about forty-five minutes. Johnny turned onto a secondary two-lane road. He stayed on this road another ten minutes until he came to a narrow dirt road leading to what looked like nowhere. Very thick underbrush made for limited visibility. I was skeptical of what lay ahead. Johnny pulled into a clearing that possessed one of the most beautiful waterfalls I had ever seen. The water overflowed into a series of smaller pools. From there, the smaller pools of water overflowed into a stream that flowed down the mountain.

I said to Johnny, "This looks like something you would see in a Tarzan movie. How did you ever find it?"

"A girl who used to work at the resort brought me here. She grew up around here. She ran off with a cook about three months ago. It's funny how people think there's a better place somewhere else."

"Are you looking for a better place, Johnny?"

"I'm looking to have a picnic with a beautiful woman right about now. Why don't we unpack our things and get started?"

I sensed Johnny was having mixed emotions about his life. I didn't push the issue.

As we spread a blanket, Johnny told me the water in the pools came from underground springs in the mountain. It wasn't as cold as it could be, had it come from the snow that was melting at the top of the mountains. He said, "I don't like to swim in really cold water. I went swimming in the ocean in Maine when I was about twelve years old. I put my feet in the water, and it was so cold, my ankles went numb. I couldn't swim there."

"What were you doing in Maine?"

"My father brought us to Maine quite often. He would try to hustle pool all over the state. People in Maine love to shoot pool, my father always said."

"Where did you grow up?"

"Anywhere and everywhere. We never stayed in one place for a long time. My father was in search of the ever-elusive 'big score' as he called it. He dragged my mother and sister and me around the country looking for something he could never find."

"What makes you say that?"

"My father didn't have the talent or guts to play the best. He made his money from the small timers. He was afraid to step up and play with the big boys. The little money he was able to win he usually lost back once he started drinking." Johnny was silent for a moment before picking a wildflower and handing it to me. "Let's talk about something else. Why don't we get into our bathing suits and go for a swim?" Johnny, once again, shut the door to his past in my face. I didn't press the issue, again. We changed and headed for the water; we dove from a rocky plateau. We swam for a short time, then as Johnny had his back to me watching the waterfall I decided to get a little promiscuous. I took my top off and swam underwater towards him. I surfaced close enough to him to yell so he could hear me. Exposing my breasts, I yelled, "Hey, big boy, think your fast enough to catch me before I get to the other end?" He turned and saw what I was up to. He began a hot pursuit of his prize. I made the chase long enough to create excitement; I even pretended to fight him off when he caught up to me. We began to kiss passionately. He suggested we make love in the water, but I had other ideas.

"Why don't we go back to the blanket, Johnny? I have some baby oil for our skin, and we can put the oil on each other." As Johnny started to head back for our suits, I told him, "Leave them where they are. I've always wanted to be this secluded with someone so I could walk naked. This moment may never come again. Why don't we be daring, Johnny? We weren't ashamed last night. I want this to be just as exciting." We emerged from the water, hand in hand, and ran together to the blanket. We pulled the sides of the blanket around ourselves to dry off a little. After a few minutes of squirming around, we decided the blanket was too small to cover us. We exposed ourselves and applied oil to the sensitive parts of our bodies. With Mother Nature as our only witness, we made love again.

I said to Johnny, "I've never been with anyone who makes me feel more alive. Go get our suits and I'll unpack our lunch. I hope the rest of the day is as exciting as the beginning."

"I can't make any promises, Katie. This would be hard to top." He got up and got our suits, while I wrapped the blanket partially around myself. He teased me slightly before giving me back my suit. I enjoyed Johnny's teasing. He had a nice laugh and smile. Life had been too serious for too long for me.

While eating lunch, I asked, "Why did you bring me here? You couldn't have planned on what happened."

"Did you ever see the movie, *The Hustler?*"

"No."

"Well, Paul Newman took Piper Laurie on a picnic in the movie. It was the best part of the movie. Paul Newman, 'Fast

Eddie Felson,' explained to his girlfriend what the feelings of a pool player are really like."

"Are we just here so you can live out the fantasy of your favorite movie? Is that all it meant to you? Can't you do anything without involving the game of pool as part of your motive?"

"Pool has been the best part of my life. I'd hate to have to tell you some of the other things I've experienced. It might ruin the rest of the day."

"We're here, Johnny. Why don't you tell me what it's like? I'll be Piper Laurie. Tell me what you feel."

"Eddie talked about—"

"I don't want Eddie's version, Johnny; I want yours. Tell me your thoughts, your feelings. Describe it to me, *Johnny*; I want to know what it's like."

Johnny started out slowly. "The game of pool is a game that demands total concentration. The better the concentration, the more in tune you become, and the deeper it gets." I felt Johnny begin to remove himself, consciously, from where he was. He began to speak as if in a trance; his mind was no longer his own. He said, "Once you have reached total concentration, the game is no longer a game. It's like the time I was in Boston with my father. We went to the Esplanade for the fireworks. The Boston Pops orchestra was led by Arthur Fiedler. He was in front of the orchestra looking like a man possessed. Every time he called on any of his players, he got the immediate response he was seeking. A pool player and a symphony conductor have a lot in common. The conductor uses his baton to call upon different instruments at the precise time he needs them. A pool player, when his game is in total synchronization, will use his cue stick in the same manner. Whatever he may ask the cue-ball to do, he will always get the response of a finely tuned instrument. The pool player uses his cue-ball to orchestrate his own symphony. The precision involved can only be appreciated by those who are doing the orchestrating. It's the sensitivity, feeling, and timing involved that people tend to overlook in a great performance. The truly great players know the experience I'm talking about."

I started to tap Johnny's shoulder to bring him back from the state he has been in...

Johnny is tapping his mother on the shoulder, bringing her out of her trance.

"Where'd you go, Mom?"

"The player on TV just reminded me of someone I grew up with. Who's winning, anyway?"

"The younger player, Rico something, has taken over the match," says Johnny. "He's in the process of humiliating the older player. He keeps taunting him more with each rack he wins. I never realized how ugly some people can get during a pool game. The announcers said these two were best of friends at one time. The younger player is a prodigy of the older man. They say he taught him everything except manners. They parted ways some time ago. The younger player is now calling him a loser: 'No wonder your name is Billy "The Bridesmaid" Bates. You're nothing but a second-place finisher. You never have and never will win a major title. That's the reason I got away from you. You could teach me how to play, but you could never show me how to win.'"

The young man is shooting the final balls to win the match and the tournament. Billy Bates sits with his head down taking more abuse. As he lines up his final shot, the young man walks past Billy and states, "This is the one shot you never get to shoot." The young man takes a little extra time. Again, he starts with a speech, "This is the final nail, Billy," he says. A voice from the crowd calls out to stop all the extra nonsense. "We came to watch a pool game, not a funeral," the voice cries out. The younger player comes up from shooting. Given a chance to humor the crowd, he answers, "I thought my opponent would show a little more life than he did. Therefore, I treated him as a corpse." Again, the young man goes into a shooting position. This time, he pockets the nine-ball and wins the tournament. The crowd is applauding as the younger player takes his victory walk around the tournament area. As this is going on, Billy Bates still sits with his hands covering his face. The crowd is chanting the young player's name. The sounds of "Rico, Rico" fill the room.

As Johnny and Elaine watch, Johnny feels sympathetic towards Billy. "How can these people only care about the winner here? Doesn't finishing second mean anything?"

"It's a little like a bullfight. One person feels the pain of the bull, the other the glory of the matador. The crowd just acts accordingly." Elaine turns towards the television. The camera is focused on Billy. His head is still down, with his hands blocking his face. She takes the remote and shuts off the TV. Billy uncovers his face as the picture fades. She feels the pain on Billy's face in her heart. She has seen this look before. His face fades on the set. It is after midnight. Elaine makes her way to the bedroom. Her husband is away at a convention. She lay in bed, and Billy's face comes back in her mind. She tosses and turns a good part of the night. Finally, she falls asleep. Her dreams tell the rest of the story about Johnny Ames.

After bringing Johnny back to reality, our picnic was suddenly interrupted. The mountain air changed quickly and the skies were threatening. We gathered up our belongings and headed for the car. Johnny hurried to put the top up on his convertible. I put the picnic basket and everything else into the back seat.

The rain began to pound the roof of the car. The skies completely opened up with a mid-afternoon shower. We were a blur inside the car. The windshield wipers were working at full speed. He drove away from our secluded paradise. What was a bright, sunny beginning became a dark, gloomy end.

I spent the ride back to the resort regretting my deception. If only the would-have-beens and the should-have-beens had started differently—I never anticipated falling in love. The car sped along the damp highway, back towards the resort area. I remained secluded in thought for most of the ride back. Johnny broke the ice and asked me, "Will I see you tonight?" I wanted to be alone for a few hours, so I told Johnny to call me in a few hours and we could decide what to do with our final evening together. Johnny respected my need for privacy and dropped me at my bungalow. I kissed him lightly on the lips through his open window. As Johnny drove away, I turned toward my bungalow, tears filling my eyes. I ran inside to my bed and buried my head in my pillow. I was still crying when Cindy came in.

Cindy rushed to my side. "What did he do to you? What's wrong, Elaine?"

I turned to Cindy, tears flowing from my eyes. Sobbing as I spoke, I told Cindy, "He didn't do anything. It's all my fault. I couldn't tell him the truth. I've fallen in love with a man who doesn't even know my real name. How can I expect him to ever believe me?"

"If he loves you, he will understand. Why don't you tell him tonight?"

"I've waited too long. He's very sensitive. He'll think that I've used him. He doesn't seem to trust many people. I need some time to figure this out. I'm going back to the school. Can you get a ride back, Cindy? There are plenty of people from school up here."

Cindy assured me that she would have no problem finding a ride.

Hurriedly putting my things together, I told Cindy, "Tell Johnny I have a family emergency and must return home. Tell him I will be back in a few days." I finished putting everything into the car. I left the resort area and headed for the highway. As I came to a stop to enter onto the highway, a sign read "Aden 80 miles." I had an aunt that lived in that town; I had always told her my problems as a child. Instead of turning left and heading back to school, I turned right and headed up the highway towards Aden.

Cindy later told me, "Johnny came back to our bungalow a few hours later. He noticed my car was missing and started to call out for me as he approached. I came to the door and tried to explain to Johnny what happened. Johnny told me that I was lying and insisted on knowing the truth. I asked Johnny to sit down, have a cup of coffee, and I would talk to him about you. He settled down and took me up on my offer.

"My exact words were 'I know Katie will hate me for telling you this, but she is engaged to be married. She's been engaged to this guy for more than four years. He keeps stringing her along and making excuses to set a wedding date. It's one of those teenage relationships that start out in high school and continues through college. I don't know why she stays with this guy. He basically treats her like shit, cheats whenever the opportunity is there, and has an ego as big as Alaska. The big problem that Katie has is that their parents are best of friends. This is a kind of modern-day pre-arranged marriage. Another problem is he is wealthy and studying to be a doctor. We are talking a little security for the future. I know Katie likes you an awful lot, Johnny, that's why she has gone to think about her future. Would you be willing to give up everything she has going for a person you hardly know? These are the things she's trying to sort out right now. Why don't you give her the time she needs? She will be back in a few days. Katie has never lied to me. There is no reason for her to start now.'

"Johnny then told me, 'I guess she does have a lot weighing on her mind right now. I will try to wait, but, I'm not that patient when I have to sit around. I hope I can last. What if she doesn't come back? Am I supposed to just forget about the past few days? Why don't you at least give me her address? If she doesn't return, I'd like to at least go to her and tell her my feelings for her. I think I deserve that much.'

"I think about it for a minute. *Katie doesn't lie, so telling her address won't make any difference.* I give him your address at the sorority house in East Los Angeles. He pauses and says that he'd better write it down. 'It's too big of a city to start looking for someone and I'd hate to forget it.'

"So I hand Johnny a paper and pen and repeat the address. He writes it down and puts the paper in his wallet. He gets up from his chair and thanks me for the coffee, address, and the truth in that order.

"What Johnny did that night I don't know. The next morning he came by my bungalow and left me a note. *Sorry, Cindy. I can't wait. I'm going to find Katie. I'll tell her I made you give me her address. Please forgive me, Billy.*

"I woke hearing the sound of Johnny's loud engine. I heard the screen door shutting as I rushed to get my robe on. Johnny was too fast for me. As I opened the door, Johnny's car was heading up the dirt road towards the highway. I ran with the note in my hand, yelling, 'Katie's real name is Elaine Crawford!' I know he saw me in his rear view mirror, but continued on his way. I stopped my pursuit at the top of a small hill."

# CHAPTER 2

The next few weeks continue in the same fashion as the past few months. Johnny's father, Dr. Clifford Jordan, Chief Surgeon at Belleview Hospital in Beverly Hills, California, is constantly arguing with him about his future. His father is insisting he go on to medical school after completing his college education. Johnny simply doesn't have the desire, ambition, or ego to be his father's protégé. Living in the same house with his father has been hard enough all these years. How could he work with this man and be under his constant scrutiny for many years to come? The master plan Johnny's father had laid out for him includes his eventual replacement. Most children would have been honored to have their father wanting them to walk in their footsteps. Johnny knows his father wants these things for himself, and not for Johnny. Anything else would be unacceptable in his social circle.

In the meantime, Elaine keeps busy trying to track down Billy Bates. ESPN had shown the match again on TV, and Elaine had taped it. She has made several phone calls, and through the Professional Pool Player Association located in Florida, found out that Billy is living in Lexington, Kentucky, and owns a bar called *Stripes and Solids*. She tells them she wants Billy's address for his class reunion. She also tells them she has seen Billy on TV and wants to make sure he receives his invitation.

From time to time, Elaine puts the tape of Billy playing pool into her VCR, constantly stopping the action to examine Billy. The years have brought about a few changes in his appearance, comparing it with the picture Cindy had taken of them in the mountains. His hair is now salt and pepper, he sports a moustache, and is about twenty pounds heavier. Staring at Billy's face, she feels the emptiness of a fisherman who has let the big one get away.

Facing the toughest decision she has ever had to make, Elaine knows she has to tell Johnny about his real father. The problem is, how and when to tell him? The next few days help Elaine solidify her decision. The bickering between Johnny and his father is getting ugly. Cliff knows Johnny has spent a great deal of time at Razz's poolroom and he resents the fact he's paid a ton of money to further Johnny's education. He lays into Johnny Tuesday night after dinner when Johnny states his intentions of meeting friends there later that night.

"Why don't you just move in the poolroom along with the rest of your loser friends? The only time we see you anymore is when you get hungry and there's a free fuckin' meal sitting on the table for you."

Pushing aside his plate Cliff stands, comes at Johnny and pushes him firmly in the chest. Johnny doesn't bend much and he comes back and pushes Cliff even harder. Both men raise cocked fists before Elaine jumps between the both of them. They're both strong willed, and Elaine knows they may someday throw punches.

She screams fearing this may be the time they go too far, and tells Johnny to leave and go meet his friends.

"That's right, Elaine. Tell your little boy to run away from his problems. Mommy will fix everything for him. She always has, and she always will. I'm out of here myself. I'll be at the country club."

This is the final straw. Elaine figures if Johnny goes to Kentucky to look for his real father, they can tell Cliff he has returned to school. It's the basic "out of sight, out of mind" theory. Elaine notices her husband has a three-day convention in San Francisco starting on Monday. With her husband away, the opportunity to talk alone with Johnny will be easier. Hopefully, during the next few days, Cliff and Johnny won't kill each other.

The next few days go by less eventfully. Cliff spends most of his free time at the country club. Johnny is with his friends at Razz's. This provides Elaine a little quiet time. It's better than refereeing pushing and shouting matches between a father and "son."

Elaine has also confided in her psychologist and has told him the dilemma she is facing. The decision hasn't been an easy one. Elaine feels she owes her son the truth. Knowing the whereabouts of his father has made her choice easier.

One more person also knows what's going on—Cindy, her best friend. She was the only other person who had known the truth all along about Johnny's real father. Elaine brings the tape of Billy playing pool to the Saturday afternoon bridge game at Cindy's house. A totally unsuspecting Cindy comes out with a typical Cindyism; she tells Elaine, "Why the hell don't you go find him? You're the one who always told me he was the only man who made you feel like a complete woman. Go for it yourself, Elaine; Johnny might scare him off."

"I had my chance. Johnny deserves the same opportunities. I hope he doesn't resent Johnny because of me."

Cindy tries to convince Elaine it wasn't her fault she and Johnny were separated. "After all, the son of a bitch was lying about his name. What's his name anyway, Billy 'The Bridesmaid' Bates? What's this 'Bridesmaid' mean, anyway?"

Elaine explains to Cindy that it's his nickname. "I guess he's famous for finishing second. I don't think it's a very flattering name."

Cindy reaches out her hand to Elaine. "Maybe this time will be different. You and Johnny may be the parts he has missed to be a winner. Keep me informed. It will help us get through these boring bridge games every week." Elaine looks at her watch and finds the time is getting late. She tells Cindy, "I have to get going. I'm meeting Cliff at the country club for dinner."

Returning home, Elaine hurries to get herself ready for another typical Saturday night at the country club. For the past fifteen years, she has dragged herself to these overstuffed, boring dinner parties. It hasn't been easy watching the same drunks get drunk every Saturday night. Having the same men try to hit on you and telling the same women how lovely they look when you know damn well they are forty pounds overweight and homely as hell. This is all part of the social expectations of the chief surgeon's wife.

Arriving at the country club at 7:45, Elaine has the valet park her car and hurries into the lounge to meet Cliff. It's not a pretty sight when Elaine walks in. Cliff has spent the afternoon trying to hustle the new barmaid. He is all over her. Elaine spends the next half hour trying to drag her husband home. It's been a while since Cliff has been *this* bad. Elaine apologizes to the barmaid for her husband's behavior. "Just because he spends about $2,000 a month here doesn't mean you have to tolerate this kind of behavior. Next time this happens, treat him like a bum on the street. Call the cops."

The valet has to help Elaine get Cliff into the car. He tries to apologize to Elaine and sucks up to her as she starts to drive away from the country club. Elaine asks, "What happened to your good friend, Dr. Silva?"

"He got beeped on the third hole for emergency heart surgery. It was his weekend for coverage."

"So you decided to spend the day trying to make it with the new barmaid? I thought we'd outgrown this kind of behavior, or at least agreed you wouldn't carry on in public like this anymore? I don't care what you do when you go off on your business trips, but for God's sake, couldn't you have the decency not to humiliate me at the same place you expect me to have dinner with you every Saturday night?"

"The booze and the long wait for you." He tries to put his arm around Elaine, and she pushes aside his advances.

"This is the last time, Cliffy baby, and this time I mean it. I won't stand for this anymore."

Cliff turns toward the window murmuring to himself, "Ya, ya, same old threats." He curls up in a ball and starts to pass out from the alcohol.

"I mean it, Cliff; this is the last time."

While driving, Elaine starts thinking about Billy. She wonders what it would be like meeting him again. Would Billy want to see her again? What if he's happily married and has eight kids? This could change everything. The only thing it won't change is her telling Johnny the truth. It's just a matter of time. He has the right to know about his real father. Pulling her car into the driveway, she reaches for the remote and opens the garage door. Cliff is curled up in a ball and snoring. Having lived this same scenario many times, Elaine leaves Cliff in the car and goes inside. She's hungry so she makes herself a salad and goes into the family room. She watches a movie. During the movie, Elaine makes herself a couple of drinks and relaxes, soon feeling the effects of the alcohol. The movie is a love story with a happy ending. Elaine wishes her own story could have been different, and she cries when the movie ends. She ponders her thoughts of Johnny (Billy Bates) while she goes to the bedroom to get his tape and watch the match again. She sits there bubbling every time she sees Billy; her one true love has possibly come back into her life. She closes her eyes and remembers Northern California. She snuggles under a blanket on the recliner, deep in her thoughts, and drifts off to sleep...

It's about one o'clock in the morning when Johnny comes home from being with his friends. He pulls into the garage and spots his father sleeping in his car. It's an all-too-familiar scene to Johnny. He goes into the house and makes himself a sandwich. He decides to go upstairs and watch a little TV before going to bed. As Johnny heads toward the family room, he sees the changing of light coming from the room. *A typical Saturday night at the Jordan's. Dad's passed out in the car; Mom's fallen asleep watching TV.*

Light always affected Johnny's ability to fall asleep, so he decides to turn the TV off and go to bed. As he reaches to turn off the TV, he notices his mom has been watching a tape. He decides to take the tape to his room, having no idea what was on it. After rewinding and hitting play, the pool match he had asked his mother to watch suddenly jumps out at him. He suspected his mother was more interested in the match than she had let on. She had sat there glued to the television watching the pool match. He decides to confront his mother in the morning as to why she had made the tape.

Arguing can be heard by Johnny as he comes downstairs for breakfast. Cliff is hung over and in no mood to listen to Elaine tell him she will no longer come to the country club on Saturday or any other time. Johnny comes into the kitchen as Cliff tells Elaine, "Fuck you, fuck this! I don't have to spend my day off listening to your bullshit. I'm out of here." With his stomach turning, Johnny takes the easy way out and goes back upstairs to eat. He knows it's just a matter of time before his father will slam the door and walk out. Johnny hears his father's car start and the garage door open. His car is squealing its tires as he drives away. He waits for a while before coming downstairs. His mother is sitting at the kitchen table with tears running down her cheeks. In an effort to change the mood, Johnny takes the VCR tape out of his pants pocket. "Hey, I found this in the VCR last night. Since when do you like pool? I've never heard you say a word about it. You could have told me the truth."

Grabbing a few tissues, Elaine gets up from the table and begins to walk around the kitchen floor. "It's funny you should mention the truth. When people lie, it can affect them the rest of their lives." Elaine stops walking around for a moment. Taking the Kleenex, she wipes away the tears from her face as new tears begin to form. She is quick to catch herself from falling apart. Johnny sits somewhat confused. "I haven't told a lie in twenty-four years about anything important, Johnny. The last time I lied, it cost me a little too much. It's time you found out the truth." Starting out, Elaine says, "I could tell you I taped it for your birthday and you'd probably believe me." Elaine begins to nervously pace the floor; she's stalling to collect her thoughts. She reaches for the pot of coffee and pours herself and Johnny a fresh cup. Johnny notices her hands trembling. She says, "I think I better sit down for this." She pulls up a chair beside her son and starts to tell him the story of Johnny Ames and Katie Starr. She takes her son's hand and squeezes it tightly as she begins to tell him most of her story. She hesitates near the end gathers herself and shoots from the hip.

"I guess what I'm trying to tell you, Johnny, is that the man in the match is your father."

Johnny is dazed and confused. He feels numbness in his body and starts to pull himself away from his mother. Elaine reaches out to try to console her son. He brushes her hand away and tells her, "Right now I don't like you very much. He begins to move away from the kitchen table. Johnny vents his anger, running his arm across the kitchen table, knocking everything to the floor. Then he tips over the kitchen table, gets up off his chair, and runs for the back door. He leaves, slamming the door, and runs into the woods. He has trouble running. His legs are like spaghetti. He falls as he runs along the pathway into the woods. Johnny curls up into a ball and starts to tremble. His heart is aching. Johnny hasn't felt this bad since his pet dog, Bandit, of fifteen years, died. He pulls himself to his feet and heads back into the woods. He knows his destination: *The Big Rock.* This is where Johnny would head when he was troubled. The big rock is located about five hundred yards behind his house. It is on a small incline; from the top, you can look out onto a small lake. As a child, Johnny would run to the big rock with his dog whenever he was troubled. He would sit on the rock and drown his sorrows while clutching his dog to his side. When he gets there now, he feels a desperate need to hold someone or something. He sits for many hours looking out on to the lake. He has lived a lie for twenty-three years. A million thoughts run through his mind. *Is this the reason me and dad never got along?* The sun's reflection on the lake near sunset starts to bother his eyes. He climbs down from the rock and starts to make his way back to the house. He turns and looks back at the big rock. This has been his longest visit to his childhood sanctuary in many years. He has somehow left his hurt and his youth in the same place. Feeling stronger with each step towards his house, Johnny decides it's time to face reality.

As Johnny gets close enough to his house, he hears his parents arguing again. Evidently, his father had returned home while he was down at the big rock. He hears his mother ask Cliff, "Are you meeting one of your regulars, Dr. Jordan, or did you talk the new bar maid into spending the night with you?" Elaine tells him she'll have his bags packed and sitting outside in the garage when he returns from San Francisco. Cliff has gotten away with murder in his relationship for many years. He ignores what he considers more idle threats. With a small suitcase and overnight bag in his hands Cliff heads for the back door. He turns to his wife and says, "I'm staying at the airport tonight for two reasons. So I don't have to listen to anymore of your cheap shit. The other reason should be pretty easy for someone of your high intelligence to figure out." Elaine wants to tell Cliff about Billy and scream at the top of her lungs she no longer feels any love for him. She refrains because she knows the whole neighborhood will hear her if she unloads her anger. Cliff slams the back door and gets in his car. The garage door opens, and he drives away. Elaine sits at the kitchen table crying her eyes out. Her life has turned into a soap opera.

Opening the back door slowly, hoping his mother doesn't notice him, Johnny tries to sneak inside. The screen door creaks loud enough for Elaine to hear Johnny come in. She sits at the table looking up at Johnny. "It's all my fault, Johnny. Everything that's happened. It's my fault."

Johnny rushes to his mother's side. "It's not your fault, Mom," Johnny whispers, trying to console her. He kneels at his mother's side, embracing her. After a while, Elaine is finally starting to settle down. Johnny pulls away from his mother and looks her squarely in the eye. "I never understood why you took so much from Dad, whoever he might be. Now I know that you did it for me, Mom, so that I might grow up with a mother and a father. You don't have to go on like this anymore."

"He doesn't know he's not your father, Johnny." Elaine gets up from her chair and starts to move around. "I was going to write you a letter explaining all this to you. I write things down better than I tell them." Elaine pushes herself away from the table. She puts her arm on the captain's chair and sits with her hand on the side of her face. She stares off into some distant place and starts to recall her childhood and how she met Cliff. "I'll never forget the first time I saw him. We had just moved into the neighborhood. My father and his father had been college roommates, and his father had convinced my father to move to California from Seattle and open up a sporting goods store. We were busy unpacking and unloading our U-haul when Cliff and his father pulled up in their car. It was in late August, and Cliff was coming from football practice. He had on a black uniform with white numbers. His face had dirt patches all over it. He instantly became my knight in shining armor."

"Was he attracted to you?" Johnny asks.

"He said he was a few years later, but the two-year age difference meant a lot when he was fourteen and I was twelve. He was already going steady with the head cheerleader for the freshman football team. I was just a skinny, underdeveloped seventh grader with a mad crush on the boy of my dreams."

"How long did it take you to finally get a date with him?" asks Johnny.

"It took three years," replied Elaine. "In the meantime, our parents were enjoying great business success. They had expanded from one to three stores. We were always at each others' homes for one reason or another. If it wasn't a cookout, it was a birthday party. We saw quite a bit of each other because of our parents. The problem was most of the time when we went to the Jordan's house, Cliff would have his girlfriend, Sandy, over. It wasn't easy trying to compete with a girl his own age. It used to tear me apart inside to see the two of them together. Sandy used to love to make out with Cliff right in front of me. She would laugh, giggle, and constantly tease him. She would get him all hot and bothered, and then tell him, 'Not here, Cliff. We don't want little old Elaine here to be seeing things she's not ready for, now do we, Cliff?' I spent many nights crying myself to sleep, feeling sorry for myself. I'm sure I wasn't the only girl in the world in this situation. But when you're between the ages of twelve and sixteen, you think you're the only one. I spent a lot of time feeling some big-time hurt.

"I was like a young actress waiting for her first big break. Finally, after what seemed a lifetime, my chance with Cliff happened. He had broken up with Sandy, or so he told me. Actually, Sandy had dumped him in favor of a college man. Whatever had happened really didn't matter to me. I was the one who was going to the big spring dance at the country club with Cliff. Feeling I was still competing with Sandy, I persuaded my mother to let me wear a low cut dress with no back. My womanly assets had developed considerably over the winter, and I wanted to be sure Cliff would notice.

"When Cliff came to pick me up that evening, I was sure I was being noticed. He had brought me an orchid corsage. When he tried to put it on me, he was all thumbs and became a little flustered. My mother had to finally step in and come to his rescue. This episode sure did a lot for my confidence. At long last, Cliff Jordan had noticed me. The rest of the evening went by in fairytale fashion. Cliff and I had already established a good friendship and found it easy to talk to each other. We had many similar interests and spoke the same language. Intellectually, we were on the same wavelength.

"That night, he and I were the toast of the dance. I also believe we were the talk of it. The best part for me was that I was accepted by Cliff's older friends. At one point during the dance, someone tried to cut in on us while we were dancing. Cliff kindly told the boy this was our first date and I was no longer available. I stood there feeling the best I had ever felt about myself. When we started to dance again, I just melted into his arms. Cliff pulled me closer to him. I put my head on his shoulder and closed my eyes. The people moving all around us were just blurs when my eyes were open. I was caught up in the moment, the time, and my dream.

"The dance was over at midnight, and Cliff drove me home. I had moved closer to him on the ride home. Cliff put his arm around me and pulled me closer to him. I rested my head on the side of his shoulder. The ride home took only fifteen minutes, and I was home before I knew it. Cliff got out of the car and came to open my door. He took my hand and helped me from the car. As we started to move towards the house, Cliff gently swung me around, and I landed in his arms with my head about neck high. He gently put his hand under my chin and raised my head, putting his lips to mine. It was beautiful and romantic and my first meaningful kiss, the perfect ending to a perfect evening.

"When the kiss finally ended, we started to head for my front door. One again, Cliff put a halt to our progress. This time was for a different reason. 'Elaine,' he said, 'I wasn't sure about what this evening was going to be like for me. This was the first time I went anywhere for a long time without Sandy. I must be honest and tell you I was very nervous about the whole thing. Thank you for helping me relax and have so much fun tonight.' It was then and there I realized my knight in shining armor was human after all.

"After another meaningful kiss, Cliff opened my front door and came inside for a few minutes. We made plans to go for a ride the next day. When Cliff finally left after what seemed to be a million good-nights and a million goodbyes, I stood at my front door watching him walk back towards his car. He started his car, put his lights on, and beeped his horn. I stood in the doorway waving frantically as he drove away. As his tail lights faded, I quietly closed my door.

"My next move was quite obvious. I ran up the stairs to my mother's bedroom. I had noticed her light was on when Cliff and I were coming up the driveway. She lay there watching TV—and couldn't wait to hear all about the evening. She quickly had me shut off the TV and made room for me to sit by her side on the bed. We talked for about two hours. During that time, I finally began to unwind and started to feel tired. About two-thirty in the morning, my mother convinced me it was time for bed. I remember asking my mother why Dad wasn't home yet. She told me he played poker once a month with some of the other local businessmen and usually got home about five in the morning. 'It's his monthly escape from reality.' I thanked my mother for not meeting me at the door when Cliff had brought me home. She explained, as long as I acted like a grownup, I'd be treated like a grownup."

"It sounds like Grammy was a pretty modern woman for her time," says Johnny.

"She was the most understanding person I've ever known. No matter what problems we faced, she never lost control of the situation. I guess my ability to deal with Cliff for so long must have come from her."

"It sounds like you started out good with Dad. What happened?"

Elaine takes a short stroll around the kitchen and sits back down. Taking a deep breathe she lets out a sigh of relief. Johnny can't wait for the explanation. He's focused on his mom and all ears as she starts to speak.

Again Elaine pauses. "I've had some time to think about what I'm about to tell you and some of it contains sexual content but," Elaine sighs again, "my life with Cliff has been about a physical attraction. He never let me get close enough to find out what made him tick after we married. He always accused me of analyzing him. It was his excuse to lock me out of his life. I think he never warmed up to the fact I was pregnant when we married. Enough of trying to speculate what happened in our relationship. These are the cold hard facts, so here we go.

"The first two months of our relationship were the best days of my life," answers Elaine, "because I think Cliff had respect for me and my family. When we were out on a date or when we went to the beach, there was never any pressure put on me about sex. Now and then, if we were making out, he would try a little something, but if I asked him to stop, he would. It was nice to know he was interested, but I couldn't afford to let my guard down. I would be the one walking around pregnant, not him. Of course, Cliff would experience a sudden mood swing if he couldn't get his way. He would take me home; a lot of our dates would suddenly be over.

"It wasn't easy for me. I was trying to hold onto the boy of my dreams. I finally went to my mother with my problems. I told her what was going on with Cliff and me. What happened after that was completely unexpected. My mother asked if I loved him. Of course, I said I did. She told me about birth control pills. I stood there confused from what my mother was saying. I couldn't believe she was actually condoning sex.

Then she took me by the hand and explained everything I was wondering about. 'Elaine, I know what it's like to go through this stage of your life. You sometimes forget I went through the same things. It's the hardest time of anyone's life. Your body and mind are telling you one thing and your morals are telling you something else. I didn't have someone who was willing or able to help me during my teenage crisis years. I wish I could have had the advantages of this generation. I can't say whether things would have changed in my life, but you never know what might have taken place.'

"My mother went on to tell me how her first sexual experience was the night she was married. This was the reason she got married at such an early age. She and my father couldn't wait any longer. She also explained that people of her generation married at a younger age for two reasons. One of the reasons was they couldn't wait. The other reason was they didn't wait. 'A lot of people I went to high school with got married because of a pregnancy. I don't think you should start your marriage carrying this heavy load.' Grammy pulled me in close to her and hugged me. 'My little girl,' she said as tears started to fill her eyes. Again, she said, 'My little girl is no longer my little girl. You're a woman, Elaine. I'll call the doctor in the morning and set up an appointment. As I told you before, Elaine, when you act like an adult, you will be treated as an adult. I'm not doing this so you can experiment with sex anytime and anywhere. I'm doing this so you may experience sex with the man you love without the fear of getting pregnant. It should help you relax enough to enjoy the experience. It will also help you determine if Cliff is a man you want to be intimate with and who will suit your needs for the rest of your life.'

"Hugging me very tightly, my mom suggested we both go to our rooms and get some sleep. The next day was going to be a busy day. I went to my room, but I had a lot of trouble falling asleep. At first, I lay awake thinking how lucky I was to have such a caring and understanding mother. Then I started to wonder if I was making the right decision about Cliff and myself. After tossing and turning for what seemed like forever, I finally sat up in bed and asked myself a few questions about what was going on in my life. The first thing was whether or not I wanted Cliff to be my first partner. I felt he was the one. I loved and wanted to be with him the rest of my life. Then I asked myself if I was ready mentally as well as physically for such a large step in my life. It was there and then I made my decision to keep the doctor's appointment the next day. The only thing different would be I was making the decision for myself. I wasn't doing this so Cliff would get his way. I also made the decision the sexual act would occur where and when I felt the time was right. With all this decided, I was able to fall asleep."

Interjecting, Johnny tells his mother, "It's really not necessary for you to explain your sex life to me, Mom. From what you have told me, I understand why you did the things you did." Johnny gets up from his chair and walks toward his mother. Elaine gets up and the two embrace. The emotions are running high and tears are filling their eyes. It takes a while until Elaine and Johnny regain their composure. They have each told one another many times how much they love each other. Finally Elaine pulls herself together enough to continue the story.

"I'm not telling you this so you know about my sex life, Johnny. I'm telling you so you understand how people sometimes fall into traps when they let their emotions dictate their lives. I let my love for Cliff make all of my decisions at this time in my life. I was willing to do whatever it took to hold onto my man. I thought he was the only person who could make me happy and fulfill my dreams. I didn't know people would prey on people like me and use and manipulate them so they could fulfill their own personal needs. I was a naïve young lady, Johnny. I wanted to believe in everyone and everything. Reality sent a major shock through my system when I finally recognized the truth. I was the last of a dying breed. My generation is full of users and takers. They grew up getting everything they wanted and expect it to go on forever." Elaine catches herself getting off the beaten path and gets back to her situation.

"Okay," Elaine says, "where did I leave off?"

"You had just decided you would be the one to control your destiny after thinking about it lying awake in bed one night. The next day you were going to see the doctor."

Elaine takes the time to say to Johnny, "For someone who doesn't care about my sex life, you remember the details pretty well." They share some much-needed laughter. "I went to the doctor the next day, and he put me on the pill. I started taking it in about two weeks.

"In the meantime, Cliff was starting to show less patience. He was hell-bent on getting what he wanted. I was beginning to wish I had not decided to have sex with him. Then one night at one of our dances, things took a turn for the better. Cliff became very affectionate. He told me how much he loved me and how he wanted to spend the rest of his life making me happy. He went on the entire evening complimenting me, saying and doing all the right things. I was melting in his arms. I found out later that Cliff had taken a few belts of whiskey in the men's room during the dance. It was the alcohol doing the talking for him. I had no clue what was going on, being as I said very naïve. The more he poured on the sweet talk, the easier it was for me to submit to his desire later on that evening."

Elaine again goes off on a small tangent. "I guess I should have known all along how Cliff was going to behave when he drank. After all, I was the first to experience it. I submitted to him that evening. Maybe I gave him the confidence along with the alcohol. I guess it really doesn't matter anymore. His behavioral patterns aren't about to change." There's a strain as she is talking. Anger is apparent as she snaps a pencil she's been holding. "Why should he change? This approach has helped him screw many women."

Johnny comes to comfort his mother. He's not feeling as sorry for himself anymore. The story his mother is telling has clearly opened his eyes. He's more interested in the truth, encouraging his mother to go on because he needs to know what really happened.

"When the dance finally ended around 11:30, Cliff and I went to his car. When we got into the car, I moved in close to him. We started our usual making out and things went pretty much the same until we got to the point where I usually stopped him. Like the time before, and the time before that, I told Cliff to stop what he was doing. I waited for him to get a little upset. Then I put my finger to his lips to stop him from going too far with what he might say. He became attentive at this point. Then to his utter amazement, I unbuttoned my blouse and loosened my bra. I asked if he could drive us to a place a little more secluded.

"Cliff had the car started in no time flat. We headed towards the dirt road that runs through the golf course. The lights from the country club were a distant glare as Cliff pulled his car into a small clearing near the fifth green. There was a full moon that provided plenty of light and set the stage for a beautiful night. Cliff sensed what was about to happen and was having problems controlling himself. I wanted to slow the action down. I suggested he get the blanket we used at the beach and told him to find a nice comfortable spot. With Cliff busy outside, I took the time to remove my inner clothing. I had also removed my bra. Cliff found a level area about thirty feet from the car. He was sitting on the blanket yelling for me to hurry up. I opened the car door on his side so I was not in his full view. I walked toward him, seductively at times pulling my skirt farther and farther up my legs. Finally, I reached the point of no return. I came close enough for Cliff to reach out and grab me. Moments later I lost my virginity on the fifth hole." Elaine gets up from her chair doing a little pacing; trying to convince herself it wasn't so bad. "After all, a lot of my friends in college told me real horror stories about their first sexual experience. I tried to make mine as wonderful as I could in the situation presented. After we had finished, I scurried to get all my belongings together. Cliff was busy getting his pants on. He got his things together and folded up the blanket. By the time he finished, I was in the car with everything back together.

"Cliff got into the car and started the engine, using only the parking lights to draw less attention to his car moving through the woods. I had snuggled in close to him. Cliff had put his arm around me. I was feeling the chill of the night air. We finally got back to the parking lot. Cliff put his headlights on and we sped away from the country club. The ride was uneventful. I sat there thinking to myself about what had happened. I guess Cliff must have been doing the same. We hardly spoke at all.

"I was late for my curfew when we pulled in my driveway. I was supposed to be home at 1:00 a.m. The announcer on the radio had just said the time was 1:15 a.m. I used the time as an excuse to hurry into the house. We did kiss good night. Cliff also told me he loved me. We walked together to my door. Cliff again kissed me and hugged me, telling me again he loved me. I opened the door and went inside. Cliff went to his car. I ran upstairs to my bedroom, opened the window, and yelled to Cliff as he got to his car, 'I love you, too, Cliff. I love you, too.' I must have said it twenty times. Cliff drove away, waving his arm he disappeared into the night.

"All the noise coming from my bedroom got my mother out of bed. She came to my room and knocked on my door, startling me for a moment. I guess I had forgotten how late it was. When I opened the door, my mother was in the middle of a yawn. The light coming from my room made her eyes wince. I guess she knew what had happened. Her only question was, 'Are you all right, Elaine?' I told her I was fine. 'Cliff and I are in love.' She opened her arms, and I rushed to her side. We hugged for a little while and my mother ran her hands through my hair. We shared some small talk for a while. After she left, I got undressed and put on my pajamas. I went in the bathroom and did all my before-bedtime duties. I was laughing and singing to myself, having the time of my life. I went to bed and lay awake half the night recalling the entire evening. I wanted it to last forever. It took a while for me to fall asleep."

Still pacing, Elaine looks up at the clock. "My god," she exclaims, "it's ten thirty. Have we been talking that long, Johnny? What time did I start?"

"It's been a couple of hours, Mom," says Johnny. "I'm not tired, so please go on."

"Could I please go on," repeats Elaine. "Let's go into the family room..

"Cliff and I became frequent visitors to the fifth hole. I thought I was doing the right thing. I honestly believed Cliff was committed to me the way I was to him. Our relationship was running smoothly, and the age difference wasn't an issue.

We rolled right along: no problems, no issues, and no fights. It was a few weeks before graduation, and Cliff had applied to numerous colleges. He was a candidate for a full scholarship to many of them. I had known all along about these things. Still, when the news hits home you don't know how you will react. It was a Saturday afternoon, and Cliff was standing with an envelope in his hand. He said, 'I've been accepted to Stanford, Elaine, full scholarship.' I stood there thinking of a million things in about ten seconds. I tried my best to be happy for him, for us. I tried to rationalize everything in my mind. I grabbed Cliff by both hands and started to dance around the room singing the Stanford fight song. I wanted him to feel good about going to school. Why should the both of us be miserable? This is when more bad news started to filter its way into the story. 'Well,' I said, as I reached and pulled him close to me. 'At least you're all mine until September.' Cliff cleared his throat a little and pulled away from me. 'Not exactly,' he said. Not exactly was not exactly what I wanted to hear. While I frowned he said, 'I've been given a football scholarship. The team starts working out the first week of August. I'm going to have to leave the end of July.' This became a common phrase in our relationship, *Not exactly*.

"The next few months were busy with prom, graduation, and parties. I tried not to dwell on the inevitable. A lot of the other girls I knew were losing their boyfriends to the Army, Navy, or Marine Corps. My guy was only headed north to Palo Alto. At least I was still within striking distance.

"July 4th came and went. I was getting a little depressed. What would I do? How would I occupy my time? I didn't even have school for another two months. I would cry myself to sleep just thinking about it.

"I was at home, and it was a week after the 4th when the phone rang. It was Cliff's mother. She was planning a surprise, going-off to college party for him and wanted my help inviting all of his friends. Cliff's mother was a kind, loving, giving parent. Our relationship grew closer, and we became good friends. I miss her. She deserved a better life. We also had a lot of things in common. Our husbands were built from the same mold, and we were both pregnant when we married. She was always there for me.

"The party was more like an event. There were over three hundred who attended. It was a very hectic evening. I spent most of the evening helping Cliff's mother. It was Cliff's party, so I figured I would let him roam free all evening. This proved to be a big mistake. I caught him coming out of his room with a girl. He denied cheating. It was the first of many public humiliations I would suffer. The sad part is I let him talk me into believing his story. The sickest part is that I had sex with him later on that night.

"The next week, Cliff left for college. We had said our goodbyes, made promises only I intended to keep, and talked about our future together. Cliff was headed out in the world on this wild adventure, and I was to sit home in self-inflicted solitary confinement. I chose my own destiny. I would be faithful to my man. While the rest of my classmates were having the time of their lives, I was either home studying or working. A few boys asked me out, but I wasn't available. I would remain true blue.

"I managed to see Cliff on holidays, spring break, and the summer. I even traveled up to Stanford with his parents for football games. It wasn't like he was completely out of my life. I even set up a few secret rendezvous with him on weekends. He would drive halfway home to Monterrey, and I would drive up to meet him. We were two young lovers in a town where no one knew us. It made for exciting times. We did this about three times a year.

"So I got through my first two years without Cliff. It was a struggle, but I made it. I drove myself academically so I could go to Stanford and be with him. If I had only known I was wasting my time. I had done well on my SATs and was a well-rounded student. I was vice-president of my class and also participated in French club, drama club, and played basketball and field hockey. I also maintained a three point six grade point average. How could Stanford refuse me?

"As it turned out, Stanford didn't refuse me. I had to refuse Stanford. My father and Cliff's father didn't like the idea of me attending the same college as Cliff. They both had their reasons. Cliff's father didn't want his son to have any distractions. He was doing well with his grades and football. Cliff was also starting to study that year for medical school. His father felt he would need all his time to get through his first year. My father didn't like the idea of his little girl being away at school with her boyfriend. Although I was accepted at Stanford, I had to settle for UCLA. This didn't help our relationship. I also resented the fact I worked so hard to get where I wanted to go and I was held back by his father and mine.

"The next two and a half years were even worse than the previous two. Cliff and I saw even less of each other. We were starting to drift farther and farther apart. Cliff had become a 'big man on campus.' He was a good-looking football star who loved to prey on young women. If it wasn't for my sexual availability during the summer, I think he would have dumped me.

"I was even starting to branch out myself. I had sex with a couple of different partners. One was a fellow student who I met in my psychology class. We were great friends who, through a great closeness, responded to each other's sexual needs on a few occasions. The other person was a co- worker. I later found out he was married and had a small child. I was ashamed and disgusted with myself. I really liked this guy. I thought we might have had a further together. This was a slap in the face I needed.

"We are coming to the part where I meet your father, Johnny." The grandfather clock in the next room is sounding twelve bells as Elaine begins to talk. "There are a few small details you should know about before I get to that part. I had taken myself off birth control six months earlier. I figured a child would bring Cliff and me closer. I was losing him, and I became desperate. I didn't think he had the right to just throw me away after six years. I was sure I was doing the right thing. We had made plans to spend spring break in the mountains. I went up to Stanford a few weeks earlier to confirm everything with Cliff. I got there on a Friday night. The subject of spring break finally came up after two days of sexual exploitation for both of us. Remember, I was trying to get pregnant. Cliff then proceeded to tell me that his father had bought him airline tickets to fly to Daytona Beach. He wanted his son to have a great vacation before starting his final year of med school. Cliff said he was sorry and apologized a million times. Deep down, I knew he wanted to go. Once again, he had taken advantage of me. I tried not to show my hurt as I put my things together. I told him to have fun. How foolish of me. I cried on the drive back home.

"The next day, I called Cindy. We talked about what had happened. She talked me into going on spring break with her. Two weeks later, I headed for the mountains. It seemed so innocent at the time. Cindy and I had gone away a few times before. We had one agreement: nobody asks too many questions. This was Cindy's request. She was there to have fun, always seeking the perfect mate. We arrived at the resort late Saturday afternoon. We rested for a while, ate, and then headed for the night spot. It didn't take Cindy long to catch someone's eye. They headed for the dance floor, never to return.

"I sat in the background, minding my own business. A few guys asked me to dance. I politely refused, and they went on about their business. Then this pest shows up. He was very big and very drunk. He wouldn't leave me alone, and I was at the point where my only choice was to dance with this goon. All of a sudden, out of nowhere, I'm getting some help from a total stranger. He dragged this guy away from me towards a pool table. I found out later he made a bet with the drunk about a certain shot. I also found out later that I was the stakes. This didn't set too well with me. Of course, he made the shot, which sent the drunk quietly on his way. I was grateful for the help and asked him to sit down and have a drink with me. He graciously accepted my offer. We had a lengthy conversation. He asked my name, which I lied about; I asked his, and I guess he did the same." Elaine suddenly stops everything and leaves the room. "I'll be right back." She runs to her bedroom and back. She has the VCR tape in her hand and puts the tape into the machine, fast forwarding the tape. She turns the TV on, and the pool match with Billy Bates is flying by. Suddenly, Elaine stops the fast forward and comes to one of the few spots when Billy is at the table, looking good. She freezes the action. Billy has a smile on his face. "This is the man I fell in love with, Johnny. He told me his name was Johnny Ames. He's also the man you were named after. Through a crazy series of events, he's back into our lives. I think you should go to meet him. You both deserve a chance to get to know each other."

Johnny sits quietly while Elaine lays back in her recliner. Johnny finally breaks the silence. He says, "You've carried around an awful lot for a long time, Mom. It must feel good to finally get it out."

"I haven't felt this much relief since I gave birth to you, Johnny."

"What happened when you found out you were pregnant? How did you convince Dad, Cliff, the baby was his?"

"Cliff ended up in the hospital when he went to Florida. He fell asleep on the beach and got a bad sunburn. That's the original story he fed me. I found out at one of his class reunions he passed out on the beach with some bimbo. The both of them were bare ass and suffered second degree burns after lying, passed out, on the beach for several hours the next morning. He came back early from Florida and, of course, I felt sorry for him and guilty about my exploits with Johnny. I slept with him as soon as he was up to it. The rest of what happened, happened fast. Three months later, I'm walking down the aisle. I don't think he wanted to marry me, but I think his mother got the final say on that one."

Elaine tells Johnny she has put money into his checking account that will either pay his tuition or his expenses for his trip east. "I'll be gone when you get up tomorrow morning. I'm going off with Cindy for the day. You can call me in a few days and tell me which choice you made."

Coming to his mother's side, Johnny kneels next to the recliner. He hugs his mom like a little boy. There are tears in his eyes as he tells his mother he will always love her. He also tells her she should have no regrets and feel no shame about what happened. It wasn't her fault.

"I wish I could have told you this story sooner. My only regret is that it took this long to find your real father. I tried in the beginning to find him, I really did. I just didn't know where to look. I did go back to the resort, but he left no forwarding address."

It is two in the morning. Elaine finally puts an end to the conversation and manages to fall asleep. Johnny goes to his bedroom and lies awake while making his decision. He will head east in the morning.

# CHAPTER 3

As Johnny packs, he finds an envelope with a note inside. *This is a picture of Billy and me taken by Cindy. This will prove to Billy who you are. I'm not telling you to go to him. I just think you should. I've deposited your college money into your checking account. Call soon and let me know where you are. I know you will make a good decision. Love Mom.*

After eating breakfast and showering, Johnny gets his stuff together and packs it into his car. He writes his mother a quick goodbye note, then gets into his car and heads for the local poolroom. He wants to say goodbye to friends. He also had to get his cue, which he kept in a locker there. When Johnny gets to the poolroom a little past one o'clock in the afternoon, the place is reasonably busy. He walks around saying goodbye to some of his new friends, telling them he's headed back to school.

He talks to Larry Walker, an elderly man who took a little time to help Johnny with his game over the course of the summer.

'Hey Larry, you're here early today what's going on?"

"My cars in the shop being worked on, my daughter dropped me off on her way to do some shopping at the mall. I could say the same thing to you; you're not usually here until after dinner time."

"I finished up working my summer job last Friday; I'm on my way east as soon as the sun starts to set. I'm entering my final year of college."

In the meantime, a ring game of nine-ball has started to develop. The players are some of the guys Johnny has played with regularly in the room. He sits and watches for a while.

The stakes are two dollars on the five and five dollars on the nine. The players in the game are from the same affluent neighborhood as Johnny, so money is virtually no object. It passes freely from hand to hand in the next few hours. Johnny sits around, not wanting to get involved.

While he waits, the room becomes busier. The ring game is still going strong. The money has gone around in circles most of the time. Two players drop out, but are easily replaced. All of a sudden, a local wise guy, Louie Salvi, enters the room with a couple of young Mexicans. They get the table next to the ring game and start talking trash and making fun of the players. Louie tells everyone in the game, "My friend, Miguel, will take all of you guys. Nobody here can shoot like him, and I do mean *no*body."

One of the players in the ring game drops out, claiming he can no longer stand all the commotion around him. Miguel infiltrates the game and begins to dominate the playing. He is also receiving help on the sidelines from Louie. He's taunting the players as they are shooting while also asking to raise the stakes after every rack. The three players in the game are clearly rattled—Miguel has taken control of the game.

While sitting and watching the ring game, Larry points out to Johnny how the players in the ring game have reacted to Louie and Miguel. "These guys have really lost their composure. All they have to do is relax and play the way they can play. Your friends could easily compete with this Mexican boy. The only way this game is gonna change is if somebody is bold enough to shut Louie and Miguel up."

Johnny says, "I don't think anybody here has the fire power to throw at the guys."

"There's somebody sitting here watching his friends take a beating. You're the best young player in the room, Johnny. You're supposed to defend your territory."

"I'm headed back to school. I don't have time to get involved with this pool game."

"You better leave now. On the way back to school, think about the game you should have played." Larry takes Johnny's cue in his hand. "I thought you were different from all of your rich friends. I thought you had guts. I guess I wasted my time with you this summer. Go ahead, kid, go out the door. You once told me you wanted to be a pool player. I'm going to tell you what it takes to be a player, kid. It takes action, risks, and combat. A pool player is like a fighter. Until you get into the ring and fight, all you've done is train. This is your chance for a good fight, kid. All this training you did this summer is wasted if you walk away now."

Johnny is embarrassed. He hadn't been prepared for such a speech. He takes his cue and starts walking toward the door. At this time, he hears Miguel in the background saying, "I'm going to wipe up this poolroom just like Rico Sanchez wiped out that guy Billy 'The Bridesmaid' Bates."

Louie yells, "I told all you guys that nobody here could beat Miguel."

Coming back to the railing separating him from the poolroom, Johnny looks down at the people left in the ring game. Shouting from a distance, he asks if there are any openings in the game. Louie looks up at Johnny in his best, yet weak impression of Don Pardow and says, "Come on down."

Larry asks, "What changed your mind?"

"He insulted my father." Larry looks at Johnny somewhat bewildered. "It's a long story, and I don't have time to explain. I'm going into combat."

"Hold on. Hold off getting into the game until Miguel is breaking. That way," explains Larry, "he will be following you in the rotation. It's important who you follow in a ring game and who follows you."

Taking Larry's advice, Johnny takes his time getting ready to play. It doesn't take long for Miguel to make a nine-ball and win the break for the next game. Johnny announces he's in the game. He is now one of four players in the game. The stakes have changed since the game started. It's up to five dollars on the five and ten on the nine. The game is ragged for the first hour Johnny plays. The money goes back and forth among the players.

Suddenly, Johnny hits a hot streak. The player he is following misses the eight-ball and hangs it in a corner pocket. He easily makes the eight and nine. He breaks the next rack and sinks the nine. The nine-ball comes back on the table. Johnny then proceeds to run out the rack. He collects $25 from each player. He dominates for the next hour. The only other player making any money is Miguel. Louie's chirping has diminished somewhat. The sounds of *no*body beating Miguel have quietly disappeared.

Louie continues his efforts to raise the stakes. He finally succeeds—the stakes are doubled. It takes Johnny and Miguel another hour to get the other two players in the game to quit. Johnny is happy and satisfied to just end the game. He doesn't know Louie and Miguel feel differently. Johnny starts to unscrew his stick. Louie snaps quickly at Johnny, "And where do you think you're going? We're not finished playing."

Louie looks at Miguel. "Did you say you were through, Miguel?"

"I never said I was through."

Louie and Miguel continue a verbal interchange, demeaning Johnny. Larry sits on the sidelines listening to all that is being said. Finally, after he has heard enough, he calls Johnny over. Louie and Miguel have a few more things to say as Johnny heads in Larry's direction. When Johnny gets close enough,

Larry asks, "Do you want to play this guy heads up for a lot of money?"

"Were you hoping something like this was going to happen?" asks Johnny.

"I wasn't hoping; I was praying. Now let's go get these guys."

"I don't want to have to listen to Louie the whole match."

"You'll be able to hear a pin drop, Johnny. I guarantee it. I have a few things to tell you before you go out there to play this guy." Larry gets closer. "He's strictly a shot maker. His position play is going to cost him at least one or two games in a race to eleven. All you have to do is win the games you're supposed to win. Your safety play is also important. Tie this guy up in knots whenever you can. It will frustrate him. Remember, this guy wants to shoot at everything."

"You make it sound easy."

"It's not easy, Johnny, but that's the game plan. You need to know how you're going to play against different players. It's important to know their strengths and weaknesses. You'll make better choices when you have more options on a shot. Now put your cue together. We're going to get this guy."

"Miguel and Louie are getting impatient."

"That's part of the plan," says Larry. "Let them get a little itchy. It will give them a good excuse when they lose."

The time of day and where Johnny has to go is no longer a concern. He is caught up in what's going on right now. The excitement of playing Miguel has his adrenaline flowing. He and Larry are headed into the playing arena. A small crowd has gathered in anticipation of the match.

At this time, Larry takes control. "We're here to play, Louie. The game is one race to eleven. The stakes are one thousand dollars. Are you prepared to play for this kind of money, Louie?" Larry pulls out a large roll of hundred dollar bills. He counts out ten bills and hands the money to one of the spectators sweating the match. "Do you have any problem with this guy holding the money?"

Louie and Miguel are scrambling to come up with enough money to cover the bet. They have moved to a corner in the room. They are fishing through all their pockets to find enough money to play. They finally emerge. Louie is still counting the money when handing it to the spectator. "I have no problem with this guy," says Louie. "He can hold the money. What about a referee, Larry? We should have a ref. There may be some close hits."

Larry says, "Go ahead, you pick the referee." Louie looks around. He doesn't have many friends in the room. In the back, he spots Willie Smith—the house man from noon until six o'clock. "I want Willie to ref the match," says Louie. With a little prodding and a fee of twenty-five dollars, Willie agrees.

Larry stands up and tells a stirring crowd, "Get all your bets down, ladies and gentlemen. There's a lot riding on this match, and I don't think the players should have to listen to any haggling while they are playing. In fact, I don't think they should have to deal with any kind of distractions. Don't you agree, Louie?"

Louie looks at Larry. "Ya, ya, whatever you say, Larry. Let's get things going for Christ's sake."

Johnny and Miguel lag for opening break. Miguel wins.

Miguel breaks the first rack and pockets the two-ball. It doesn't take long for Johnny to understand what Larry was talking about. Miguel pockets his first two shots, making very hard shots. His position play is virtually non-existent. After pocketing the three-ball, Miguel has left himself safe and is kicking at the four-ball. He manages to make a difficult hit, but Johnny comes to the table with a simple six-ball run out. He proceeds to clear the table. After pocketing the nine-ball, he walks over to his seat. His mouth is a little dry and he takes a drink of Coke.

Larry notices Johnny is trying to clear his throat. He gives Johnny a stick of chewing gum. "This will take care of your dry throat."

Willie racks the balls while Miguel sits on the edge of his chair awaiting another chance. Willie is lifting the rack from the balls as Johnny comes back to the table. He proclaims game one to Mr. Jordan as he throws a bead across the overhead score indicator. Johnny picks up the cue-ball and places it on the table. He has recently started to break from the side rail. Johnny knows the importance of a good break. He takes his time stroking and making sure he feels right. He thrusts the cue-ball forward. There is a loud sound as the balls separate on impact. They seem to be running for the pockets. The cue-ball has jumped back off the rack and squatted near the center of the table. Johnny has executed a textbook break. He has a clear shot at the one-ball and has pocketed two balls. He runs the table easily.

Willie proclaims, "Mr. Jordan now leads two games to zero."

The mood of the match has been set. Johnny wins game three. He is feeling more confident, stroking each shot clean and smooth. Games four through seven are split evenly. Miguel enters game eight trailing five to two. He has one thing going in his favor. He is breaking.

Once again, Miguel becomes his own worst enemy. He makes the rack harder to run with each shot. He eventually breaks down on the six-ball, trying to draw back a long, straight shot, and it wiggles out of the corner pocket, working its way back up the side rail. The ball settles in front of the side pocket. Johnny comes to the table. Again, he starts with an easy shot with fairly easy position play. This is obviously the difference in the match.

This proves to be a big game; instead of a score of five games to three in the match, the score is six to two, in favor of Mr. Jordan. At this point, Johnny puts on his finest shooting display. He runs the next two racks in convincing style. He is truly in a zone. All parts of the body machine are in total sync. He controls the cue-ball as if it were on a string. A natural high has his senses totally aroused. The crowd has been applauding some of his finer efforts. He prances around the table after making a difficult eight-ball shot to set up an easy nine-ball shot. Johnny raises his fist in a show of dominance. In Johnny's mind, the match is over.

A small comeback is mounted by Miguel. He wins four of the next six games, bringing the score to ten to six. The break fails Miguel in the next game, and the game is there for the taking. Johnny has a good shot to start his run out. There are two balls tied-up, but Johnny solves this problem, breaking the five and six open while pocketing the two-ball. He opens up the run out and still has a good shot at the three-ball. The rest of the rack soon becomes history. Johnny ends up with an easy side pocket nine-ball shot to win the game. Willie announces to the crowd, "Game, set, and match to Mr. Jordan." The crowd cheers loudly in Johnny's favor. He had rightly defended his poolroom's honor.

Louie comes out of his subdued state. He is barking at Johnny and Larry that he will be back the next day to play again. Larry says, "This kid is headed back to college. You're going to have to wait until next year for a rematch. Miguel will have time to practice."

Johnny tells Louie, "Miguel is no Rico Sanchez."

"You're no Billy Bates either."

"You're right," says Johnny, "I'm not Billy Bates, but I'm a lot closer to being Billy Bates than Miguel is to being Rico Sanchez. Someday, you and everybody else here may understand what I just said. I'm headed to Kentucky and the poolroom he owns when I leave here." Johnny thanks Louie and Miguel, a little sarcastically, for paying for his gas to drive there, then he unscrews his stick and puts it away.

He and Larry gather their things and collect their winnings. They head out of the playing area and sit at Larry's table overlooking the poolroom. The crowd has dispersed. The activity in the room is back to normal. Johnny looks at the clock in total disbelief. "I can't believe it's ten thirty. I lost track of everything while I was playing."

"You never lost track of the cue-ball, Johnny. Your position play and safety play was great. I got a better player than I expected. You were fantastic."

"How did you know I was going to win?"

"I wasn't betting on you to win. I was betting on Miguel to lose."

"What do you mean?"

"It's nothing personal, Johnny. You played a great match. The biggest difference between you and Miguel was that he had the cards stacked against him. Why don't we do a quick instant replay of the whole day? You'll have a better idea of what I'm talking about. Louie and Miguel came in talking all kinds of trash. Nobody was good enough to beat Miguel. Then you got into the ring game. It didn't take long for them to realize that not everyone in the room was a chump. They took notice of the way you played. When the ring game broke up, they tried to intimidate you. That's when I stepped in. I made them bet more money than they were prepared to play for. They had to go into all their reserves to put up the thousand dollars. The fact they had one race to play put all the pressure on Miguel. I'm the type of person who likes things in my favor when I bet. Don't think these things weren't on Miguel's mind when you were playing. It wasn't the reason you won, but if it came down to a close game, it might have helped."

Larry takes the thousand dollars from his pocket and gives it to Johnny.

"What's all this money for?" asks Johnny.

"It's what you won," says Larry.

"That wouldn't be right," says Johnny. "You're the one who put up all the money."

"Just take it," says Larry. "I made twice as much betting on the side. I'm a little confused though. You said earlier you were going back to school, and a few minutes ago you said you were on your way to Kentucky to see Billy Bates."

"Why?" says Johnny. "Do you know him?"

"Know him?" says Larry. "Everybody who spent time in poolrooms in the seventies knew of him. He's a legend. I knew him better than anyone did. I was his backer. We hustled all over California and parts of the southwest together. He was the best. The only flaw he had was he could never get over this girl he met up in the mountains."

"Was the girl's name Katie?" asks Johnny.

Larry's eyes narrow in disbelief. "How did you know that? How the *hell* did you know that?"

Johnny says, in a much lower voice, "Katie's my mother."

"Well I'll be a horse's ass," proclaims Larry. "And I suppose you're going to tell me Billy's your father."

"That's right," says Johnny. "Billy Bates is my father."

Larry has come all the way out of his chair. He is pacing the floor as he talks to Johnny. "Ya know, there were things I saw in you that reminded me of someone. I just never put it together. The way you walk around the table, the way you get down to shoot, and the way you chalk your cue. Now that I think about it, who else could it be? The one final clincher could be your hands. Billy had huge hands. Let me see the size of your hand." Johnny places his hand up against Larry's. His fingers and palm are a half inch longer than Larry's. "I guess there's no denying it. You must be Billy's kid," says Larry.

"Could you tell me a little about Billy? I don't know much about him."

"He's a typical pool player, hard to figure and harder to get close to. It's the makeup of the animal. Billy had a bunch of bad luck when he let his guard down. He has a hard exterior, but if you get to know him, he's a really good guy. The only problem is he's a tough nut to crack. Be patient with him and remember what you're dealing with. It might take you a little while to be accepted. At least you'll have an advantage. You know more about him than he knows about you. Let's keep this between us. I'd hate to have Billy find out the news before you reach Kentucky."

Getting up from the table, Johnny shakes hands with Larry and humbly thanks him for all he has done for him. He even offers to return the money Larry has given him. Larry refuses to take the money, saying, "There's only one thing you owe me, kid. Say 'hello' to Billy for me. Tell him Last Call Larry said hello. He's the only one who ever called me that name. Tell him about today. He appreciates a good poolroom story. God knows he certainly has a few." Larry looks up at the clock. "It's eleven o'clock. If you let me keep rambling on, I'll go on forever."

Johnny collects his things and heads through the door. Larry turns his attention back to the poolroom. It's back to business as usual for Larry.

# CHAPTER 4

Johnny's in no hurry to get to Lexington. The first stop he decides to make is Las Vegas.

He can't believe how a simple trip to the poolroom to get his cue turned into such a bizarre affair. He's glad the whole thing happened. Any doubts about going to find Billy are out of his mind. Johnny discovered things he never knew. The feeling of playing with a large crowd of people watching excited him. All his senses were keener. Of course, he felt a little nervous at first, but it was a good nervousness. After the first few shots, it went away. He also liked the ability to control his own destiny. He sees how anyone could get caught up in this type of lifestyle. The fast "easy money" he made could easily lure anyone into believing this could happen all the time. Johnny knows better. It took all the right circumstances for him to involve himself in such a game. After all, he spent a good part of his summer playing in Razz's poolroom. That was his first encounter. If it wasn't for Larry, the match would never have taken place. He thinks about Miguel and Louie. If they didn't act the way they acted, again, no match. Johnny gets a clearer picture of how the pool world works. If no challenge is issued, another challenger cannot step forward. Johnny only wishes it were more civilized. The taunting and degrading remarks made him uncomfortable. Perhaps, such is the intention!

After hours of driving, the Vegas lights are in sight. Johnny's foot suddenly weighs more. His friends at school were right. Vegas makes Lake Tahoe and Reno look like shanty towns. Johnny heads for the main strip. The automatic controls are shutting down the lights with the coming of daylight. Johnny passes many hotels then spots a sign at the Frontier. Single rooms $37.95—a good price with an appropriate name. This is Johnny's new frontier; he pulls in, checks in, and takes a long nap.

Later, he showers, then heads to the busy casino. The place is busy. Johnny finds a table with an opening. He knows the routine; he takes three one hundred dollar bills from his pocket.

"Change please?"

"Changing three hundred," announces the dealer to the pit boss. He wishes Johnny good luck as he moves his chips in front of him.

The minimum bet is ten dollars a hand. The money goes back and forth when all of a sudden Johnny's luck changes. It's actually a combination of a cold dealer and a hot player. He increases his wagers. Betting as high as twenty-five dollars per hand, Johnny manages to run his money up over seven hundred dollars. He takes the rest of the day off and enjoys his surroundings.

Noon, the next day, the method of procedure remains the same, except for one variation. Johnny takes his suitcases to his car and checks out. He will play blackjack again, then leave town. It takes five minutes to find a good seat at a table. He loses two hundred and sixty dollars, leaving him holding six one hundred dollar chips. He bets one on the next hand and wins. Dumb luck takes over. For the next half-hour he can do no wrong. He gets so hot he starts playing two hands. The betting escalates to one hundred on the first hand and two hundred on the second. He's on a roll. The only person not having any fun is the pit boss.

The black chips continue to pile up. He's so involved, he has no idea how much he is winning, so he starts betting even higher amounts. The first hand is now two hundred and the second has gone as high as four hundred. Johnny is using the first hand to protect the second, taking all his chance cards on the first hand. It works out well. He has yet to lose the larger bet.

All of the decisions Johnny makes work in his favor. Then the inevitable takes place. A pair of aces is dealt to the second hand. The rules of the game are plain and simple. Always split aces. Johnny has a four hundred dollar bet on this hand, and he isn't ready for this hand. It breaks his rhythm; his concentration becomes distorted. Eventually, he splits the aces, but he becomes nervous about the bet. He senses something is wrong. The dealer gives Johnny two down cards. He never looks at either card. He focuses his attention on the dealer's cards. The dealer has a four showing. He flips his down card over and it's a nine. He has to take at least one more card. The dealer turns over a deuce, giving him fifteen. Again, the dealer flips a card. This time it's another nine. The dealer busts. Johnny wins the hand. He has been holding his breath the whole time. He exhales, pushing himself back into his chair when the dealer busts. Three hands later Johnny feels his luck has changed, he pushes his chips at the dealer and asks, "Cash me in please?"

The pit boss starts a conversation with Johnny as the dealer tallies up his winnings.

"We can give you a credit on your room account for the amount of chips your cashing in if you would like, I'm sorry I don't know your name. What's your room number?"

"My name is Johnny Jordan and I'm sorry but I've checked out. I'm walking to the parking lot as soon as I cash these chips in. I'm headed east and I'm in a hurry to get where I'm going."

"What if the casino comped you a room for the night? Maybe threw in tickets to a show, and if you're traveling solo found you an escort to help you enjoy it possibly, even more?"

"Sorry, I made a commitment when I woke up today, I was leaving as soon as I finished playing and I'm done."

"I have to make this offer to big winners to try to keep them here. Good luck Mr. Jordan, thanks for the action. Maybe if you come through Vegas again you'll stop and give us another play?"

"It's not a case of if; it's a case of when. I love this town, and this place. I'm sure I'll be back."

Johnny cashes in $5,800. He has never carried this kind of money around; it feels awkward. He heads for the men's room. Once inside the stall, he takes the money and divides it into four even piles. Then he puts a pile into each of his four pant pockets. The thought of carrying around this kind of money makes him nervous. He runs to his car and quickly drives away from the parking lot.

# CHAPTER 5

Johnny makes it to Albuquerque. The city sits high in the mountains, and he is a little surprised by its size and elevation. Johnny decides to have lunch at a bar. He spots two eight-foot pool tables, but heads for the bar to get some change to call his mother first. He sees a young lady sweeping the floor. She's absolutely beautiful, and Johnny gets a little distracted. He walks into a chair, knocking it over, and then fumbles through his pockets trying to find his money. He locates some and asks for change for a five dollar bill.

The barmaid watches the scene. She is actually flattered by Johnny's reaction to her. Wanting to save him from more embarrassment, she breaks the ice by saying, "You're not the first person to knock over something in here. I guess it takes a little time for your eyes to adjust to the light."

While she talks, Johnny manages to pull himself together. He picks up the chair he knocked over and gets his bearings. Taking advantage of what the barmaid has said, he squints a little as he hands her his money, asking for five dollars in quarters.

"Are these for the pool tables or the video machines?"

"Honestly, I need them to make a phone call."

"I'm not supposed to give out that much change for phone calls, but in your case," she teases Johnny a little, "if you promise not to tell anyone and have lunch here, I'll give you what you want."

Agreeing to the barmaid's terms, Johnny orders a small salad and cheeseburger, asking her to put his lunch on hold while he makes his phone call.

After telling him she would hold his cheeseburger till after his call, she asks him to call her "Flo" instead of "hey you."

"Is Flo short for Florence?"

"No, it's short for Little Flower. I'm part Indian. What's your name?"

"Johnny Jordan, but all my good friends call me J.J."

"Make your call. You're salad will be waiting for you when you come back." Winking at Johnny, she asks, "Is that alright with you, J.J.?"

Taking all his change from the bar, Johnny heads for the phone booth.

"It's me, Ma."

"I had to run in from the garden; I'm a little out of breath." After a few seconds, Elaine settles down. "Where are you?"

"Albuquerque, New Mexico."

"Albuquerque," says Elaine, "that's a long way from Stanford. Are you lost, Johnny?"

"No, Ma. I'm following my heart. I'm going to find my father."

"Tell your heart to hurry up; it's not traveling very fast."

He starts to tell her about his trip, about his day at the pool hall, and how he played for a thousand dollars and won. He also tells her he met someone who knew Billy. "The guy's name is Last Call Larry and hangs out at Razz's poolroom. Maybe you can go down and introduce yourself to him. He told me Billy had never gotten over you."

"You went to the poolroom and met a friend of Billy's? I find that hard to believe."

"That's not the way it happened. I've known this guy for some time and just happened to mention Billy's name in passing. That's when he found out it's a small world."

Johnny's three minutes are up and the recording lets him know his time is allotted.

"Are you calling from a payphone?"

"Yeah, I didn't want dad to see a call from Albuquerque on the phone bill."

"Are you kidding, Cliff check out a bill from the phone company, or any other company? His secretary, who happens to be me, handles all the bills. Call me back on your cell phone."

Johnny takes care of his additional charges and calls his mom back. His phone rings and his mom answers. She jumps right back into the conversation.

"Okay, you met a friend of Billy's. That was two days ago. What else have you been up to?"

"I drove to Vegas. Won a bunch of money between the pool game and playing blackjack. I know all this sounds crazy, but you asked."

"You're becoming quite the gambler."

"Not really," says Johnny. "I was just as lucky as it gets for half an hour. Besides, after I took my chips and cashed them in, I was so nervous carrying around all the money I wanted to get out of town as fast as possible, so I drove to Flagstaff last night. This morning, I drove to Albuquerque and here I am, in a small bar, waiting for my lunch and talking to you. Speaking of lunch, it must be ready by now. I have to go."

"Why the big hurry?" asks Elaine.

"Well, to tell you the truth, Ma, there's a beautiful Indian barmaid here who took my lunch order, so I should be getting back. She's probably thinking I ran out the back door."

"Don't go starting something you're not prepared to finish. Remember why you're in Albuquerque."

Johnny wishes he had never mentioned the girl at the bar. The conversation goes on for another few minutes. Johnny changes the subject and asks his mother how things were going between her and Cliff.

"Things have been great. Cliff's been away in San Francisco and not due back until Thursday."

"I know why you've put up with him all these years," says Johnny. "You did it for me and you felt guilty. You've more than paid your debt to him. Why don't you leave him?"

"I'm in the process of starting a new life. I've applied for a few jobs around town, and if I can get one, I'll stay here until I save enough money to leave. I wasn't going to tell you this for a while, but you asked." Elaine starts to get emotional, but she catches herself. She says, "Here I go again telling you all my problems. Are you sorry you called?"

"Naw," says Johnny. "It feels great just to hear a friendly voice. I'll keep in mind what you told me," Johnny says in a very warm, reassuring voice. "I love you, Mom."

"I love you, too, Johnny." They both say goodbye and hang up.

Back to the bar, the lunchtime crowd has arrived and the scene has changed. Evidently, Johnny has picked a lively spot. He sits down to find his salad waiting for him. Even though Flo is busy with the rest of her customers, she manages to look at Johnny from time to time. He finishes his salad, and she quickly comes over to take his bowl away.

"Can I get you something else, J.J.?" asks Flo.

"I think I'll change my order to two cheeseburgers and a ginger ale. I'm going to move, so could you bring my food over there?" Johnny asks, pointing to a small table near the pool tables. "I want to play a few games of pool while I eat," says Johnny.

"Don't tell me you're a pool hustler," says Flo.

"I'm not a hustler," says Johnny. "I just like to play."

"Are you good enough to play for money? There are a couple of guys here looking to play nine-ball. Would you like a small ring game, for short money?"

"Sure," says Johnny. "Sounds like fun. Let me go get my stick out of the car."

As Johnny turns to leave, Flo grabs his arm saying, "If you just use a house cue they won't think you're a player. These guys I'm setting you up with don't play very well, so just take your time and you'll make some real easy money." Flo beckons across the room to the two locals. "Hey, Frankie, hey, Joey, got a nine-ball player here. He's looking for some action. You guys wanna play?"

Frankie and Joey quickly get to their feet and head in Flo's direction. They reach Johnny, and Flo takes care of the introductions. After everyone is introduced, they head for the pool tables. Johnny heads for the two eight-foot tables he had noticed earlier. Flo tells him those tables are for ball-bangers and league play that requires you play on smaller tables. She tells Johnny to take a right and walk past the men's room where there are more tables. Johnny, Joey, and Frankie head down the dark hallway and Flo throws the light switch, which lights up a larger room with nine-foot tables. Johnny is pleased the room is well lit and there's plenty of space between each table.

Flo says her goodbyes and wishes each player good luck before returning to work. "Take it easy on the new guy, fellas; we want him to enjoy Albuquerque."

Frankie and Joey are anxious to start playing and have already flipped coins on the table saying to Johnny, "Odd coin wins the break." The coins are all flipped and Joey has won the right to break the first rack. Frankie will follow him and Johnny will shoot last.

Playing only a few games, it's obvious to Johnny that both players are terrible. Frankie is a slasher who rides the money balls (five and nine) at every opportunity and often hits the object-ball hard into the five or nine, hoping to luck one into a pocket. Joey tends to "choke" when he is shooting a money ball. They're also starting to guzzle down the beers at a pretty good rate. Johnny is almost embarrassed to be taking their money.

Poking her head in the room from time to time, Flo checks on how things are going. She even brings a free pitcher of beer in for Joey and Frankie. Johnny sticks to soda. Flo promises to join in the game once the lunch crowd goes back to work. Johnny pulls Flo aside to tell her he's winning close to fifty dollars in a little under an hour. "These guys aren't going to get angry and want to fight, are they?"

"They come in here all the time and lose to me. They just like to play and have a few laughs and beers. Of course, I usually have on tight jeans and my blouse is unbuttoned. I'll tell you what," says Flo, "why don't you start missing a few shots on purpose if you're afraid they might start to resent losing their money to a stranger. Loosen up, and buy them some beers. Be their friend, and they'll stay longer and lose more money."

Uncomfortable in his situation, Johnny starts to play the way Flo suggests, but he doesn't like this strategy. A few timely misses have Joey and Frankie losing their money at a slower pace. A pitcher of beer from Johnny takes whatever tension he was feeling completely out of the game. The boys are laughing and joking like they had played together for ten years.

At 2:30, the crowd has all but disappeared. Flo makes her entrance into the room. Johnny notices a few changes right away. Her hair is in a ponytail and she smells nicer. Flo has a two-piece custom-made cue and proclaims to the boys, "I'm all yours, guys. My relief came in early, so let's play." Still putting her cue together, she asks as Johnny is shooting and making a nine-ball, "Who do I follow?" Johnny doesn't know it, but Flo has timed her entrance into the game.

Johnny says, "You follow Frankie." Johnny breaks and makes a ball, but has no shot at the one. He kicks at the one, but fails to pocket a ball. Joey and Frankie manage to get to the four-ball between them, but Frankie misses on the five. Flo gets to the table and runs the five through nine rather easily. Johnny is impressed and says to Flo, "You make this game look easy."

"You're not afraid of a little competition are you, Johnny?"

"I've never seen a lady play like that before."

"Did I ever tell either of you guys I was a lady?" Flo takes her cue and strokes it as if masturbating a man. She flirtingly says to them, "I just like something hard in my hands. I guess a pool cue with a hard shaft is all I need." Flo laughs as she gets ready to break the next rack. "Well, guys, I guess I got your minds exactly where I want them." She breaks, and the cue-ball is sent rapidly at the one-ball. Flo pockets a ball. Before she proceeds to shoot, she again takes time to tease and have a little more fun with the boys. Taking the chalk into her hand, she lightly applies it to the cue tip. While chalking, Flo gently blows on the tip of the cue, making sure to accentuate her large, beautiful lips. "Well," Flo proclaims, "I guess it's time to let my game do a little talking."

The game goes on for an hour and a half, and Frankie and Joey continued their losing ways. Johnny has managed to win a little more, but Flo has won the majority of the money since she entered the game. She's managed to keep Johnny in check by being the person Johnny has to follow. Frankie and Joey finally go to the rack and call it quits. Flo consoles them a little as they head for the door. "You guys didn't get many rolls today," she says. "This new guy was pretty lucky. Come back soon, and we'll play again."

Frankie and Joey head for the door, mumbling to one another. They say to Flo, "Next time we come in we're going to win the cash. Our pay day is coming."

Joey looks at Flo, his eyes glassy from the beer and his voice raspy. He points his index finger at Flo saying, "You're the best, Flo, you're the best." Frankie and Joey head for the door arm and arm.

# CHAPTER 6

Facing an awkward situation, Flo breaks the ice and asks Johnny, "So, J.J., what do you want to do now? You want to play some heads-up, just you and me?"

"What kind of stakes do you have in mind?"

Flo looks Johnny square in the eye. "I've always had this fantasy to play a guy for an evening of love making. How much are you willing to put up for your part of the bet?"

"You know, in the last five hours, you've really cheapened yourself. When I saw you, I said to myself, this has got to be one classy lady. What kind of money do you think you're worth? After what I've seen and heard in the last few hours you must already have a going rate. How much?" asks Johnny, pulling a wad of bills from his pants pocket, "a hundred, two hundred, perhaps five hundred."

Angry at Johnny for what he has just said, Flo gets in his face telling him, "I'm not usually like this. I'm a little desperate right now, and desperate people sometimes need to take desperate measures. I'm no two-bit whore you can talk to like that."

"Well," says Johnny, "why have you acted the way you're acting? What's going on?"

"You don't want to know."

"Why don't we sit for a while and you can tell me your story? I'm a good listener."

At the table, they order margaritas and nachos.

"Why don't you tell me what's going on?" says Johnny. "Maybe I can help."

Flo hesitates and collects her thoughts "I'm so ashamed of the way I acted today. I hope you will understand after you hear my story." She holds back tears. "My boyfriend walked out on me six months ago. Says he tired of living in New Mexico. My choices are to go with him or stay behind."

"Why didn't you go?"

"He went on the road to play pool, cards, the horses, anything he can bet on. Then he tells me if we go broke," Flo raises her voice, "I could be his fuckin' prostitute and he'll pimp me off if we need money. I spent two years with this guy. I gave him money when I could, put up with his cheap bullshit when he comes home drunk, and tried to make him happy." Flo has caught the attention of a few people sitting at the bar, she lowers her voice. "This is what I get for trying to do the right thing and make this relationship work. I can really pick 'em. I've been going it alone trying to pay my rent and the rest of my bills, but things are starting to get out of hand. I'm a month behind on rent, and my home phone has been disconnected. I'm trying to hustle some money any way I can. I don't like the person I'm becoming trying to survive. I called a good friend of mine a while back and this is what he told me, hustle. Use my womanly assets and my pool cue, and I should make a good living. Problem is, there's no money to be made in this area. Guys like Frankie and Joey are few and far between. Men around here have a hard time losing to a woman, especially an Indian woman."

"I can give you some money to help you out. I'm on a hot streak and money isn't a problem right now. I won some money in the last three days. Why don't you let me help you get straightened out?" Johnny takes out fifteen hundred dollars and offers it to Flo. "Is this enough to get you out of your crisis for now?"

With trembling hands, Flo reaches out to take the money from Johnny. "It's only a loan. I'm a proud American Indian. I'll find a way to pay you back."

"Is this all you need to get you back on the right track?" asks Johnny.

A long hesitation from Flo produces, "Well, there is one more thing."

"I know," says Johnny, "you've got three kids and they all need new shoes and their clothes are all ripped so you need another thousand."

"Naw," says Flo, "if I had three kids I'd be on welfare and Uncle Sam would give me food and clothing. I wish it were that easy. I need five hundred dollars to enter the women's tour event that comes through here in a few weeks. It's a chance for me to break into the tour and play with the top female players. You saw me play this afternoon. I'm as good as 90%, maybe 95% of the women out there playing. The only thing I lack is a sponsor. I have the playing skills to compete at that level—"

"Why haven't you entered in the past?"

"I wasn't good enough two years ago. Last year, I was all set. I had the money, my game was right where I wanted it to be, and then my boyfriend decides the horse in the fifth race was a better bet than me. He threw my chance to play with the big girls right down the drain."

"So how do I know you won't blow this five hundred if I give it to you?"

"I guess you don't."

"Two days ago, I was in Las Vegas. I went to the blackjack tables and won several thousand dollars. I took a chance, and I got lucky. I'm ready to take another chance. I'll give you the entry fee, but I want half the money you win if you do well."

79

Flo is so excited she lunges at Johnny, forgetting there is a table between the two of them. A glass crashes to the floor, but Flo is too busy hugging Johnny to even notice. Realizing what she's done, she scrambles to pick up the pieces of glass. As she's picking up the pieces of broken glass, she tells Johnny, "Before today, my life was like these pieces of glass, broken apart. I will take this glass back to my apartment, and as my life gets better, I will put the pieces of this glass back together to symbolize my newfound life. I will also remember you, Johnny, for helping me to find my way."

Later, Flo suggests she and Johnny take a ride to the outskirts of town. "Albuquerque has beautiful sunsets."

"I suppose they also have some beautiful sunrises, but I can't stay around for either. I'm a product of a one night stand, and I'm not about to have some kid tracking me down years from now telling me that I'm his father. I'm on my way to Kentucky. I've already taken longer than I wanted to get this far. I'd love to spend more time with you, but it's time I moved along. Why don't we exchange cell numbers and we can keep in touch by phone. You can tell me how your life's going and I'll do the same."

After they exchange numbers, Johnny gets up and heads towards the door. Flo goes along with him to his car. As he starts to get into his car, he says to Flo, "I'm thinking of driving straight through to Kentucky. I don't know if I can take another episode like this for a while."

Flo leans into the window and gives Johnny more than just a friendly kiss. "My people say, 'When two people's paths cross in life, it will happen again if it's meant to be.' I believe our lives are now bound eternally." She takes her hand and kisses her index and middle fingers, then places them on Johnny's forehead. "The gods are in control of our destiny. They will find a way for our paths to cross again." Johnny looks at Flo and feels a little freaky. She has gone into a trance while speaking to him. "*Via Con Dias*," Flo says to Johnny. He backs away with Flo standing in the parking lot.

As Johnny drives, Flo walks slowly back into Giuseppe's. She can't believe her life has changed so much in such a short time. She takes the money Johnny has given her from her pocket. Looking at it in disbelief, she lets out a huge sigh, knowing how much easier her life will become.

# CHAPTER 7

After what seems like a week of driving, Johnny pulls off the interstate for a break. He approaches a place named Rosie's and gets food, then books a room. He then calls his mother.

"I thought I might hear from you today," she tells Johnny. "I was starting to worry. So, where are you now?"

"I'm in a small town in Missouri, about seventy miles from Jefferson City."

"So you got out of Albuquerque okay. You had your eyes on a pretty barmaid."

"You know," Johnny says, "I hate it when you remember everything I tell you. A lot happened, but nothing happened, if that makes any sense."

"Why don't you tell me what happened and let me figure out if nothing happened?"

Johnny tells her about Albuquerque except for his act of generosity, and then asks, "What's been going on with you, Mom?"

"I thought you'd never ask. With all our kids are back at school—I didn't tell her you might be going east. With all the free time we both have, Cindy and I decided to join a fitness club today. We even have a personal trainer. He set up a schedule for us Monday, Wednesday, and Friday from 9:30 to 11:30. I've always wanted to do this and now I'm going to. It's time to think of myself for a change." Elaine catches herself and says to Johnny, "My selfishness doesn't include my son. I'm always here for you, Johnny."

"It's time you did more for yourself. Don't ever feel guilty about taking some time for you. You've more than paid your dues." Johnny's cell phone battery starts to die, and their words are beginning to sound garbled. The conversation ends.

Shortly after, 8:00 a.m. Johnny eats and starts his traveling again. After a few hours, he plugs his phone charger in and scrolls down to Flo's number, then calls. "It's Johnny. I figured I'd give you a call to see how you're doing."

"Things have been happening fast in the last two days. I asked my boss for a raise, and he gave me ten percent more. I also asked him if I could change my hours so I could play in some of the local tournaments during the week. He said okay.

"I went across town last night to play in a handicap tournament. There was a field of thirty players, and I won the whole thing. I took home $150 dollars. The big tournament is coming to town in a few weeks. When I signed up, they said the field was full and put me on a waiting list. A couple of hours later, my phone rings. One of the girls backed out, so now I'm in the tournament." Flo takes time to catch her breath. "I'm putting the pieces of that glass back together in a hurry. You helped me turn my life around. Things right now couldn't be better."

The air is not only back in Johnny's balloon, he's floating on cloud nine. He takes this time to tell Flo, "I've thought about you often. You've helped make a long, lonely ride a lot more bearable."

Flo suddenly interjects into the conversation. "I'm in the parking lot at work. The cook and the cleaning people are at the door, so I have to run. Call me tonight after seven, and I'll have time to talk."

He disconnects, then throws the cell phone in the passenger seat; it bounces and falls to the floorboard. Johnny shakes his head and grips the steering wheel tightly, then punches the horn. "Damnit!" He lets out a deep breath through gritted teeth. "Why can't I just tell the girl how I feel?" After a few more miles down the road and a few good songs on the radio, his grip on the wheel loosens and he starts to relax. *When I talk to her tonight, I'll make sure I tell her! I must! The fuckin' cat that always seems to grab my tongue has to loosen up. I want to get to know this girl, really get to know her.*

Johnny has crossed into Indiana, and the final stretch to Lexington is in reach. His anxiety builds up as he thinks about meeting his father. His palms are sweaty and his adrenaline is flowing. In an effort to calm down a little, he calls his mom.

"I figured out my plan for getting to know Billy. I can ask him for lessons."

"That's a great idea, Johnny. What made you think of that?"

"I know Cliff took golf lessons, and you took tennis lessons. I know this may sound stupid, but if I'm paying Billy, he'll have to give me some of his time."

"That's not the best reason I've ever heard of. Why don't you look at it as a way of breaking the ice, getting to know one another?"

"I think that was my original plan. Forget what I just said to you. That was pretty stupid. I'm not thinking too clearly right now. I'm feeling a little anxious, and all this driving isn't helping either."

"Open the windows and get some fresh air, or pull over and walk around."

Johnny assures his mom the deep breaths and fresh air is more than enough to settle him down. He also says, "I guess I just needed to hear a calming voice. I'll be fine the rest of the way."

"When you finally meet Billy, you'll know who he is, but he has no idea who you are. Don't be too judgmental and keep an open mind."

A horn starts blowing in the background of Elaine's phone. "I have to run. Cindy is in the driveway. We're off to do some shopping; I've already dropped a pound; the workouts are going great."

Johnny congratulates his mom, then says, "I just saw a sign for Lexington, Kentucky, and it's only 180 miles away."

"Keep an open mind."

There's plenty of daylight left when Johnny reaches Lexington. This is a good thing for Johnny; he doesn't like driving in the dark in unfamiliar territory. He finds a motel just off the highway on Cox Street and decides to rent the room for a week. Johnny unpacks all his stuff and puts everything in its appropriate place, then takes a nap. His cell phone rings.

"I thought you were going to call me," says Flo. "After I finished work I was worried stiff thinking you might have had an accident or something crazy like that."

Johnny is still yawning when he finally asks Flo, "What time is it?"

"It's eight o'clock here and you were supposed to call a little past seven. I'm about to start playing a match, and I didn't want to be worried about you while I'm playing pool."

"I'm sorry about that. I dozed off." He sits up in bed. "I appreciate you caring enough to be worried about me." Johnny is suddenly awake as his heartbeat quickens. "I've thought a lot about you and a lot about the last moment we were together in the parking lot." He lets out a deep, anxious breath. "Your kiss has made it hard to keep driving east."

Flo is touched by Johnny's honesty. "I sat in the parking lot for some time hoping you would come back." With their feelings for one another more out in the open, they share some small talk for a few minutes. "They just called my match. I have to go play."

"I'm going to be busy the next few days. I'm going to meet my real father, and I want to concentrate all my efforts in that direction. I don't want you to feel I'm avoiding you, but I've got twenty-three years to catch up on."

"I'm on a hot streak. I've got a tournament to win. Call me when you get the chance. I can see the guy I'm playing is growing impatient. Let me go kick his ass. I'll let you know how I make out next time we talk."

Johnny gets directions to the poolroom, then grabs his cue and heads out the door. Johnny goes to the front desk and asks the clerk if there are any restaurants still open in the area. Noticing Johnny is carrying a cue the clerk asks, "Are you headed for *The Stripes and Solids?*"

"Yeah."

"They have everything there," says the clerk. "You can get a full course dinner if you want. It's quite a place. A young guy like you should really have fun there."

Johnny thanks the clerk for his help and walks to his car.

# CHAPTER 8

The ride to *The Stripes and Solids* is a little too short as far as Johnny is concerned. The parking lot is just about full, but he manages to find a spot. He sits in the car for a while before getting out. His stomach is feeling the effects of not eating for several hours and being nervous at the possibility of meeting his real father. When he gets out of the car, he takes a few deep breaths to settle his nerves. He walks across the parking lot towards the main entrance. There are people standing outside the doorway. As Johnny makes his way to the doors, he takes a very deep breath. His five-day journey is complete.

He starts to walk around, looking for the eating area. The clerk at the motel wasn't kidding. *This place has everything,* Johnny thinks to himself. There are two full-size bars at each end of the room. He counts sixteen pool tables arranged in four rows of four spread across the room. The place where Johnny is standing is about six feet higher than where the tables are. It's a mezzanine that goes around the entire poolroom. This provides a beautiful view of all the tables in the room.

The room is full of young people, probably college students. The music is loud, and a lot of the tables have couples playing and having fun. The rest of the room is comprised of boys looking for girls or girls looking for boys. For someone looking to play serious pool, this isn't what Johnny had anticipated.

Johnny opens a door and can't believe what's on the other side. There are at least twenty booths set in a dining area. He sits at one and has something to eat. Across the dining room is a large counter. The sign above the counter reads "Action Central." Next to the counter is a large board, and written on the board are all kinds of pool games. It's like being in a casino. The games listed are nine-ball and one-pocket. The dollar amounts range from $10 to $500. Johnny sees a few names on the board looking for games. One player wants to play one-pocket. Another has his name under the nine-ball sign for $50 sets. After his meal, Johnny walks over to "Action Central" telling the person at the counter, "I'm willing to play the person looking for $50 action."

The person at the control desk opens the microphone and calls Jim to come to the counter. After a few minutes, Jim is at the counter. He asks Johnny, "You the one looking for some $50 action?"

"I'm your guy."

Jim says, "You sound pretty anxious. Maybe I should wait around to see if someone else comes in. I don't remember seeing you here before. You're not some out of town hustler come to take advantage of us country folk, are you?"

"I'm from California and like to play nine-ball, and your name was the only name on the board. If you don't want to play I'll just wait around for someone else."

"I like your honesty, kid. Come on, I'll try you a couple of sets. The money goes up front with the cashier. This way nobody runs out the door without paying." Jim reaches into his pocket and pulls out a roll of hundreds that would choke a horse. Johnny has his money in a few different places, but doesn't want to draw attention to himself by flashing a large bankroll. He goes into his left front pocket and takes out his money. He has a few hundreds in his stack and makes sure Jim sees he has a good amount of money when he hands over his fifty dollars. The two players gather their things together and head for the tables.

Jim tells Johnny, "We have to pay the table time up front. We both pay twelve dollars apiece, and we're good till eight tomorrow morning."

"We can play all night for just twelve dollars? How do they stay in business?"

"Volume. You stick around here long enough and you'll see how they stay in business."

With the table time paid, Johnny starts to head back in the direction he saw all the people playing pool. Jim heads in a different direction. He calls to Johnny, "Where the hell are you going?"

"To the poolroom across the dining area."

"That's the entertainment area. The poolroom is this way." Jim is pointing with his cue case. "Follow me, it's through this door."

The first door leads to a small hallway, which leads to a second door. When Johnny opens the second door, he has a hard time believing his eyes. The room is the exact replica of the other room, only twice the size. There are thirty-two tables instead of sixteen. There is more space between tables and no loud music. In fact, Johnny can't hear any noise because the room is completely enclosed. The mezzanine is there, but has Plexiglas all around it, reminding Johnny of a hockey rink. Johnny and Jim open another door on the mezzanine and enter the room. Finally, the sound of clicking pool balls enters Johnny's ears.

The room is half full with people playing. There is a large center aisle that separates two groups of sixteen tables. Jim tells Johnny, "We're on the right side of the room. The left side is for people playing one-pocket." Johnny thinks to himself, *What a perfectly conceived poolroom.* As he's putting his cue together, he notices another great thing about this room. He can't see back through the Plexiglas to the mezzanine. There's some kind of tint in the glass that prevents him from seeing back out of the room.

Johnny and Jim end up playing on table number eight. It's the last table in the first row. As they're putting their cues together, a young lady comes to the table carrying a rack of pool-balls. Placing the balls on the table, she asks, "Can I get you fellas something to drink?"

Jim tells the waitress, "I'll have a bourbon and water."

He offers to buy Johnny a drink. Johnny tells Jim, "I'll take a bottle of water, thanks."

Consumed by his surroundings as he and Jim start to play, Johnny loses the coin flip and racks the balls. He asks Jim, "Does Billy spend much time here?"

"There's a lot of different Billy's that come in here. Which Billy are you talking about?" Before Johnny can reply, Jim stops pulling his leg. "Of course," Jim says. "You're talking about Billy Bates. He'll be here sooner or later. Usually comes in between midnight and one. That's when the real action starts around here."

Jim and Johnny finally get around to playing nine-ball. Johnny's game is sluggish starting out. His shoulders are tight from all the driving during the past few days. He loses the first set to Jim 7-5. Jim is a slow, methodical player, and Johnny has trouble adjusting to the pace of the match. The second set is close the whole time. Johnny wins a tough rack to bring the score to six to six ("hill-hill"). He breaks the next rack. He has made his best break of the night and pockets two balls. His first shot is an easy one-ball in the corner pocket. The two-ball went in on the break. There is an easy three-nine combination sitting near the side pocket. Johnny makes the one-ball, bringing the cue-ball off the back rail and in perfect position for the combination. He chalks his cue, takes his time, and pockets the nine off the three-ball. Johnny wins the second set 7-6.

Two drinks have been consumed by Jim during the two first sets. Before they start the third set, Jim takes a bathroom break. Johnny figures he might as well use the facilities along with Jim. Johnny asks, "Is it safe to leave our stuff here when we use the restroom?"

"They have cameras all over this place. Besides, I know the people playing on table six, and I'll have them keep an eye on our things."

The trip to the men's room is over, and Jim and Johnny are back to their table in five minutes. Johnny has been so involved with playing that he hadn't noticed how full the room is getting. There are only four empty tables. Johnny offers to buy Jim another drink before they start playing a third set. Jim accepts Johnny's offer. Johnny also orders a beer for himself.

As Johnny gets ready to flip a coin to start the third set, Jim asks Johnny, "How about we raise the bet to a hundred a set?" Johnny thinks for a while and agrees to raise the bet. Jim takes a fifty dollar bill from his pocket and places it on the light above the table. He tells Johnny, "It takes too long to go back to the cashier for fifty dollars, so we usually put the money up here."

Johnny reaches into his pocket, gets two twenties and a ten, and hands it to Jim. Jim places the money on top of the light. Johnny finally flips the coin to start the next set. Jim calls tails, and the coin comes up heads. Johnny wins the first break. As Johnny is placing his cue-ball on the table where he usually breaks from, there is a small disturbance in the room. Billy has made his usual nighttime entrance. He walks around the room, quietly recognizing each of his patrons. Johnny finds himself getting anxious as Billy makes his way towards his table. Johnny holds off breaking the rack long enough for Billy to get to his table.

When Billy gets close enough, Jim takes over the introductions. Johnny finds out that Jim and Billy are a little more than acquaintances. Jim says to Billy, "We got ourselves some fresh blood here, Billy. Boy shoots pretty straight. He's come all the way here from California."

Billy extends his hand to Johnny. As the two shake hands, Billy says, "I'm Billy Bates. It's nice to meet you."

In his eagerness to make a good impression, Johnny says, "I know who you are. I saw you play Rico Sanchez on ESPN."

Billy points out to Johnny, "That wasn't one of my finest moments in life."

Johnny changes the subject. "My name is Johnny Jordan, but my friends call me J.J."

"I've got a bunch of people here tonight, and I've got to get on with business. I'll let you and Jim get back to your game. Perhaps we can talk a little more some other time." Billy takes the time to make one more comment to Jim. "Take it easy on Johnny or J.J. or whoever he is. We need all the customers we can get. Don't chase him out of here."

Jim assures Billy, "I don't think this kid is afraid of me. We just upped the bet from fifty to a hundred. I figured I'd see if he's got any heart."

Johnny is starting to get annoyed listening to Billy and Jim talk. He gathers himself and remembers what Larry had told him when someone tries to rattle him. Larry had told him when someone is trying to get into your head, they are showing fear. They don't feel capable of beating you with their ability. Take advantage of the situation. Play the game the way you always play. You already have your opponent's attention, and he's the one feeling the pressure. Pool is truly a game where actions speak louder than words.

The rest of the night turns into a nightmare for Jim. Johnny dominates play through the next four sets. Jim is foolish enough to keep on drinking while trying to play and his game is suffering the consequences. Jim also insists on raising the bet again. After the first three sets for a hundred, Jim pushed the bet to two hundred for the fourth set. Johnny is comfortably sitting in the driver's seat; he's ahead of Jim five hundred dollars. Jim has also gone through a personality change, developing a temper and constantly complaining. Johnny is getting all the rolls in his favor.

Time passes quickly—normal in a poolroom. It's five-thirty in the morning and Jim decides to make one final stand. He offers to play Johnny one final set, a race to nine games for a thousand dollars. Johnny hesitates to play the game. He has won five hundred. If he loses this race, he will end up losing five hundred. Jim gets impatient waiting for Johnny's decision, making a comment just loud enough so Johnny can hear him. He accuses Johnny of not having the guts to play for a thousand. Johnny finally decides he's had enough of Jim's bullshit. He takes out the money he needs to cover Jim's bet and places it on top of the light. Johnny asks Jim at this time, "Would you like to bet more than a thousand?" Johnny has turned the table on Jim, showing far too much confidence.

Jim tucks his tail in and says to Johnny, "A thousand dollars is enough."

Jim doesn't want to flip a coin for the first break. He insists on lagging for the first break. At this point, Johnny doesn't care how they determine who gets opening break. All he knows is there's two grand sitting on top of the light waiting for the winner. Jim wins the lag, earning the right to break the first rack.

Jim's break, as has been the case for most of the night, is weak. He fails to make a ball, and Johnny comes to the table. The rack is difficult, but Johnny uses it to his advantage. He makes the balls he can pocket and plays safe when it's the best option. He quickly gains a three game advantage using this strategy.

The fourth rack turns out to be quite an experience for Johnny. He's shooting at a five-ball, which is close to the eight-ball. He miscues shooting the shot. The cue-ball appears to hit the object-ball, but it's close; Jim comes to the table claiming Johnny's cue-ball hit the eight first and says he has ball-in-hand. Johnny argues his case, saying he hit the five. Jim threatens to take back the money and call off the match if he doesn't get his way. With a three game lead already established, Johnny relinquishes and gives Jim ball-in-hand. Jim takes advantage of the situation and runs out the remaining five balls on the table. The score is now 3-1 in Johnny's favor.

The argument swings the momentum of the match in Jim's favor. He wins the next rack, making the score 3-2. Johnny sits in his seat and is starting to get pissed off thinking about the way Jim has manipulated him. His frustration continues to grow as Jim makes his way through the next rack. Jim is shooting a five-ball into the side pocket, making the five, but leaving himself a difficult shot on the six. It's a tough side to side cut shot away from the rail about three inches, a diamond below the side pocket. Jim shoots the shot but fails to cut the six enough. It hits the side rail and bobbles out of the pocket. Johnny comes to the table with an easy shot to start. He makes the six- through nine-balls to win the game.

Jim never recovers from missing the six-ball, although Johnny gives him a few good opportunities. Johnny wins the set 9-5. Johnny takes the money from the light. As he puts his cue in his case, Jim manages to make a few more excuses to Johnny as to why he lost. He also tells Johnny, "If we play again, I'll need a little weight."

Johnny doesn't want to rub it in Jim's face, so he simply states, "I think we can make a game."

Johnny collects all his things and starts to walk out of the room. It's about 7:00 a.m. and the room is busier than it was at 10:30 the previous evening. Some of the people playing acknowledge Johnny as he walks from the room. One of the guys playing tells Johnny, "Don't see Jim take many losses. It's about time someone gets some of his money." Johnny senses Jim isn't the most popular person in the room. If he acts the same way he did with Johnny, it's easy to understand Jim's lack of popularity.

Nine and a half hours of playing pool mentally and physically drains Johnny. He needs a good breakfast desperately, so he takes a seat and orders. While Johnny sips a cup of coffee, he reads a local newspaper someone had left in the booth. He has his head down and is reading an article when he hears a voice. It startles him. It's Billy.

"That's the kind of concentration it takes to play pool. Maybe you've got what it takes. Mind if I sit down?"

Nervous as he's ever felt, Johnny tries to get out of the booth to show Billy some respect. In the process, he hits the news paper and spills the rest of what's left of his coffee all over his pants. *Oh! Fuck, He's going to think I'm an idiot.* Billy slows Johnny down, telling him, "You don't have to get out of your seat for me. I'm nobody special."

"My parents always told me to show respect," says Johnny.

"Mind if I sit down? I hope you weren't always this clumsy," Billy jokingly says. "It might have been dangerous being around you."

While wiping his pants and wiping up his mess Johnny thinks about Larry's and his mother's advice, he considers coming right out with the fact he is Billy's son, but holds off. He laughs to himself at Billy's comment about being around him, before stating his false purpose of getting to know Billy better.

"To be honest, I'm a big fan of yours. I came here hoping I could take some pool lessons from you. I watched all of your matches on ESPN, and you are by far the best player I've ever seen."

"The last person I taught to play humiliated me on national television. I'm not in that business anymore. That little ungrateful bastard, he couldn't beat anybody till I taught him the game. Furthermore, I was the one who beat the best players in the tournament." Billy catches himself rambling on. "I just watched you play for about five hours. You beat up on Jim pretty good. The problem is you probably lost 95% of the action you're going to get in this place. You might have been better off losing."

"I made fifteen hundred dollars. That's not chicken feed."

"I've got a couple of guys who come in here regularly. If you had lost to Jim, they would have given you at least the eight, maybe even the seven. You could have easily beaten them for five, maybe ten thousand. Now the word will be out, and those guys won't go near you. The news isn't all bad."

"What do you mean?"

"I like what I saw out there. You have some talent and I'd like to take you under my wing, tell you who to play, and what kind of games to ask for from them. I think you and I can do some hustling, make some easy money."

Johnny is skeptical of the arrangement Billy wants to make hustling people. But he also realizes this may be his only chance to get to know Billy, so he agrees to meet Billy's terms.

"Where you from? Is that a West Coast accent I'm hearing?"

"Just outside of L.A."

Billy mentions that he has spent a few years in California. Knowing what Johnny knows, Johnny tries to avoid talking about Billy's time in California. Billy then makes a comment that gets Johnny's attention. He says, "I spent a long time looking for someone I lost." Johnny is happy to see Billy has a human side to him. He sits and chats with Johnny a few more minutes before his name is announced over the intercom. He is needed at Action Central. Billy gets up to leave, then tells Johnny, "I'll see you tonight around nine o'clock. There's a room across town that a couple of big betters go to. Maybe we can find you a game."

Before Johnny finishes his breakfast, Billy is back at his table. Billy is mumbling to himself as he sits down, telling Johnny, "People who come in here never cease to amaze me. This guy just played pool for fourteen hours and doesn't understand why he should have to pay twenty dollars for table time. I told him it's ten dollars every eight hours. It doesn't matter if you play eight hours and one minute, or fifteen hours and fifty-nine minutes, the price is still the same. I wouldn't mind," says Billy, "except the guy won three hundred playing one pocket. I told him next time, go play somewhere else. I don't need the aggravation." Billy suddenly turns his attention back to Johnny. "Oh yeah," he asks Johnny, "Where are you staying?"

"At the motel on Cox Street."

"That's good, you can get here quick. You never know who might come through the door or what time of day they might come in." Billy asks for Johnny's cell number and tells Johnny that cell phones are great tools for hustlers. "We can both be in a poolroom two hundred feet apart, talking about who to play and what kind of spot to ask for, and no one is the wiser." Johnny isn't sure what Billy is talking about, but he gives Billy his number. The waitress shows up with Johnny's check, but Billy tells her to put Johnny's bill on his tab. Billy tells Johnny, "If you're hustling for me, I pay the bills." Johnny thanks Billy for breakfast. He takes a ten dollar bill from his pocket and leaves it for a tip. Johnny gathers his belongings together and goes out the door.

The streets of Lexington aren't busy at eight-fifteen on a Saturday morning, and it takes less than ten minutes for Johnny to get back to his room. He wants to call his mother, but realizes it's only five-fifteen on the West Coast. The good news will have to wait till later. Johnny decides to take a hot shower, hoping it will help him relax before going to bed.

After sleeping, he calls his mother. "I met Billy last night. In fact, he bought me breakfast."

"How does that work?"

Johnny tells her about the night, and then says, "Billy wants to teach me how to hustle people."

"I don't like the sound of that," says Elaine. "It sounds seedy to me."

Johnny assures his mother there's nothing seedy about what he and Billy will be doing. "Billy knows all the players around this area. He'll just make games that put me in a good position to win. Besides, I had to take whatever he was offering if I wanted to get to know him."

Elaine understands Johnny's line of reasoning and says, "I wish he had agreed to give you lessons. It would have made me feel better."

"I have another call; hold on a minute." Johnny clicks over to the other line.

It's Billy. He asks Johnny, "How soon can you get here? There's a guy here looking for action, and you can beat him pretty easily."

"I'll be there in ten minutes." He clicks back to his mom. Johnny tells her Billy is on the other line and wants him at the poolroom right away. "I'm headed over there. I'll call you tomorrow. Talk to you later, bye."

He calls Billy back. "I'm in the parking lot."

"He's still here talking to my waitress. His name is Walter, and he's on the board looking to play hundred dollar sets. Come in and put your name in at Action Central. Tell them you'll play for a hundred, and Walter will seek you out. Tell him you'll try him for a set or two, and then you can adjust the game if you have to. You're probably capable of giving this guy the seven-ball. Make sure you keep the sets close, even if it takes missing a few shots on purpose. It might not be a bad idea to lose a set." Billy goes on to tell Johnny, "Oh yeah, I put up all the money. That's the good part for you. The bad part is I get sixty percent of the winnings."

What Johnny says next catches Billy off guard. "I don't need the money. I'd play for nothing; I just like playing pool."

Billy doesn't have time to figure this out. He tells Johnny to hurry up and get his name on the board.

Once Johnny gets his name on the board things go exactly the way Billy said it would. Walter seeks out Johnny, and they start to play. Play by both players is sloppy in the beginning. The first six racks seem to take forever. The score is three to three. Johnny is having trouble playing. He's constantly thinking about what Billy told him earlier. Keep the games close. Walter has an easy out of four balls to win the seventh game. Somehow, he misses an easy six-ball and Johnny wins the rack to go ahead four games to three. Johnny breaks the next rack and makes the nine on the break. He now enjoys a two-game advantage.

Breaking the next rack, Johnny pockets two more balls. Fortunately, he has a difficult shot on the one-ball, and it's a bank shot. He plays the shot, knowing he's not creating a long enough angle off the side rail to make the shot. He misses, leaving Walter an easy shot to start out. Walter makes two balls and creates a dilemma for Johnny when he misses the next shot. With five balls on the table, Johnny has to find a way to screw up without making it too obvious to Walter. Johnny makes the five- and six-balls. His position for the seven-ball comes up short; he manages to safe himself behind the nine-ball. Unable to make a clean hit on the seven-ball, Johnny shoots the cue-ball into the cushion. He makes sure he misses the seven-ball completely. Walter comes to the table. He has ball-in-hand with three easy shots remaining. He makes the balls to make the score six to five, Johnny's favor. The next game Johnny wins after he and Walter miss several shots. Johnny's misses are on purpose.

The rest of the night continues in the same fashion. Johnny starts to make a game out of how to look bad enough at pool so Walter will continue to play him. He either leaves himself in a bad position for highly miss-able shots or leaves himself safe on critical position shots. Walter is none the wiser to Johnny's little game. Walter tells Johnny on numerous occasions that he's lucky to be winning.

Johnny has won all seven sets. Walter had upped the bet to two hundred after the fourth set. Johnny's up one thousand dollars entering the eighth set. Walter plays his best set of the night and wins the set seven to four. He proclaims to Johnny that he finally found his stroke. He offers to up the bet to four hundred a set; Johnny accepts. Walter's game does improve in the next set, but Johnny steps up his game to win a close match seven to six. The hard-fought match takes the wind out of Walter's sails after losing that match; he loses two more sets before calling it a day.

While paying for the table time as a good will gesture to Walter, Johnny considers his next move. He's as hungry as a horse, so he walks over to one of the booths and sits down to order his breakfast. He figures Billy will be coming to join him at any minute. To Johnny's surprise, Billy doesn't come to his table; he calls him on the phone instead. Not wanting to raise any suspicion, Billy tells Johnny, "There's another player sitting two booths away from where you are sitting. He has been watching you and Walter play for hours. I don't want to come near you right now; sit tight for a while. The guy might ask you to play."

"I'm too tired to even think about playing anyone else today."

"You're not about to play him right now. What you want to do is make an appointment to play tonight. If he asks you to play, tell him you need a spot of at least the wild eight-ball. He just witnessed you win two thousand dollars from Walter. He'll be anxious to play knowing you're carrying a good amount of money."

After Johnny hangs up, it only takes a few minutes for the man Billy was talking about to come over and introduce himself to Johnny. As he puts his hand out for Johnny to shake, he says to Johnny, "My name is Bobby Wilder. Are you interested in maybe playing a few cheap sets?"

Bobby's as cute as a used car salesman, and Johnny sees right through him. He makes the excuse.

"I've been playing all night with Walter, and I could use some rest."

"Maybe we could get together tonight?"

Johnny doesn't want to appear anxious, he also doesn't care for Bobby's bedside manner. So he hems and haws while making a few awkward faces, before saying to Bobby, "I'll play, but I'm going to need the wild seven."

Bobby's not happy; he disgustingly walks away and thinks for a minute. The cat and mouse game continues when Bobby goes back to where Johnny is sitting. He wants to know why Johnny's asking for such a big spot.

Johnny says to Bobby, "You watched me play Walter for some time. You saw my game, and now you're asking me to play. You obviously think you're better than me, or you wouldn't be asking me to play; that's the reason I need a lot of weight."

This time, it's Bobby's turn to hem and haw after a short deliberation. "I'm not so sure I can give you that big of a spot."

"Those are my terms. If you want to play, be here tonight at ten o'clock."

Bobby counters, saying, "I'll play races to nine for two hundred dollars a set; those are my terms."

"I'll see you at ten o'clock."

Bobby gets up from Johnny's booth and walks towards the door.

As if from out of nowhere, Billy appears at Johnny's booth. He congratulates Johnny on the way he handled Walter and says, "Walter will probably want to play again; he might come back chasing his two grand. People who play this game have a lot of bad tendencies, and he happens to be one of those people." Before Johnny can get a word in, Billy asks him, "What about Bobby? Did you manage to do anything with him?"

"I'm meeting him here tonight at ten o'clock; we're going to play races to nine for two hundred dollars a set, and he's spotting me the wild seven. I didn't like him so I asked for a bigger spot than you suggested and he took the bait."

Billy explains to Johnny he's not happy with the situation. "I love the fact that you're getting the weight you're getting, but Bobby has been known to take a shot at people with short money." Billy figures Bobby has maybe four to six hundred dollars in his pocket. He says to Johnny, "When Bobby shows up tonight, tell him you want to freeze-up a thousand dollars."

"Freeze-up?"

"It's actually called a freeze-out. It requires both people to freeze-up a certain amount of money. Then play starts, and now you know your opponent has at least the amount of money you freeze-up in his pocket and you play until someone wins or losses it, or both players agree to quit. It's basically an insurance policy that guarantees you your opponent isn't playing with a small amount of money in his pockets." Billy's last instructions to Johnny are for him to come to his private room early in the evening so he can practice in private before Bobby comes to play. "Oh, by the way," Billy says, "you owe me twelve hundred dollars." Johnny starts to take the money from his pocket. Billy says to Johnny, "Hold on to a thousand; you may need it tonight if you're going to be playing Bobby."

Johnny hands Billy the two hundred dollars he asked for and says, "You trust me holding a thousand dollars of your money?"

"I trust you like you're my son."

Johnny thinks about what Billy has just said. He mutters to himself as he gets up to leave the booth he sitting in, "If you only knew."

Later that night, Johnny's only focus is on the pool table in Billy's private room. He notices the pocket size is much smaller than they typically are. "How come the pockets in this table are so much smaller?"

Billy tells Johnny, "This is the pocket size the pros are shooting at when they play. When I was practicing to go out and play in a pro event, I had my mechanic make the pockets the same size."

"Why should I practice with small pockets? I'm not playing in any pro events."

"The reason you should practice on a table with small pockets," says Billy, "is because if you can start consistently pocketing balls on this table, when you play on a normal size table you will have that much more confidence in your ability to pocket balls." Billy starts to make a few suggestions for Johnny to consider changing to improve his game. The first thing Billy talks about is Johnny's stroke. He tells him, "Your stroke is too short, and your bridge hand is too close to the cue-ball; it should be eight to ten inches behind the cue-ball."

"I read a bunch of books on this, and they said my hand should be six to eight inches behind the cue-ball."

"What the books fail to explain is that they were all written by people who grew up playing straight pool. Straight pool is a game that requires far less cue-ball movement than nine-ball. If you lengthen out your stroke, you'll move the cue-ball better with far less effort. You'll be using your cue as it was meant to be used, instead of whacking the balls like it's a hammer when you need to do more with the cue-ball." While he's on a roll,

Billy's next suggestion to Johnny is about how high his head is over his cue when he's shooting. Billy takes Johnny's stick and demonstrates to him where and how high his head should be when looking down his cue to shoot a shot. Billy's chin is resting right on top of the cue, and it's directly under the middle of his chin.

Johnny asks Billy, "Are we in here so you can pick my game apart?"

"Naw, I'm trying to improve your skills, so if you ever need to make a tough shot, you'll have more confidence when you pull the trigger."

"If all I'm ever doing is hustling people, why should I improve my skills?"

"If you improve your playing skills, we can start hustling better players. Better players play for more money, and some even have a stake-horse."

"What's a stake-horse?"

"A backer or a guy with a lot of money. They usually run around with people who have talent and can play this game. So if you can improve all your skills, we may be able to make the right game and win us a good chunk of change. I know you don't need the money," says Billy, "but I could always use some extra cash."

Johnny can sense Billy is growing tired of fielding all of his questions, but Billy is polite enough to allow Johnny one more question..

"Why is everything we do such a big secret?"

Billy takes a seat, starts rubbing his forehead, and wiggles around in his chair a little before explaining himself to Johnny. "Why," he says, "is everything such a big secret? I'll tell you why. A few years ago, I brought a guy in here just like you. The word got out in my room I had a hustler playing for me.

I lost a lot of my steady customers because they thought I was robbing them."

"Isn't that what just happened between me and Walter when we played yesterday? You knew I was much better than him. Isn't that robbing someone?"

Billy smirks a little, then says, "Yes and no. For the sake of argument, let's review what happened since you first hit town. You played Jim and won fifteen hundred dollars. Jim has spent the last part of five years beating up my customers. The loss he suffered the other night might have been his first loss in my room. Then came Walter, who was going to lose his money to someone; he always does. Why not lose it to me? If he loses it to Bobby, the money is either at a race track, card game, or bet on a sporting event. I can't control what people do with the money that changes hands in my poolroom. I have people who come in here all the time; they play amongst themselves and are steady customers. I never try to hustle any of them. It's the short-enders. They walk into my place looking to rob people so they can run and blow the money somewhere else. These are the people I want you to take care of for me."

"Makes sense. Is there anything else about my game I should change?"

Billy shows Johnny what he should look like when he is shooting a shot. Johnny has a clear visual of what Billy is explaining to him. As Billy talks, Johnny starts to get a better understanding of what he's saying because Billy is also giving him a demonstration by placing some balls on the table and shooting them into pockets. For the next few minutes, Billy talks about how Johnny needs to get down lower on his shots. He demonstrates to Johnny how it's done by bending his legs, not his back. "Your legs are much stronger than your back, and if you play this game for many hours, it will take a toll on you."

Johnny has formed a picture in his mind of the things Billy has been demonstrating. As Billy hands the cue to Johnny, he says, "Don't make the changes I told you to make all of the sudden; do them slowly, a little at a time."

While all this talking and instruction was going on, Johnny's dinner had been brought into the room. Billy tells Johnny, "Hurry up and eat your dinner; it's getting cold. After you eat, try to practice some of the things we talked about. I'll keep an eye out for Bobby in the other room." Billy leaves the room, and Johnny eats his dinner. Afterwards, he practices one thing at a time. The first thing he starts to do is lengthen out his stroke, and he notices results immediately. His cue-ball is moving effortlessly around the table. His follow-through is smoother and longer than it was in the past. The next step Johnny takes is trying to lower his head. He makes sure he feels the cue on his chin while stroking the shot. Johnny starts to notice he's seeing the contact point of the object-ball better from this vantage point. He starts firing balls into the pockets.

Time once again passes quickly. Billy comes back into the room to tell Johnny, "Bobby's in the house." As Johnny gathers up all his things, Billy reminds him, "We're only playing if Bobby freezes-up the thousand dollars."

"Why are you taking such a hard line on posting a thousand dollars?"

"Because Bobby might have as little as two hundred dollars in his pocket; we can't give him big odds on his money. If I am willing to lose a thousand dollars, I want to be able to win the same amount."

Although Johnny is more anxious than ever to play, he honors Billy's request. He says to Bobby, "I've left a thousand dollars at Action Central; if you want to play, you have to match my thousand."

"We never discussed anything about putting up a thousand dollars."

"It slipped my mind."

Bobby starts to yell at Johnny: "I drove for an hour to play tonight. I'm not about to drive home and get more money. Next time you want to play, make sure nothing slips your mind." Bobby grabs his cue case and heads for the door.

Johnny has second thoughts about playing Bobby. He would love to beat him out of any money he might have brought with him. The paging system immediately erases any thoughts of playing Bobby as a young lady announces over the loudspeaker, "Johnny Jordan, please come to the practice room."

Johnny is fuming as he gathers all his things together and walks in the direction of the practice room. He's not used too walking away from anything, and he's not sure he'll be able to control himself if the situation comes up again. He wishes he could have played Bobby with his own money. He would have enjoyed burying the little bastard and taking his money. He arrives at the practice room opens the door and slams it as he walks inside. Billy can see Johnny is upset, so he asks, "What's wrong with you?"

"Bobby yelled at me and made me look stupid. I wanted to play him with my own money. I don't know if I can handle our relationship."

Billy's not happy with Johnny, but he keeps his cool. "You don't have to do everything I tell you to do. I just strongly suggest you do. It's a lot more fun when you win playing this game. If you want to go back on your own, be my guest."

*Johnny, you're not here to be a hustler; you're here to get to know your father!* "I'm sorry, Billy. I need to work on not getting upset at every little thing. You're sticking your neck out for me here, and

I need to respect that." Johnny swallows hard—part spit, part pride.

"I accept your apology, but remember, there are a few emotions that don't belong in a poolroom, and anger is probably the worst one of all; it gets you doing many stupid things. The night you played Jim you controlled yourself and didn't let him get under your skin. If you show someone you're prone to get angry, they'll take advantage of you by needling you whenever they can."

"So," says Johnny, "what do I do for the rest of the night? I slept all day anticipating playing Bobby. It's ten forty-five, and I'm wide awake."

"You've had action two out of the three nights you've been here; you're spoiled. I've sat in poolrooms for days at a time waiting for a game. Why don't you practice the things we talked about earlier and maybe someone will come in to play in the next few hours?"

Johnny spends the better part of five hours on the table. The novelty starts to wear off, and Johnny is starting to get bored. Just in the nick of time, Johnny's cell phone starts to ring; it takes a few rings before he answers. He's pleasantly surprised when he hears the voice on the other end of the line: it's Flo.

"Did you forget about your investment? I'll have you know I'm playing the best pool of my life. I hope it continues through the tournament. I won another local tournament tonight, and I beat one of the best players in the area. He was spotting me two games in a race to seven, but I beat him five games to four. He was a little annoyed that I beat him, even." Flo catches herself babbling on about her life. She takes a deep breath before saying to Johnny, "So, what's been going on with you?"

"I've turned into a vampire," says Johnny. "I sleep all day and play pool all night, but I've managed to make some money. I have a backer who's teaching me how to hustle; his name's Billy Bates."

"Is that the same Billy Bates who played Rico Sanchez?"

"That's him," says Johnny.

"How in the world did you manage to hook up with Billy Bates?"

Johnny fills Flo in on all the details since he arrived in Kentucky and how Billy approached him after he beat Bill out of fifteen hundred dollars..

"Sounds like things are going to work out well for you, Johnny."

"I just wish I wasn't hustling people. I don't like the way it makes me feel. I've had to miss some shots on purpose to keep things close. I don't like playing that way."

"Is it as bad as when you were playing Frankie and Joey?"

"Not quite," says Johnny. "The people I'm playing here are a little bit better than those two. I don't want Billy to think I'm ungrateful, but I'd like to start playing fairer games. I'm trying to improve my game, and I want to know if I've got what it takes."

"I have an idea," says Flo. "Why don't you get out of town for a little while?"

"Where would I go?" asks Johnny.

"Why don't you try Albuquerque? I know a nice little Indian lady who wouldn't mind some company for a few days. I could set up a few matches, and you could play some of the better players in the area. Kinda put yourself through a test and find out how good you are playing. Plus, the fact that I would have someone here for moral support when I'm playing in my tournament. Did I mention it starts in four days?"

"I don't know," says Johnny. "I'm just getting to know Billy. I don't want him to think I'm walking out on him."

"You could say someone in your family passed away, and you have to go home for the funeral."

Johnny appreciates Flo's scheme, but he's also reminded of the reason he's in Kentucky. Although it hurts to turn down Flo's invitation, he says to her, "I'm going to stick it out here for a while and see what happens." Johnny is feeling some pain about his situation with Billy so he asks Flo the infamous question: "Flo, can you keep a secret?"

"How big is this secret?"

Johnny lowers his voice and says, "It's huge. If what I tell you ever gets out it could change my life, suddenly. If I tell you my secret, you have to promise to never tell anyone else unless I say it's okay."

"You're really serious about this secret of yours, aren't you, Johnny? Okay, I promise."

"I drove from California to Kentucky to meet Billy Bates. It's very possible that he is my biological father."

Flo has a hard time grasping everything Johnny has just said to her. It takes a few seconds before Flo says to Johnny, "Can you prove he's your father?"

Johnny tells Flo about the picture he has with him that was taken in California. He explains briefly about his mom and Billy and the affair they had in the mountains. He goes on to explain about his plan and how he came here just to get to know Billy and see if things could work out between them. Flo understands why Johnny would want to stay in Kentucky and get to know Billy. Before she hangs up the phone, she says, "I'll understand if you don't come, but I'm really hoping you do."

Johnny's phone starts to beep so he tells Flo to hang on while he answers the other call. When Johnny clicks over to the other line, he discovers Billy's the one calling. Billy tells Johnny, "A possible game just showed up. It's not big action, but it's someone to play."

"I'd rather not play at this time because I'm on the line talking to a friend in Albuquerque. Do you mind if I get back to my other conversation?"

Billy says, "Did you know that there is a major tournament for women starting there next week?"

"I know. I'm sponsoring a friend, Flo. She asked me to come to Albuquerque and be with her during the tournament."

"So I take you under my wing, we start making some money and you want to run off to Albuquerque? Is this the kind of thanks I can come to expect from you?" Laughing aloud Billy tells Johnny, "Maybe it's a good idea. If you leave town for a while, people might forget you beat-up on Jim and Walter.

"I wasn't sure if you would understand my leaving."

"Understand?" says Billy. "I can tell you really like this girl. Let me see, how would I like to spend my time, with a broken-down pool hustler or a pretty young girl? Get back on the phone and tell the young lady you're flying out tomorrow. I'll drive you to the airport."

Johnny's excited. He struggles to find the right words to thank Billy. Billy interrupts and says, "You better get back to your call and let her know what's going on. I'll talk to you some other time."

Clicking back to Flo, Johnny asks, "Are you still there?"

"Yeah, I'm still here, but I was starting to doze off lying on my bed waiting for you to come back and talk."

Johnny gives Flo the good news about his conversation with Billy. Flo's no longer close to falling asleep. She's running around her apartment. She's singing the words to Johnny repeatedly on her cell phone. "Johnny is coming to Albuquerque to watch me play. I knew our paths would cross again, someday."

When the singing finally stops, Johnny and Flo talk for a few more minutes before he says to her, "I have a lot to do before I can go to New Mexico." They spend a little more time saying their goodbyes before they both hang up.

After Johnny hangs up, Billy comes into the practice room. He tells Johnny, "I have an empty apartment in the building. I'll rent you the place for thirty dollars a week when you get back from Albuquerque, if you're interested."

Johnny, does the math, and tells Billy, "I'll move in when I get back."

"Go and get everything you're not taking to Albuquerque and put it in the apartment before you leave; that way, you don't have to pay for a motel while you're gone."

Johnny thanks Billy for his generosity.

Billy says, "These acts of generosity are also business investments. If I can make your life easier, you will perform better. I hope the lady in Albuquerque is also willing to keep my investment happy."

Johnny sees no future in discussing his love life with Billy. "I'll let you know how happy I am when I get back from Albuquerque."

Less than fifteen minutes later, Johnny's on his way back to his motel. The first thing he does is book a flight to Albuquerque. Johnny then packs his things and checks out of the motel. He's back at the Stripes and Solids at 8:30 a.m. The place is busy when he gets there. When Johnny comes through the door, Billy comes over and tells him, "Go back outside to your car and drive around the building as far as possible. The entrance to the apartment is back there; I'll come around to meet you there in a few minutes."

When he gets to the apartment, Billy is inside straightening up the place. He says to Johnny, "My housekeeper will be by at the end of the week. I'll have her come in and clean the place while you're gone. It's been awhile since someone has lived in here. I'll have her change the sheets and it wouldn't hurt to air out this place for a few hours." Johnny hustles to get the rest of his belongings into the apartment.

Johnny asks Billy, "Where is your car parked?"

"I always park where my car can be seen by potential customers. If I don't, people will think the place is empty. Nobody wants to walk into a poolroom if they think it's empty. Fortunately for me, this place hasn't been empty since the day I opened. I also tell the day crew to park there so the place looks even busier. That's another feature of the room you provide. I can promise someone a game in a short period of time, as long as I have you on twenty-four hour call."

"I have everything I need ready to go into your car."

"Boy that was fast. How did you pull off packing all your stuff in such a short time?"

"I've been doing it for years attending college."

"When do you find time to attend college?"

"I'm not enrolled this semester. I waited too long to enroll in the fall. I'm not starting classes until January. I figured I'd come here early, find a place to live, and get familiar with my surroundings. I even considered the fact that I wanted to improve my pool game, seeing as I have time to play and practice."

Billy unknowingly starts to give Johnny some fatherly advice: "Finish school and get your degree. If you think there's any future in the game of pool, you're grossly mistaken. It's a great hobby, but, unlike golf and games like that, the money just isn't there for pool players."

"You've done pretty well for yourself."

"Why don't we bring your things to my car, then have breakfast. I'll tell you some of the story of how I became part owner of this business."

"Aren't you afraid someone might see us together?"

"Naw," says Billy, "you're going out of town for a while. If anyone sees us together they won't remember it."

Billy and Johnny sit down in the farthest booth in the restaurant area. Billy starts telling his story about how he had become a poolroom owner. "I spent a good part of my life living day to day. One day, I was in a poolroom clear across town and a stranger came in, and I started trying to hustle him. We played for a few hours, and I ended up beating him out of a few hundred dollars. After we played, we had a few drinks together. Ralph, the stranger, now my partner, starts talking to me and telling me he's thinking about opening up a pool hall or 'billiard parlor.' He told me there was a pool movie coming out next year, and he wants to get in on the ground floor before the movie hits the big screen. He also said he needed someone to run the business and asked me if I would be interested. I asked him, 'Why me?' He told me he liked the way I handled people and said I had the gift of gab; a good businessman needs these qualities. I told him I had run a few small rooms in the past and asked him what kind of room he had in mind. He told me about this place, and I couldn't believe the kind of money he was willing to invest. A few weeks later, he buys the building, hires an architect, and together we designed the entire building. The poolroom opened a month before the movie hit the theaters. That was twelve years ago, and the business has been going pretty strong ever since. Of course, my television experience helped out a lot."

"I guess it did. You're famous now."

Billy downplays his fame to Johnny, before he tells him the story about how he ended up on television. "I gotta tell ya, kid, the only reason I ended up on television was that I made a bet with my partner. I bet half of *my* half of the business, I could finish in one of the top four places in a Pro Tour event. My only stipulation was, I wanted to play in five tournaments to improve my chances of winning the bet. My partner took the bet, and I was down to my next to the last chance before I finally won the bet. That's the tournament you saw on television. The increase in business after my television appearance more than made up what my partner lost making the bet. He basically made a bet he couldn't lose, and here I am thinking *I'm* the hustler."

There were a few more parts to the business story. Billy says, "I received a salary, a decent one, until my partner got back his original investment, and that took some time. Once he got his original investment back, we became partners. I'm also here sixteen to eighteen hours a day."

"Why so many hours?"

"I tried to cut back a few times, but it's hard to find good, honest people. Every time I hire someone to run the place, my numbers go down the tubes. I have to be here." Billy smiles, ready to change the subject. "This girl in Albuquerque must be pretty special."

"I'm not sure yet. I have only known her for a short time."

"I met a girl in California and knew right away; unfortunately, things didn't work out the way I wanted." Billy doesn't offer any more information on the subject, and Johnny refuses to pry. He is happy to hear Billy remembers his mom and thought she was special. There's a smile on his face as he digs into the rest of his meal.

Billy and Johnny leave the restaurant and walk to Billy's car. On the way to the airport, Johnny remembers he still has Billy's thousand dollars in his pocket. Johnny takes his money from his pocket and starts to count out what he owes Billy. Billy asks him, "What are you doing?"

"I'm giving you back the thousand dollars I was holding to play Bobby."

"Aren't we still partners? Take the money with you to Albuquerque. If you find some action, use the money to play. Seeing you're out there on your own, making all the decisions, you get sixty percent of the winnings and I get forty."

Later, at the airport, Billy extends his hand to Johnny. They shake hands. Billy says, "Good luck. I hope all goes well for you and the girl."

"I'm going there not expecting much; that way, I won't be disappointed if nothing happens." Billy puts his window up, beeps his horn, and drives away as Johnny walks towards the airline terminal. He calls Flo from St. Louis while waiting to board his next flight. She's too busy, at work, to talk, so the conversation is brief. He does manage to tell Flo his next flight is delayed and he has no idea when he will be taking off.

# CHAPTER 9

Johnny's flight finally arrives in Albuquerque. After getting a rental car, he calls his mother.

"Is something wrong, Ma?"

"There sure is," says his mother. "I am desperately out of shape. I've been on the treadmill for fifteen minutes. How are things going in Kentucky?"

"Things are going great. I'm actually in New Mexico."

"What the hell are you doing there? Is Billy there with you?"

Johnny explains the situation.

"You've been making a lot of impulsive decisions lately. Are you sure you know what you're doing?"

"The rest of the week will tell the story, but I think this may be my special lady. That's what Billy told me you were, his special lady."

"When did Billy say I was his special lady?"

"When I told him about Flo. That's when he told me he had once met a special lady once in California; unfortunately, Billy said, she slipped through his fingers."

Suddenly, Elaine is choked up. "What's going on with Billy?"

"Things are fine with Billy. I moved into an apartment he has inside the poolroom before I left. He's only charging me thirty dollars a week; in fact, we've become business partners. Billy sets up all my pool matches along with providing the finances. So far, we're ahead of the game two thousand dollars."

"Is this all you plan to do with your life, play pool and gamble?"

"It was the only option I had to get to know Billy, and we're getting along very well. I think he might even be starting to like me, and he's teaching me a lot about pool." Johnny now says, "I just pulled into the parking lot at Flo's restaurant. Flo thinks I'm still at the airport in St. Louis. I keep calling you at the wrong times. We never get to talk about what's happening with you."

"Give me a call in a few days, and I'll make sure I fill you in on all the details. Go make Flo's day; women love to be surprised."

Before making his entrance, Johnny decides to disguise himself with a hat, flipping up his collar, and sunglasses. Johnny sits for a few minutes Flo's busy with customers at the other end of the bar and she's really hustling. He takes a salt shaker and raps on the bar. In a deep voice, he starts calling out, "What's a man gotta do in this place to get a drink?" Flo has finished with the people at the other end of the bar, but chooses to ignore Johnny. He raps the salt shaker even louder and calls out even louder. "What's a man got to do to get a drink in this place?"

Flo is hopping mad at this point. She starts coming at Johnny with fire in her eyes. Johnny bends down as if he's trying to tie his shoe. Even though Flo loses sight of Johnny, she starts a verbal assault on him. "Who the fuck do you think you are? Can't you see I am busy waiting on other customers?" Flo is looking over the edge of the bar, but Johnny still has his head down. Flo continues to pepper Johnny. "Hello," she says, in a sarcastic voice. "I'm here now, and I am not in the mood for your fucking games, mister."

Johnny takes off his hat and glasses, then he looks up at Flo. "Would you mind getting me a drink of water?"

Knowing she's been had, Flo stands there looking at Johnny with her arms folded. She's not a happy camper as she asks

Johnny, "Is this the kind of thing I can grow to expect from you?" Before Johnny can answer, Flo bursts into laughter. She extends her arms, and they both hug one another. "Go sit in one of the empty booths, and I'll get you something to eat."

In a few minutes, Johnny falls asleep.

Flo finishes her shift, then takes a few minutes to freshen-up. She always keeps another blouse handy and changes her clothes. She then gathers up her hair and puts it into a pony tail. When Flo gets over to the table with Johnny's food, she puts her fingers into a glass of water and flicks the water right in his face. It only takes one try for Johnny to spring-up from his sleeping position. He falls off the seat and lands under the table. "Are you okay?"

Johnny peeks out from under the table and says, "I guess that makes us even."

"Are you always that jumpy?"

"I've had some bad experiences in college after falling asleep. I actually got painted one night. I passed out from drinking, and my roommates thought it would be funny if I wet the bed. Someone had been given the idea if you put a person's hands in warm water they will wet the bed. Of course I didn't cooperate, and all this did was lead to a more devious plot. My roommates found a can of red stain and put some in an eye-dropper, then started to drop small amounts on my chest. Then they started tickling me so I would rub the paint all over myself. I woke up thinking I was bleeding. I jumped out of bed and ran in the bathroom to look in the mirror. I couldn't believe what they had done to me. It did teach me a great lesson. I never got drunk enough again to pass out."

"It sounds like college can get a little crazy."

"We had our moments."

"Do you miss going to school?"

"Apparently not, because this is the first time I've even thought about it. But enough about me; what's been going on with you?"

"I've been trying to get myself ready to play in the tournament. I've spent almost all of my free time practicing or playing in local tournaments. There's a tournament tonight that I was hoping to play in. It's in a bar about a mile from here."

"What time does the tournament start?"

"Eight o'clock. I thought you might be too tired and not want to go."

"I slept for almost an hour. I'll be good for six or seven more hours before I even start to feel sleepy."

Flo is suddenly excited and gets up from the table. "I have a few more things to take care of before I can leave."

It takes a few minutes to get to the car. "Which direction are we headed?"

Flo turns and looks at Johnny. She's opening and closing her eyes at a rapid pace. She leans across and kisses Johnny. Then she says, "That depends on which direction we choose to take. To get to the tournament we have to take a left leaving the parking lot."

It's almost seven-thirty in the evening when Flo and Johnny get to the poolroom. They both go directly to the main desk and register for the tournament. The tournament director knows Flo and asks, "Is this guy a ringer?"

"Would I bring someone in here to rob you guys? I hope you know me better than that."

"What's his handicap?"

"Six."

Johnny intervenes. "What's the highest handicap a player can have in this tournament?"

"Seven," says the director.

"I'll play as a seven handicap. I don't want to hear anybody complaining about my handicap."

They pay, grab a set of balls, and start walking towards an open table to start practicing. Johnny tells Flo, "I didn't mean to overrule what you were saying to the tournament director, but my game has really improved since the last time you saw me play."

Tilting her head while looking at Johnny, Flo asks, "Didn't I take control of the ring game we played in with Frankie and Joey? I thought I was giving you extra credit when I told the tournament director you were a six handicap." Johnny tries to defend his actions by simply stating to Flo, "You've only seen me play once, and that was in a ring game. I'm a much better player in a head-to-head match; besides, I don't like confrontations. If someone starts questioning my handicap, I may get upset and lose my temper. I don't want that to happen, and my opponent won't like if it happens; he may end up getting hurt."

"Let's see the improvements in your game."

Johnny is ready for Flo's personal challenge, as Flo lifts the rack from the balls, He takes the cue-ball into his hand and places it in the position from which he will break the rack. He proceeds to run two racks. A cross-side shot with the object-ball squeezing between two other balls is the feature shot of the two racks.

"All right," says Flo, "you've proved your point. I'm a believer." She says, "I'd like to get a little practice in myself so I can show you my game has also improved." Flo breaks the rack and runs it out. For the next twenty minutes, Flo and Johnny put on a shooting clinic when they get to the table.

The tournament director starts announcing the matches. After Flo's match is announced, she turns to Johnny and states, "I'll see you in the finals."

Things go according to plan despite Johnny and Flo struggling to win a few of their matches. They meet in the finals. Flo says to Johnny, "I don't want any pity; play me as tough as you possibly can. The girls I'll be playing this week won't be missing any balls on purpose, so I want your best game."

The match starts slow the first four racks. The score is tied at two, and Johnny is breaking. He catches stroke the next five games. He completely shuts down Flo's game. When he's not running out the table, he ties her up by playing well-executed safeties. In the end, he ends up winning the match by a score of seven games to two games. Shaking hands, Flo complements Johnny on how well he has played. Johnny tries to console Flo by telling her she didn't get many breaks in the match.

Flo laughingly tells Johnny, "I know when my ass has been whipped, and Johnny boy, you just whipped it."

Marty Rosen, the tournament director, walks over to Flo and Johnny and hands them each an envelope, then congratulates them. Then he says to Flo, "A lot of people are starting to complain to me about your handicap. I think I'm going to have to move you up to a six."

Flo surprises Marty when she says, "That's fine with me; the higher my handicap the better I'm playing. I hope to be a seven handicap someday."

Flo suggests they go into the lounge for a drink. When they get to the lounge, Flo goes to the ladies room. The sound of country music fills the air. People are dancing, whooping, and hollering and having one hell of a time. Johnny stands there thinking to himself, *This isn't so bad.* He looks down at his foot and he can't believe it's actually tapping to the beat of the music. As he sits, he hears a loud voice to his right. It's a man who has drunk too much. He yells to Johnny, "Hey, bud, who won the pool tournament tonight?"

Johnny politely tells the man, "I did."

"Who finished second?"

"Flo."

"It's about time someone beat that half-breed bitch. I've lost to her so many times I stopped playing in the fuckin' tournament." The man moves over closer to Johnny and says, "It's embarrassing losing to a girl, especially some half-breed girl, if you know what I mean. Of course, there is one nice thing about her; she's awfully pretty to look at." The man next drunkenly slurs out in front of all his friends. "I wouldn't mind boning the little bitch." The man's friends all share a laugh, at Flo's expense.

Taking a quick survey of the situation, Johnny knows he's completely outnumbered. He also knows Flo will be showing up sooner or later, and he doesn't want her to get in the middle of anything. The DJ has stopped playing music and things have quieted down. Johnny yells to the man who had berated Flo, and says, "Ya know, that half breed you been talking about for the past few minutes, she happens to be my date tonight, so the only boning you'll be doing will be with your fist."

Some of the stranger's friends find Johnny's comment amusing and they start to laugh. At this point, Johnny has managed to get his attention. The stranger is a much larger man than Johnny, and he probably figures he has his friends to back him up, so he stands up and yells down the bar to Johnny, "Do you want to take this problem we seem to be having outside?"

Johnny gets up for the chair and asks the stranger, "Is it going to be me and you out there by ourselves, or am I going to have to fight all your friends?"

Belittling the stranger in front of his buddies only pisses him off more. He gathers all his cronies together and starts walking towards the back door. Before he gets too far away from Johnny to hear him, he turns around and points his finger at him and states, "If you're not out in two minutes, I'm coming back in to get ya."

With all the commotion going on, Flo rushes from the ladies room to Johnny's side and asks him, "What the hell is going on here?"

"I'm about to go outside and fight someone."

"Who the fuck are you going to fight?"

"I don't know. He's about six foot two and wearing a black cowboy hat."

"That's Jim Bob," says Flo. "Is he waiting out back for you?"

"Yeah," says Johnny. "How did you know?"

"It's a trap. When you go outside, the cars are so close together that Jim Bob will just grab you, then it's all over. He's big and strong. The last guy he took outside got hurt pretty badly."

Handing Flo his cue and keys, he says "When I give you the signal, I want you to pull up the car."

Flo just shakes her head. "I hope you know what the hell you're doing."

"I'm smarter and quicker than Jim Bob; plus, I hold several degrees in self-defense. I better know what the hell I'm doing." Johnny insists Flo go out the front way and have the car ready when he needs it.

One of Jim Bob's cronies comes back inside and asks Johnny, "Are you chickening out of the fight, boy?"

Johnny reassures the crony he'll be out side and a few seconds. Flo kisses Johnny on the cheek and tells him, "Good luck."

"If this is going to come down to luck, I'm probably in trouble."

When Johnny gets to the back door, he's able to survey the situation through the glass door. He has a few things working in his favor. The back door opens inwardly; plus, there is a large truck parked on the right-hand side of the door. Knowing what Flo has told him about Jim Bob, Johnny opens the door and takes one step forward. He can see a group of people gathered to watch the fight. There is a light across the parking lot, and it's shining on the backdoor. Johnny sees a large silhouette of a man charging at him. It's Jim Bob, and he figures he's got Johnny cornered, so he's coming in for the kill. Johnny waits until the last second, then jumps onto the hood of the truck as Jim Bob lunges to grab him. As Jim Bob swipes at Johnny, he grabs Johnny's shirt tail and pulls Johnny towards him. Johnny is on his side on the roof of the truck. He's able to get his feet between himself and Jim Bob, and he kicks Jim Bob in the face several times before Jim Bob lets go of him. Johnny gets to the flatbed of the truck. The flatbed has two long posts with a bar running across them. Johnny grabs the bar and swings himself out into the parking lot. He has made his way to an open area. The crowd has formed a circle, and Johnny stands right in the middle.

Jim Bob has collected himself and pushes through the crowd. He has fire in his eyes as he stalks Johnny. Johnny decides to tire out Jim Bob. The circle the crowd has formed is large enough for Johnny to move around. He gets Jim Bob to chase him around for a few minutes; finally, Jim Bob loses his patience. He charges Johnny with his arms flailing. Johnny ducks under Jim Bob's arms and grabs Jim Bob's shirt with both hands. Johnny falls to the ground, taking Jim Bob with him. He puts his feet in Jim Bob's stomach. Using his body as a catapult, he sends Jim Bob flying through the air. Jim Bob lands on the hood of a car, then falls to the ground. Johnny gets to his feet and runs to Jim Bob. He proceeds to place his foot on Jim Bob's throat.

"Are we through here?" Johnny is in complete control, so he tells Jim Bob to just nod his head if they are through. Having little or no other choices, Jim Bob nods his head. Johnny tells Jim Bob the fight was between the two of them, and he shouldn't bother Flo anymore. Jim Bob agrees to Johnny's terms.

Looking around the parking lot, Johnny spots Flo standing on the top of his rental car. He signals to Flo to drive over and get him. When Flo pulls up, Johnny quickly removes his foot from Jim Bob's throat and jumps inside the car; he and Flo speed off.

Flo has a hard time believing how Johnny has just handled the situation. When they finally slow down, Flo says, "So what's next, Johnny? How many things can you do in one day to impress a girl?"

"Jim Bob was saying a lot of nasty things, and I couldn't just sit there and listen anymore. He was calling you a half breed. Then he made a comment about what he'd like to do to you sexually. I couldn't take it anymore, so I said a few things back to him. All of a sudden we're headed outside."

"What'd he say?"

Johnny fills Flo in on the details. Flo tells Johnny how grateful she is that he defended her, but she also reminds Johnny she still has to live in these parts.

"When I had Jim Bob pinned on the ground and my foot on his throat, I told him our little disagreement had nothing to do with you and that he better not start harassing you. Jim Bob agreed."

They stop at a diner. "Where did you learn how to fight?"

"I took martial art classes for a little over five years out of necessity; I got tired of being picked on by the local bully. I was his personal whipping boy my entire sixth grade year. Every day at the bus stop, Charlie Gray would find some way to personally torture me. He was an eighth grader, and I used to wonder, *How does he think of all these things to do to me?* I knew he wasn't smart. I later found out that he was victimized by a bully when he was in sixth grade. I guess it had become a tradition for an eighth grader to torture a sixth grader at my bus stop."

"What did Charlie do to you?"

"At first," says Johnny, "Charlie started out ripping up my homework, but I started to make copies, so Charlie's game started to progress. He knew I had a crush on a girl named Kelly, who was also one of the kids at our bus stop. He would sneak up behind me at the bus stop. Before I knew it, my pants would be down around my knees; it was so humiliating. Charlie eventually moved out of town, but before he moved, I got even. In high school, he was sitting in the cafeteria with a bunch of fellow football players and a group of cheerleaders. One of the cheerleaders was Charlie's girlfriend. I walked up to the table they were all sitting at with a straw in my mouth. The straw was full of milk, and I proceeded to spit all the milk right in Charlie's face. Charlie then made the same mistake as Jim Bob; he came out of his seat and ran right at me. I grabbed his arm and flipped him right over my shoulder, and he landed flat on his back in the middle of the cafeteria. The teachers jumped in before anything else happened, and I ended up getting two weeks' detention. It was worth every second. Charlie never bothered me again, and I became very popular. Charlie, I guess, had picked on more than just me." The story ends as the food hits the table.

"Are you staying at my place tonight, Johnny? I have a pull-out couch that's comfortable."

"Sounds good to me. I hate looking for a room at this time of night."

Johnny pays the check, and they leave. Flo's apartment is small, but more than adequate for one person. Flo tells Johnny, "Go take a shower, and I'll get your bed ready."

Realizing she's only fooling herself about Johnny's sleeping on the pullout couch, Flo takes out a book of matches and lights a few candles. Then she takes off all her clothes, except her thong, puts on a long undershirt, and rushes to the bathroom before Johnny finishes his shower. When she gets to the bathroom door, she can hear the sound of running water. Flo opens the bathroom door slowly and quietly steps inside. She peeks her head in and covers the rest of her body with the shower curtain. Johnny has his eyes closed standing under the shower head. Flo takes a few quick glances at Johnny's body and she likes what she sees. Johnny suddenly opens his eyes and jumps back in surprise.

"Mind if I join you?"

"Na-na-not at all."

Flo pulls the shower curtain about halfway back. She slowly removes the long t-shirt she is wearing, and all that remains is a bright yellow thong. She turns around to show Johnny how her backside looks. "Do you like what you see?" She doesn't need any answer from Johnny. She looks down to see he's aroused. Flo removes the thong and steps into the shower.

Johnny and Flo began to kiss and caress different parts of each other's bodies. From there, Flo takes a bar of soap and starts to lather Johnny's chest, occasionally moving down to his sensitive area. Flo turns her back to Johnny and asks if he would wash her back with a face cloth. Johnny starts to rub the soap on Flo's back; he also massages her neck muscles. They rinse off and move away from the shower head. Johnny pins Flo up against the wall of the shower and begins to kiss and touch the tender parts of Flo's body. Passions run high, but there's a more comfortable spot twenty feet from them. Flo suggests a trip to the bedroom. Johnny agrees and shuts off the water. He and Flo each take a towel and quickly dry off. Then they walk hand-in-hand from the bathroom into Flo's bedroom.

Flo shuts the door behind them; the candles help to enhance the moment. Johnny pinches himself to make sure he's not dreaming. Flo's actions reassure him what's about to happen between them isn't make believe. They pull down the covers on the bed and get in. They look at each other; words are no longer needed. Two young lovers that have built a passion for each other since that fateful day at Giuseppe's put their lips gently together. It ignites a spark in their bodies, and their animal instincts take over. They soon discover all they have fantasized about each other is even better than they thought. Johnny has very soft hands, and Flo soon discovers he knows how to use them. Flo likes her neck kissed, and she encourages Johnny to take some time kiss it. Johnny moves close to Flo and tilts her head back to make room for Johnny to caress her neck. This is the final straw for Flo. Her desire to feel Johnny inside her becomes overwhelming and she says to him, "I can't take anymore," she emphasizes as she whispers into Johnny's ear. "I need to feel you inside me." Johnny tries to maneuver Flo's body to where he thinks she wants him. Flo has different thoughts. She prefers to be on top. A few more hugs and kisses and Flo's ready to accept Johnny's love. She gasps a few short breaths and rolls her eyes back as her warm, moist body accepts all Johnny has to offer. In an upright position, she starts to rub herself against Johnny. He has no problem staying stimulated, and he entertains Flo's nipples with the tips of his fingers. Flo begins to moan and groan louder as all the passion her body is feeling reaches an uncontrollable state. She can't hold back any longer; her body reaches its heightened state. Flo's body experiences a minor shock as she releases an orgasm that runs through her body and curls her toes.

Johnny has felt the passion Flo's created. They change places, and he begins to slowly move in and out of her body. It doesn't take long for them to start expressing the desires their bodies are feeling. Between the sensations, Flo says several times, "Oh, Johnny, Johnny, you make me feel so good." Johnny looks down at Flo and she's moving her head back and forth. She has a strained look on her face as he begins to move faster. He can no longer refrain. His body reaches the point of no return. "Oh, baby, baby, I'm coming." He collapses into Flo arms moments later.

The passion they have felt for one another lasts long after the sexual act.

"I hope we didn't wake the landlord."

"The landlord's son was no dope; he made the bedroom soundproof. I met him once, and he told me he could never have had sex if he thought his parents could hear it."

"I wish I had known that a few minutes ago." Flo and Johnny hold each other tightly before they drift off into a deep sleep.

The next day, before she goes off to work, Flo gives Johnny directions to a popular poolroom called Snooker's. As he pulls into the parking lot, he calls his mother.

"I had to get a restraining order on Cliff. He didn't hurt me or anything, but a week or so after you went back to school, the credit card bill came to the house. I don't usually look at every transaction, but one of them caught my eye. It was a motel charge. I asked what he was doing at the motel. He made up this cockamamie story and expected me to buy it. He told me he went to play golf near this particular town. After the round of golf, he had lunch, and while driving back home, he started getting sick to his stomach. 'It was so bad,' he said, 'it started coming out both ends.' So he decided the smartest thing to do was to check into a motel. He told me the whole thing passed in a few hours, then he got back in his car and drove home."

"I hope you didn't buy that story."

"Not for a minute," says Elaine. "But it may have been one of the most creative lies Cliff has ever told me. He tried to be so convincing talking about the vomiting and the diarrhea. People like Cliff become such good liars; I think they start believing their own lies."

"Did you do anything to try and find out what really happened?"

"I hired a private detective to follow Cliff, and it only took him a week, one fuckin' week." Elaine takes some time to regain her composure. "The detective came back with enough pictures of Cliff and his lady friend to fill a scrapbook. She's a doctor. When I confronted Cliff with the pictures, I told him to pack his stuff and get out. He did what I asked, but he called me drunk. He promised he would change, but I told him the marriage was over, and I was filing for divorce. He didn't believe me until he was served with papers. That's when he came to the house and confronted me. When I wouldn't let him in the house, he broke the screen door. I called the police and got a restraining order. He called after I got the restraining order, and what he said to me wasn't very nice. I've become afraid to answer the phone because I think Cliff may be the one calling."

"Why don't you just change your phone number and get an unlisted number?"

"I thought about doing that, but I would have to call all my friends and tell them I've changed my number and tell them why. I'm not ready for the whole world to know my problems."

Johnny feels terrible about what his mother is going through. "Would you like me to come home?"

"You're being here wouldn't change anything. You're better off staying right where you are." Elaine manages to perk up. "Where are you, anyway?"

"Albuquerque. I'm staying here with a friend."

"The girl from the restaurant. How's that going?" She knows that they've been intimate.

Johnny confesses, then says, "I have a good feeling about what's happening with Flo. She's easy to talk to, and we have a lot in common. This isn't the first woman I've experienced in my life, but I think she could be the perfect match."

Elaine is emotional and sobbing openly, but she manages to say to Johnny, "I hope so, Johnny."

"I know it's early in my relationship with Flo, but I'm starting to get the feeling she's definitely the right fit. Do you know what I'm talking about? Have you ever felt the way I feel, Mom?"

Elaine quietly says to Johnny, "Once at a resort in Northern California. I met a guy named Johnny—you know the rest of the story. Don't make the mistakes we both made. Be open and honest with each other, and if you think this may be the girl for you, grab her and hold on tight because it may turn out to be the ride of your life." After another short pause, Elaine says, "I'm happy that you're happy, and don't let what's going on with me bring you down. I feel better when I get things out in the open."

"I feel better, too."

Letting out a sigh of relief, Elaine says, "I'm glad that's over, but there is something else I'd like to tell you. I'm going anyway for a few days. I'm taking a little R and R. Cindy and I are flying down to Acapulco for a few days. We're leaving on Friday and coming back on Tuesday. We're going to a health resort, and they're going to pamper us to death. I not only need this, I deserve this. I've made a commitment to myself to start being good to myself. I know it sounds selfish, but it's something I have to do right now. So unless it's a national crisis, don't call me again until after next Tuesday."

"Your request shouldn't be a problem because I plan on being busy with Flo the whole weekend."

Elaine is starting to choke-up once again. "Have the time of your life." She starts to weep openly. She tells her son, "I love you, Johnny."

Johnny has succumbed to his mother's emotional status; he is also teary-eyed. "I love you, Mom; I always will. Goodbye."

Collecting his emotions, Johnny heads towards Snooker's with his cue case in his hand. Several tables are in use. He goes right to the control desk to rent a table. After the houseman gives Johnny a set of balls and assigns him a table, he takes the liberty to ask Johnny, "Are you looking for some action?"

"I wouldn't mind having some company at my table."

"Do you want expensive company or inexpensive company?"

"I'd be willing to play races to seven, nine-ball, and I'm willing to start at fifty or a hundred a set."

"You play any one-pocket? We've got some one-pocket players here right now."

Johnny doesn't play one-pocket, but he doesn't want to say that to the houseman. Instead, he says, "Nine-ball, races to seven. If anyone in here is interested, I'll be playing on the table you just assigned me."

"I'll see what I can do to find you some company."

Less than fifteen minutes go by, and Johnny's already been asked to play three times by three different people. He has turned each offered down, wanting to talk to Flo first. He calls her. "I've been approached by three guys looking to play." Johnny describes the first man as being about six feet tall and maybe forty years old with black hair.

"That's Bill," says Flo, "he's the best player in the room."

"I kind of figured that because he was the first to ask me to play." Johnny describes the next person: fifty years old, mustache, black hair, and Spanish.

"That's Paco," says Flo, "he's the local bookie. He shoots well, but he has a tendency to dog-it in close matches. He may be the guy you want to play because he has plenty of money. Who's the third guy?"

"He's a young guy, probably in his early twenties; dirty blonde hair, looks cocky."

"If it's who I think it is, don't play him. He's been out of town on the road, and if he's back home, he's probably broke. He's also a pain in the ass to play."

"Thanks." When Johnny goes back out into the room, he hits a few more shots before he walks over to Paco and asks, "Are you still interested in playing some nine-ball?"

"There were two other guys who asked you to play. Why play me?"

"I figured you were the oldest of all three players, and if I can't beat you, I should be able to learn something."

Paco tells Bill and the younger player, "This guy wants to play me because he figures he can learn something." Paco accepts Johnny's challenge. "How much money do you want to play for?"

"How about if we play races to seven for a hundred a set?"

"You've got yourself a game." The next issue isn't settled quite as easily. Paco wants to play on the table he's playing on, but Johnny doesn't want to concede to playing on Paco's table. He offers to flip a coin to see what table they will eventually play on. He also tells Paco, "The loser of the flip table gets to break the first game of the set they're about to play." Paco agrees to Johnny's terms so Johnny flips his coin. Paco calls heads, and the coin lands on heads. Johnny has at least salvaged the first break of the set; he grabs all his equipment and comes over to Paco's table. Before the match starts, Johnny brings back the rack of balls he was using to the houseman and pays for his table time. After that, he goes back into the room to begin playing.

A few sweaters have already gathered to watch the match. Winning the opening break is the best thing that happens to Johnny in the first set. Paco wins the first set in convincing fashion by a score of seven to two. Johnny takes a few minutes after the first set. He's not sure if he is in over his head. He decides to give Paco another game. The second set is the kind of game Johnny had hoped for. It's a tight dogfight, where neither player ever holds more than a one-game advantage. Eventually, the match comes down to one game. Johnny is breaking, and he makes the seven-ball on the break. Unfortunately, he doesn't have a good shot to pocket the one-ball. He elects to play a push-out. He shoots the cue-ball up table, close to the back rail. He leaves Paco with two options: a difficult shot or a difficult safety play. Paco comes to the table and elects to play the difficult safety. He shoots the cue-ball at the one-ball, slicing it very thin. The cue-ball goes down to the opposite end of the table and ducks behind the five-ball leaving Johnny no direct shot to play the one-ball.

Johnny has two choices at making contact with the one-ball. He may use the rails to hit the one-ball or he may masse, or curve, the cue-ball to make a hit on the one-ball. Johnny's cue is elevated, and he likes the way he feels stroking the shot. After several practice strokes, Johnny decides to play the masse-shot. He lowers the tip of his cue onto the cue-ball. The hit is clean, and the cue-ball curves around the five-ball and proceeds up table. The cue-ball strikes the one-ball, sending the one-ball off the back rail and caroming back down to the other end of the table. The cue-ball ends up behind the three-ball. Johnny has turned the tables on Paco, and he comes to the table trying to figure out a way to hit the one-ball. Paco kicks at the one-ball by going two rails and manages to make a legal hit. The only problem is that Paco has left Johnny a good shot at the one-ball. Johnny pockets the one-ball through the five-ball easily. The three balls that remain on the table are the six-, eight-, and the nine-ball. The six-ball to the eight-ball position play has two options: Johnny can either follow off the six-ball three rails or draw the cue-ball side to side for position. Johnny studies the shot closely and decides to play the three rail position shot instead of going side to side because side to side presents a chance of scratching. Johnny has done enough thinking, and he goes to the table to shoot. He lines up the shot using high-left hand English. He strikes the cue-ball and sends it on its way. The cue-ball makes contact with the six and sends it down the rail and into the corner pocket. The cue-ball travels the desired three rails, landing in perfect position to pocket the eight-ball. Johnny makes quick work of the eight- and nine-ball to win the game and the set.

Johnny wins three more sets in a row, and his confidence grows with each win. Paco has the look of a beaten man, but he offers to play Johnny one last set double or nothing. Johnny feels very strong so he accepts the terms of Paco's proposal. The only change Johnny wants to make is the amount of games required to win. Johnny proposes they play a race to nine games to determine the winner. Paco is facing little choice in the matter; he agrees to play the longer race.

Paco says, "I would prefer if we lagged for the break this set instead of flipping a coin. Johnny agrees and grabs the one-ball out of the pocket and hands the cue-ball to Paco. The two players shoot their respective balls at the back rail. The balls bounce off the back rail and come back towards the two players. Johnny's ball comes to rest an inch from the back rail. Paco's ball hits the rail and bounces away, farther than Johnny's ball. Johnny wins the lag and the right to break in the first game.

A fast start is what Johnny is hoping for, and it's exactly what he gets. He pockets the nine-ball on the break. Paco lets out a loud groan as he comes to the table to rack the balls for the second game. Johnny is feeling even stronger than before. All of the pool he has played lately is really paying off. He has plenty of bounce left in his step as he moves around the table. When Paco comes to the table, he is lifeless, and everything he does seems to take more life out of him. Johnny has no trouble winning the final race with Paco. The score ends up being nine games to four.

As Paco hands Johnny six hundred dollars, he asks, "How would you like to play Bill tomorrow night? I'm willing to back you against him."

"Are you serious?"

"Of course I'm serious. I'm a businessman, and I think you're good enough to beat Bill. He has a backer who likes to bet big money, and we would probably start out at five hundred dollars a set. If you play the way you played against me, you should have no problem winning the money."

Johnny thinks about it for a while, then asks Paco, "What would be a good time to get here?"

"About three in the afternoon." Paco gathers his stuff together and starts walking away from Johnny.

"I'll pay for the table time and see you here tomorrow."

For the past few hours, Flo has quietly been playing pool on the other side of the poolroom. She has matched-up with one of the girls in the tournament. She has managed to win two of three sets from the girl, and is currently involved in the fourth set. It takes a few more racks to finish before she has a chance to talk to Johnny. She has won the fourth set, and as she begins to talk to Johnny, the girl she is playing starts to shoot her mouth off. She starts to complain she's getting bored because they are only playing for twenty-five dollars a set. She gives Flo an ultimatum: "We either raise the stakes or the game is over."

"We can play for fifty dollars a set if you want to."

"You're still boring me, little girl."

Johnny butts in. "How about two hundred a set? Is that enough money to keep your mind on the game?"

The girl doesn't like that Johnny has invited himself in to the conversation. She asks Flo, "Who the fuck is this guy, anyway?"

"He's my backer. So do you want to play for the two hundred or not?"

To save face, the girl agrees to play Flo for the two hundred dollars.

Flo has funneled all of her focus and attention on playing her best game. She completely dismantles her opponent for the next two sets. She wins in convincing fashion by scores of seven to two and seven to three. The girl has already told Flo she refuses to play anymore pool on this particular day. As Flo receives the money for the second set, she can't help gloating. "I'll be here tomorrow night if you feel lonely. I'd hate to think you might be *bored*."

The girl breaks down her two-piece cue and makes like she's ringing Flo's neck as she takes it apart. "I'm not through with you. I'll be back tomorrow." Then she turns away from Flo and walks towards the control desk in a huff. She yells back at Flo, "I hope you're paying for the pool." Flo holds out the all the money she has won so the girl can see it. "I'll pay for the pool because I have a lot more of your money than I would have if you didn't get bored so easily." This only enrages the girl even further. She walks quickly to the door and slams it on her way out.

Johnny asks Flo, "Do you even know who that girl was?"

"Karen Black. She's rated in the top sixteen players on the woman's tour."

"That's a good sign, beating a ranked player on the women's tour. I have a good feeling about how things will go in the upcoming tournament."

Flo looks into Johnny's big blue eyes and leans over and kisses him lightly on the lips. "I also have a good feeling about my chances in the upcoming tournament."

After leaving Snooker's, they go to a restaurant. Before Flo starts talking, she reaches across the table and takes Johnny by the hand. "I was a lost soul wandering aimlessly with no direction. I was on the verge of making some very bad decisions with my life. Then you came along, and everything has changed for the better." A small tear starts to form in the corner of Flo's right eye. Johnny reaches across the table and wipes the tear away, then they kiss.

Johnny and Flo begin to eat as a small band starts walking around the restaurant playing music. At first, the music is lively, and the patrons clap their hands to the beat of the music. After a few songs with lively music, the mood of the room suddenly changes. The lights are dimmed, and the band goes from table to table to serenade all the couples eating their dinner. When the band gets to Flo and Johnny's table, they play a beautiful ballad that has a wonderful Spanish guitar solo. The music consumes Johnny and Flo, and they sit, holding hands, listening to the beautiful melody. When the band finishes playing, they start moving on to the next table. When the bandleader goes by Johnny, Johnny reaches into his pocket takes out a twenty dollar bill and gives it to the bandleader.

After dinner, Flo and Johnny return to her place. He goes in to take a shower expecting the same results as the night before. Flo has a problem staying awake. Johnny comes out of the shower to find her asleep on the coach. He picks her up and carries her to the bedroom.

The next day, Johnny tells Flo about Paco's offer to back him against Bill. "Paco told me to meet him at Snooker's around three." With over four hours to kill after they eat, Flo and Johnny take a walk to a local playground. There are swings in the park and they make their way over to them. Flo sits on one and Johnny starts pushing her back and forth. They strike up a conversation.

Flo asks, "What was your childhood like, Johnny?"

"I'm an only child. Up until recently, I thought it was pretty normal. I went to private school, played a lot of different sports, spent a lot of my time at the country club where my father belonged. That's how I got to see him. He's a doctor. My mom had to do the things he liked to do if we wanted to spend time together. He used his job as an excuse to get his way. In my teens, I played a lot of baseball. I was good at it. My mom and I spent a lot of time driving around California. What was yours like?"

"The opposite of yours, more or less. I grew up on a reservation. My grandfather and uncle raised me. I didn't have time for sports. I worked as soon as I was old enough." Flo dismounts the swing and they leave the park. While walking, Flo says, "I want to buy some new clothes for the tournament, so I can drop you off at Snooker's and take your car to go shopping. I figure most guys don't like shopping."

"You got that right."

The fairytale for Johnny continues when Flo says to him, "We do have some time on our hands so why don't we go back to my place and see what happens?" Johnny gets the message; the pace of the walk increases dramatically. They get back to Flo's and she goes into the bedroom alone. After a few minutes, the bedroom door opens slowly and Flo has changed into a see-through negligee. She walks past Johnny sitting on the coach and models the negligee. Once past Johnny, she walks as far as she can into the kitchen. She turns like she is on a runway and walks past Johnny, back to the bedroom. She opens the bedroom door, straddles it, looks back at Johnny and says in a very sexy tone, "I'll be in my playground if you wanna ride my see-saw, little boy." She clears her throat and corrects herself, saying, "After the other night, I should be calling you big boy."

Flo enters her bedroom then peeks back around her door. Using her index finger, she signals Johnny to come in and join her. Johnny gets off the coach and walks slowly into the room. They close the door. If Flo's bedroom walls could talk, they would tell the tale of two young lovers totally consumed by each other's desires and a commitment to satisfying them.

She says, "I hope you enjoyed our little roll in the hay because, from this point until the time I get knocked out of the tournament, we will be abstaining from sex because I need to concentrate on playing pool."

"I guess I'll be rooting for your opponents."

Flo tries to hit Johnny with a love tap, but he blocks the punch and holds her down on the bed. They start to hug and kiss again.

Time has gotten away from them. The excursion into the bedroom has pushed the clock past one o'clock. They make it to Snooker's by two-thirty, then Flo goes on to the mall.

"There's no need to hurry," said Paco. "Bill's backer won't be here until four o'clock." Johnny is relieved. He and Paco get together for a conference. Paco lays out the ground rules for Johnny when he plays Bill. The first rule he stresses to Johnny is, "Don't play Bill on his favorite table; he knows table one like the back of his hand. I have to insist there's no game if he won't play on a different table."

"What if he won't budge?"

"He has to budge because games like this, for this kind of money, don't come along every day for Bill. There is no way he can sit around and wait for a better offer." Paco gets the set of balls for the table he and Johnny had played on the night before. As he hands the balls to Johnny, he tells him, "You're going to be playing races to nine for five hundred dollars. How do you feel about playing for that amount of money?"

"I feel great. I've played for more money than that before, and it didn't bother me." Johnny takes the tray of balls from Paco and starts practicing.

When the backer finally arrives, he and Paco barter for some time before the ground rules are decided. In order for Bill to play on a different table, the backer insists the races are increased by two games. The stakes are also changed; instead of playing for five hundred dollars, they are going to play for one thousand dollars.

Starting the match, the two players cordially shake hands. Bill has already taken a coin in his hand and tells Johnny to call in the air. Bill tosses the coin into the air and Johnny calls heads. The coin lands on heads, and Johnny wins the right to break. As Bill racks the balls, Johnny takes the cue-ball and places it in his typical breaking position. He lines up the shot, and after a few strokes of his cue, he sends the cue-ball, as fast as he can in the direction of the one-ball. The action on Johnny's break isn't the typical reaction. Johnny has received a bad rack from Bill.

The race to eleven turns into a test of will rather than a test of skill; Johnny has to examine every rack Bill puts up on the table. Bill is also a slow, methodical player and takes at least ten to fifteen practice strokes on every shot. The race also produces a few very close hits involving object-balls. Bill argues with Johnny until he gets every call his way. Bill's backer even manages to get into the act. He never shuts his mouth the whole time Johnny's at the table. After playing for over two hours, Bill wins the race to eleven by three games.

Paco pays Bill's backer the thousand dollars, then comes down to talk to Johnny. He apologizes to Johnny for the way Bill and his backer have behaved. Then he tells Johnny, "I'm getting out of the action. I wasn't prepared for this kind of nonsense. I thought we were playing a pool match and dealing with gentlemen. It's up to you whether or not you want to continue to play."

Johnny doesn't like the fact that he has lost Paco's money. He tells Bill and his backer, "I'll continue to play, but I insist we have a referee to call any close hits." Johnny asks Paco, "Is there anyone in the room that I can trust?"

"Pablo's the most honest guy in the place, but you'll probably have to pay him."

Johnny asks Bill and his backer, "Do you have any problem with Pablo refereeing the match?"

Bill and his backer agree to Johnny's terms. Johnny asks Paco to negotiate a price with Pablo if he's willing to accept the job as referee. Everything gets done and Pablo's price is twenty dollars a set. Johnny tells Bill and his backer, "Whoever wins the set will pay for the referee." Johnny makes one more request before the match starts. He wants Pablo to hold all the money. Johnny takes the thousand dollars he's betting out of his pocket and gives it to Pablo.

Bill's backer asks Johnny, "What's the matter? Don't you trust us?"

"I don't want any misunderstandings about how much we're playing for."

Bill's backer counts out to his thousand dollars and says to Pablo, "I hope you understand this is only a temporary loan."

A small crowd has gathered. This starts to excite Johnny, especially after he wins the coin flip. He duplicates his break from the first race, but the balls scatter and run for the pockets. Johnny has a much better feeling in his stomach starting the second set. He goes on to win the first three games of the set before he loses game four. Johnny manages to right the ship in games five and six and enters the seventh game leading by a score of five to one.

Scratching on the break isn't the way to keep your momentum going. Bill makes two easy shots before making a carom-shot off the three to pocket the nine-ball. Bill's now in control of the pace. He manages to catch Johnny after they have played fourteen games. With the score tied seven to seven, the match becomes a race to four. Johnny sits lifeless in his chair. He knows he's in serious trouble. Bill breaks the fifteenth rack and makes a ball on the break. He has a decent shot at the one-ball to begin his run-out. When he starts shooting, Bill makes the one- and two-balls; the three went in on the break, and Bill is facing a shot on the four. The four-ball shot is a long one, and it requires Bill to draw the cue-ball back. Bill is taking even more time to play the shot. He knows if he can make the four and get position for the five, he will probably run the table.

Executing a long draw shot requires a perfect stroke of the cue stick. Bill hits too low on the cue-ball, and it goes airborne and lands on top of the four-ball, then bounces on the table and up onto the back rail, eventually leaving the table. Johnny comes out of his chair like a shot as Pablo retrieves the cue-ball and hands it to him. There are still six balls remaining on the table, so Johnny collects himself and places the cue-ball where he wants it. He proceeds to run the rest of the rack and take a one game lead.

In the next game, Johnny fails to pocket a ball on the break, and Bill has another good look at a very run-able table. The first two balls go smoothly, but his position on the three is out of line. After another long deliberation, Bill pockets the three and tries to bring the cue-ball around the six-ball, for his position to shoot the four. His plan doesn't work. The cue-ball catches the side of the six and changes its path. The cue-ball rolls close to the eight-ball, leaving Bill without a clear shot at the four. Frustration can be seen all over the Bill's face, but he still manages to kick and hit the four-ball. The only problem is the four rolls around the table and stops near the nine-ball. Johnny is left with a dead combination shot, and he comes to the table and fires it into the pocket. Bill never recovers; he loses the set eleven games to seven.

Pablo takes a thousand dollars from his pocket and gives it to Johnny. Then Pablo turns to Bill's backer and asks for another thousand dollars from him if the match is going to continue. The backer calls Bill over; it's their turn to have a shot conference. After the conference, Bill's backer insists they play the next set on Bill's favorite table. Johnny feels Bill is starting to tire so he makes his own counter-proposal. He agrees to move over to Bill's table, but he wants to guarantee he and Bill will play at least three more sets. The backer is reluctant at first, but Bill convinces him he has a big advantage playing on his favorite table. The backer takes three thousand dollars from his pocket and gives it to Pablo, as does Johnny.

Before play starts, Johnny notices Flo. "I hope you don't mind, I've taken a few liberties. I'm locked into playing at least three more sets with Bill. What time does the tournament start tomorrow?"

"The players meeting starts at two o'clock, and the first matches start play at four. As long as you get me home so I can get seven or eight hours sleep, I'll be fine. I want to play at least two or three more hours in this ring game to get ready for tomorrow. It's only nine o'clock, so why don't you go back to the table with Bill and do what you have to do."

"How is the ring game going?"

"I'm up a hundred dollars; we're playing for ten a game. The word's out that I beat Karen Black, and the girls I'm playing are shaking in their boots." Flo smiles, then glances at her table. "It's my shot. I gotta get back to work." Flo gives Johnny a quick kiss on the cheek and says, "Go kick some ass."

Shortly after nine o'clock, Johnny and Bill resume play on table one. The first two sets they had played lasted more than four hours. The next three sets, played on Bill's favorite table, are over in less than three and a half hours. It wouldn't have mattered if the games were played on the moon. Johnny dominates Bill in all phases of the game. He wins by the scores of eleven to four, eleven to three, and eleven to two. Bill extends his hand to Johnny to congratulate him. "I never thought in a million years I'd get beat that badly in this room on my favorite table." Bill's backer isn't as gracious; he storms out of the room. Pablo comes over to Johnny and hands him all the money he has won. Johnny asks Pablo, "How much money do I owe you?" Pablo has collected the balls and is holding the tray containing the balls.

"Eighty dollars."

Johnny hands Pablo two hundred dollars, then asks, "Do you think that will cover what I owe you plus the table time?"

Pablo smiles. "There's more than enough money to cover everything. Thanks."

"You did a great job; I couldn't have done it without you."

Johnny notices Paco is still hanging around, so Johnny calls him over. He comes over to Johnny and extends his hand to congratulate him. Johnny takes money from his pocket and tries to give Paco back his original thousand dollar investment.

"I would be cheating you if I took the money. I just made as much money as you did booking bets on the side. I got back on you after the second set. When you switched tables, I made Bill a two game favorite to win the match; everyone watching bet on Bill to win. After you beat him, the line was even, and, again, everyone bet on Bill. The last set I made you a two game favorite, and, again, everyone bet on Bill." Paco takes five hundred dollars from his pocket and gives it to Johnny. "I might have made more money than you did. I want you to take this money and buy the little girl you're with something nice." Johnny's now the one thanking someone for being generous. Being a bookmaker, Paco says to Johnny, "I don't want you to tell anyone what's going on here because I have a reputation to maintain. I'm a businessman, and I don't like people to know I have a soft side; it could ruin me." Paco laughs openly as he turns around and starts walking towards the door to leave the poolroom.

Johnny makes it just in time to see Flo ending her game. He hears one woman tell her, "You made a believer out of me tonight, honey. I hope we don't meet up in the tournament."

Flo thanks the girl for the compliment. Then she announces to all three of the girls, "I'll take care of the table time."

Johnny asks her, "How much money did you win?"

"I'm not sure. I lost track. I just kept stuffing money into my pockets." She starts taking out the money in her pockets and putting it on the pool table. "I started playing with two hundred dollars." Johnny counts the money. "Everything I have in my hand is profit."

Johnny finishes, then asks, "How much money do you think you've won?" Before Flo can answer, Johnny adds, "If you can guess the amount within twenty dollars, either way, I'll double your money."

"I don't know, four hundred maybe four-fifty."

"I need a firm number."

"Four twenty-five."

As Johnny hands the money to Flo, he makes a fake buzzing sound with his mouth. He says to Flo, "The lady's bid is four twenty-five. The actual amount of money the lady has won tonight." Johnny makes more sounds with his voice. This time, the sounds a bell would make fill the air. As he hands Flo the money, he says, "Seven hundred and forty dollars."

Flo's hands are trembling as Johnny hands the money to her. She gives Johnny a big hug and kiss before they leave the playing area. As Flo pays the table time, Johnny hands the houseman the tray of balls.

It's a short ride to Flo's place. "I'm not taking any chances tonight; the cues are coming with me into the house. I'd be sick if someone came along and stole our cues. I'd rather they took the car."

Johnny has a feeling Flo is starting to get nervous about the tournament. They move onto the couch and start watching television. It takes a while for Flo to fall asleep: a little after three in the morning. Johnny goes into the bedroom and brings back a pillow and a blanket. First, he covers Flo with the blanket, then places her head under the pillow. He shuts the television lights and goes into Flo's bedroom. He takes his clothes off and gets into bed. Johnny tosses and turns for a while as he thinks about his mom and Billy. He wonders how they're both doing and if they'll ever get together. The long, hard day and too much thinking finally takes its toll: Johnny falls asleep.

# CHAPTER 10

The next day, Johnny and Flo head to the tournament. Registration for the players is going on in the main lobby. Flo opens her purse and takes out an envelope. Johnny asks Flo, "What's in the envelope?"

"It's my confirmation notice. It shows I've already paid my entry fee, and I'm guaranteed a spot in the tournament. Thanks to you, I was able to prepay. I heard there are several girls on the waiting list to play here. They're hoping some of the girls don't show up who normally play on the tour."

"I'm going to run to the bank. I'll be right back to see you play," says Johnny.

After going to the bank and buying some clothes, Johnny passes a jewelry store that's having a clearance sale and decides to look. A gold medallion in the shape of a flower catches his eye. The flower looks like it could possibly be a rose petal that has blossomed. He buys it and a chain for Flo.

Johnny puts his things in the car, then goes inside the hotel; it is 3:22. He finds Flo playing on table seven. Johnny finds his seat and watches from a distance. She spots Johnny sitting in the stands and calls him over. "Most of the top players in the world have come here to play," she says.

"How are you feeling?"

"I'm a little nervous, but I have a strange feeling I might make it to Sunday and play in front of the television cameras. Call me crazy, but you asked and that's what I'm feeling"

"Billy told me if I get nervous to take some long, deep breaths. It relaxes you."

"Gee, thanks; I'll try that."

155

Things are running right on schedule. At 3:30, the lights dim. The lights on the practice tables are completely shut off. On a large screen on the wall, the first bracket of sixteen players' names is listed. Flo's name is announced for a six o'clock match. Her opponent is from Minnesota, Emily Patterson. Johnny and Flo take time to grab a quick bite to eat. Then they return to the practice area.

After Flo's settled in practicing, Johnny goes to get her necklace. He figures this is probably the best time to give her the medallion. She still has over an hour before she will begin to play. Johnny wants to give her enough time to regain her focus after he gives her the gift. After Flo finishes racking the balls for her opponent, Johnny holds out his hand to Flo and she spots the jewelry box. "The waitress in the restaurant thinks this might have fallen out of your purse." He hands the box to Flo; she takes the wrapping off and opens the gift. She sees the flower medallion and goes nuts. She lets out a loud scream and jumps into Johnny arms. She starts kissing him all over the face and telling Johnny how much she loves the gift.

Everyone in the practice room has turned their attention to them. Flo notices what's going on and she collects herself, then apologizes to everyone for creating a disturbance.

Flo's hands are trembling as she tries to put the chain on her neck. She comes over to Johnny and she's teary-eyed and asks Johnny if he could put the necklace on her. Johnny is upset; he feels he might have ruined any chance Flo has of winning her first match. "Why are you so excited?"

"Nobody has ever been this nice to me." Flo's warm-up partner has played her rack, and Johnny tells the girl to play another while Flo collects her emotions.

While putting the necklace on Flo, Johnny starts to tell her the story behind the necklace. He says, "The other night when

I got through playing Bill, Paco and I started talking. He told me he had made a lot of money betting on me against Bill. He gave me some money and told me to buy you something nice." As Johnny finishes putting the clasp together on Flo's necklace, he turns her around and says, "I'd like to take all the credit for the necklace, but I would be lying if I said it was all my idea. It's supposed to be a good luck charm and not the reason you lose your first match."

Regaining her composure, Flo gives Johnny a kiss. As she starts to head back to the practice table, she says, "This is a good time to see if taking a few deep breaths really helps." When it's Flo's turn to play a practice rack, she takes the cue-ball into her hand and stands back from the table. She is inhaling and exhaling heavier than usual. Sound advice creates a sound player. Flo breezes through the rack.

The announcement comes over the speakers that the six o'clock matches may go to their assigned tables. As Flo gets her stuff together, Johnny makes his way towards the entrance of the ballroom. Flo takes a few minutes to catch up to Johnny. She is all business as she and Johnny walk into the main ballroom. After a quick kiss from Johnny and a wish of good luck, Flo heads in the direction of her assigned table.

Emily wins the right to break. There are only two referees, so each player must rack the balls for their opponents. Flo racks the balls and walks back to her seat as Emily comes to the table preparing to break. Before breaking, Emily checks the rack and she sees all the balls are properly touching. She returns to the far end of the table and places the cue-ball on the table. The cue-ball is struck by Emily's cue. It races down table towards the one-ball. The collision between the cue-ball and the one-ball occurs. Flo and Emily's race to nine has officially started.

Emily's cue-ball doesn't make a solid hit on the one-ball, which causes the cue-ball to fly into the air and leave the table. Emily's isn't the only player whose cue-ball ends up on the floor. Two other ladies get off to the same bad start. Poor aim and high acceleration aren't good combinations when it comes to breaking a rack of nine-ball. The situation Emily finds herself in is a common result of such a problem. She has to leave the table and relinquish it to Flo.

"Ball-in-hand," the referee proclaims as he places the cue-ball on the table. Flo has come out of her chair like a shot after seeing Emily's cue-ball leave the table. The referee walks back to his chair and sits down. Although Flo has virtually run to the table, she gathers herself together and takes the time to calm down. Despite Emily making poor contact with the one-ball, she had managed to pocket two balls on the break. Both the seven-ball and the eight-ball made their way into different pockets. Although there are only seven balls left on the table, the four-ball and six-ball are tied up close to the rail. There is a positive side to the situation. The two-ball is sitting near the right-hand corner pocket close to the back rail. The one-ball sits three inches past the left-hand side pocket, four inches off the rail. Offense is always Flo's first choice when playing. She puts the cue-ball at the proper angle to pocket a one-ball in the side. She strokes the shot several times using high right-hand English. The cue-ball is propelled into the one-ball by Flo's cue. The one-ball goes into the side pocket and the cue-ball has enough energy to head down the side rail towards the four- and six-balls. The cue-ball strikes both balls, and Flo has a perfect shot on the two-ball. The traffic jam created by the four-ball and a six-ball no longer exists. Flo runs out the rest of the rack to win the first game.

For racks two and three, Flo's engine purrs like a kitten and she goes ahead in the match by a score of three to zero. When Emily does come to the table, she's kicking at the object-ball just to make hits. Rack four is a different story; Flo suffers her first brain fart. Her position play to pocket the four-ball isn't her best effort. She misses the shot and Emily wins her first game.

Five games later, the score is six to three, Flo's lead, and she has broken the next rack. She has pocketed two balls, but she's unable to play a shot on the one-ball. She has to play a push-out. Flo looks around to find a spot to shoot the cue-ball, which will force Emily to play a difficult shot. Leading six to three, Flo figures she will play the percentages. She shoots the cue-ball off the side rail, and it rolls to the back rail and bounces off the back rail about half an inch; it's close to the corner pocket. The one-ball is three inches below the side pocket and two inches out from the rail.

Emily elects to come to the table, and the position of the next object-ball plays a major role in what shot she may decide to play. If Emily makes the one, her position for the next ball looks pretty good. She takes a lot of extra time looking over the shot. The importance of the shot causes Emily to come out of her shooting position. She seems to be concerned with the position the five-ball has taken on the table. She regroups and gets down to shoot the shot. After several strokes, the cue-ball is sent in the direction of the one-ball. The one goes down table and splits the corner pocket. Emily's concerns about the five-ball are soon validated. The cue-ball comes across the table and hits the five-ball. It changes direction and rolls into the side pocket. Emily stands beside the table slumped over with her hands against the side rail. Fate has dealt her a terrible blow.

Knowing how sick Emily must be feeling, Flo waits until she is back to her seat before she comes to the table. Feeling sorry for her opponent wouldn't be in Flo's best interest. She puts her game face on, and the six balls left on the table quickly begin to disappear. After Flo pockets the nine, she looks at Emily. She is slumped over in her chair and has the look of a beaten player. When Emily finishes racking, she has a strained look on her face as she lifts the rack.

Game eleven also goes in Flo's favor, and she sits on "the hill." The next game Flo wins would put her over the top, and the importance of the game seems to have an effect on her. She makes an uncharacteristic mistake and misses an easy shot at the six-ball in the side pocket. Emily is all but convinced the match is over and springs from her chair. She pockets the remaining four balls on the table and wins the rack.

Momentum is in Emily's favor, and she wins another rack. The score is now eight to five in Flo's favor. She starts to squirm in her seat as Emily starts clearing balls in the next rack. She cruises through the first four balls, but makes a mistake playing position from the five to the six-ball. She's straight in on the six. She cinches the six, leaving a long, straight shot on the seven. Emily hits the shot easy hoping the speed of the shot helps if she's not completely accurate. Emily misses and hangs the seven.

Three balls remain on the table, and that's what stands between Flo and victory. She comes to the table and chalks her cue while observing the situation. She plays the three shots in her mind. The first sign of nerves shows when Flo makes her bridge with her left-hand and rests it on the table. Once again, Flo remembers Johnny's advice and backs away from the table. She takes a few deep breaths; when she returns to the table, her hand is much steadier. She proceeds to pocket the seven-, eight-, and nine-balls to win the match.

Spattering of light applause is heard as Flo makes the winning shot. Johnny looks around to see who is clapping. A couple of faces in the crowd are familiar to him. It's Frankie and Joey, the two men Johnny had played with in the ring game the day he met Flo. Several other people come to congratulate Flo as she leaves the playing area. Johnny sits watching the other matches still in progress. The two ladies playing on table six are of special interest. The winner of that match will be Flo's next opponent. The match is tied at seven games apiece, and Johnny has caught glimpses of this match while Flo was playing. Both women have struggled, and Johnny feels Flo can compete with either one of them if she plays the way she just played against Emily.

Coming back into the spectator area, Flo is stopped several times by admiring spectators. A few even ask Flo for her autograph. She's on cloud nine when she finally gets to where Johnny is seated. Johnny stands up as Flo gets closer, and he gives her a big hug and kiss. Flo is beaming. "I thought you would be the first in line to congratulate me."

Johnny tells Flo, "If the match on table six were finished, I would've been the first in line."

"What's so important about table six?"

"You play the winner in your next round of play."

As the match on table six goes to hill, Flo says, "Do you have a scouting report for me?"

"How do you know about scouting reports?"

"My uncle was a football scout and talked about scouting reports all the time. He was a full-blooded Indian and scouted for the Dallas Cowboys."

Johnny does all he can do from holding back laughing out loud. "Sit back and watch the final rack of the match. I'll give you my report when the match is over."

Table six is the only match yet to be decided, and everyone left in the spectator area focuses on the match. The player's sense what's going on and play becomes slow and ragged. Each player gets more than their fair share of opportunities to win. The worst part comes on the nine-ball. Both players miss, although they are difficult shots, on the nine-ball. In the end, Flo's next opponent will be Jackie Lane from Alabama.

Players in the next round start to filter into the playing area. As they do, Johnny starts to give Flo his scouting report on Jackie. "Jackie missed several kicks on safety plays and some weren't even that hard. She also had trouble banking balls. She shoots combinations well. She won two games by making combination shots on the nine. Overall, I think her game was weaker than the girl you just beat."

"We'll find out tomorrow; my match is scheduled for two in the afternoon."

Exhausted, they rent movies, grab some take-out, and go to Flo's home.

"Was it as exciting playing in the tournament today?" he asks her. "I was envious of you. I've never played in a tournament of that magnitude, and I know after watching you in that arena today that that's what I want to do. You were magnificent. I watched a lot of the other girls at various times, and you carried yourself as well as anyone I saw play. You should be proud of what you've accomplished today."

"Today was the best I have ever felt playing; I found a level of concentration I didn't know existed. Of course, the conditions were perfect: new cloth, excellent lighting, and plenty of space between tables. I never had to wait while someone on the other table was shooting a shot." Flo takes Johnny's hand and squeezes it then she says. "I just hope I can carry today's play into tomorrow."

Johnny pulls Flo close to him and gives her a big hug. "I'm sure you'll do just fine."

"Would there be a problem with Billy if you started playing in tournaments?"

"There could be a problem," says Johnny. "Billy thinks the best way to make money is by hustling people. I told him I didn't care about making money playing pool. The problem is, Billy seems to be obsessed with money. I have to go along with him because it's my only way of getting to know him. Let's watch the movie. That's enough pool talk for one night."

Day two is an instant replay of the previous day. The only differences are the clothes Flo and Johnny are wearing. Flo plays another strong match and beats Jackie Lane 9-3.

Johnny had made a bet with a big-mouth, who turned out to be Jackie's uncle and a decent guy. He quickly paid up the $500 he lost betting against Flo.

After collecting the money, Johnny then looks around the ballroom for Flo, who is nowhere to be found. He figures she must have gone to the ladies room. Johnny makes his way to there. A young girl comes from the ladies room and Johnny asks the girl if Flo is inside. The girl tells Johnny, "There isn't anyone in the ladies room." Johnny starts to get worried and goes back into the ballroom. Flo is still nowhere to be found. Johnny gets out his cell phone, and he starts to dial Flo's member. Suddenly, he feels someone tapping him from behind. He turns around quickly and discovers its Flo and she has a grin on her face from ear to ear. Although Johnny is glad to see Flo, he's a little upset he couldn't find her. "Where the hell have you been all this time?"

"In one of the conference rooms with a reporter from the local newspaper. She's going to write a story about me playing in the tournament. There's also a camera crew from the local news channel coming in today at six o'clock, and they want to do a live interview." Flo grabs Johnny and gives him a hug, then starts jumping around, full of excitement. "I am having the time of my life; I can't believe all that's happening to me. So much, so fast, and I owe it all to you, Johnny. Not only the financial support you've given to me, but the confidence to go out and play as well as I have played my first two matches. I couldn't have done this without your support." She grabs Johnny and pulls him inside an empty conference room. After locking the door, she grabs him and starts kissing him passionately. "After I'm knocked out of this tournament we're getting a room upstairs and making love till our bodies have no more to give."

"You sure you don't want to get a room right now? We have until ten o'clock tonight before you play your next match."

"I'm not about to change my plan. I need to focus on playing. It's only for two more days."

A knock on the door interrupts Flo and Johnny. By the sound of her voice, the person knocking is the reporter that interviewed Flo. When Flo opens the door, she takes time to introduce Johnny. "This is the reporter from *The Chronicle* I was telling you about, Virginia Graham."

Johnny and the reporter exchanged pleasantries. "I have a photographer coming by. Is there a place where we could take some shots of you at the table?"

"We could try the practice room; it's set up with four tables inside it. You could ask for permission to take some pictures."

Virginia says, "I've already talked to the tournament director, and she said we could use whatever facilities we need, just no flashbulbs. We're ready when you are."

"Will you come with me?" Flo asks Johnny. "I've never done anything like this before, and I could use all the reinforcement I can get."

"I'll be there in a little while. I want to call Billy because I haven't talked to him since Monday. I promise I won't be long. I don't want him to think I forgot about him."

"That's a good idea; you'd probably be bored watching me pose for pictures." Flo and Johnny give each other a quick kiss before going their separate ways.

"You've missed out on a lot of action the past few days," says Billy. "A couple of brothers came into the room and both thought they could play. They started throwing around plenty of money, and I'll tell you how bad they play. Walter beat the better player for twelve hundred." Billy pauses. "When will you be coming back to Lexington? I don't know how much longer these two brothers will be staying around."

"My flight leaves Monday."

"Call me when you're leaving St. Louis, and I'll come and get you at the airport."

"That'd be great."

"How's the tournament going?" asks Billy.

"Flo's played two matches and won both of them."

"That's pretty good. When's she playing her next match?"

"Ten tonight."

"What time did she play her last match?"

"Two this afternoon. Why?"

"It's a long time in between matches, and way too much time to think. Keep her busy; better yet, try to get her to sleep for a while. The time will go by faster and she'll be more alert while she's playing."

"Keeping her busy might be easier than getting her to take a nap. She's already done an interview with a local newspaper, and now she's having some pictures taken in the practice room. Later, they're doing a live telecast on the local channel and want her to do an interview."

"I don't like it. Way too many distractions. I know this is probably the biggest thing that's ever happened to her. I just hope she can regain her focus when it's time to play. How has she played so far? Has she played well or have her opponents played poorly?"

"She's dominated play in both matches. Neither opponent has come close to beating her."

Billy lets out a big sigh. "I hope she can keep her head from getting too big. This whole ordeal can be hard on a person. I hope when she gets knocked out the cloud she's on isn't so high she falls hard to the ground. If she falls hard, you have to be there to make sure she doesn't hurt so bad she can't recover." Billy is silent for a moment. "Have you found any action in Albuquerque?"

"I never thought you'd ask. I'm up about fifty-one hundred."

"Who did you beat out of that kind of money?"

"I beat a couple of people and also won a side bet on one of Flo's matches." Johnny starts to elaborate more on how he played Paco and Bill, but Billy interrupts.

"I have to go, the meat delivery guy is here, and if I don't watch his every move he screws up everything."

"We have to talk when I get back to Lexington."

Billy doesn't understand how serious Johnny is and shrugs off what Johnny has said by saying, "Yeah, yeah, kid, we'll talk." Billy says goodbye and hangs up before Johnny can get another word in.

Annoyed that he didn't get to tell Billy more about his money matches, Johnny slams his cell phone closed. He feels he's missed a good opportunity to talk to Billy about what his aspirations are in a game of pool. Johnny knows he's definitely not a fan of the hustle game. He has had a taste of the big time pool tournaments, and he likes what he sees. He knows he wants to test the waters of the men's professional tour so he can get his feet wet. Johnny walks towards the practice room to reunite with Flo.

Entering the practice room, Johnny sees the photo shoot is still in progress. Johnny and Flo make eye contact, but that's as close as Johnny gets. He sits and watches while listening to some of the girls playing in the practice room. They seem a little upset at the attention Flo is getting from the media. Johnny overhears one girl saying to the other, "This girl has two career wins and she's front page news. Her opponent tonight, Becky Slater, was in the practice room when the camera crew came in to set-up. Becky's the number two player in the world and thought they were going to take pictures of her. She wasn't too pissed when she found out the photo shoot was for her opponent tonight. She had a few choice words for the darling of Albuquerque."

When the session finally finishes, Johnny walks over to Flo. Having listened to the local gossip, Johnny takes the slow approach. "So," he asks, "how did everything go?"

"My photo shoot might turn out to be a huge mistake. The girl I'm playing tonight already hates me. The photographer made her stop practicing on the table she was on. He said it had the best background for taking pictures. She blew up and started yelling at me and tells me I won't be smiling after the match tonight."

Johnny feels the need to step in and calm Flo down. He tells her that Becky is just blowing off steam. "She's upset because she's not the one people are talking about and getting all the attention." Flo starts to break down as Johnny pulled her close to him. A tear comes from her eye as she looks up at Johnny. Johnny takes his hand and smoothes it across Flo's face, wiping her eyes.

Johnny tells Flo, "None of what's happened here is your fault. You shouldn't be the one who's upset. Becky's the one with the problem."

"Becky was the number one player in the world for over a year, but she recently fell to two."

"That's probably part of the problem. She's the one used to getting all the attention, and she can't stand to see anyone else get any."

"What time is it?"

This is the first time Johnny has seen Flo's unpleasant side. He figures he'll give Flo a little cooling off time before he answers. Johnny pretends not to know where his cell phone is located. He finally reaches into pants pocket and pulls it out. "It's time you and I went for a walk. There are some fountains outside the hotel. Why don't we take a walk outside and sit for awhile?"

Knowing what Johnny has said makes a lot of sense; Flo sheepishly says, "Let's get out of here for awhile."

Sitting by the fountains, they take it all in before Flo gets the idea of taking her shoes off and wading into the water. Johnny does the same thing, and soon they are splashing each other with their feet. The splashing escalates a little before Flo comes to her senses and reminds Johnny she has a television interview at six o'clock. Johnny pulls out his cell phone and checks the time. It's five-thirty, and he and Flo get their shoes back on. They sit for a little while in the sun trying to dry off.

The camera crew is busy setting up when Flo and Johnny get back inside. The tournament director calls her over to meet everyone. Johnny decides to take a back seat and finds a comfortable area to watch. Flo meets the woman doing the interview. Flo looks nervous as she and the interviewer start doing a quick rehearsal. She settles down as the interviewer asks her a few questions. The makeup people come in and do a quick fix on Flo and the interviewer before they go on the air. As they count down the seconds for the interview, Flo takes her place alongside the woman doing the interview. Everything goes well.

To keep Flo's mind off the stress, Johnny takes her to a movie, then to get something to eat. When they get back, they find that the matches have been delayed. Flo takes advantage of the delay and practices.

Finally, the players are introduced with a spotlight shining upon them. Becky's anger towards Flo comes to light before the match starts. As they start to lag for break, Flo extends her hand to Becky's for the traditional handshake. Becky doesn't even acknowledge Flo's being at the table. She takes her object-ball and goes into her shooting position. Flo backs away from the table and takes a few deep breaths before she snatches her object-ball from the table and puts it into position to lag. Then she crouches down beside Becky and gets ready to lag. After a few strokes of the cue, each player sends a ball down table. The lag is so close they need a referee to decide which ball is closest to the rail. Using the ferrule of the cue to measure, the referee decides in Flo's favor.

Slamming her cue on the floor to vent her frustration, Becky reluctantly leaves the table. Flo jumps out to an early lead but a series of bad breaks hurts her tremendously and she loses nine to five. At this time, Becky takes the time to go to Flo and shake hands. She also reminds Flo of her earlier statement. She quietly whispers to Flo, "I told you I would be smiling now," as she flashes a big grin before walking away from Flo.

Not knowing what kind of mood Flo will be in, Johnny takes his time getting through the crowd. A few of the spectators are busy consoling Flo as Johnny makes his final approach. The typical lines are coming from the mouths of the spectators. The consolation of getting no breaks or receiving any rolls does little to change losing a match. Still, Flo is very gracious and carries herself with dignity despite her defeat.

Gritting her teeth while keeping a smile, Flo says to Johnny when he finally gets close enough to hear, "She's afraid of me."

"What?" says Johnny.

"She's afraid of me. Now let's get out of here, and I'll explain what I'm talking about on the ride back to my place."

They get in the car, and Flo says, "This may sound crazy, but I think Becky respects my game so much that she's trying to irritate me to make me want her to beat her for personal reasons." After a pause, Flo asks Johnny, "Do you think I'm crazy for thinking that way?"

"I was in a similar situation the day before I started to drive east. I went into my local poolroom just to get my cue, and all of a sudden, through a series of events, I'm playing this big mouth that came into the poolroom for a thousand dollars."

"What happened?"

"Well, this guy, Larry, told me the loudmouth was running his mouth for the same reasons—"

"Did you win the thousand dollars?"

"I beat him either eleven to five or six. I'm not sure."

They get to the house and order a pizza.

"Let me tell you the way I look at my situation," says Flo. "Two days ago, before the start of the tournament, my goal was to win one match. I know I told you I wanted to play in front of the cameras, but that might have been unrealistic. I just wanted to be able to say I won a match. If you told me that day

I'd be playing on the third day of the tournament, I wouldn't have believed it could happen. I could feel sorry for myself and say I could've beaten Becky with a few breaks. Looking back at my first match with Emily, she could've beaten me with a few breaks. Tomorrow, I'm going to play a match I never counted on playing. I have nothing to lose and nothing to prove; I've already exceeded my own personal expectations."

Knocking on the door interrupts Flo. It's the landlady. She tells Flo, "I saw you today on the six o'clock news and couldn't believe it was you. You're playing in a billiards tournament at the big hotel down by the mall." Flo acknowledges what the landlady is saying. Then the landlady asks Flo, "Are you playing tomorrow?"

"I'm playing tomorrow at two."

"Do you mind if my husband and I come to watch you play?"

Surprised, she tells the landlady, "I would be honored if you both come and watch me play." Flo asks her landlady, "Do you like pool?"

"Oh yes, my husband and I watch it all the time when it's on television. In fact, we used to play at my brother-in-law's house every Friday night. I'll see you tomorrow," says the landlady. The pizza and salad they ordered shows up as the land-lady walks back upstairs. Flo takes the food and Johnny pays the delivery boy.

Johnny has already cracked open a beer and has started to put some salad on his plate. Flo asks Johnny, "Did you hear what the landlady was talking about? That's the first civilized conversation she and I have had. I can't believe we have something in common. The wildest part is it's the game of pool." Flo comes to the table and pops open a beer then she starts to eat her half of the salad.

The next day, words between Flo and Johnny get scarce because Johnny doesn't want to say anything that might upset her. Flo seems to have her game face on as she and Johnny get into the lobby of the hotel. "While you're playing today, tell yourself that the shot you're about to play may be you're final shot of the tournament. Don't take it for granted. Put as much effort into the easy shots as you do the difficult shots. I did those things the other night when I was playing against Bill and it worked out well."

Flo thanks Johnny for his advice. "I want you to sit in the first row. I don't want to have to look around to find you. You've a calming effect on me, and there may be times today when I have to remind myself to stay focused."

Soon, Flo and her opponent, Christine Ly, are at the table getting ready to lag for the break. Christine not only extends her hand to Flo, but when Flo shakes her hand, Christine bows slightly in a show of respect for her opponent. Flo awkwardly does her best to bow back to Christine to also show her respect. With the ice broken, the two ladies share a short moment of laughter before getting down to some very serious business. Although close at one point, Flo goes on to win nine to five.

Any doubt who has become the crowd favorite is answered after Flo's final nine-ball of the set falls into the pocket. She receives the loudest ovation of any player thus far in the tournament. Flo is a little embarrassed she is getting so much attention, and she downplays her accomplishment by moving her hands in a fashion like she is trying to suppress the crowd noise. She shakes hands with Christine and sits back in her chair to relax for a few minutes. Flo's next match will start as soon as the two matches still in progress are completed. Looking around, Flo spots her landlords sitting a few rows up in the crowd. Her landlady gives Flo a big smile and a thumbs-up expressing her satisfaction with Flo's performance. Finally, two o'clock comes around and the matches conclude.

Twenty minutes is what the emcee announces to the crowd for the start of the next round of matches. Flo will be playing on table number five. Luckily for Johnny, he was seated between tables five and seven and he'll be able to stay in the same seat and view Flo's match quite comfortably. The tables are brushed and wiped down so the players can start warming up for their matches. Flo shoots a rack of balls, then gives up the table to Bonnie Keegan. As Bonnie is shooting, Flo comes over to Johnny to chat for a while. She tells Johnny, "I'm playing the person who got me interested in playing pool. My uncle brought me to this tournament when I was nine years old. I watched Bonnie come through the loser's bracket; she won five matches in a row the final day of the tournament to claim victory."

"Five matches! That seems like an awful lot of matches to play in one day."

"This used to be a three-day tournament. They expanded a couple years ago for television." Flo starts to tell Johnny more about the day she was watching Bonnie play.

Johnny doesn't like the way Flo is going on about Bonnie. "I want you to go over to your chair and start thinking about what you're playing instead of who you're playing."

"You're right. I'm starting to lose my focus."

Soon, Flo takes on Bonnie. Winning the opening lag helps Bonnie pounce on Flo. She runs out to leads of two to one, and then she extends the lead to four to two. Flo has played rather poorly up until this point in the match. She has missed a couple of easy opportunities to win games. In the next rack, things get even worse. Flo has three balls left on the table and a good shot at the seven, but Flo's position play for a good shot on the eight-ball is tricky. She pockets the seven, but her effort to get position on the eight comes up short and she leaves herself safe behind the nine. Although Flo kicks and hits the eight, she leaves Bonnie a good shot at the eight with an easy position for the nine-ball. Bonnie proceeds to pocket both balls and win the game; she has also taken Flo's biggest ally, the crowd, out of the game.

Two more games have passed and the score is six to three in favor of Bonnie. She breaks the next rack but fails to pocket a ball. Flo comes to the table and notices a good chance to win the game early. The three-ball and the nine-ball are near the side pocket. The one-ball, however, is difficult, a bank shot. Without any easy way to play safety and trailing by three games, Flo elects to play aggressively and goes for the bank-shot. She splits the pocket banking the one and the cue-ball starts down table towards the back rail. The four-ball and a six-ball are the obstacles the cue-ball must avoid in order for Flo to get position on the two-ball. The cue-ball splits the four and six like a football player kicking a field goal. It goes to the back rail and bounces out a little for a good shot at the two-ball. Flo's next shot is much easier; she pockets the two-ball, and the cue-ball comes off the back rail and side rail in a perfect spot from which to play the three-nine billiard shot. Flo plays both the three and a nine on the same shot. She pockets the three, and the nine crawls towards the side pocket. It sits on the lip of the side pocket before it falls. The crowd comes to life on Flo's behalf.

Igniting the spark that has been lacking, Flo shifts the momentum in her favor. She runs off a series of games to take the lead. The next rack Flo misses the intended pocket with one of her shots but the ball finds its way to another pocket. Flo looks over at Bonnie and shrugs her shoulders. Bonnie shows no emotion. A veteran knows luck sometimes plays a major role in who wins a nine-ball match. Although Flo is visibly nervous, she manages to prod her way through the rest of that rack and the final rack to win the match.

The emcee comes over the microphone and announces, "The winner of our final match of this session is Miss Flo Stevens from right here in Albuquerque." The crowd noise is so loud it's hard to hear the announcement. Flo makes her way over to Bonnie. She starts to tell Bonnie how sorry she is about lucking in the two-ball. Bonnie gives Flo a little sisterly advice. "Don't ever feel sorry for or apologize to your opponent for winning a match. If you get a break to win a match, it's because you're the one at the table. The breaks usually go in the favor of the best player. The last six racks we played, you were the best player." Bonnie takes Flo's hand and raises it up to her adoring crowd. Then she bends over and whispers into Flo's ear, "I remember when I was the one hearing the applause."

Flo yells above the noise to Bonnie, "Fifteen years ago, I sat in the stands and applauded your victory. You're the reason I started playing this game."

Bonnie is humbled by Flo's honestly and gives her a last few words of advice. "I hope you make better decisions than I made. Enjoy what's going on around you right now with the crowd because they love to root for the underdog. Use the energy they give you to climb to the top. But, remember one thing, when you get to the top, the crowd will look for a new hero. Good luck." They shake hands and go their separate ways.

The crowd is still buzzing as Flo starts to unscrew her cue and put it into her case. Most of the people in attendance get up from their seats and start heading for the exits. There are a few stragglers lined up waiting to see if Flo will sign any autographs. Knowing he has no chance at pulling Flo away from the autograph seekers, Johnny decides to buy better seat tickets.

Walking back to the main ballroom, Johnny sees the landlord and the landlady and makes his way to them and introduces himself. "Hi," he says, as he extends his hand to the landlord, "I'm Johnny Jordan."

The landlord stands up to shake Johnny's hand. "I'm Pedro Garcia, and this is my wife, Marie."

"Would you like to come and sit down front closer to the action? I have purchased two extra seats in the preferred seating area for the next match."

Marie asks Johnny, "Are you sure? We wouldn't want to make Flo nervous."

"Flo won't mind. She likes looking in the crowd and seeing friendly faces."

Marie says, "Our conversations were not always the friendly type. We've had our disagreements in the past."

Johnny tells Marie and Pedro to stay where they are, and he walks down to the preferred seating. When he gets there, he calls Flo over and explains the situation. She looks up into the stands and signals for Pedro and Marie to come down and sit with Johnny.

"Who's the young lady you're going to be playing?" asks Johnny.

"Kelly Munnice. She's supposed to be one of the up and coming stars on the woman's tour." As Flo starts to say more about Kelly, the emcee comes over the speakers calling for the players to go to their assigned seats. He makes his introductions and the players start their matches.

Kelly wins the lag for break and shows right away why she's so highly regarded on the women's tour. She runs out the first two racks to take a two-game lead. But Kelly all of a sudden seems to be having a problem. She takes a bathroom break and is gone for some time. When she returns Flo wins eight games in a row and two games later closes out the match. As she walks over to shake Kelly's hand, a large part of the crowd stands to applaud. As a show of good sportsmanship, Flo takes Kelly arm and raises it to the crowd. Kelly tells Flo her nerves got the best of her and that's why she went to the ladies room. Flo and Kelly then shake hands and Kelly wishes Flo the best of luck in her next match.

Even with a five-minute break, Flo's match and all the other matches are over by nine-thirty. Flo comes over to chat with Johnny, Marie, and Pedro. Some of the people sitting in the preferred seats ask for autographs. Flo is nice enough to oblige many of them. Flo's next match will be played on table three, and she watches as they place her name on the lights above the table. The name on the other side is familiar to Flo. It's Karen Black, the girl she had played at Snooker's. After the tables are cleaned, the players start to practice for the next match.

Minding her own business, Flo goes to the table and starts to hit a few balls. Karen is nowhere in sight after Flo plays one rack, so she starts to hit a second rack. When Karen finally shows up, she has a small entourage following her around. Some of them are already touting Karen as the winner of the match. She approaches Flo and asks, "How about we bet the four-fifty you beat me out of the other night at Snooker's on this match?"

Flo's not sure what to do, so she confers with Johnny. After a short deliberation, Flo comes to Karen with a counter proposal. "The bet is either six hundred or two hundred. You can take your pick."

"I'll bet the six hundred."

Action on the side has been scarce since Flo's second match. This match between Karen and Flo has ignited a spark amongst the spectators. Johnny has found two people willing to bet on the match. One person has bet two hundred on Karen, the other bet a hundred. Marie and Pedro even get in on the action. The person sitting next to them wants to bet fifty on Karen. Marie insists they bet at least a hundred. A lot of the spectators in the crowd are still haggling over bets as the light starts to dim for the final introductions of the night.

Twelve players remain: four are undefeated and the other eight have one loss. The introductions don't take very long. When it comes time to introduce Flo, the emcee adds a little extra when he announces her name. He gives Flo a nickname of The Comeback Kid. Flo's introduction receives the loudest ovation.

"Comeback Kid," says Karen, as she and Flo come to the table to lag for the break. "The only comeback that's gonna happen is when you come back to your chair and watch me shoot."

Flo tries to block out anything Karen has to say. She's busy trying to find the concentration and energy to play her fourth match of a long day. Before her match starts, Flo takes out her medallion and kisses it for luck. Just before she takes her stance at the table to lag, Karen reminds her, "In case you don't know, the winner of this match gets to play in front of the television cameras tomorrow."

"I know what's riding on this match. The more you have to say, the more incentive I have to kick your ass." Flo is miffed at this point. "If you want to bet more money on this match, say so right now. If you don't want to bet anymore, it's time to put up or shut up." Karen is either out of money or she's lost her nerve. "Just like I thought, Karen, you have no balls, and that's what you're going to make when we play, no balls."

Visibly shaken by what Flo has said, Karen's lag barely makes it back to the spot on the table. Flo's lag comes within an inch of the back rail. She takes control of the match by winning the right to break. Flo has the speed of the tables down pat and has gotten into stroke. After she steamrolls her way through the first four games against Karen, the crowd has reached a frenzy rooting for Flo. Flo has Karen by the jugular and is not letting go. Karen manages to win one game, but Flo hits her with another haymaker by winning four more games in a row. With the score eight to one, Karen wins two meaningless games. Embarrassing an opponent is something Flo would never usually consider doing, but Karen has shown no class every time they have played. With a simple shot left to close out the match, Flo takes several strokes, then stops to chalk her cue before going back to shoot the nine-ball into the pocket. One of Karen's supporters starts to boo Flo for her antics.

"How many times are you going to stick the knife into your opponent? She's on the ground dying!" yells an audience member.

"As many times as it takes." Then she pockets the nine to close out the match nine to three.

Six crumpled up hundred dollar bills are placed into the corner pocket by Karen. When she walks past Flo, she murmurs, "You haven't seen the last of me. Why don't you come out and play on tour instead of hiding in your hometown?"

"If I had thought all the players on tour where as easy as you, I would've played years ago."

After Karen storms away and heads out of the arena, Flo sits back and watches the rest of the ladies play. Her opponent, the next day, will be the winner of the match being played on table four. It's a close game, but the victor ends up being Lori Cole, a respectable player unlike Karen.

In the meantime, Johnny and Marie have kept busy by collecting bets they were able to get on the match. The long day ends, and when Johnny and Flo come outside the hotel, the valet has a surprise waiting for them. Their car is sitting in the carport already started. The valet tells them, "I was inside watching Flo's match. When it ended, I came outside and got your car. I figured I would save you some time." Johnny's thanks the valet for being so considerate, and he hands him a generous tip. They jump into the car and drive back to Flo's place.

All of her emotions catch up with her as Johnny pulls the car into the driveway. She starts to weep openly as she leans over and puts her head against Johnny's shoulder. He tries to console Flo and reminds her she still has to play the biggest pool match of her life in about thirteen hours. Flo and Johnny talk for a while about their future together.

Johnny tells Flo, "I have found out a few things about myself during all this. I know I want to play pool, professionally, and I also have found the woman I want to spend the rest of my life with." Hearing these words from Johnny changes her emotional state. She starts to kiss Johnny intensely.

Flo whispers into Johnny's ear, "I know I said I wanted to remain abstinent until the tournament was over, but I'm beginning to have second thoughts about my decision."

Johnny comes back with an answer that catches Flo off guard. "I think we should wait until you're through playing. You need to save as much energy as you can. If we start to make love, you may be late for your match tomorrow. After you're through playing, we'll have plenty of time to makeup for what we've been missing."

"All of the guys I've been with would have me in the back seat of the car by now. They would be afraid I'd change my mind if we went into the house. You're different. You intrigue me. I guess that's why I'm so attracted to you." Flo kisses Johnny on the lips one last time. Then she says, "Let's go inside, I'm a little hungry. Maybe I can throw something together for us."

"That sounds like a great idea. I could eat something; I could definitely eat something."

When Flo and Johnny get inside, they find a note on the apartment door: *Flo, I hope you don't mind, but I took the liberty of making some food for you and Johnny to eat. I have put it in the refrigerator, all you have to do is heat it up.* The note is signed by Marie. *P.S. I really enjoyed watching you play today. I never knew how well you played, and I look forward to watching you play tomorrow. I also enjoyed meeting Johnny, he's a really nice guy and good looking too. You two make a nice couple. I hope you like fajitas.* A small tear flows from Flo's eye; she is happy to think she and her landlady are finally becoming friends.

Handing the note to Johnny, Flo reaches into her pocketbook to get her keys. As she opens the door and goes inside the apartment, Johnny finishes reading the note. His response to the note is more typical of what Flo is used to hearing from a man. He says to Flo, "I don't know about you, but I love fajitas." Flo's faith in Johnny's manhood has been restored.

"When Karen wanted to bet on the match, why did you give her the option of betting either two hundred or six hundred?" asks Flo.

"I just wanted to throw her off stride and give her something to think about. She was obviously comfortable betting the four hundred fifty, thinking if she won, she was getting back the money she had lost at Snooker's. I didn't want her to have that piece of mind. The two hundred bet made her feel she couldn't get her money back. The six hundred probably put more pressure on her to win because she would be losing even more money to you."

"Whatever it was, it sure worked."

"What I did had nothing to do with the fact that you kicked Karen's ass. In fact, you played that match with a little anger in your game. Maybe you should play that way more often. If you keep falling behind in all your matches, it might come back to bite you in the end. I know it's not as dramatic, but I wouldn't mind watching you beat some of these girls, nine to nothing."

"That will be impossible. The rest of the matches we play are races to seven. They shorten the match's two games for television in hopes of getting everything in an hour."

"All the more reason to jump on your opponents early; there's less time to come back."

Flo smiles and kisses him, then goes to the bedroom.

Lying on the couch, Johnny thinks how can he fix his life. His mother is living in California, his father in Kentucky, and his girlfriend in Albuquerque. Johnny lies awake for a while trying to figure out a way to make everything work. Unable to find a clear solution, he goes to sleep.

While waiting in line to buy his seating tickets, Johnny hears a few people talking up Flo's opponent, Judy Rosa. Johnny listens for awhile before he approaches Judy's fans. He asks, "Do any of you have enough faith in Judy to place a bet on her?" Johnny, as in the past, is a little surprised at how much faith some people have. In no time whatsoever, Johnny has covered seven hundred dollars in bets.

After all the betting has concluded, a fan of Flo's asks Johnny, "Do you know who Judy Rosa is? She won the last tour event two weeks ago. She beat all the best players. I hate to say this, but Flo has her hands full playing this lady."

"She may have her hands full," says Johnny, "but it's her heart that has gotten her to where she is today." Not wanting to sound like a jerk, but willing to defend Flo's honor, Johnny asks the man, "Do you want to bet on Judy?"

"Oh no," says the man. "I wouldn't bet against Flo. She's made me a believer."

Inside the playing arena, things have changed. They are down to using one table.

A large crowd has already gathered. Johnny looks around and sees Pedro and Marie coming into the arena. He motions for them to come down and sit with him. They split the action on Flo.

Right from the opening break, this match features two heavyweights at their best. Flo and Judy go at it toe to toe. Each player delivers and lands many punches in the form of bank-shots, combinations, and safety play. Flo throws in a brilliant two-rail billiard shot on the nine to win one game. Judy manages to make a jump shot, along with making a beautiful masse-shot. The crowd is really into what's going on in the match. Although they favor the local player, they have also recognized Judy's great play. When one player manages to take a small lead, the other player counters and catches right up. It all comes down to one game. The match is all even at six games apiece.

It boils down to one final rack, and Judy has control of the table, she's breaking. Being the only game in town, all eyes follow the cue-ball as Judy sends it towards the one-ball. She makes a square hit and pockets two balls. That's the good news for Judy. The bad news is the six and seven are tied up and all the low balls are at the opposite end of the table. The best Judy can do is run to the six and play safe. She does exactly that and plays a safe—and what a safe.

Flo comes to the table scratching her head. After taking an extension, Flo figures she has one chance at hitting the object-ball. She will have to elevate the back of her cue and masse the cue-ball to create a longer angle off the side rail to hit the six, which is down near the opposite back rail. Flo takes several practice strokes trying to get a feel for the shot. It doesn't happen. Flo asks for and is granted her last extension. She is worried about fouling the seven-ball with her follow through so she goes at the shot at a more difficult angle. She will be forced to masse, or curve the cue-ball even more.

Flo's stroke of the shot is true and pure. The cue-ball travels several inches sideways before it starts to bend at a severe angle. It runs up table before it strikes the side rail. Flo has managed to get an amazing amount of speed on the shot. The cue-ball glances off the side rail before it heads up table towards the six. It contacts the six and sends it towards and into the corner pocket. The cue-ball comes off the back and side rail in perfect position to pocket the seven-ball.

As the cue-ball slowly comes to rest, a thunderous roar is still going on in the room. It's a great show of sportsmanship when Judy politely claps her hands in appreciation of Flo's shot. Three balls still remain on the table. Regaining her composure, Flo tries to get the crowd to settle down before she resumes playing. Flo has no extensions left, so she has to go to work, even though the crowd is buzzing about her last shot.

Deep breaths help Flo settle back down. She pockets the seven and the cue-ball moves into a position where the eight-ball is fairly simple and she makes the shot. Her position on the nine is almost perfect. The importance of the shot makes it seem more difficult. Flo studies the shot, takes one final deep breath, and goes about her business pocketing the nine-ball.

The crowd explodes with the same intensity as it did when Flo pocketed the six-ball. Flo and Judy shake hands and exchange a few words before going their separate ways. Judy quietly makes her way out of the playing arena while Flo leans back and closes her eyes. Although Flo will get a break before playing her next match, she stands quietly trying to conserve as much energy as possible.

Johnny comes over and asks, "Are you all right? You look a little funny to me."

"My legs feel funny, and I'm a little lightheaded. I think the last match might've gotten the best of me."

"It sounds like you're dehydrated to me; drink some water."

She drinks some water, then does a television interview while Johnny collects his money from bettors.

Feeling a tap on the shoulder, Johnny turns around; it's Marie. She says, "What a shot, what a match, it was unbelievable. Look at me, I'm still shaking, I don't know how many more matches I can take."

Johnny takes three hundred and fifty dollars from his pocket, and he places it in Marie's hand. "Maybe this will help settle you down."

"It's not about the money. It's about watching someone you care about pulling themselves up from hanging over a cliff on the tips of their fingers. I thought for sure Flo had no chance of hitting that six-ball. Never mind making it and winning the game." As Marie takes out her purse and puts the money into it, she says, "The money does make it a little sweeter."

Johnny grabs Marie and gives her a hug. It's an emotional moment, and he says to Marie, "Thank you for caring."

"I cared too much for Flo, and that's why we never got along. She and I had a lot in common. We were young, attractive women, and we had the knack of finding losers. I kissed a lot of toads before I met Pedro. I'd like to tell you the whole story, but I don't think we have the time right now. Maybe later."

Another hug ensues, then Marie goes to the bathroom.

Flo finally returns, and Johnny asks, "How did that go?"

"Great. They have a new show on ESPN called Instant Classics, and they want to show my match with Judy as soon as possible. They told me I get three hundred the first time it is aired and two hundred every time after that."

"Maybe it's time you considered hiring an agent and PR person. The more matches you win, the more leverage you will have when you start talking to sponsors. The most important match of your life is your next match. You have to convince everyone that what you've done here the last four days is no fluke."

"Once again," Flo says, "you have managed to say all the right things. Now give me my weapon. A great warrior would never go into battle without having a weapon." Johnny hands Flo her cue.

Marie makes six hundred dollars worth of bets on the next match, then goes and tells Johnny, "There's someone else in the crowd who wants to bet a thousand dollars on Jessica. I wasn't sure if you wanted to make a bet as heavy as a thousand. One more thing you should know. The person that wants to bet is a woman."

"Sure. Will you set it up for me but when it comes to paying or collecting the money the job is all yours, Marie?" She does, then comes back to watch the match.

Excitement fills the room once again. Jessica wins the lag and hits Flo with a haymaker on the first break of the match. The nine-ball comes out of the center of the diamond and journeys into the left corner pocket. With one stroke of her cue stick, Jessica Conners has built a one-game lead.

She continues to make balls on the break and stifle Flo's ability to get started in the match. In what seems like a flash, Flo finds herself trailing Jessica four games to one. Everything is going Jessica's way as she prepares to break the balls to start game six. Her break is getting stronger as the match goes more in her favor. On this break, once again, the nine comes out of the pack and heads right for the right-hand corner pocket. It's not traveling at the same speed as the opening break, but it looks like it has a good chance to make it to the pocket. Miraculously, the nine-ball seems to strike a small spec of dirt; it comes to rest on the lip of the corner pocket.

Counting the balls from her seat, Flo comes up with the right number. There are still nine of them remaining on the table. Flo has a very make-able shot on the one-ball, and the two is in a good spot to make the nine-ball with a combination. After sitting for so long, Flo takes extra time before she goes into her shooting position. Although the one-ball shot isn't as hard as the few shots Flo has seen, the importance of the shot makes Flo's stroke a little tentative. When she shoots the one, it catches the jaws of the pocket and wiggles around a little before it drops out of sight. Jessica has come halfway out of her seat thinking Flo had missed the shot. As Jessica sits back in her chair, Flo goes to the table and makes the two-nine combination to win the game. The crowd responds to Flo's good fortune with a nice ovation.

Unlike Jessica's sprint, Flo's pace is that of a marathon runner. She manages to control the action and keep Jessica at bay with some fine shooting and excellent safety play. It's tied at five games apiece after Flo makes a difficult cross-side shot on the nine-ball.

Flo has the momentum on her side, but Jessica has a wealth of experience. Flo breaks to start game eleven, but nothing finds its way into the pocket. The best thing Flo has going for her is Jessica doesn't have a shot at the one-ball. Studying the table, Jessica plays a safety-shot. She executes the shot to perfection. With danger lurking in every direction, Flo figures a two rail indirect shot is the best way to make a hit on the one-ball. She goes with her gut feeling and sends the cue-ball on its way.

Flo makes the hit, but she still needs a ball to strike a rail. The cue-ball creeps slowly towards the rail. Looking right over the cue-ball as it nears the rail, the referee is in perfect position to make the call. The cue-ball barely gets to the rail and the ref makes the call.

Jessica limps over to the table because she knows she's not going to like what she sees. The cue-ball is about a half-inch behind the seven-ball and a good path to strike the one-ball isn't available. Jessica tries in vain to contact the one-ball. The referee declares "Ball-in-hand for Miss Stevens."

Flo goes on to run out a very pressure-packed rack of balls to take the lead. She also wins the next rack and claims her victory. Thunderous applause is heard around the arena. Flo goes to Jessica and raises her arms into the air, telling the crowd Jessica was more than a worthy opponent. The crowd gives Jessica a great and well-deserved ovation. When the two ladies turn and face the crowd, they look like two heavyweights who have just slugged it out for twelve rounds. The crowd starts to settle down as both players shake hands for the last time. The emcee announces the next match will start at 7 p.m.

Several autograph seekers surround Flo before Johnny has a chance of fending them off. Flo signals to Johnny she's okay with what's going on. Johnny feels a tapping on his shoulder as he stands waiting for Flo to come clear of her admirers. Turning around, Johnny sees a hand holding some money. It's the lady who made the bet, and she says to Johnny, "I believe I owe you some money."

"The other lady was supposed to collect the bet."

"I know, but after I told her I was an agent for most of the ladies playing on tour, she thought it might be a good time for us to meet. I know you're very busy, so I don't want to talk about anything right now." She hands Johnny the money and a business card. "I represent several of the women on tour. I've written their phone numbers on the back of my card. Before you call me, call them; they will tell you how much I've helped their careers. A few of my girls make well over six figures. Personally, I think Flo has the best earning potential of any girl I've seen so far."

"Why are you talking to me? Why don't you talk to Flo?"

"I'd love to talk to Flo, but I'm on my way to California. I stopped here because I heard there was a new hot commodity I should take a look at in person. My plane leaves in an hour. I have to rush to the airport. All I want you to do is consider what I have to offer. I'm totally connected in the pool world, advertising, television, and I even know some people in the movie business. Flo is, by far, the best thing I've seen in the last ten years." The lady extends her hand to Johnny. "My name is Liz Dennehy. I know I rushed my pitch, and I wish I had time to sit and talk with you and Flo. I'm not a bullshitter. I know I can help this girl's career."

Flo comes over and asks, "Who was that?"

"The lady made a bet on your match with me, and she just came over to pay me."

"You were talking with her for a while. What was that all about?"

"She was asking me to bet on the next match, so she could try to get even. She was trying to get some weight, so I told her I'd think about it. She gave me her cell phone number and told me to call her if I wanted to make the bet."

"Oh," says Flo. "How much did you win?"

"When you're through playing, I'll let you know. Right now, you need to get ready for your next match. Let's go find Pedro and Marie. I have a surprise for them. I ran into the manager of the hotel and he offered the four of us dinner in the gourmet room compliments of the house. He thinks your being seen in the dining room will be good for business."

Scanning the lobby, Johnny sees Pedro and Marie talking with a small group of people. As he and Flo start to walk towards them, Flo says to Johnny, "I'll be right back."

Johnny goes to Marie and Pedro and says, "I hate to break this little gathering up, but when Flo comes out of the ladies room, the four of us are going to take some time to have dinner." He then tells them to keep quiet about the agent.

They eat and have pictures taken, then Johnny asks Flo, "Do you want to head straight back to the tournament room?"

"I think I want to freshen up a little."

Marie tells Flo, "Count me in; I'll go with you." They agree to meet in the tournament room afterwards.

When Marie gets back and sits down, Johnny asks, "What took so long?"

"Flo and I had a nice talk. She said she feels like Cinderella. The only problem she has is its fast approaching midnight, and she's afraid her fairytale is coming to an end. She started to break down a little, and I had to pull her out of it pretty quick. I told her you, Prince Charming, were not about to run away from her. I guess that was the wrong approach. She reminded me you were leaving tomorrow for Kentucky. I wish I hadn't said what I said, when I said it. This led to a few tears. I asked her why you were leaving and she told me about your father, or the man you think may be a father."

Before Marie can say anything more, Johnny interrupts. "Is Flo going to be able to play her next match?"

"I think she'll be all right. I had her laughing as we came out of the ladies room. I told Flo, if you run off and don't come back, I would go with her to hunt you down and we would cut your balls off."

"What did she do?"

"She laughed. You must realize a woman's heart is a very delicate place. There are only so many times it can withstand the pain of being broken before it shatters completely. Flo's heart is at the breaking point; one more bad relationship will put her over the top."

"I don't know how I'm going to get everything that's going on in my life to work. I know it won't be easy. The one thing I'm absolutely sure of is that the most important part starts and ends with Flo. I've rented the honeymoon suite for later tonight so we can enjoy each other one final time before I have to leave town."

Marie and Johnny are hugging each other as the lights start to dim. The next match is about to start.

Lost in all the confusion are a few subtle changes made in the playing arena. More seats have been added, and for the first time ever on television, a woman's match is being aired live. The crowd is at fever pitch when the introduction of the players starts. Both players have won over more than their fair share of fans. Flo's opponent, Barbara Wiggins, a room owner outside Milwaukee and known for her defensive game, receives a rousing ovation as she is introduced. When Flo is introduced, everyone comes to their feet. Long after the lights are brought back to their normal brightness, people stand applauding Flo. Flo grabs a tissue and wipes a small tear from her eye before grabbing her cue and coming to the table to lag for break.

Flo wins the lag, but her break is her worst of the tournament. This plays right into Barbara's strength. She plays her first of many safeties that help her jump to an early lead. Flo gets frustrated after missing a hit with the score four to one, Barbara's favor. She's out of character; she appears tired and Johnny catches her eye as she returns to her seat signaling her to try to relax. Lucky for Flo, Barbara tries a nine-ball combination and misses. More luck for Flo, Barbara leaves a simple combination on the nine and Flo makes it to win the game.

Any doubts about Flo's physical or mental state for this match are soon put to rest. She's, all of a sudden, in dead stroke. Barbara gets limited chances the rest of the match. Flo receives a resounding ovation as she pockets the nine to win her final game. The crowd leaves nothing to speculation as to who they favor. There's little time to bask in her glory. The last match on the winner's side of the chart is about to start. Flo's next opponent will be the loser of the match.

Undecided about what to do while the match is being played, Flo finds a seat next to Johnny, but she starts to get antsy. She asks Johnny if he would mind if they take a walk outside for a few minutes. Johnny is quick to oblige Flo, as he doesn't want her to sit and watch the match. He figures Flo is better off getting away from what's going on; she might get stale if she sits around watching.

The fresh air feels good. There is a slight breeze, which makes the night air feel even better. Sitting on a wall that surrounds a fountain, Johnny and Flo listen to the rushing water. Flo suggests to Johnny that they lie down on the wall and look up into the sky. The down time feels good.

Loud yelling can be heard from someone coming across the street. It's Marie, and she's in a big hurry. When Johnny and Flo can finally make out what she's saying, she's repeats, "It's a blow-out! It's a blow-out! Becky's getting killed. If you want a fair share of practice time, you need to get in there as soon as possible."

Flo rushes to the playing arena. When Flo gets ready to hit a few balls, she has already lost several of her practice minutes.

Becky makes things even worse as she stalls making the last few balls of a practice rack. When Flo finally gets to the table, Becky has one of her patented wisecracks waiting for Flo. "I thought you might have headed back to the reservation."

Flo has a glare in her eye and is tempted to punch Becky right in the mouth, but she decides to fight fire with fire. "I was on my way back, but the radio announced some loud-mouthed bitch named Becky Slater was getting her ass kicked by Kathy Kramer, so I figured I'd come back and do the same thing."

Becky doesn't like the fact that Flo has stood up for herself. She comes at Flo, and the two women stand toe to toe until the referee comes between them. He tells Becky to go to her chair and give her opponent a chance to warm up. Becky takes the cue-ball and bounces it on the table. The crowd has seen enough, and they start to boo Becky for her antics. Becky gets out of the referee's sight and flips the bird at the crowd. She has sealed her own fate; the crowd starts to boo her even louder.

Cheap moves continue on the part of Becky. She pretends to be nice to Flo saying they will lag when Becky counts three strokes of her cue-stick. On the count of three, Flo strikes her cue-ball, but Becky has no intention of doing the same thing. She waits for Flo's lag to hit the back rail and starts back up the table before she sends her ball forward. The scummy play by Becky backfires in her face. Flo's ball ends up almost frozen on the back rail. Becky slams her cue on the floor.

Picking up right where she left off against Barbara, Flo takes command early in the match. She has learned many lessons thus far in the tournament, but the safety play she learned from Barbara is carrying her through the first few racks. When faced with a choice between playing a difficult shot or playing safe, Flo is executing perfect safeties. Becky is the only one the arena who isn't enjoying Flo's dominance of the match. With a score of four games to one in Flo's favor, the crowd senses Flo is well on her way to claiming a victory.

In game six, Flo makes a ball on the break and has a shot at the one-ball. Flo's cue-ball has ended up in the middle of the table near the spot. The only problem is the eight-ball is close to the cue-ball, and she's having trouble finding a comfortable place to put her bridge hand. She uses an extension to figure out what to do with the shot. She finally raises her bridge hand and comes over the eight-ball to shoot the shot. Flo makes a perfect hit on a one-ball, and it goes towards and into the corner pocket. The cue-ball goes down table in a forward motion. It strikes a six-ball and glances off it. The cue-ball falls into the right-hand side pocket. It feels like the air has been sucked out of the room as Flo turns and walks back to her seat.

Quick as a bunny, Becky is at the table picking the cue-ball from the side pocket. She knows she has just gotten a major break, and she has to take advantage of it. Becky runs out the balls that remain on the table to make the score four games to two games. Becky thrives at the table; she goes on to run two more racks and tie the score at four games apiece. Becky breaks the next rack, but fails to make a ball. Flo comes to the table after sitting through almost three racks.

Exhaustion seems to have set in while Flo was sitting waiting for her next chance. She tries to play an easy safety, but over-hits the cue-ball. She leaves Becky a good shot at pocketing the one-ball. Becky barely breaks stride as she makes the one and runs the rest of the rack. With all the momentum going in her favor, Becky breaks the next rack and makes the nine in the left-hand corner pocket.

Needing to win the next three games, Flo is in serious trouble. She manages to get back to the table, but she's facing a very difficult shot.

Razor-like precision is what's required to pocket the three-ball. That's exactly what Flo provides as she slices the three ever-so-thinly, and it starts its trek to the corner pocket. The crowd erupts as it senses Flo has executed the shot. The cue-ball has come off the back rail and is traveling at a rapid pace. It strikes the seven-ball and changes its course. Its new course has the cue-ball heading towards the four-ball and a nine-ball, which are close to the left-hand-corner pocket. The cue-ball first strikes the four-ball, then hits nine-ball. After hitting the nine, the cue-ball deflects into the corner pocket. A numbing silence has transformed its way into the crowd. The two balls that conspired against Flo, the four and the nine, present the perfect combination for Becky to win the match.

Initial reaction from Becky is what Flo was expecting. She sprints from her seat, to the table, and grabs the cue-ball out of the corner pocket before the referee even has a chance to do is to his job. She places the cue-ball on the table and takes several strokes to shoot a simple combination. The crowd starts to react with displeasure because of Becky's antics. She makes matters even worse when she asks for an extension to play the shot. As the crowd starts to boo loudly, Becky takes an unexpected stroll over towards Flo. Flo wants to get out of her seat and punch Becky out, but she maintains her cool. She figures, whatever Becky has to offer right now will only degrade her image even more. Flo braces herself; she figures Becky will come with one final round of insults before putting the final nail into Flo's coffin.

Assuming what's about to take place, Flo starts to unscrew her cue. She's not in the mood to sit around and be humiliated. Becky does something Flo is definitely not expecting. She comes near Flo and start addressing the crowd. She starts out by apologizing for her crude behavior. She tells the crowd how she had become annoyed and jealous because Flo was an unproven player and she was getting so much attention from the media. She goes on to say, "I watched this girl play several matches after I put her on the loser's side of the chart. There were many occasions she could have given up and gone home. She didn't give up and she fought and fought till the very end." Becky comes closer to Flo. She tells her to get up from her seat and take a bow. Then she tells the crowd what many of them already knew. "Ladies and gentlemen, I give you a future star of the women's pro nine-ball events, Miss Flo Stevens."

The crowd comes to its feet and gives Flo one last standing ovation. In all the confusion, the referee has lost track of Becky's allotted time for her extension. He tells Becky she has ten seconds in which to go to the table and execute a shot. At this time, Flo takes her towel and flings it onto the table. After Flo performs her act, the referee tells the crowd that Miss Stevens has conceded the game to Miss Slater. Therefore, the winner of the match is Becky Slater. The crowd responds in a positive fashion to recognize Miss Slater's victory. The emcee comes over the microphone and asks the crowd for one final ovation in appreciation of the play of Miss Stevens and Miss Slater. The crowd lets loose with all it can muster before Flo makes her final walk from the playing arena.

While waiting for Flo to get clear of her admirers, Johnny turns his attention to Pedro and Marie. "Are you two going to stick around and watch the finals?"

"The shows over as far as we're concerned. We're both tired. I think we're going to just go back home." Marie takes a bag from under his seat. With a tear in her eye, she hands the bag to Johnny. She tells him, "I got something for you and Flo for when you get up to the honeymoon suite."

Johnny takes the gift and puts it under his arm. He shakes Pedro's hand and gives Marie a final hug. Marie is an emotional wreck. Before she finally walks away, Johnny asks, "Hey, Marie, were you serious about cutting off my, you know whats?"

Marie manages to crack a smile. "Let's hope we never have to find out."

When the last of the autograph seekers has been dealt with, Johnny sneaks up from behind and taps Flo on her shoulder. He asks her what it felt like when the cue-ball entered the corner pocket. Flo looks to the ground and says, "It was like I had hooked the biggest fish of my life, and as I was starting to real it in, the fish snaps the line and you're left with a feeling of total emptiness."

Johnny smiles, then looks her in the eyes. "Have you ever made love on a pool table?"

She giggles, then gives Johnny a wink before saying in her sexiest voice, "I think I'm going to plead the Fifth Amendment on that question." Flo pulls Johnny close.

Exhausting all they could from this situation they were facing, Johnny and Flo reach the same conclusion. They both agree it's time to move ahead.

"Any regrets?"

"In a way, I'm glad I lost to Becky. If I had gone on to win this tournament, I might start thinking I don't need to make any improvements in my game. This way, the fire and desire will burn inside me to get good enough to win."

Johnny has never been able to find positives from negative situations. As he and Flo walk to the hotel lobby, he thanks Flo for opening his eyes.

Handing Flo the bag Marie had given to him, Johnny stops at the main desk. Flo asks Johnny, "What are you doing?"

Johnny asks Flo. "Did you forget about your promise?"

"I'm not sure," says Flo, "remind me."

"After you had been knocked out of the—"

"I'm going to take you to a room and we're not leaving until our desires for each other are exhausted."

Flo rings the bell at the front desk. She laughs as she says, "What's a lady got to do to get some service around here?" Flo laughs again as she reminds Johnny, "Didn't you use that line on me at my restaurant the other day?"

Ring two of the bell finally gets the clerk's attention. Johnny hands the clerk his receipt for the honeymoon suite. He gets the key, and escorts Flo to the suite.

# CHAPTER 11

Flo takes a short nap in a warm bathtub to recharge her batteries. While she's bathing, room service arrives with some complimentary food. Johnny becomes a charming French waiter who seduces Flo while serving her dinner. As if anything else is needed to enhance the moment. Johnny tells Flo he loves her. Flo asks Johnny if the French waiter is speaking or is he speaking. Johnny confesses he sent the waiter home so he could tell Flo how he felt about her. Tears of joy come down Flo's cheeks as she says to Johnny, "I didn't think this day could get any better." She moves close enough to Johnny to hug and kiss, and Flo tells him "I love you, too." They make their way into the bedroom and explode with the passion and desire that has built in the past few days.

Morning comes first for Flo, and the best she can do is write Johnny a note before quietly slipping out the door.

*My Dearest Johnny,*

*The past four days, you showed great patience and understanding. When I was playing in the tournament, you never once thought of yourself because you knew how important it was to me to focus on playing well. I intend to have the same patience and understanding for you when you return to Kentucky. Getting to know your real father is what's important to you right now. I'm here if you need me; I'll always be here. Until I see you again, I will remember all the days and nights we spent together. I will cherish the medallion you gave me and never forget our night together in this beautiful suite. My emotions are starting to get the best of me, so it's either wake you up or go home to my place. I'll start to miss you the moment I close the door.*

*Love always,*
*Your Little Flower*
*P.S. I'll send you a check for the money I owe you from the tournament.*
*When you get back to Kentucky, call me and give me your address.*

# CHAPTER 12

Johnny is touched by Flo's ability to understand his problems. He folds up the note and puts it into his pocket. This will be a keepsake and a reminder of how strong the bond is he and Flo have built the past few days.

Johnny gets to the airport and makes his trip to Kentucky. He leaves his mother a brief message about his trip and that he's in love with Flo.

Billy picks him up and quickly drives him to the poolroom. The brothers' are already there and looking for action.

"Grab your cue and cell phone and go inside and wait for instructions."

Johnny asks, "What are the brothers' last names?"

Billy laughs aloud as he tells Johnny, "They're black; I don't think they're related in any way, but you never know. One's name is Ernie, the other Willie. If you get to play one of them, hold back. Offer Willie a game in a race to nine. Ernie won't bet as much, but he'll play you even. Now get inside and let's see what happens."

Following orders has never been something Johnny prefers. When he gets inside the poolroom, he goes directly to Action Central. Looking at the board, he sees Willie's name under the people willing to play for two hundred dollars a set. Johnny tells the girl in charge to call Willie to the counter. The girl announces Willie's name and he comes forward. Johnny notices a scent of liquor on Willie's breath as they start to engage in a conversation. Willie is first to talk, and he says to Johnny, "You're new around here, aren't you?"

"I've been out of town for a while."

"How are we going to workout a game? I've never seen you play before."

"That makes us even; I've never seen you play either. Is there anyone in the room you have played before?"

The conversation is going nowhere fast Johnny needs to find a solution to his problem.

Looking out into the room Johnny spots Walter playing Ernie, Willie's buddy. He tells Willie, knowing Willy has played Walter, he says, "I played Walter even and I was lucky to beat him. He had a bad night."

"I played even with Walter before, but he beat me. He was lucky to win but I still want a game on the wire in a race to six. Johnny tries to get Willie to compromise, but he won't budge. More people are starting to filter into the room and Johnny figures he better get Willie down to the playing area before he loses him altogether. He makes Willie aware he's not happy about the game, but he agrees to play.

Stake money of two hundred dollars is left at the counter by Johnny and Willie. They gather their equipment and walk down into the room. Johnny starts to walk over to one of the tables he's played on before, but Willie has different ideas. He walks in a different direction. It becomes a Mexican standoff. Eventually, Johnny and Willie manage to reach a compromise. They will flip a coin. Willie wins and picks the farthest table in the back of the room. The waitress comes and delivers the rack of balls. Both players order their drink of choice, Willie prefers a bourbon, straight-up, Johnny sticks to a beer. Play begins after each player hits a warm-up rack.

Johnny forgets to check Willie's rack and sends the cue-ball heading down table for the opening break. A dud is the best way to describe the action Johnny gets after the cue-ball hits the pack. Willie comes out of his chair when all nine balls come to rest on the surface of the table.

Willie is obviously a person of little scruples. He has given Johnny a bad rack, and he comes to the table like nothing has happened. With little movement of the balls, the one and nine end up in close proximity. Willie has a good chance to make a combination, and he also has a seven-ball near the corner pocket, which would help guide the nine into the pocket if he comes close to the shot. Lining up the shot, it appears Willie is trying to make the one-nine combination and win the game. He slams the one, which hits the nine. He hits the shot so poorly the nine-ball hits the side rail and caroms across the table into the opposite corner pocket. As Willie puts up his game, he takes a sip of his drink. After that, he proclaims to Johnny, "It looks like tonight might be my night."

Dentist chairs have been a more comfortable place for Johnny than playing a game of pool with Willie. Every shot Johnny plays, Willie talks about anything he can to distract Johnny. When Johnny is in Willie's vision, a strategic part of why he picked this table to play on, Willie finds a reason to move when Johnny is in the middle of his last stroke. One of the shots Johnny plays is a very close hit. Willie calls it no hit and takes ball-in-hand. Johnny has just taken a three game to two lead; he figures if an argument ensues Willie will probably quit. *Is two hundred dollars really worth this kind of aggravation?* He manages to keep the score close. He wins the first set six games to four. When Willie takes out his money to pay, Johnny sees why Billy had driven like a nut to get back to the poolroom. Willie is carrying a wad that would choke an elephant. Johnny doesn't have as much as Willie, but he's packing pretty good himself. He pulls out his roll and makes sure Willie gets a good look at it.

Renegotiating the next set takes twenty minutes. Willie wants another game, but Johnny refuses to give any more games. He offers Willie the break in the first three games of the set, plus a game on the wire. Willie accepts the game on one condition; he wants the stakes increased from two hundred to five hundred dollars. Johnny calls the waitress over and gives her an additional three hundred dollars. He makes sure Willie does the same thing.

Checking Johnny's racks gets to be Willie's latest obsession. He makes Johnny re-rack five times. Johnny stands with a disgusted look on his face twirling the rack as Willie examines it closely. To Johnny's utter surprise Willie accepts the rack. Willie shows a much better break this time. He pockets two balls, but doesn't have a good shot at the one-ball. Safety play wasn't a factor in the first set—both players shot at just about every shot. Willie's opening move of the first game has Johnny tied up in knots. He banks the one-ball down table near the nine on the back rail. He leaves the cue-ball behind and between two object-balls close to the side rail. Johnny has no chance to break up the combination. He tries in vain to make a three-rail kick-hit on the one-ball. Pausing before he leaves the table, Johnny thinks, has Willie sucked me into a stupid bet? Willie takes ball-in-hand and makes the easy one-nine combination. Johnny senses a real urgency to step up his game.

Breaking balls are what Willie turns out to be good at both on and off the table. This rack only takes four re-racks before Willie decides to break. Pocketing only one ball still keeps Willie in control of the game. Playing safety is still his first option to keep Johnny from gaining any momentum. The first three breaks prove to be a big advantage for Willie. He holds a three to one lead in the match.

In the next game, Willie makes Johnny re-rack the balls seven times. Johnny gets so frustrated with Willie's antics he throws the rack on the table and tells Willie to rack the balls himself. Willie has no problem with Johnny's request. He gives himself what Johnny has yet to experience: a nice solid rack. He cracks it open, makes two balls, and has a pretty easy run-out. Willie pockets four more balls in the rack, and only three remain on the table. The last three balls look so easy from where Johnny is sitting, he almost concedes the rack. Willie pockets the first ball, but his position for the next shot isn't as good. The shot is difficult for both the right-hand side pocket and also the corner pocket. Willie, after a long deliberation, elects to cut the eight-ball into the side pocket. He slices the shot too thin, and the eight-ball hits the outside point of the side pocket. It comes across the pocket and hits the other point of the side pocket. With no place else to go, it sits in an easy place for Johnny to come to the table and finish the rack. Before Johnny can even come to the table, Willie takes his cue and smashes it on the table. His anger not only costs him the game, but a new shaft will be required to continue playing.

It gets the room's attention. With everyone in the room staring at Willie, he gets even angrier. He verbally challenges more than one of the people staring at him with the words, "What the fuck are you looking at, motherfucker?" He even makes an obscene gesture at one person in the room as he screws in his new shaft. Billy had been watching Willie and Johnny's match very closely, but was distracted when Willie smashed his shaft. He doesn't find out until the waitress comes by and explains to him what has happened.

A person out of control in a poolroom is never a good thing. Billy makes his way into the room and walks down towards Willie and Johnny. Billy shows great diplomacy when he asks Johnny and Willie, "What's going on down here, boys?" Willie calms down. He tells Billy he missed a key shot, got angry, and busted his shaft. Billy takes control of the situation and tells both Johnny and Willie, "I'm going to sit over here in the corner. Any more outbursts, and I will be forced to throw somebody out of here." Willie and Johnny agree to Billy's terms, and the game continues. The new shaft becomes Willie's next excuse. He becomes better at making excuses than he does at making balls. Johnny buckles down his play and wins four of the next five games. He wins the second set by the same score as the first set, six games to four.

Murmuring under his breath things like how much he thinks Johnny sucks and saying Johnny can't play at all, Willie is unsure if he wishes to play another set. Johnny can hear loud and clear what Willie is whispering. Tired of all the nonsense, Johnny comes back with a formal challenge. He offers Willie three games in a race to nine along with the first break. Billy is cringing over in the corner as he listens to Johnny make a very stupid game. Willie knows a good thing when he hears one. He asks Johnny how much money he'd be willing to bet. In Billy's eyes, Johnny comes back with a very foolish statement. He offers to play Willie for whatever he's willing to bet. Willie moves into the corner, pulls out his wad of money and starts to count it. After a long deliberation, he comes back and puts twenty-five hundred dollars on the table. Willie looks at Johnny and thinks he may have just scared him off with such a large bet. He makes a shaking motion with his hands that suggests Johnny is deathly afraid to play for this kind of money. Backing down from anything isn't in Johnny's vocabulary. He takes out his money and places it on the table. Billy sits in the corner rolling his eyes. If Johnny makes a strong showing, he's doomed for anymore action in the room. If Johnny loses, Billy is out eighteen hundred dollars.

Johnny gets control in the race to nine. After Willie fails to make a ball on the opening break, Johnny comes to the table and runs out the rack. Then he proceeds to run three more racks. Johnny has gotten the lead before Willie has had his first opportunity to come back to the table, Johnny breaks rack number five and makes a ball, but doesn't have a shot at the one-ball; he pushes out. Willie comes to the table looking at a length of the table cut-shot. He has no desire to take the shot, so he gives it back to Johnny. Johnny makes a paper thin hit on the one-ball, and it rolls across the back rail and into the corner pocket. Johnny is really feeling it right now. He runs out the rest of the rack and strings two more racks together. Willie has only broken the first rack, and he trails by seven games to the three games Johnny had spotted him. The rest of the match is all academic. Willie manages to win two games, but it's not enough; Johnny wins the set nine games to five.

Thirty-two hundred dollars has a numbing effect on Willie. He sits in his chair looking the part of a broken man. Johnny can't help himself. He asks Willie, "Have you had enough?" Willie gets his stuff together and walks from the poolroom.

Elated about the way he has just played, Johnny starts to walk quickly from the room. He looks over in the corner where Billy was sitting, and he is nowhere to be found. Johnny figures Billy will catch up with him later. He figures Billy has probably left the room to keep their relationship a secret. He leaves the room and goes up to Action Central to collect his winnings. There is a large group of people Johnny has to wade through on his way to the counter. Johnny doesn't know it, but they were all watching him play his match against Willie.

Five grand takes a while to count out. Johnny stands patiently until the final bill is placed into his hand. When that happens, he reaches into his other pocket, takes out a twenty dollar bill, and hands it to the house person. Johnny then goes to his apartment.

Changes have been made in the apartment in the past week. There is scent of fresh paint in the air and the rug on the floor looks different. There is even a new and bigger television set.

The bed Johnny lays down on has all new blankets, and when he folds them down, he sees it also has new sheets. Johnny lies on the bed and almost doses off before he hears a loud knock on the door.

"Beautiful, just fucking beautiful," are Billy's opening remarks as he comes through the door.

"Did I do something wrong?"

"Wrong?" Billy gets louder. "I'd like to know what you did right." Billy rushes his words and gets even louder. "I sent you out there to play Willie with a certain game in mind." Johnny tries to plead his case, but Billy won't have any of it. "I'm trying to teach you how to hustle. I'm telling you everything you need to know, and you go into the room and start doing everything and anything *you* think is right. Did you notice all the people standing around when you left the room? They were all potential customers of yours. Now, thanks to your stupidity, you won't get a game with any of them."

"Are you through?"

Billy gets in Johnny's face and says, "What happened to you in a week? Did you forget about the deal we made? You live here for practically nothing and you work for me. I get you games and teach you how to hustle." Billy's voice is as loud as it can get. "What the fuck happened?"

Johnny yells at Billy as he throws Billy's money into the air. "Hustle, hustle, hustle, is that all you ever think about? I bet you would hustle your own mother."

"I wouldn't hustle mine, but I might hustle yours."

Johnny's boiling point has been exceeded. He takes the picture his mom had given to him out of his back pocket and whips it at Billy. The picture hits Billy right in the chest. As Billy looks down to try to catch it, Johnny hauls off and hits Billy right in the face. Billy goes down, and the picture lands on his lap. Johnny comes over to Billy and grabs him by his head of hair. Pulling Billy's head back and raising it up so he can see Johnny, Johnny gets in Billy's face and, gritting his teeth, says, "You already have." He shakes him a few times. "You already have."

Slamming the door behind him, Johnny goes out into the parking lot. He gets into his car, starts the engine, and drives off. He wants to get drunk, but nothing is open at four in the morning. He drives around for a while listening to the radio. As the sun begins to rise, he goes to the only other place in town he knows, the hotel on Cox Street.

Booze is plentiful where Billy is located. When he gets back on his feet, he takes a good look at the picture Johnny threw at him and decides he needs a few drinks. He can't take his eyes off the picture. He had almost put Katie out of his mind. He begins to swill down another shot of whiskey, but he changes his mind. Alcohol never solved his problems. He decides to get some sleep and try to find Johnny when he wakes up.

In the morning, with the help of a friend at the police station, Billy tracks Johnny down. He knocks on the motel room door.

"What the hell do you want?"

Billy suspects Johnny has had a few beers, so he tries not to antagonize him. "I've come to apologize. I never should have said the things I said or yelled at you way I did. I had no right to do any of those things, and I'm sorry." Billy takes out the picture and hands it to Johnny. As Johnny takes the picture from Billy's hand, Billy says to Johnny, "You once asked me to teach you how to play pool. If you're still interested in learning, I'll teach you everything I know about the game. When and if you're ready to make a total commitment to me and the game, come back to my place and we can go to work." Billy turns to walk back down the stairs, then stops, keeping his eyes pointed away from Johnny. There's a long, awkward pause. "How is she?"

"She's okay," says Johnny. "It hasn't been easy for her, but she's okay."

Billy continues to walk down the stairs.

Johnny calls Flo and tells her what happened. Flo has a hard time dealing with the fact Johnny has punched Billy in the face. She tells him he should've been the one apologizing to Billy for what he had said and done. Johnny agrees with Flo, saying it was also wrong he came to Billy's life under false pretenses. What happened was a result of him lying to Billy in the first place. He tells Flo he's going to take Billy up on his offer.

"Liz Dennehy," Flo asks Johnny, "do you remember the name?"

"Oh shit."

"She called me yesterday. She told me she had given you her business card and a bunch of names as references. Can you explain it to me?"

Johnny tells Flo about Liz. "I forgot about her. I guess the wrong head was doing the thinking once you were knocked out of the tournament."

"Are you sure you're in the right frame of mind right now? You're going to be tied up with Billy."

"Yes, absolutely." They exchange goodbyes, then hang up.

Walking back into Billy's poolroom isn't the easiest thing Johnny has ever done. He's not proud of the way he acted the last time he was in Billy's presence. Billy knows the look. He's been in the situation a few times in his life. He notices Johnny is flexing his hand so he uses it as an opening line. He asks Johnny, "Is your hand a little sore today?"

"Yeah." Johnny wants to show some concern for Billy so he asks him, "How's your eye?"

"You throw a pretty good punch. Where did you learn how to punch?"

Johnny tells Billy he practiced martial arts for several years.

"Really?" says Billy. "I did the same thing. I got my ass kicked in the poolroom one night. I figured it was time I learned to defend myself. It's going to take a couple of days before you can start hitting balls. In the meantime, there is an exercise bike in my apartment." Billy flip's Johnny his keys and tells him, "Put it your apartment. For the next couple of days, you can start to strengthen your legs."

Johnny obeys him, knowing it is all in an effort to help his game.

Downtime is something Johnny isn't used to. He puts up three quick miles on the bike and takes a break because he doesn't want to overdo it. He thinks about starting to make all the calls to the people Liz has suggested. Johnny makes his first two calls, and the people on the end of the line are very responsive. They tell Johnny she is a very hard worker and gets all she can on the player's behalf. Johnny likes what he hears about Liz. As Johnny contemplates making his third call his phone rings. It's his mother.

She starts out telling Johnny about her trip. How much fun she and Cindy had had and how just relaxing and receiving some special treatment, at the spa, helped her to forget about all her other problems. "It was great," says Elaine. "People were waiting on *me* for a change. How about you, Johnny?"

"I'm not so sure you'll want to know." The vagueness of Johnny's statement has an Elaine's mind thinking a million different thoughts, none of them good.

Long pauses aren't usually followed by good news. Johnny tells her everything.

Elaine is flabbergasted "You threw the picture at him? What made you to do such a foolish thing?"

Johnny tells her about the yelling and what Billy said to him.

Balling her eyes out, Elaine tells Johnny, "Maybe this was all a bad idea. Why don't you come home? I don't like the way things are going."

Johnny gets his mother to settle down when he tells her he and Billy both apologized to each other and things are fine now.

"What did he say to you about him being your father?"

"Come to think of it," says Johnny, "the subject never came up. He never said he was, but he never said he wasn't. He did ask about you and how you were. I just said you were doing okay, and we left it at that."

Elaine let's out a huge sigh and says to Johnny, "I had plenty of time to think while I was in Acapulco, and I know I want to see Billy again. He's not married or with a girl hanging around, is he?"

Johnny tells his mom, "If he is, he's hiding it pretty well. He works crazy times, crazy hours, and the look on his face when he handed me back your picture, I think he's flying solo."

"Can I depend on you to control yourself long enough so if the situation arises I can come and visit the both of you? I'd love to be part of your lives."

"I feel terrible about what happened, but he yelled at me so loud."

"From what you tell me he's over it. When do the lessons start?"

"As soon as the swelling goes down."

"I can hear Cindy beeping her horn outside; I have to run."

Boredom is setting in a real quickly. Billy comes over to keep him company.

"News travels fast," says Billy. "A couple of hot shots from Louisville came in here today. They heard all about what happened between you and Willie, and they were looking to play. I told them they were a day late or three months too early. It's funny they looked at me the same way you're looking at me right now. If they had shown up here yesterday, we might have been able to hustle them, or should I be more modern and just say the 'H' word?" He chuckles, then says, "Three months early means it will take that long, if not longer, for you to be able to learn and execute everything I'm going to teach you."

"So, I'll be practicing for three months and never get to play anyone?"

"You'll have all the competition you're gonna need. After the first couple of weeks, you and I will be playing pretty regularly."

"How can I keep busy the next few days?"

"I'll have a list of things for you to do tomorrow morning. Until then, take care of any unfinished business you might have. I'm going to get some sleep."

Alone at the table, Johnny takes out his phone and starts to call the names that remain on the list Liz gave him. All of the calls, except one, are positive. This lady seemed to think Liz would roll out a red carpet for her just because she signed on, Johnny looked up her name on the women's tour and the last two years she has one top ten finish. Johnny knows Liz isn't to blame for this girls problem. Johnny decides to call Flo and recommend she get involved with her.

They have been separated for only two days, and Johnny's already missing Flo. As he dials the number, he thinks about how much he enjoyed being in her company. He never felt like he couldn't say or do anything he wanted. She even started to enjoy some of his stupid pranks. Johnny hits the send button after he dials the last digit of her phone number. The phone rings a couple of times, and Flo picks up.

"I was hoping you would call me back today. What happened when you went back to the poolroom?"

"Nothing eventful. I think Billy recognized that I was feeling bad about what happened, and we eventually shook hands. Then he told me to start using an exercise bike to strengthen my legs. Not as exciting as the last time we talked, is it?"

"It sounds like you two are starting to get along."

"Yeah. By the way, I called all the numbers on Liz's list. Only one person had anything bad to say. I think it would be a smart move if you hooked up with her. She impressed me. I don't think there's anyone out there doing a better job." Johnny senses Flo is nervous and asks her, "What's wrong?"

"I'm not very good at understanding stuff that's written on paper. Remember, I had to go out and work at an early age and my grandfather and uncle couldn't read at all so I had no one to help me learn."

"That could be a problem. You don't want to start signing things that you don't understand. Maybe I can help; when Liz sends you the contract, forward it to me. I'll read it, and if there is anything I don't like about it, I'll give you the information and you can iron it out with Liz. How's that sound?"

"You'd be willing to do that for me?"

"I'd be doing it for both of us. Your future and your happiness will play a big part in my future and my happiness. Teammates have to help each other out. Oh, shit," says Johnny, "I just became my high school baseball coach."

"Baseball coach, hockey coach, I don't care who you are; you're the best thing that's ever come into my life. I'm used to guys who do nothing but take."

"One thing I never had to do in my life is struggle. If I wanted something bad enough, my mother made sure I was able to get it. I appreciated what she did. I wasn't spoiled, and she knew it. I was a person who performed better when things in my life ran smoothly. When I would hear my parents fighting and arguing, I would be an emotional wreck for the next few days. That's when I would struggle. I know the importance of stability in a person's life. Those are the things I'm trying to provide for you. If I can help satisfy some of your smaller needs, you'll have an easier time satisfying your bigger needs."

"Who gets credit for that last bit of information?"

"I winged that one. That was a Jordan original. How did it sound?"

"It sounded like it came from the kindest and most generous person I have ever met."

"I hope I can live up to my reputation."

"I know you can," says Flo. "I'll talk to you later. I love you."

"I love you, too. Bye."

For three days in a row, Billy has Johnny up early. His list of jobs includes washing every set of balls and vacuuming the rugs and tables, cleaning the booths, emptying the trash, and cleaning the men's room and parking lot.

# CHAPTER 13

Day four is different. Johnny says, "I'm ready to start."

"Okay," says Billy, "when you got a horse that's ready to run you can't keep it tied up in the barn. Let's get started. Go down to the practice room and get ready."

Billy joins Johnny twenty minutes later.

"I hope your ready for all this, I'm going to explain everything I do while I'm playing in full detail and give you demonstrations and reasons why you should do the same thing. Fundamentals—that's where it all starts. It's like building a house. The more solid the foundation, the easier it is to go on from there."

For more than an hour, Billy talks about and demonstrates everything involved while shooting a shot. How to get down on a shot, the importance of bending your legs. His aiming technique, the importance of a longer stroke. He stresses to Johnny the importance of his bridge hand. "It lines up every shot. If it isn't comfortable on the table, it's telling your brain it doesn't like the way the shot is lined up. Listen to it." When to think is another point Billy emphasizes. "Always think when you are away from the table. Don't go to shoot unless you know how you are going to play the shot you're attempting. Look at and line-up your shots from a distance.

Billy wraps it up and asks, "Any questions?"

"I don't think that's necessary. I've got a lot of work to do. You present this game in a different fashion. None of the books or tapes mentioned what you talked about and demonstrated. How long do you want me to practice every day?"

"As much as you can stand. Personally, I hate to practice. All I want you to do is make sure you get between eight and ten hours sleep a night and keep exercising. I'll give you more to do in three or four days. The next time we get together, we will try to improve your break."

After working with Billy the first day, he goes back to his room and sets up his schedule.

At one-thirty in the morning, Flo calls.

"I need the address of Billy's poolroom. Liz wants to mail you my contract. We had a long conversation and she has offered to pay all my expenses to play in the next four women's events. She says if I do well, it'll help us get more money when we start negotiating with sponsors."

"Does this mean you are signing on with Liz?"

"I'm leaning heavily in that direction. What you think, Johnny? Do you think I should?"

"I think it's a great opportunity. You're hot right now, and you should strike while the iron is hot. I say you should go for it."

"There's more good news. Two of the tournaments are in the east. I may be able to see you. It depends on when I can get off from work. My boss is all for me going out and playing. His business has never been better. We're having a tournament tomorrow night, and twenty-five people have already pre-paid their entry fee. We're expecting thirty-five to forty players. I don't want to brag, but I think my success is helping with his increase in business."

"Of course, it's helping him."

"Even Marie and Pedro came in and prepaid. Then they started to play, Marie hits 'em pretty good. She ran six balls while I was watching." Johnny yawns uncontrollably. "I forgot it's a two-hour difference. Let me call you later. I love you, Johnny."

"I'm sorry. I'm just exhausted. I love you, too." They hang up.

Lunchtime comes and goes, and Billy still has yet to make his anxiously awaited appearance. After he exercises for the second time of the day, Johnny goes back to the practice room. Billy is sitting on a chair when Johnny enters the room. Johnny is first to speak. "I wasn't sure if you were coming or not."

Billy has been taping Johnny's practices. "I've been busy. I've made a big investment and have been watching its every move. How has your day been going?"

"I've been okay," says Johnny.

"Really?" says Billy. "You didn't start getting impatient waiting for me to show up? You didn't start whacking balls around and losing your focus about eight o'clock this morning?"

"What, have you got a crystal ball or something?"

"Naw," says Billy. "Just a camera. I've been watching your every move for the past three days."

"Why?"

"I'm looking for reactions," says Billy. "I want to see how dedicated you are. You passed that part of the test. The second part you failed miserably: How you react when things don't go your way. You expected me to be here early today. I told you things would happen at my pace. I know it's cruel, but I have to prove a point. How you react when things aren't going your way in a pool game is crucial. Getting upset leads to making bad decisions; bad decisions lead to missing balls; missing balls gets you a front row seat to watch your opponent beat the shit out of you. Now, your break." Billy takes the rack in his hand and places it on the table. "The lessons are not always about improving your game. They are also about improving your mind. You're headed into shark-infested waters. Everyone you play from now on is going to want to chew you up and spit you out.

They're all going to be man-eaters. The worse part is after they are through with you, you don't die. You wish you were dead, but you're not dead. The game of pool is the only game played where you may never get a chance, there's no guarantees. Any other game, you're guaranteed a chance. You may have to sit through some awful beatings, when your opponent has landed punch after punch after punch. How you handle such a beating will determine how far you go playing this game.

"Wanna get the balls out of the pockets?" Billy says to Johnny.

Johnny is starting to understand what Billy is talking about. He tries to talk to Billy, but Billy stops him, and says, "I'm trying to save you the years of frustration most people go through trying to master a game that can't be mastered. Now give me the balls, and let's get going with the lesson."

Lecturing starts once again, and once again Johnny is all ears. Billy starts out by explaining to Johnny how important the break is in the game of nine-ball. "It's all about control. If you make a ball on the break you keep control, if you fail to pocket a ball, you lose control."

Billy racks the balls and takes the cue-ball in his hand. The first thing he explains is the importance of hitting the one-ball square. He places the cue-ball on the table and tells Johnny, "You line this up the same way you line up all your other shots, from a distance." Billy elevates the back of his cue and chokes up on his grip. He tells Johnny, "It's like throwing a punch. A shot quick stroke with a long follow through is what creates the power." He makes several long strokes of the cue telling Johnny to watch how his cue tip always returns to the same spot. He tells Johnny, "That's because my bridge hand is tight. It locks you in on the cue-ball." Billy rears back and lets the cue-ball fly. A loud crack can be heard as the balls come apart and scatter. Two of them find pockets.

Handing the cue to Johnny, he tells him, "It's your turn." Billy points out to Johnny, "The hardest part of practicing your break is getting someone to rack for you." Johnny breaks several racks and Billy makes a couple of minor adjustments to his break. Billy points out to Johnny that he's breaking too much by using just his arms. Billy tells him face the rack as if you could walk up on the table after you contact the cue-ball. He also tells Johnny to pull his weight back on the final stroke before contacting the cue-ball. Showing a great deal of patience, Billy racks several racks for Johnny. Then it happens: Johnny puts it all together and crushes the rack. His sound is louder than the one Billy made.

Billy asks Johnny, "Did it feel like as soon as the cue-ball left your cue it struck the rack?"

"That's exactly the way it felt."

"That's the right one. Now let's try to do it again."

A couple of duds precede another explosion. Billy racks for another half hour before calling it quits. Johnny has the break down pat.

Billy says, "I'll have someone here to rack for an hour for you tomorrow. I don't want you to think I don't want to spend time with you, but I also have a business to run."

Billy has shown far greater patience and is a much better teacher than Cliff was when he tried to teach Johnny how to play golf. He tells Billy, "I didn't want to own you when I asked you to teach me to play. I'm satisfied with renting you for now."

It's the first time they look at each other and smile. A chill can be felt down both of their backs.

Before leaving the room, Billy hands Johnny a folded up piece of paper. "This is your goal. I hope you're ready when the time arrives. It's a flyer advertising the United States nine-ball championships."

Johnny checks the dates, and it's less than six months away. Johnny's phone rings.

"Are you scared?" asks Billy.

"I'm a little nervous."

"Don't worry. I'll get you ready to fight the big fight. After lessons are over, we're headed on the road."

"I better get practicing then."

Johnny digs out Flo's contract. Sixty/forty seems like more than a fair share of percentages. Johnny likes everything he's reading. There's no bullshit or terminology he's unable to understand. The contract represents what his first impression of Liz was: honest and straightforward. He recommends that Flo sign on with Liz after he's finished reading.

Six o'clock comes and Johnny has called back to talk to some of his old buddies at Razz's. Johnny goes into Billy's office. He wants to surprise him with the voice of an old friend. "I've got your old friend, Larry, on the phone." He leaves to give them privacy.

Billy is surprised and snatches the phone. Billy and Larry start talking like two guys who went through school together at their first class reunion. When they get past talking about their lives together, all of the news isn't good. Billy learns Larry's wife had passed away from breast cancer five years ago. They go on to talk about their old pool days. "I still do okay with the side action. I still know a winner when I see one."

Billy asks Larry, "What do you think of this kid?"

"I think he could be a hell of a player."

"That's what I am seeing, too," says Billy. "I'm taking him out on the road in a few weeks to play in some small tournaments and maybe some heads-up action. What are you doing these days? How would you like to come here while I'm gone and baby-sit my poolroom?"

"I could use a change of scenery. When do you want me out there?"

"A week from now would be good."

"Sounds good." They finish up, then hang up.

Billy gives Johnny the good news, then tells him, "Get back to work. Things are going to start happening pretty fast, and we have a lot to cover in a short time."

A few days later, Flo calls. She has a bunch of good news. "I'm signing on with Liz. I'm going New York City for a couple of days, but on my way back to Albuquerque, I'll be able to see you! Are you comfortable with what I plan on doing?"

"When do you plan on coming to Kentucky?"

"In six days."

"Great. I won't have started on the road by then."

"Guess what's going on the second day I'm in Kentucky?" Flo lets Johnny think, then blurts out, "ESPN will be airing the first match I played at three p.m. Remember, I made the masse shot on the six-ball."

Johnny decides to tease Flo. "I don't remember the shot. Oh, you mean the best shot in the entire tournament; of course I remember. It will be great to see you; I really miss you."

They talk for a while longer before Johnny goes back to the grind, feeling much better now that he's talked things out with Flo.

Two more practice sessions are given by Billy; one that explains all the different shots and another that covers the strategy for playing nine-ball. It's back to the grind.

# CHAPTER 14

It's finally time for Billy and Johnny to practice head to head. Rounds one, two, and three go exactly the way Billy would have probably predicted. He gives Johnny some big-time beatings. Scores of eleven to two and two scores of eleven to four do nothing to help Johnny's ego. He is totally deflated after his third consecutive thrashing at the hands of Billy. He's almost ready to pack it in and give up his dream. The fourth time he and Billy square off, Johnny starts off way behind again. He's down by a score of six games to one, and he misses an easy shot on the eight-ball. He gets angry and starts going off on a tantrum. Billy starts laughing. "What took you so long? You should be pissed off, but are you pissed off at the right person for the right reasons?

"I've come in here and hit you with punch, after punch, after punch. You haven't come back and hit me with anything. When someone is beating you to death in this game and you curl up the little ball and let them keep hitting you, that's what they will continue to do. Be a man! Fight back. Land some punches of your own. Get your opponent's attention. If you don't, they will do what I've done to you every time we've played so far. If you must take a beating, figure out how the player giving you the beating is doing it. You might be able to learn something. Don't just sit there like a little baby feeling sorry for yourself. If you want me to start missing on purpose to make you feel better, I can do it. But when you're playing big-time pool players, they're not going to feel sorry for you; they're going to play you like you're not even there. Part of the lesson plan was for you to get past being intimidated by any player. I was hoping you would come around on your own. You can't go to the table being concerned about who you're playing. You have to focus on what you're playing. The game can be difficult enough. If you think you can't make a mistake because Billy Bates is going to make me pay, you're going to make a lot of mistakes. If you're at the table, it's because Billy Bates has made a mistake. Take advantage of the opportunity; make me pay. As long as I'm sitting in my chair, I can't do anything to hurt you."

Sinking in slowly but surely is how Billy is evaluating Johnny's progress. The next two times they play, the final scores are much closer. Billy wins by three games the first time and two games the next time. They finally call it a day.

The following day, Billy is set to pick up Larry and Johnny to pick up Flo.

# CHAPTER 15

"Do you like my new look?" asks Flo. "Liz took me to a beauty and health spa, and they gave me a complete makeover."

"I love it. You look incredible. I'm not so sure I want to let you out of my sight anymore. Guys are going to be hitting on you left and right."

Flo moves over as close to Johnny as she possibly can and puts her arms around him. "They can hit on me all they want; if it isn't you, they will all strike out."

They pull up to the poolroom. "Billy's inside waiting for us. He's dying to meet you."

Billy and Pete (the boy who racks for Johnny an hour a day) are in the practice room playing, but they stop once Flo and Johnny come into the room. Billy has no problem breaking the ice and starting a conversation. He extends his hand to Flo and she to him, Billy kisses her hand. "You never told me Flo was gorgeous, Johnny."

Flo's a little embarrassed, but she loves the attention.

"Johnny tells me you're one hell of the pool player. Isn't that right, Johnny? He hasn't stopped talking about how you played in Albuquerque since he's come back to Kentucky." He turns and points to the food table. "Are you hungry?"

"I'm starving."

"Well, help yourself. We have plenty."

After they eat, Billy asks, "Anyone care to play a game of partners? I've got time for a quick race to seven before I have to get Larry."

Johnny and Flo versus Billy and Pete. Johnny and Flo win the flip for the break, and Johnny chooses to get things started. Three balls on the break make the first game an easy run-out for Johnny and Flo. Billy sits back and watches as the youngsters work in perfect harmony dissecting the rack. When Billy gets a chance to shoot, he's kicking at the four-ball in the second game of a race to seven. He makes a good hit, but Johnny and Flo never break stride and they run-out the rest of the remaining balls on the table.

Game three is Flo's first chance to break the rack. If Billy wasn't already impressed, this would be the clincher. Flo breaks the rack as well as most men Billy has played. Her cue-ball jumps back off the rack and stops near the middle of the table. Billy looks over at Pete after Flo has broken and rolls his eyes. Any advantage they thought they might have had with Flo breaking is quickly put to rest. Pete and Billy manage to win three games, but it's obvious they are no match for Flo and Johnny.

"Spectacular," is the word Billy uses to describe Flo and Johnny's play. Because the race was played so well, Billy has a few minutes to spare before he has to leave for the airport. He compliments Flo on her playing ability and says he hopes to see more of her in the future. He extends his hand once again to Flo and this time, he only shakes her hand. He says to Flo, "I'd kiss your hand again, but I think Johnny was a little jealous the first time I did it, so I won't do it again." Billy looks at Johnny and says, "I'm taking Larry up to Louisville; he's never been to Churchill Downs. I'll be back late tomorrow night. Your game is really starting to improve, and I'm not just saying that because your girlfriend is here. I really mean it. Your game has come a long way in a short time." Before things start to get to melancholy, Billy grabs his keys and slips out the door.

Later, Johnny makes copies of the training tapes for Flo, then takes her to dinner.

"What else went on in New York?"

"I had a photo shoot, and Liz introduced me to a bunch of different people. One man runs a modeling agency, another is in the advertising business. The last person we met with represents a shoe company. Liz is trying to get this company to design a shoe for pool players."

"It sounds like Liz is really on top of things."

"She's aggressive, but she's not pushy. How do you think you and Billy are getting along so far?"

"Considering I punched him a couple of weeks ago, I think we're getting along pretty well. He's a great instructor."

"Whatever he's doing is definitely working."

"What do you think of Billy?"

"I think he's charming. A helluva pool player, too."

The food comes and they enjoy their dinner, then go dancing. Johnny shows more versatility; he sings Flo an Elvis song and they return to the room for a night of passion. The next day is more of the same; they can't take their hands off each other. Before they know it, Flo's visit is over.

Eyes wide open before Johnny's alarm has a chance to sound, Flo shuts off the alarm and quickly and quietly moves around Johnny's apartment gathering her things. Before she leaves, she manages to scribble out a quick note: *Thanks for a great two days, Elvis. Keep those hips in shape because I'll be back for more.* Flo goes over to the bed and kisses Johnny lightly on the lips, then leaves.

# CHAPTER 16

Fishing around with one hand after waking up, Johnny comes to the reality. Flo has managed to slip out the door early on him once again without waking him up. He is reluctant to get out of bed, but he knows the honeymoon is over, and it's time to get back to work.

Billy and Larry make their way to the restaurant. Larry says, "You have quite a place here. Have you ever had a big tournament here?"

"I've thought about it, but there's so much involved. I wouldn't know where to begin."

"I was involved in running a few on the West Coast. I know a bunch of people who would be willing to help. Think about it for a few days and let me know if you're interested in hosting a tournament."

"You know I've never done anything half-ass. If I were going to put on a tournament, it would have to be the biggest and best in the history of the game."

"Your name still carries a lot of weight in the game. People would come out of the woodwork to play, and sponsors would line up at the door."

"Money," says Billy, "there would have to be the biggest payout in the history of the game. I'm sick and tired of watching these guys play their hearts out for a measly ten or twenty grand."

"Pool has to take a lesson from the poker tour. They run qualifiers with some small entry fees to get more players."

"That's all well and good," says Billy. "They have these tournaments online, and people from all over the country are participating. The action is fast; if you try to do that in a poolroom, the tournaments would last a month."

"What if they had qualifiers all over the country?"

"That might work. We have two hundred and fifty-six people win qualifiers to play in our tournament. If they could each earn their entry fee, plus some money for expenses, they would be willing to come and play my tournament. If the entry fee is five hundred dollars, we start out with a guaranteed one hundred and twenty-eight thousand dollars. That's just in entry fees. We have to be able to find ways to get more money." Billy pats Larry on the back and says, "Call all your friends and get the word out. Billy Bates is going to have the biggest and the best tournament in the history of the game. You do realize, Larry, this is going to keep you here for the next few months."

"It doesn't matter. I can stay here as long as I want. My kid and his wife live in my house. They'll take care of things while I'm gone. I could use an extended vacation. If you play the tournament, we would have no problem attracting sponsors."

"My playing days are over. There is a whole new generation of players. Let's give them a chance to show the world how great they can play the game. I'll be sitting on the sidelines enjoying myself. I wanna watch the kid play."

Johnny comes into the poolroom with all smiles as he extends his hand to Larry.

"The guys back at Razz's all told me to say hello; they miss having you around. That guy you beat before you left hasn't been back."

Billy says, "I ran into one of the players from Louisville who had come looking to play you for money. I told him you would be ready to play him Wednesday night between seven and eight o'clock. We're gonna start out at five hundred a set. You think your game is good enough to beat this guy?"

"I'm not sure. I've never seen the guy play."

"The other day when we played the partner game. Was that you're typical game or a fluke?"

"Typical."

"Well, after playing against you the other day, I think you can beat anybody. That's why I told Alex to come down here Wednesday night. Now get back into the practice room and start working on your game." Before Johnny leaves, Billy casually mentions, "We're having a pool tournament here two weeks before the U.S. Open. If you can think of any ways to raise some money, I'd appreciate any help. Larry is going to be the tournament director."

"How about raffling off a car?"

Two days later, the plan is implemented, only there are two cars instead of one; tickets are selling like hot cakes at twenty dollars apiece.

Larry keeps busy trying to set up qualifiers across the country to play in Billy's tournament. All of the major pool publications get ready to run full-page ads for Billy's tournament. Larry also suggests they have a woman's event in the other side of the poolroom, which is approved by Billy easily.

Wednesday night creeps up on Johnny and Billy before they know it. Alex, from Louisville, is in the house and looking to play. Johnny loses the coin flip, and Alex breaks. He starts strong by winning four of the first five games, but Johnny makes a comeback and wins the remaining eight games.

Alex's mood has changed from the first five games. He is starting to complain about his inability to get a good leave from Johnny. Johnny knows he has strategically played every shot exactly the way they came out. He pays no attention to the bickering Alex is throwing out.

Punishment is the way Johnny decides to handle all the bullshit Alex is throwing at him. Before the second set starts,

Johnny sets his goal at shutting Alex out. He comes close to attaining his goal. A fluke scratch on the six-ball in the eighth game gives Alex a chance to win two games. Johnny gets back to the table when Alex fails to pocket a ball on the break trailing seven games to two. He takes advantage and runs out the eighth and ninth racks to win the set.

Johnny figures Alex should quit, now that he has been dominated for the past nineteen games, but he asks Johnny if he wants to double the bet. He is more than happy to oblige and wins the set nine to six.

Surprisingly, Alex still wants to play. Things continue to go in the same fashion. Johnny dominates from start to finish. After the conclusion of the last set, Johnny just looks over at Alex. He doesn't want to provoke him by breaking down his cue again. Alex has the look on his face of a beaten man. Mercifully, he says to Johnny, "The match is over now, kid; you just broke me."

Six thousand dollars is a hell of a night's pay. Johnny tries to give Billy half the money, but Billy tells Johnny to hang onto it. "We're going to need the cash. We're flying up to Providence on Friday. You'll be playing in a tournament starting on Saturday. By the way, you played real well against that guy, and you also handled yourself well; you didn't let his antics bother you. It's a great sign of maturity on your part. You've got a day and a half to get ready to leave. Get a good night's sleep."

Johnny tells Flo the good news.

"That's great, Johnny."

"What's been going on with you?"

"Sponsors have been calling Liz left and right trying to make deals to have me represent their products. Liz is holding out with some of the cue makers hoping they will increase their offers. Table manufacturers are also coming in with different offers. The photo shoot I did in New York is paying huge dividends. Liz says there's a clothing line interested in using me as a model, and here's the clincher. A major shoe company loves Liz's idea of producing a shoe strictly for pool players. If I can crack the top sixteen in the standings on the women's tour, I've got one of the contracts to represent the shoe company."

"Life for me has been pretty boring compared to what's been going on with you. Billy is hosting a major tournament in his room, and he's going to make it the largest payout in the history of pool. We are leaving Friday for New England to start playing in some smaller tournaments. Billy wants me to get my feet wet and prepare myself to play in his event."

"I'm playing in a tournament in California in two weeks."

When Flo gives Johnny the name of the town in California, Johnny tells Flo it's only a half hour from where his mother lives. Johnny suggests to Flo she should get together with his mom.

"I was hoping you would suggest that. Ask your mom if she can come to watch me play."

"I'll do what I can." He also tells Flo that she has no reason to be nervous. Her game is good enough to compete with any woman playing on the tour.

They finish up the conversation, then call it a night.

# CHAPTER 17

On the flight to Providence, Johnny and Billy have a long conversation about Johnny's life.

"I was going to Stanford as a pre-med student."

Billy has a problem understanding why Johnny would drop out of college in his final year to pursue the dream of being a pool player.

"I was trying to meet Cliff's expectations."

Billy understands where Johnny is coming from. He knows a person's happiness is far more important than trying to please other people. They chat a little more, then land in Providence and make their way to the poolroom.

Billy runs into a loudmouth named Frankie in the men's room and challenges him to play his "nephew," Johnny, they freeze-up 1500 and play for five hundred a set. He figures it will be good practice. Johnny goes on to win the first set nine games to five.

The action attracts a crowd. One person even figures it out that the older man with the young man is Billy Bates. The buzz works its way to Frankie's partner, who in turn tells Frankie what's going on. Whatever chance Frankie had to win the second set just flew out the window. The fact that he has been had by Billy and Johnny is eating away at Frankie. He starts an open conversation with himself about how stupid he was to get trapped by Billy's little game. He openly admits he let his big mouth get him in trouble. Frankie has lost all hope of winning the set and concedes the match, then tries to take the remaining five hundred he had posted and stop playing. Billy is not about to let Frankie walk away, but does agree to make a change in the game. Frankie wants to be spotted the wild eight and the first break of the set. Billy does Frankie one better. He offers him the wild seven-ball and the first break, but the stakes have to be doubled. Frankie goes back to his buddy for more money. His buddy is reluctant to give up the money, but Frankie convinces him to part with the dough. Billy's actions have created a little more interest in Frankie and Johnny's match. Two bystanders approach Billy to make side bets on Frankie. Billy takes the action, but limits each bet to one hundred dollars. Billy is risking two hundred dollars to win twenty-two hundred dollars.

Johnny makes quick work of winning the set amidst Frankie getting extremely upset. Snapping his cue apart, Frankie has a few more choice words to say to Johnny before walking away.

Billy approaches Johnny from a distance. He is surrounded by newfound friends he made while he was off eating his dinner. Johnny just stares at Billy in amazement as he proceeds to introduce everybody to him. He knows all their names, and some he gives a small history lesson about as part of the introduction.

Collecting the money Johnny has won is Billy's next priority. Before he goes to find the other guy, who bet on the side, he takes the money Johnny has won and puts it into his pocket. Billy tells Johnny he's entered in a mini-tournament that will be starting in about half an hour. "It's a good warm-up for tomorrow. It's only a race to five, single elimination, eight players, the first-place finisher gets one hundred and fifty dollars. I've been watching some of the player's practice, and you'll need to bring your A-game."

Later, announcements come over the intercom assigning two players to four different tables. Johnny has some ups and downs, but eventually wins the mini-tournament, his first major victory since being coached by Billy.

# CHAPTER 18

The next morning, Billy and Johnny get ready for the big tournament. After breakfast, they head to the poolroom. Players start to filter in by the dozens. Johnny notices a lot of the players are renewing old acquaintances.

Mike Zuglan comes over the microphone. He announces to everyone seventy-five players have signed up to play. Mike thanks the sponsors that help make the Joss Northeast Nine-Ball Tour such a huge success. "Ladies and gentlemen," says Michael, "Let's put our hands together for the host and hostess of this wonderful event, Steve and Regina Goulding, the owners of Snooker's Billiard Club."

Receiving a first bye, Johnny's first opponent for the tournament is none other than the tournament director himself, Mike Zuglan. Johnny loses the coin flip, so Mike sets up to break as Johnny racks the balls.

Mike is considered one of the tournament favorites, so there's a lot of attention at table number three. Right from the opening break, Johnny knows he's got all he can handle playing Mike. The first game Mike makes the seven-ball on the break. He runs up to the four-ball and has what Johnny considers a difficult five-nine combination. Mike shoots the combo like it's a hanger. The nine-ball splits the corner pocket, giving Mike the first game. Johnny does what he has to do. He comes to the table and racks the balls for the next game. A nine-ball on the break is the next thing that happens in Mike's favor. When Johnny sees his first legitimate shot of the match, he's already trailing by two games, and he's kicking off the side rail and back rail just to make a legal hit on the three-ball.

Control is something Billy had always talked about with Johnny. Mike, up until this point of the match, has been the one in control. Johnny picks his spot on the side rail with which he wants to shoot the cue-ball to make a three-rail hit on the three-ball. Coming in from behind the three, off the back rail, Johnny makes a clean hit on the three-ball. The three makes it way down table and collides with a six-ball. The collision changes the course on which three-ball was traveling and it finds its way into the left-hand corner pocket.

Skill was involved in making a hit on the three-ball. A little bit of luck and good fortune was what it took for the three to find the corner pocket. Unfortunately, Johnny still has a very difficult bank-shot facing him on the four-ball. With no place to hide, playing safety, Johnny has little choice left but to go for the bank on the four-ball. He looks at the shot for a while before he makes his commitment. Knowing the rest of the table presents a fairly easy run-out if he misses the bank shot, Johnny commits to playing the shot. Several long strokes are made before Johnny strikes the cue-ball. It moves quickly across the table and strikes the four-ball. Johnny hears the sweet sound of the ball hitting the backside of the pocket. Mike taps his stick on the floor and says to Johnny, "Nice shot." The rest of the balls remaining on the table are what the players refer to as sitting ducks. Johnny picks them off one-by-one and wins his first game of the match. He takes a deep breath to get rid of whatever jitters he is feeling.

Unleashing possibly his best break ever, Johnny pops the corner ball from the left-hand side of the rack into the corner pocket. When the dust settles, Johnny has a manageable one-ball shot and a reasonable rack to run-out. Things start out well for Johnny; he makes the one-ball, two-ball, three-ball and the four in fairly simple fashion. Weak position on the five-ball, however, makes for a difficult shot. Johnny makes the five, but the position play starts to have a snowball effect. Johnny has little chance but to play a safety on the six-ball. Johnny banks the six-ball from the racking end of the table to the breaking end of the table. His cue-ball creeps over near the eight-ball but not behind it. Mike comes to the table. Without much hesitation, he banks the six back-up table and into the right-hand corner pocket. Johnny taps his cue and compliments Mike's effort. Mike makes the rest of the balls on the table to take a three game to one lead.

Two games behind keeps Johnny looking for opportunities to win more than a single game at a time. His big chance comes when Mike misses a difficult cut shot on the seven-ball with the score seven games to five, Mike's lead. Pouncing on the opportunity, Johnny goes on to win that game, plus another, to even the score.

Undaunted by what's taken place the last two games, Mike nonchalantly comes out of his chair and racks the balls. He knows he's been in these situations many times before and it's out of his control.

Johnny doesn't make the most solid strike on the one-ball, and the balls react accordingly. Mike comes to the table. He doesn't have an easy shot at the one so he plays a safety on Johnny. Earlier in the match, Johnny had turned one of Mike's safety plays into his advantage. This time, there's no such luck. Johnny does manage to make a legal hit and shot on the one-ball, but he leaves Mike with a simple shot to start his journey through the rack of balls. The one-, two-, three-, four-, five-, and six-balls leave the surface of the table. Mike has left himself with a seven-ball shot that has all the makings of a miss. The cue-ball is just below the head string spot in the middle of the table. The seven is just above the other spot on the table.

The eight-ball is about three inches off the back rail near the right-hand diamond. Mike takes his time shooting this obviously critical shot. The deliberation is short-lived; Mike goes to the table and shoots the shot. As if in slow motion Johnny watches as the seven-ball buckles the right-hand corner pocket. It spits out, but it travels across the table behind the eight-ball and into the left-hand corner pocket. Johnny sits in his seat, wanting to puke, as Mike cleans-up the eight and nine to take an eight games to seven lead.

Good players stick the knife in you. Great players, like Mike, stick the knife in and give it a twist. The next rack is all academic: Mike makes two balls on the break and goes on to run-out the rack. He consoles Johnny after a tough loss when he tells him, "I got lucky on you, kid." Johnny just sits in his chair for a few minutes. He's emotionally spent after playing his first match. It's been a while since Johnny's has suffered a loss, and he has a sick feeling in his stomach. He has very little time to sit around feeling sorry after losing his match. Two new players have shown up at the table to begin a match. Johnny gathers his equipment together and starts his long walk to face Billy.

Johnny gets back to where Billy is sitting and sits down expecting to hear a sermon. Billy starts to say something, but Johnny interrupts telling him. "Mike was lucky to win. He missed the shot, and the ball went into the other corner pocket—"

"Losers make excuses for losing a match; winners learn from the losses. You made a couple of poor safety plays and your position play wasn't that good. Your break eluded you at a key game in the match. I didn't want to scare you, but you just played a great pool player, extremely tough." Billy knows the feeling of losing a tough, grinding match. "I want you to remember how awful you felt after losing that match. It's the worst feeling in the world, if I remember correctly. The best way to avoid the feeling is to win matches." Johnny can't believe it, but his next match has just been called. Before he goes out to play, Billy says to him, "Now you're playing for something."

"Are you betting on this match?"

"If you lose another match you're out of the tournament, which means you're playing for your tournament life. That, to me, means you're playing for something."

Nestled in the far corner of the poolroom is table twelve. Johnny's next opponent is already hitting some balls. His name is Tommy Jag, a local player. Tommy and Johnny spar for the first four games. Then Johnny catches his stroke and lays a run of five games on Tommy. Tommy never recovers from Johnny's heavy barrage. Johnny goes on to win his first important tournament match nine games to three.

History has a way of repeating itself: Johnny's future matches start having a lot of repetition: close in the beginning, then Johnny catches fire to run at least three racks at a time. He plays and wins six more consecutive matches. His average score per match is nine games to four. It's almost three-thirty in the morning when Johnny finishes playing. They finally call it a night, and the tournament resumes at noon the next day.

Johnny sees Billy as the Mr. Miyagi of pool, being a big fan of the *Karate Kid* growing up. His martial arts background and his own usually being the underdog in most of his fights had taught him to respect how hard work and the right technique gets you through anything. Billy's similarity to Mr. Miyagi is that he gives you something to do, like riding the bike, which seems to make no sense. At the point when you need to know why you've been doing what you've been doing, he tells you so it all makes sense.

Parking at the poolroom is easy. Johnny can't believe they have virtually the pick of any spot, they want, in the lot. He questions Billy if anyone but the players will be showing up today. Billy assures Johnny, "There will be a good-size crowd, but they won't be showing up for a while. Most people around this game aren't early risers. The only ones who will be here at noon are the ones who have to be."

Ticked-off for not having Mike Zuglan announce he will be hosting the biggest tournament in the history of the game on Saturday, Billy makes sure before play starts on Sunday that Mike gets the news. Noon time comes and there's a formal introduction of the players to the spectators. The first four players are the ones on the winners' side of the chart.

The next player introduced is Johnny's opponent, Bob Busa. Bob and Johnny have chatted for a few minutes before they started the introductions. Bob is from Massachusetts. He tells Johnny, "I had some great battles with your Uncle Billy many years ago. I think I might have even beaten him out a few times." Johnny watches as Bob warms up. He sees that Bob has a tendency to draw the cue-ball to play position.

Before the match starts, Billy calls Johnny over and tells him, "Don't take this guy too lightly; he knows how to play the game." Introductions for all the players are concluded. Mike makes the announcement about Billy's tournament. He has Billy stand-up and be recognized by the people in the room. Billy gets a strong ovation from all the players and spectators.

Bob wins the coin flip and comes out firing, maintaining control early into the second rack. He makes the first three balls, but his position on the four-ball comes up a little short. He tries a bank shot but misses it by a small fraction. The four-ball sits in the jaws of the pocket as Johnny comes to the table. Bob is busy mumbling to himself as he makes his way back to his seat.

Sitting-ducks have a nice way of making your first visit to the table a little more enjoyable. Johnny pockets the four, and his cue-ball sets up the five nicely. For his first shot of the day, Johnny is happy with his results. The execution remains steady for the remainder of the first rack. Johnny wins the game to even the score.

Twelve more racks are played in the set before Johnny ends up winning nine games to five. When the match concludes, Bob tells Johnny, "I missed one ball, the four-ball, cross-corner in the second game and you beat me by four games." Bob goes on to commend Johnny for his strong play. He shakes Johnny's hand to congratulate him on his victory. "At least I didn't beat myself; I lost to a terrific young player."

Familiar faces are battling it out on the first table. It's Joe T. from the other night in the mini-tournament; Johnny has since found out his last name is Tucker. He's playing another player Johnny victimized in the mini-tournament, Steve T., or, as Johnny has also come to find out, Steve Tavenere. The match is a very close, hard-fought battle, but Steve prevails over Joe. Johnny will play Joe as soon as the matches have been completed.

Joe's not as fortunate as Bob Busa on the flip of a coin. Johnny wins and immediately takes full advantage of his good fortune. He strings together the first three racks right out of the gate. Joe sits for a long time before he finally gets a chance at the table; he's almost wishing he weren't there. He's facing a nasty safety Johnny has laid upon him. Joe manages to make a legal hit, but he may have been better off missing the one-ball. It rolls up table and comes off the rail, leaving Johnny a very easy one-nine combination. Johnny is right back at the table and easily puts away nine-ball to claim another game.

Deficits can be overcome, but not when you're consistently kicking at balls. Joe is victimized by Johnny's offensive and defensive capabilities. The total package has Johnny sitting on the hill leading eight games to one before Joe manages a late rally. After winning two games in a row, Joe starts to run a third rack, but he gets a bad roll after making a tough shot. It leads to a scratch. Johnny closes out the match. A small smattering of applause can be heard around the room, even though he beat one of the local heroes.

Johnny starts to feel agony as he watches the match that will decide his next opponent. Both players make a few mistakes down the stretch, but Mike Zuglan pulls out another close decision.

Now it's a rematch between Mike and Johnny. Mike shows the signs of working and playing for two days. His shooting skills are greatly diminished, and he misses shots he had made look easy the day before. Johnny gets caught up in Mike's sloppy play early in the match, but then starts thinking about the day before and how he let it come down to who got the final break to win the set. With the score tied at three games, Johnny flicks the switch and ignites the after-burners in his engine. A four-pack leaves Mike gasping for air the next time he comes to the table. Mike is running on empty; he fails to convert a chance in the next rack, and Johnny goes on to win nine games to four. Mike congratulates Johnny for his fine play and thanks him for playing on his tour. "We need all the new blood we can get on this or any other tour. I hope to see you around in the future."

"I think my uncle has me lined up to play next weekend in New Jersey."

"Great, maybe I'll see you there. Is there any chance Billy might come and play in a few more tournaments?"

"He's pretty upset about the way Rico taunted him on national television. I'm not so sure he wants to put himself through that again."

"That's too bad. Billy's a huge asset to the game and probably the greatest nine-ball player to ever pick up a cue."

"Did you ever play Billy?"

"Many times. Most of the time, Billy came out on top. There was the one time in a major event I managed to beat him out in the finals. Unfortunately, I helped to contribute to his not-so-admirable nick-name." The conversation comes to an end between Mike and Johnny. It's getting near the end of the match between Kid Delicious and Steve Tavenere. Steve makes a late charge at Danny, but loses nine to seven.

Back in the Green Room, Johnny locates Billy. He's having a drink, sitting and talking to his old friend Mike X. about his upcoming tournament. Johnny mumbles out, "I'm nervous." Billy and Mike look at each other and start to laugh.

Billy asks Johnny. "What the hell took so long?"

Mike says, "The first tournament I played in, I felt the way you feel right now from the very beginning." The match is being called, and Johnny has little time before the match starts.

Billy says, "You've already exceeded what I did playing in my first tournament. Why don't you just relax and go out and have some fun?" Johnny goes back through the crowd feeling a little better. He's taking deep breaths as Steve finishes his warm-ups. The introductions are concluded and play starts after Steve wins the coin flip.

Johnny loses, and Steve makes Johnny pay a heavy price. He runs the first four games right out of the chute. When he does let Johnny come to the table, he's got Johnny locked up in a nice safety. Johnny manages to make a nice hit, but the cue-ball finds its way into the side pocket. Another two racks and Steve has built a six-game lead. Johnny manages to mount a counterattack off Steve's first legitimate miss of the set. He strings together a run of three games, but Steve's big lead is too much to overcome. Johnny ends up losing nine games to five. As Johnny shakes Steve's hand, he notices his nervousness is long gone. Johnny congratulates Steve on a match well played. The crowd shows its appreciation for both players with a loud ovation encouraged by Mike Zuglan.

Johnny knows he was outplayed. Steve took control from the start and never looked back. When Johnny gets back to where Billy is seated there is a big smile on Billy's face and a nice cold beer, Johnny's favorite, sitting on the table. Billy gets up from his seat to applaud Johnny's efforts. Johnny couldn't be happier at the way Billy is conducting himself. He was never able to satisfy Cliff unless he was the best at anything he tried. Mike X. is still sitting with Billy and also gives Johnny a boost of confidence when he says, "This weekend, I think I witnessed the birth of a future champion." He holds his glass up and salutes Johnny in a toast. A Freudian slip caused by maybe a little too much alcohol has Mike proclaim, "To the future of Johnny Bates; may he enjoy the same success as his—"

"Uncle," he politely says to Mike. "My last name is Jordan."

Mike knows he's kind of fucked up, so he stops talking.

There's a short pause in the conversation before Johnny asks, "What's next on the agenda?"

Billy asks Johnny, "When was the last time you talked to your mother?"

"It's been a while."

"Give her a call and be sure to do it often. And give your girlfriend a call, too. Let her know how you did in the tournament."

Johnny runs down the end of the room, finds a quiet place, and does just that.

"Hello, stranger."

Elaine tells Johnny that her lawyers started to investigate Cliff's financial worth. "They found a bunch of stuff Cliff had hidden from me when he was the executor of his father's will. I'm looking at maybe two or three million in total assets on top of what I already knew about. As cruel as it may sound, Johnny, I could kick Cliff square in the balls and it wouldn't hurt him as bad as taking money out of his pocket. I'm not sure what he likes more, the floozies he runs around with or the almighty dollar. And I'm thinking of starting my own business."

Johnny knows his mom had already mentioned starting in real estate business with Cindy, but he lets her repeat the story. His grandmother started to drink herself to sleep after her husband had passed. Alone at night, although the circumstances may be different, Johnny sometimes had the fear his mother may do the same thing. When Johnny fills her in on his weekend's accomplishments, she's very impressed.

"Billy must be quite a teacher."

"He has admitted to at least being related to me. He told everyone he was my uncle. I guess the difference in our last names would have been confusing to people if he said he was my father. The thing I liked about him the most was that he was proud of me for finishing third in the tournament. Cliff would have considered me a failure. I have also given him my own little nickname, Mr. Miyagi, the guy from the *Karate Kid*." He explains why.

Elaine's spirits are lifted even higher. "So how's the gambling been going?"

Johnny hesitates to tell the truth because he knows his mother is concerned that he may be getting himself caught up in making a living the easy way. He tells his mother part of the truth. He says he only gambles to pay his expenses of living on the road and paying for his food and motel bill. He fails to mention how much money he has to play for to meet these expenses.

"I watch the tape of Billy playing Rico at least once a week. I definitely want to see him again someday. I'm starting to get the achy feeling in my heart like the time when we met. Does he ever mention me in conversation?"

"Billy was the one who suggested this phone call. He doesn't talk about it, but I bet he's dying to see you again. Maybe the time and place will come in the future."

As Johnny and his mom say their goodbyes, Elaine says, "Maybe the right time and place will present itself."

He then calls Flo.

"Hello, big boy; I was hoping you'd call tonight. I'm sitting here on my couch with nothing on but a little see-through nightie. I wish you could come on over to my house so we could play together."

Johnny gets excited. "Is that what you're really doing?"

"I'm really in my car driving home from work and have a bad headache. My legs are all cramped, and I think I'm ready to get my period. I am not looking forward to making my own dinner and eating another meal by myself. I miss you terribly and wish we were together. Where are you?"

"I'm still at Snooker's."

"Let me guess," says Flo, "it's late Sunday night and you're calling me. You sound like you're in a pretty good mood. I'm guessing you did pretty well playing this weekend."

"Third place," says Johnny, "after losing my first match."

"Copy cat," says Flo.

"What you mean by that?"

"Don't you remember how I did in my first tournament?"

Johnny feels a little foolish not making the connection. "I guess I got caught up in what was happening in my life. What's been going on with you?"

"I'm all set for my trip to California, and Liz told me she gets about three calls a week from people interested in using me in various promotions. We're holding out until after I play again."

"Sounds pretty exciting to me," says Johnny. "The agent thing may prove to be a great move on your part."

"She's really aggressive," says Flo, "and worth every penny she gets." There is a moment of silence, then she asks, "Is there any chance you could come home for a few days?"

"I'm pretty committed to what Billy has lined up for me. I know I'm playing in New Jersey over the weekend. After that, I'm not sure what he has planned. What I wanted to suggest was having my mom come and watch you play."

"Does she know anything about pool? I wouldn't want her to be bored."

"My mom is interested in the people I am interested in. It will be a good time for you two to get acquainted. If she's anything like she was at my baseball games, you'll have one heck of a rooter sitting on your side."

Mike Zuglan announces that Kid Delicious is the winner of the Joss Nine-Ball. Presentations are being made to the first and second place finishes. Mike comes over the loudspeaker and tells Johnny to come forward and receive his third-place trophy. Johnny had no idea he was getting a trophy, so he hurriedly tells Flo, "They want me at the first table; I'm getting a trophy." He rushes across the room, telling Flo, "I love you. I'll call you the next time I get a chance."

As Johnny is flipping his phone shut, Mike walks over to present him with his trophy.

Later, Billy greets Johnny and holds out his hand. "Let me see the trophy," he says. "This is a beauty. Good thing we got the big car. We're going to need all the room we can get to store trophies if you keep playing like you did this weekend." Johnny can't get enough accolades from Billy. He beams with joy every time Billy gives him any praise. Billy tells Johnny, "I've got a little more business to discuss with Mike X. It shouldn't take more than a half hour or so."

Not long after, they hit the road.

# CHAPTER 19

"There's action in Maine, so we're headed there first. I got you a game playing ten games ahead for a thousand dollars."

"Ten games ahead?" asks Johnny. "What's that? I never played it before?"

As Billy sits back and relaxes, he explains to Johnny. "It's just what it says it is. You play nine-ball, and the first one who gets ten games ahead, on the wire, wins the money."

"When's all this happen?" asks Johnny

"Tuesday afternoon," says Billy, "about three o'clock. I figured you could use a day off to relax. I have to call Larry tomorrow to make sure things are going all right back of the room. You're lucky we're making enough money so we can afford to relax for a day. Most of the people who get out on the road can't afford such a luxury."

Johnny asks, "How far are we driving tonight?"

"Maybe an hour and a half or two hours," says Billy. "I figure you can use the time to unwind a little. I know, after I used to play in tournaments, it would take a while for me to lose the adrenaline rush playing pool always gave me." After Billy yawns, he instructs Johnny to drive as far as he feels like driving. "I'm going to close my eyes for a few minutes. Wake me up when you decide you have driven far enough. We'll look for a hotel or motel to stay in at that point."

Johnny drives a while then gets a motel.

Johnny wakes to Billy's talking on the phone. Before Billy hangs up, he hands the phone to Johnny and says, "Larry's on the phone. He wants to congratulate you on how well you play this weekend."

"Hi, Larry."

"Pretend we're talking about the tournament; I don't want Billy to know what I'm telling you."

Johnny plays along, saying, "I was a little nervous playing Steve in front of all the people."

"Billy will never tell you this, but he called me and raved about how well you played in the tournament." Larry explains to Johnny why Billy will never give him the amount of praise he might deserve. "Billy's father never gave him any credit for the things he had done in his playing career. Billy had been angry about a lot of things that happened to him in his life. You've turned his life around; now he has a purpose."

"Thanks for all the helpful tips. I'll keep them in mind the next time I'm playing." Johnny hands the phone back to Billy, and he and Larry talk for a little while before the conversation ends.

"Let's head to Portland," says Billy.

In the car, Billy says, "Sorry, I didn't think I would be on the phone so long."

"Sounds like things are going well."

"Well," says Billy rather loudly, "things are going fantastic. Larry already has over two hundred qualifiers set up around the world. He's brought in a friend from California, and they're making phone calls all day to set up all these qualifiers. Plus he's gotten calls from another two or three hundred people who want to pay the five hundred dollars to ensure themselves a spot in the tournament. Your idea about raffling off a vehicle has gone bananas. Larry says we've already sold enough tickets to cover the cost of one vehicle, plus we have two thousand towards the second vehicle. We should have no problem turning a big profit once the players show up. Larry has also hired an architect; he says he can knock down a few walls and have stadium seating in the room for around three thousand people. The architect says he knows a local contractor who could get the job done for about eighty thousand dollars."

"Sounds like a lot of money to me."

"I've had the place for over twelve years. I am paying the government a big chunk of change every year, and I'm tired of looking at the same four walls every day. This will increase the value of the property. My partner is all for what Larry wants to do. They're starting the renovations in two days. Larry also told me business has been great. When people come in to buy raffle tickets, they stay and have a few drinks and dinner and play some pool. Many people have come in for the first time and say they will come back again real soon."

"Larry's got a great personality. Why didn't he open his own poolroom years ago?"

"Larry had the fear of not knowing where to start. This is a very fickle business; one day your place is jumping and the next day you can't give a table away."

"You seem to be doing okay for yourself."

"I have a few things going in my favor. My partner got a good buy on the property, so we were able to pay off the mortgage in five years. The university also helps tremendously. We have a turnover every year of about ten thousand students. A lot of them come in at least two or three times a year. I hire a lot of upperclassmen and encourage them to have their friends come in. I give them a twenty percent break on their bills. If a group of four or more girls come in, I give them a thirty percent break on their bills. If they play pool I only charge them half price."

"How come the girls get to play for half price?"

"Because girls attract boys, and boys spend money trying to impress girls. At least they did in my day. I'm not so sure the

255

same rules still applies. I've done it since I opened my doors. Why change now? A few more exits and we'll be in Portland."

At one-thirty, they make it to Spot-shot Billiards. There's a few locals sitting along the railing; they give Johnny and Billy the once over as they pass them by. Billy goes to the counter and strikes up a conversation with the person running the room. "Is Kerry around?"

"Kerry has gone off hunting somewhere. He'll be back tomorrow."

"If Kerry should happen to check-in, would you please tell him Billy Bates is in town for a couple of days."

"I thought you looked familiar. I've taped all your matches from when you played on ESPN a few months ago." The houseman extends his hand to shake. "My name is Mark Ross." Mark in his excitement introduces Billy to all the locals sitting along the rail. The railbirds are not as overwhelmed as Mark; they just put up their hands in a waving motion to recognize the fact that Billy is in the room.

"You're lucky I'm not here to hustle. I might have gotten mad at you for telling everyone who I am." Mark tries to apologize, but Billy tells Mark not to worry about anything. "I am here for my nephew's sake; he has a match all lined up for tomorrow night with Kenny Spain."

"He's a pretty tough player. I hope your nephew can play this game."

"I think he'll be able to hold his own against Kenny. I have one question, Mark. What's Kenny's favorite table?" Mark points at the table directly behind the railbirds. "How is Kenny's money situation?"

"He's probably got someone to back him if he's betting a lot of money. The man who usually stakes him typically carries quite a bit of money."

"Thanks," says Billy.

"We have a handicap tournament here tonight. It starts around seven-thirty. I'll have to give you the highest rating; we have to protect my local players, but you're welcome to come in and play if you want. It's only a twenty dollar entry fee to participate."

Johnny and Billy look at each other. Billy says, "Sounds good to me." He hands Mark a twenty and says, "Johnny will be here with bells on."

Johnny and Billy then get a motel room. Billy's impressed with, Ashley, the girl working at the motel. He gives her his business card and offers her a job if she's ever looking for a change of scenery. Billy has one last set of instructions before Johnny leaves the room. He tells Johnny to practice on three different tables when he goes back to the poolroom. "Get about forty-five minutes and on each table and tell me which one of the three you feel you played your best on." Once again, it's a Mr. Miyagi move; Johnny knows enough not to ask any questions. He grabs the car keys and goes out the door.

Later that night, Johnny returns. Opening the door makes enough noise to wake Billy.

"How'd it go?"

"I played on the first three tables on the right, and I like the middle the best."

"When we play tomorrow, Kenny will want to play on his favorite table. I'm going to insist we play on two different tables."

"What if he doesn't want to use two different tables?"

"We walk out the door. If we don't walk, we're giving him every psychological advantage in the game. We can't afford to let him play comfortably. Don't worry; he's in no position to let us walk out the door. This is his chance to make a score.

There aren't too many thousand dollar games running around this town."

"You have an uncanny way of making irrational thinking become rational."

"Don't be talking to me with all those big college words. The things I do require poolroom smarts, nothing more, nothing less. Now let's get dinner."

After dinner and on their way to the poolroom, Billy says, "When you get to the poolroom, only you will be getting out of the car. I want to take a ride. I spent a lot of time in this area when I was a kid. I want to see how much things have changed." Before Billy drops off Johnny, he gives him a few more instructions. "When you get out of the car, go for a walk around the parking lot. That way, when you go back downstairs to play, you won't feel so bloated. The exercise will help you start to digest your meal. You have my cell phone number if you need me. I should be back before nine-thirty." Johnny takes his cue from the backseat of the car and starts to walk around the parking lot.

Inside, Mark has a set of balls already in his hand as Johnny comes down to the counter. He tells Johnny, "It's two dollars to practice from now until the tournament starts." Johnny gives Mark the money and walks into the room. All three tables he had played on earlier are active so he makes his way farther into the room. Some of the railbirds who were there earlier are getting ready to play in the tournament. Johnny notices many of them are keeping a close eye on how he plays.

Seven-thirty rolls around quickly. Mark announces there are twenty-three entries in the tournament. Johnny has the highest handicap of any player in the tournament. His first two matches are against players with a five handicap each. This means Johnny must win nine games before his opponent wins five. Johnny easily wins both, nine to three and nine to two.

The next guy isn't as nice as the first two. From the start, he's all over Johnny for showing up out of the blue and robbing a bunch of hicks out of a small time tournament. The bullshit has an effect on Johnny early in the match. He makes a couple of costly errors and falls behind with a score of three games to one. His opponent is a seven handicap, so Johnny's still has time to regroup and get back in the game. Johnny is getting a little flustered when his opponent appears to be running out the next rack. Poor position, however, stops the run out on the seven-ball. Johnny comes to the table and makes a fantastic shot to help win the game.

Anger and frustration causes the man to proclaim to the poolroom, "This guy's a pro! He should never have been allowed to play in this tournament." He throws the rack up onto the table and slams a few balls as he racks them. Johnny has had enough; when the balls are put in place, he puts his cue on the table and walks over and sits in the chair beside his opponent. He takes a twenty dollar bill out of his pocket and puts it into the shirt pocket of his opponent. He politely tells him, "If I hear one more outburst like the one you just had, we'll have to step outside. I'm giving you back your entry fee, so you have a free ride at winning all the money you may earn tonight. I play this game because I like to play this game. I didn't come here tonight with a gun and mask to stick this place up. I came to play a quiet game of pool and get myself ready to play a money match tomorrow. I've taken the highest handicap of any player in the place." Johnny gets out of his seat he looks the man in the eye. "Is there anything I just said that you don't understand?" Johnny receives a meek "no" from Mr. Wonderful, then he goes back to the table and breaks.

Fire and passion are now instilled in Johnny's game. He hates that he has just had a confrontation over a twenty dollar pool tournament. He's on the table he had practiced on earlier and everything clicks in. A run of three racks, followed by a great safety play, which leads to another game has Johnny ahead six games to three. A run of two more racks has Johnny sitting on the hill and breaking the next game. He doesn't close out the match, but he does the following game. Mr. Wonderful doesn't bother to shake Johnny's hand after the match. He angrily puts his equipment away and storms up the stairs. Johnny goes over to Mark and asks him to raise his handicap.

"I can't do that; the guy you just played is used to coming in here and having his own way with everyone. You may not know this, but you just made yourself a few friends. It's about time someone came in this place that plays good enough to show that guy the door."

When Billy shows up, Johnny tells him what has happened. Billy makes light of the situation. "Every time I leave you alone you almost get into a fight." Billy also commends Johnny for sticking up for himself. "You can shut most of the jerks up by doing what you did tonight, but there will be the one guy who goes to the parking lot. I hope you're ready for that guy."

"I ran into him in Albuquerque—"

Mark calls his next match.

Johnny's next opponent has much more class than the poor sport. She tells Johnny before the match starts, "I don't care how good you play, make sure you to play your best game." After two racks of early sparring, Johnny puts on a display they may still talk about in Portland. With the score tied at one to one, Johnny breaks and runs out seven straight games. His run ends when he scratches on the break. The long wait for a shot affects his opponent. She manages to pocket a few balls, but she misses the five-ball. Johnny remembers what she told him in the beginning. He gives his best effort and runs out the rack to win the match. One thing changes for the good: Johnny gets a handshake from his opponent, and she can't find enough compliments for his shooting. They enjoy a long conversation while Johnny waits for his next opponent. In that time, Johnny learns more about the young lady. She tells him her name is Renée Brown and someday she hopes to play on the ladies pro tour.

Johnny tells Renée about Flo, and how he spent four days with her in Albuquerque. "Flo wasn't sure if she was ready to play at the level of the pros until she took the first step and entered a tournament."

"I came in second place in the last qualifier I entered. Next time, I am going to win and get to play in a pro event." She then leaves.

Thirty-six games won for the night and still another nine to go to win the tournament. Johnny's next opponent catches him by surprise. He asks Johnny if he's willing to split the money for first and second place. Johnny has second thoughts until Ned tells him, "I could really use the money; I haven't worked for three weeks." Johnny has forty dollars invested in the tournament. The total amount of money for first and second place is two hundred and fifty dollars. Johnny tells Mark to give him fifty dollars and give the rest to Ned.

Standing off to the side is Billy. After Ned thanks Johnny numerous times and walks up the flight of stairs to leave, Billy comes over and asks, "What's going on?"

"I just gave most of the money to Ned. He has been out of work for three weeks and asked me if I'd be willing to split the money for first and second place."

Billy laughs. "You just got conned."

"I'll bet you five hundred dollars he wasn't a con man."

Billy is not about to piss Johnny off when he has a big money match to play the next day. Billy tries to be as diplomatic as possible. "This is not about money, it's about who has had more experience with people who come into poolrooms. I have a funny feeling this guy, Ned, just pulled the wool over your eyes, and I'd hate to see it happen again."

Johnny settles down and asks Mark, "Who's right in this argument? Is Billy right or am I right? I want to know the truth."

Mark pauses and says to Johnny, "I hate to say it, but Billy hit the nail right on the head. Ned owns a small store down in Saco, has for years; he heard you ran seven racks, so he figured he had no shot at winning. He would've been happy splitting the money. You were the one who decided to be so generous. He did tell the truth about not working for three weeks. He just got back from Florida."

Johnny feels pretty foolish. Billy says, "Shake it off, kid; if that's the worst thing that ever happens to you in a poolroom, you'll be lucky. Let's get out of this place; it's been a long day." They both say goodnight to Mark and walk up the staircase.

Eating crow is something Johnny has never been comfortable doing. It takes a while for him to initiate any conversation with Billy. Johnny waits until he's almost back to the motel to break the ice. He finally says to Billy, "You were gone a long time. Where did you go?"

"I took a long ride back into time." There's a short pause. "I spent a great deal of time in this area when I was a kid. My father used to lug us around in a trailer from place to place. If you take Route 302 north heading out of Portland, it leads you up to the Sebago Lake region. We stayed in a lot of different parks because my father would usually stiff the owner out of the last month's rent. Bridgeton was one of the bigger towns in the area. Lots of times we would go into town, and my dad would end up playing pool all night in one of the local bars.

Sometimes, when we won, we even got to eat our dinner sitting in the booths while he got drunk playing with all the locals and the occasional vacationer. My mother would work her tail off all week long at the diner, and good old Dad would usually blow all her earnings. As we got older, my mother started to smarten up. She started to hide a lot of her tips so we could have enough money to get by." Billy starts to get some anger in his voice. "I went back into the stinking place tonight where all this used to take place. There were ten or twelve people in the place, and I bought every one of the customers, and myself, a drink. After I finished my drink, I walked out the door. When I got to the bottom of the stairs, I started to recall how we used to have to carry my dad back to the trailer after he'd gotten too drunk to walk. Usually, he would start saying nasty things to my mother, and she would start crying, which made me and my little sister start to cry. It's funny; I had a lot of great memories of these trailer parks, and all I could remember tonight were the times that weren't so great. It's crazy how those things can stick in your head. I faced a lot of old demons in my life tonight; I also stopped by another bar and had a few more drinks. I shouldn't have had the last one. I'm all done talking now." He gets out of the car and goes to the motel room. Johnny shuts off the light and goes upstairs to his bedroom.

Reflection makes Johnny starts to think. Although their lives were totally different growing up, they both have anger issues about the things their fathers had done while they were growing up. Johnny doesn't want to, but he starts to get teary-eyed thinking back at some of the incidents that occurred at his home. He considers calling his mom to talk but figures it would probably make matters worse. Emotionally spent after tossing and turning for at least an hour, Johnny finally falls asleep.

"Game day," are the next words Johnny hears coming from downstairs. Johnny gets up and ready and they head to the poolroom after breakfast.

Kenny is already at the poolroom warming up when Billy and Johnny come down the flight of stairs. The railbirds are lined up early anticipating an afternoon of entertainment. Billy says to Johnny, "Get a set of balls and practice on the second table." When Kenny sees where Johnny is going, he offers to share his favorite table. Billy picks this time to get involved in the conversation. He tells Kenny and his backer, "I thought we might play ten games apiece on each table." This wasn't part of Kenny's plan at all. He figured he was going to have a big advantage playing on his favorite table. Kenny and his backer balk at Billy's idea. Billy goes into his bag of little white lies. He says to Johnny, "Let's go. I knew we should have gone to Connecticut and played Carlos Vieira." Billy turns his white lie into something a politician might even envy. He says to Johnny, "When we get out to the car, remind me to call Carlos; maybe we can set something up for tomorrow."

Johnny doesn't get two balls back into the tray when Kenny suddenly has a change of heart. "Wait," he says to Billy, "maybe I overreacted a little."

"This is the last of it," says Billy. "I don't want to hear any complaints about how the game is to be played after the match starts." Billy takes a large wad of hundred dollar bills from his pocket. He counts out ten and gives them to Mark. He tells Kenny and his backer to do the same thing. Billy throws in one more minor detail. "The first ten games will be played on the table Johnny prefers to play on." By this time, Kenny and his backer are sick of listening to Billy; they agreed to all the terms he has laid out.

Kenny falls heavily into all the traps Billy has laid. The opening lag costs him two games right from the start. The first ten games have Johnny already ahead by four games on the wire. The first move to the other table gets Kenny two of the games back from Johnny quickly. With Johnny up by two games, a disaster hits Kenny squarely in the face. He misses an eight-ball, which would have given him a chance to close the gap to a single game. Johnny pounces all over Kenny's mistake. He wins that game, plus three more to move six games ahead on the wire. The remaining four games played on that particular table are split, so Johnny moves back to table two with a six game lead. Johnny also has a big advantage. He's breaking the next rack and takes full advantage of the situation. He makes the nine on the break. Kenny's extremely mad. Billy takes a look over at Kenny's backer, who is slumped over in his chair looking like Rocky Balboa after the first ten rounds with Apollo Creed. Billy looks at Johnny's face and sees himself back in the day. Johnny has the same desire and intensity as a cold-blooded killer. It doesn't take much more time before Kenny becomes Johnny's prey.

Louie, Kenny's backer, tries to take control of the situation and flex his muscles. He offers to play again, but this time the switching of the tables is out of the question. Billy isn't intimidated by Louie; he says to Johnny, "Let's get out of here; these people can't accept the fact they just got their asses kicked."

Louie is piping hot. "Aren't you going to give me a chance to get my money back?"

Billy goes to the counter, gets the money from Mark, and puts it into his pocket. He says to Louie, "It's my money now, and I'm not about to give it back." The railbirds all find Billy's statement amusing. Louie isn't so happy. Billy does come up with another proposal for Louie and Kenny to consider. He offers to play Kenny on the front table if they raise the bet to two thousand dollars. Kenny, Louie, and one of the railbirds go into the corner for a huddle. When they emerge, they have enough money to cover the bet. Johnny has witnessed this act before when Larry backed him. He knows Billy has put all the pressure on Kenny because he's playing with all the money he has to his name.

In the meantime, the owner of Spot-shots, Kerry Herbert, has found his way back from the hunting trip. Billy spots his old friend and discusses business while Johnny and Kenny go toe to toe on the first table. Sixty-three games and four and a half hours later, Kenny throws in the towel by conceding Johnny's easy shot on the nine-ball. Kenny is a broken horse; there is no more fight left in him. His backer tries to save face by shouting some obscenities at Billy while he's at the back of the room talking to Kerry. When all of the bullshit ends, Billy and Kerry congratulate Johnny.

Kerry and Billy go back many years. Their conversation in the back of the room wasn't all business. Billy had let Kerry in on a little secret. He told him Johnny could possibly be his son. Of course, Kerry is under strict orders not to talk about the subject to Johnny or anyone else. Kerry does, however, know Billy and Johnny are posing as uncle and nephew, and he makes it known to Johnny how excited he is to meet a family member of the great Billy Bates. While Kerry and Johnny get acquainted, Billy makes his way over to the counter to get his winnings from Mark. He counts all the money in front of Mark and commends him for keeping a good eye on the money. Billy's twenty-five dollar tip, over and above the cost of the table time, brings a nice smile to Mark's face. When Billy gets back to Kerry and Johnny, they are hitting it off. Kerry has invited them both to dinner. Johnny's excited about the idea. He's famished from not eating since breakfast. Billy says, "What the hell, let's do it."

At the restaurant, beer starts to flow, and the three men sit back and relax for a few minutes. Billy talks about the tournament that he's hosting: "Over two hundred and fifty-six players have already sent their money to play in my tournament. We have well over another hundred rooms that want to have at least one and possibly two qualifiers. That's just how things are going on the men's side. We're gonna have sixty-four women players guaranteed, and possibly one hundred and twenty-eight. Larry's trying to get a lot of the leagues across the country and the rest of the world to send the top male and female players in their leagues to play. My partner has also stuck his fingers into the pie. He has somehow gotten the University of Kentucky to donate the use of new dormitories they have built for the upcoming semester as a place to stay for the people coming to the tournament. I guess the dorms are brand new and they want to make sure any of the kinks they might have are hammered out before the students come back to school. The tournament will have to start the second week of December. With the size of the field, we anticipate it will run for ten days." Billy informs Johnny he's going to be leaving for a couple of days. "I'm flying out of Portland airport tomorrow morning at nine o'clock. I have to go back to Kentucky for a few days. I want you to drive back to Providence tomorrow. There's a handicap tournament at Snooker's tomorrow night. Thursday might be a good day to hang-out and do some laundry and maybe look for a poolroom in Connecticut. Who knows," Billy chuckles, "maybe Carlos will be around. On Friday, make your way over to New Jersey."

"I thought the tournament was in New York?"

"New York, New Jersey, what's the difference? I think the room is actually in Jersey. There is a flyer hanging on the wall at

Snooker's. When you get there tomorrow, find out the address and phone number, then call me and let me know."

They finish their beers and order another round. Johnny finally asks, "When did you decide to invite women to play in the tournament?"

"I think I decided when I saw your girlfriend—she's beautiful." He has to laugh, trying to pinch some jealousy out of Johnny. "Actually, it was Larry's idea. He says the women are more popular than the men and better to look at. I couldn't agree more."

"Your uncle Billy and I had some wild adventures in our day. Maybe I can fill you in on some of the details some day."

Johnny says, "I would like that. I'd like it a lot."

They end up staying with Kerry that night. His place is set way back in the woods, which is a nice change of scenery for the travelers. Kerry drives Billy to the airport early the next morning.

# CHAPTER 20

The next morning, Kerry wakes Johnny for breakfast.

Johnny asks Kerry, "How did it go with Billy?"

"Smooth as silk. It's nice to see him happy again." He smiles. "I know about you and Billy. He also told me about your mother, who he's never gotten over."

"Did Billy admit he's my father?"

"He said there is a good chance he may be a father. He didn't come right out and admit the fact. You gotta understand, Billy is a tough nut to crack. He's also an opportunist. He'll wait until exactly the right time and place if he's ever going to admit he's your father."

"Why was Billy so angry?"

"First of all, he hates his nickname. Billy was the best nine-ball player in the country for ten maybe fifteen years. Unfortunately, it got him nowhere. The game was on the downswing for most of those years. He used to say to me, if he played most any other game, he would have been a multimillionaire. When he got to the finals of many of the tournaments he earned his nickname from, it was more lucrative for him to lose than it was for him to win. Billy was in with a bad group of people. They would go up into the stands and get people to bet on Billy to win the tournament. When enough money was bet on Billy, they would give him the signal to dump the match."

Johnny is appalled listening to what Kerry is telling him. "He dumped against Rico?"

"No. Rico beat his brains in. The look you saw on Billy's face. That was a look of disgust for not winning when he could have won. He had many opportunities to do what Rico was doing to him to other people, but he sold out for the money. That's why he's so intent on building up the game and making it affordable to be a professional pool player. He's absolutely crazy about you and your game. The whole ride to the airport, it's all he talked about. Billy's never had anything. He's finally at the point in his life when he may be able to make a difference in someone else's life. Maybe a young pool player or two, they may be able to make enough money from the game to choose the right path in life."

They chat a little longer, then Johnny has to get on the road. Johnny extends his hand to Kerry, and as they shake, Johnny asks him, "Will I see you in Kentucky?"

"I wouldn't miss it for world."

Once on the road, Johnny calls Flo. "Did you know Billy is having a tournament at his place for both men and women starting the second week in December?"

"I saw the ad in *Billiard Digest*."

"What's the matter? You don't sound that enthused?"

"They are only taking the top sixty-four ranked players on the ladies tour, and right now, I don't qualify as one of them."

"What about the tournament in California?"

"That's my last chance."

"Don't worry. You'll do just fine, then you'll have enough points to qualify for Billy's tournament."

"I'm not so sure about that. I'm in a bit of a slump right now. Are you going to be able to come to California and watch me play?"

"Ah shit," says Johnny. "I forgot to ask Billy about next week. I didn't call my mom either." Johnny changes the subject. "What about Liz?"

"Everything with Liz remains status quo right now. She sent me my airline tickets to fly to California and paid for my room. She even paid for my entry fee. I'm just afraid that I won't play well and Liz will get stuck with a big bill."

"That's insane," says Johnny. "Liz knows a winner when she sees one. Don't forget it's not only a pool game she's banking on; it's also your looks and her ability to market you."

"If you come, I could stay at your house, but to just show up at your mother's doorstep and possibly be there for five days—I'm not so sure I could impose on someone I don't even know and feel comfortable staying there."

"Let me talk to my mother, and I'll call you back soon."

Johnny calls Billy to ask about attending Flo's tournament and doesn't get the answer he wants. Billy wants Johnny to go to Louisville and play in a major tournament the same time Flo's in California. He hopes the call to his mother will be different.

His mother thinks that Flo staying with her is a great idea, even though Cliff is still calling her when he gets drunk and bothering her. Johnny thanks his mom for offering her home to a total stranger. He eventually makes it to his destination and gets a motel room.

Later that day, Johnny runs from the parking lot up the flight of stairs leading to Snookers. He starts to meander around the room looking to find a possible game before the start of the tournament. Rejection is something Johnny has yet to experience in a poolroom. He starts getting uncomfortable from some of the looks he's getting when he's asking people if they want to warm and maybe play for fifty dollars. Johnny starts to think he's developed leprosy. One of the players that's warming up finally pulls Johnny aside and tells him, "The word is out on you around this area, kid. Any easy action you might have gotten went up in smoke last Friday night when you took down Frankie. A lot of the people playing right now were all there and saw what you did to him. They're not going to step up and play you even. Most of them wouldn't play you with a three-game spot in the race to nine. My advice to you, grab a rack of balls and warm up by yourself. Unless one of the solid A-players comes in, like Steve Tavenere, you're probably not going to get any action." At this time, the man giving Johnny the advice introduces himself. "My name is Jim Tibedo." Johnny puts out his hand and shakes Jim's hand. Before he can say his name, Tibedo says, "And you're Johnny Jordan, the nephew of the great Billy Bates. I watched you play here all last Sunday. I thought you were going to win." Johnny thanks Tibedo for his advice and his praise before going to the counter and getting a rack of balls.

Houseman Ray Mack comes over the loudspeaker at six o'clock and has all the tables clear out their table time. He also requests everyone pay their twenty-dollar entry fee for the tournament. A half hour of free table time ensues before the tournament starts. The room has really filled up, and Johnny starts to share his warm-up table with two other players. At six-thirty, play gets underway and there are forty-six total players entered. Johnny cruises through his matches, along with his nemesis: Steve Tavenere.

The two players once again meet up on table one. Steve opens up the match by scratching on the break. Johnny takes full advantage of the opportunity. The next time Steve comes out of his seat, he's trailing by three games and kicking at a tough three-ball hit. Steve makes it a hit, but the cue-ball again finds its way to the bottom of a pocket. Johnny runs out the remainder of the rack and leads by a score of four games to zero. Steve does win the next game, but fails to make a ball on the next break. Johnny runs up to the five-ball, then makes a six-ball, nine-ball combination to win the game and also the match.

Forty-six players and a one o'clock curfew aren't exactly a good mix. Johnny sits around for a while, and Ray Mack makes him an offer he can't refuse. Johnny has the option of splitting first and second place money and not waiting around another hour to play a match. It may be too late to play anyway. Johnny takes the money instead of waiting around. He knows he could use the sleep more than he could use the money. He gets the flyer information for his New Jersey poolroom, then leaves Snooker's around a quarter of one. He's back in his motel room and fast asleep before one-thirty.

Thursday morning almost completely slips away, but Johnny gets his act together and hits the road for the poolroom in Parsippany called Comet Billiards. He gets a motel room near the poolroom.

Once he opens the door to Comet Billiards and his eyes adjust to the light, he discovers a diamond in the rough. The blue interior is pleasant to the eyes. A snack bar is off to the right of the door, and a players-and-spectators seating section is on the left-hand side of the room. A couple of tables are in use, so Johnny grabs a soda at the snack bar and sits for a while to watch them play. There's not a lot of talent in the room right now. It looks like a few of the local kids, probably in high school. After watching for about twenty minutes, Johnny makes a quiet departure.

Billy calls and tells Johnny, "I'm not going to be able to get up to New Jersey before Saturday and possibly Sunday. This project is turning into a nightmare, but if it comes out as good as it looks on paper, it's going to be unbelievable. I hate to do this, kid, but, in order for this place to get done the way I want it, I think it's best I hang in here for a few more days. Larry is also starting to feel a little overwhelmed. He's been putting in fifteen to sixteen hours a day. He's doing a remarkable job getting players. We have already gone past three hundred. Larry thinks we're going to have a full field of five hundred and twelve players, plus a waiting list in case someone has to cancel last minute." Billy finally gets around to Johnny when he asks, "Where are you? What's been going on? Have you gotten any action since Tuesday?"

"Right now, I'm in a Motel 6 in Parsippany. The tournament is in Comet Billiards here." Billy hits the panic button and tells Johnny he has to go. Something big comes up, and the contractor running the show needs Billy to make a major decision.

Billy does say to Johnny, "Keep playing the way you played in Portland and Providence and you'll do just fine. If they have a Calcutta, buy yourself when your name comes up. They may not know you and you could go cheap." He then hangs up.

Johnny does miss Billy, even if he is a bit self-centered. He has flair and style in his personality. He's also an interesting person to be around.

Flo then calls. "Your mom called me last night, and we had a nice long talk. She's going to have me stay with her. She also suggested I have a friend come along, and Marie said she would love to come. Oh, Johnny, I can't believe how much my life has changed since I met you and how many good things are happening for me. When I called Liz and told her to cancel my room reservations, she told me she would send me a check for half the amount she would have paid. The money is for being honest and not taking advantage of her. Liz also said she is very close to convincing a shoe company they should design and start making shoes for pool players. She said that me and a couple of other girls she represents would be wearing the shoes while playing in tournaments." Flo giggles. "I'm also out of my slump. I played in a tournament last night and kicked everyone's butt."

Happy that Flo is happy, Johnny says, "That's all great news!"

"Your mother is going pick us up at the airport Tuesday night. The tournament doesn't start until Thursday, and your mother said she would take a sightseeing Wednesday if we felt up to it. Marie went nuts when she heard the sightseeing news. She's been a big fan of movies stars her whole life."

"Between my mother, Cindy, you, and Marie, you ladies won't have many dull moments."

"Oh, no, I'm out of time. I have to get back to work. Talk to you soon."

Later, Johnny returns to the poolroom. Comet's is busier than it was earlier, but still, there's no talent playing in the room. Johnny manages to strike up a conversation. Steve Scott, the houseman, notices Johnny is making his second visit to the poolroom in one day. He approaches Johnny and asks him, "Are you looking for a game?"

"Yeah," says Johnny. "Do you want to play?"

Steve says to Johnny, "You sound a little too anxious for me; besides, I'm working all night. I couldn't play if I wanted to. Are you here to play in the tournament over the weekend?"

"That's the plan."

"If you're looking for action, this isn't the place. Most of the action players hang out in the city poolrooms. They only come out here to play when we run a tournament. I'd be surprised if any of them show up before Saturday." Steve offers to call some of the rooms in the city to find Johnny a game. Johnny declines Steve's offer.

Johnny tells Steve, "I think I'll just go back and hang around the motel. Maybe they have a good movie on one of the pay channels. I don't feel like driving into the city. I'm not sure of where I'm going and I don't like getting lost. I'll be back tomorrow. I want to hit some balls and get used to the tables before I play on Saturday."

Steve tells Johnny, "I'll be here any time after twelve." They shake hands.

Johnny shakes Steve hand and says, "My name is Johnny Jordan." After a few minutes of small talk, Johnny leaves the room and returns to his motel for the night.

On Friday at three-thirty, he walks back into Comet Billiards. Steve has good news for Johnny when he makes his entrance. "A couple of players from the Succasunna area called, and they're coming in to play tonight to get ready to play tomorrow. One of the players has a reputation for losing decent money." Steve tells Johnny, "I was in a room once, and this guy dropped as couple of thousand. He has plenty of money, and he thinks he's better than he really is. He likes to bet it up, especially when he starts losing."

"How much do you think I should start him off at when and if we play for money?"

"I told him you were going to be here tonight. If he comes in the room, let him be the aggressor. He's got a big ego. He'll come over and ask you to play. If he asks you how much you want to bet, turn the table and say to him, 'What are you comfortable betting?' He'll try to impress you and probably bet higher than you might anticipate."

Luckily, Johnny had made a stop at the ATM machine while out on his ride. He has more than five hundred in cash in his pocket. Steve gives Johnny the bad news now. He says, "There is a slight fee I charge for setting you up with a game. I find you a game; I get ten percent of your winnings."

"Ten percent! That's pretty steep," says Johnny.

"You think that's steep?" says Steve. "I'm getting fifteen percent if you happen to lose to Harry. I gave you a break because you're playing in the tournament and living on the road."

"Is this a common practice?"

"It is around this part of the country, so you better get used to paying anybody who steers you towards any action."

"My uncle usually takes care of the business end. I just get out and do the shooting."

"Where's your uncle?"

"He's back in Kentucky tending to business. He said he would probably be here tomorrow. "

"I've been on the phone all week with Mike Zuglan he said Billy Bates and his nephew may be coming here to play this weekend. You're Billy's nephew, aren't you?"

"I guess I blew my cover."

Steve drops to a whisper: "You're secret is safe with me, but if I were you, I wouldn't tell another soul who you are and what you're doing here. If this gets out, you'll get no Harry; you'll be playing with your dick all night." Steve gives Johnny a set of balls. "Go play on table six and keep your mouth shut."

Harry and his friend come into the room at six forty-five. Johnny spots them talking to Steve and pays them no mind. Harry's entrance into the playing area is well received by a lot of the people playing in the room. He seems to know just about everyone in the room. At first glance, Johnny sees money written all over Harry. His watch, his cue case, a couple of rings he's sporting on his fingers and his clothing is of the finest quality, and he is very well-groomed. Harry and his friends have a rack of balls, and they end up on table four. There is an empty table between them and Johnny.

Half an hour later, Harry makes a move over towards Johnny's table. "Are you here to play in the tournament tomorrow?" Harry asks.

"I'm going take my chances and get in."

"From what I've been watching, your chances look pretty good."

"I've been hitting them pretty well lately; I think I'll do okay."

"I'm Harry Haroutunian." As he extends his hand to Johnny; Johnny introduces himself.

"Aren't you Armenian?"

Harry's impressed. "How do you know?"

"I had a good friend growing up that was Armenian."

Harry's says something that strikes Johnny in an odd way. "I feel like I'm with a member of the family. Why don't we play a race to nine for a hundred dollars? The only stipulation I have is that we play on table four."

Switching tables and feeling like Harry has become his friend hurts Johnny's game in the beginning. After six games, he is tied with Harry three games apiece. Harry is also a talker, and Johnny is having trouble maintaining his concentration. In the seventh game, Johnny makes a bad choice playing position and leaves himself safe on the four-ball. Angered a little by his play, Johnny kicks off the rail and makes the four in the opposite corner pocket. Johnny finds the focus he was missing and goes on to win the set by a score of nine games to five.

Negotiations for the next set take a good part of fifteen minutes. Johnny just wants to play, but Harry likes to talk. Slick and cunning, Harry ends up getting himself a great game from Johnny. Harry will get a game on the wire, plus all the breaks to play the next set.

Johnny starts to think he's been manipulated in the early games of the race. Harry pockets balls in each of the first five games he breaks. When he has a decent shot, he makes it, and when he doesn't, Johnny finds out Harry is adept at playing safeties. After the first five games, Johnny is down four games to one. He finds out racking every game leaves an emptiness in his game. Even when you win a game, you feel like you've lost, and even more importantly, you can't start stringing racks together. Harry does, however, start to fall apart. He scratches on one of his breaks and fails to make a ball on two more in a row. Johnny takes full advantage and gets back in the game. The rest of the set is hard fought until Harry squeezes a long six-ball draw-shot with both players sitting on the hill. Johnny makes a nice bank off Harry's miss and goes on to win the set.

Whirling from his miss of the six-ball, Harry throws five twenty dollar bills onto the table to pay for his losses. The game and Harry are no longer friendly. Harry had all the best of the game and couldn't put Johnny away. He tries to work another game on the wire for the next set, but Johnny won't have any more of giving up all the breaks. Johnny has a little leverage in the negotiations, Harry's two hundred dollars. He offers Harry two more games on the wire, but the break is now winner breaks and the race has to be extended to eleven. Harry ponders Johnny's proposition, then he offers to double the bet if Johnny throws in the first two breaks of the set. Johnny likes the double the bet idea, so he and Harry start their third set.

An airborne cue-ball isn't the way Harry wanted to start the match. With cue-ball in hand, Johnny sets his sights on a one-nine combination. He makes the shot, much to Harry's dismay. When Harry loses the next game, things start to get ugly. Johnny breaks and runs out the next two racks and passes Harry four games to three. Harry does squeeze out the following game, but the pressure of playing Johnny even starts to wear him down physically and mentally. Johnny goes on to win eleven games to seven. Harry starts to negotiate another game, but Johnny's not willing to give anymore weight. Harry just looks at his watch and says to Johnny, "You know what, kid, it's getting late. I think the smartest and least costly thing I could do right now is go home." He pays Johnny. "I'm looking forward to watching you play some of the hot shots from the city."

Johnny takes his money graciously and thanks Harry for the game. Fifty dollars for table time and forty for Steve cut into Johnny's winnings.

At eleven the next morning, Johnny is back at the poolroom. Constant ringing of the phone starts around eleven forty-five. With the thirty to thirty-five people already in the room, it looks like a good turnout is expected. The Calcutta will start at twelve-thirty. Johnny is sharing his table with Harry and his friend. Harry hints to Johnny he wants to buy him in the Calcutta. His reasoning to Johnny is, he can have Johnny get back some of his losses from the night before. Billy then calls and tells him that there are too may things going on in Kentucky for him to break away. Johnny is a little disappointed, but he understands. He shuts his phone off and bids on himself and the Calcutta.

True to his word, Harry has already pushed Johnny past the eighty dollar mark by the time Johnny gets into the bidding. Steve has also been active in the bidding war for Johnny. At one hundred and eighty dollars, Johnny realizes Harry is not about to give up his pursuit of Johnny. He bows out of the bidding and Harry ends up owning Johnny for the price of one hundred and eighty dollars. Johnny buys half of himself from Harry, and both men are happy with the deal.

Harry says, "I want you to know one thing, kid, I only bet on winners, and I know one when I see one." Johnny thanks Harry for the compliment.

At one-fifteen, things start to happen. Johnny is summoned to table two; his first opponent is one of the hot shots from the city. Johnny makes short work him and three more opponents on this particular day. His last match of the day is right up front and Johnny lights up the room with some sparkling play. He gets plenty of notice and finds Jersey responding very well to their newfound hero. Several people stand applauding as Johnny makes his way out of the playing area. He is besieged by fans wanting to talk to him and get to know more about him. He likes all the attention he's getting, so he's more than willing to sit down and talk to people. He's through playing for the day and has plenty of time to kill. He grabs a bite to eat and sits and talks with many of the remaining spectators. Shortly after midnight Johnny leaves the room and returns to his motel to get some rest.

# CHAPTER 21

Sneaking in the door on Sunday, about quarter of five, comes none other than Billy Bates. He has a baseball cap on and is wearing dark glasses. Johnny sees him, and Billy makes a signal to meet him in the men's room. Johnny is the first one in and Billy follows a short time later. Johnny doesn't understand what Billy is doing, but he has no time to ask questions. Billy tells him to keep doing what he's been doing. Billy does say to Johnny, "You've beaten most of the best players from the area; keep up the good work."

Wading back into the crowd, Billy acts like he's just another spectator. Johnny goes back to socializing with all the locals. In the meantime, Johnny's sitting in the "hot seat," and Tony Robles and George "Ginky" Sansoucci are battling for another shot at Johnny. Tony comes up big in the final three games of the match that was tied at six games apiece. He takes advantage of a missed seven-ball by Ginky and nails him to his chair for the rest of the set. Billy is watching, and he knows Tony has found his stroke and the speed of the table. Between the time Tony and Johnny start the final matches, Billy places several bets against Johnny. He is bold enough to give a game on the wire in the first race Tony and Johnny will play. Several people bet their money on Johnny. Harry is the biggest better; he bets all his Calcutta earnings, two hundred dollars, on Johnny to win.

Bets down, Billy sits back as Johnny does what Billy is betting he'll do. After hitting just a few balls, he says to Tony, "I'm ready to play." Tony has barely been in his seat and is coming off a two-plus run out of games of his previous match.

Billy makes a mental note to tell Johnny this may have been his biggest mistake if he loses. Shaking hands, both players take an object-ball and lag for the break. Tony sneaks in a little closer than Johnny and wins the right to break the first rack.

Steamrolling his way through the first few racks, Tony sets the tone. Johnny tries, but much to his dismay, he doesn't land as many punches as he'd like to. Tony is gaining more momentum and confidence with each rack he wins. The first set Johnny wins only four games.

During the second set, Johnny starts to think too much and fails to execute shots and position play with the precision he had shown previously. Tony becomes a silent assassin: his aim is true, and he continually makes shot after shot. The methodical way he plays leaves Johnny sitting in his chair for long periods of time. The few good chances Johnny gets he rushes to the table only to falter. Tony puts the final nails in Johnny's coffin, delivering a solid nine to three beating.

Mixed emotions are felt by many in the crowd. A local favorite, and a good guy, gives them something to cheer about, but deep down they wanted their newfound hero to win. Consoling from Tony helps Johnny feel a little better, but he still has a knot in his stomach. Steve's handing Johnny nine hundred dollars for his second-place finish and his share of the Calcutta doesn't take all the pain away, but it helps a little. What Johnny starts to witness takes all of the attention he has on his losing away. He turns his focus to what's going on with Billy.

Collecting money from several people, Billy becomes preoccupied. Johnny gets an even bigger knot in his stomach, but it's not because he has lost, it's because he figured out Billy has bet against him. He quickly gets his act together and goes out the door, slamming it behind him. He contemplates getting in the car and driving off, but he can't resist waiting for Billy.

He's hopping mad and wants an explanation right away. He sits in the car fuming as Billy takes his time coming out the door.

Nonchalantly, Billy moseys his way out to the car. He acts like nothing is wrong when he says to Johnny, "Why don't you let me drive? I'm sure you're tired from playing all weekend." Johnny just throws up his hands and gets out of the car. He can't believe someone could be so stupid and have nothing to offer Johnny to make him feel a little better. When Billy gets up on the highway, he puts the radio on and starts singing along to an old country song. This is when Johnny goes ballistic.

Pushing Billy's shoulder almost causes Billy to swerve into another car. Billy is able to recover in time, but the car is now a little bit out of control. Billy fights to pull it all together, as Johnny screams, "You bet against me, you fuckin' son of a bitch; you fuckin' bet against me." Billy pulls the car off the road before Johnny does anything else stupid. Johnny gets out of the car when Billy pulls over and runs away. He's far too angry to be around Billy right now. He's afraid he may lose it altogether and really hurt Billy.

Perched on a knoll about two hundred yards from the car, Johnny has his head down, and his eyes are glassy from his tears. Suddenly, he feels a strong hand grab his shoulder. He pushes it away and starts to run again. Billy shows his ability to vocalize. "If you run again, I'm leaving you behind." Johnny stops, but he doesn't turn around. Billy makes a small compromise and walks down to where Johnny's standing. "If it'll make you feel any better, hit me again, but remember, you'll probably be out of commission for several days again." Johnny comes back to his senses. He lets Billy convince him to come back to the car so he can explain his actions.

Father to son talks were never given to Billy, so he struggles to find the right words. After fumbling through the beginning,

Billy settles in and just tells Johnny the truth. "The reason I bet against you is because I saw a lot of what you were doing in the things I did. Believe it or not, I went to the hot seat six times and lost six times before I figured out I was doing something wrong." Billy has managed to get Johnny's attention so he starts the car and starts driving down the highway. As he drives, Billy starts to tell Johnny his history of playing in tournaments.

"Six times, Johnny, six fucking times," Billy tells Johnny. "I was coming off a long layoff and I won a tournament after two tries. It was a fluke; what never hit me was I came from the loser's side of the chart. I wasn't sitting around waiting to play for four hours. The hot seat is a special place only if you know how to handle it. After six losses, I started to take a new approach. Instead of sitting around gloating, I went for a long walk and got some fresh air. I had a small snack when I came back to the poolroom. The next thing I did was get a rack of balls and go to the table and start hitting them. The guy I was going to play wasn't sitting around waiting for me to show up. When his match did finish, I made sure he sat around for ten or fifteen minutes before we started playing. I figured I'd give him time to cool off a little and maybe time to think about who he was going to be playing and the stakes involved. When I finally cracked my cherry, I started to win on a regular basis. I was hoping I was wrong when I bet against you today. I wanted you to win. My experience and my sense of business got the best of me." Billy takes Johnny's forearm in his hands and squeezes it. He says to Johnny, "Deep down, I was praying I was wrong. What I hope comes out of this whole mess is saving you the frustration I had to go through. I'm also glad you got angry at me. If you accept what happens to you, you'll never climb to the top of the mountain." Billy has backed himself into a corner, and he tries to change the subject.

Before he thinks of a way, Johnny asks him, "You knew how to win but you started to lose again. What happened to you, Billy?" He pauses for a minute, then says, "I asked you a question, but I already know the answer. Kerry told me all about how you threw matches for the money. How could you do such a thing?"

"Deep in debt to the bookmakers, I was forced to make a decision. I could go back home with half the money I needed to pay off all my debts or I could throw the match, go home, and have some extra money if I lost. I'm playing Nick Vlahos from Massachusetts. After I hang my first ball on purpose, I have a change of heart; I'm playing to win. The only problem, I forgot to tell Nick what was going on. He puts the clamps on me and put me in a coma. By the time I'm able to do anything, he's got me beat by a score of eight games to two in a race to nine. A tough scratch later and Nick is walking away with first place money, a nice trophy, and the feeling of being a winner. My scumbag friends are up in the stands collecting all the money. I cheated people who believed in me and bet their hard earned money on a three-legged horse. I never was, and hope I never will be again, that ashamed of what I did ever again. Drugs entered my life after I came back home from throwing the match. I couldn't face who I had become so I hid behind a mask of drugs. I hope you never experience how desperate I became after becoming an addict. Throwing matches for money became easier as my daily need for drugs increased. It became hard for me to look at myself in the mirror. It went on for several years; I ran around trying to hustle anyone and everyone. I talked people into betting their money on me, and I would dump the match for half the money." Clearing his throat, Billy quietly says, "They weren't the finest moments in my life. They tell me I was shooting a three-ball in a poolroom in Connecticut. And I woke up three days later in a rehab. The only thing I knew was someone else was paying the bill. They wrote me a note: *Everyone in life deserves a second chance. If you happen to come out of your drug overdose, this will be your chance. I'm helping you because you possess a special and rare gift in your ability to handle a pool cue. When you come out of your self-induced coma, make the best of the rest of your life. I'll be watching you from a distance. Please don't go back to your old ways.* Don't ask me how or why, but I came clean with the help of God, and I've been clean ever since."

For three straight days, Billy uses the same procedure. They hit a big-city poolroom, and within the half hour, Johnny's at the table playing a big money match. Billy makes all the arrangements; Johnny makes all the shots. The system works to perfection. Johnny wins more than ten thousand dollars in a three-day span. On their way to Louisville, Johnny has had enough of trying to figure out how Billy manages to walk into a town and get big money games.

Billy laughs as he tells Johnny, "When you told me we weren't going to be hustling people anymore, I had to go to plan B." Billy pulls out a huge role of hundred dollar bills from his pocket. "Do you know what this is?"

"It's a huge role of hundred dollar bills."

"You have a fucking amazing grasp for the obvious. This is a lure that always has and always will catch the biggest fish. If you're bold enough to pull it out and show it to people in a poolroom, amazing things will start to happen. The thought of making a big score will get you a game." Billy then shows Johnny a shoulder holster with a gun. "Having this guy on your side will make sure nobody gets stupid and tries to take your money when the game is over. It's just an insurance policy. There are nice to have, but you hate to have to use them. All the games I'm getting you are with reputable people. I would never put you in jeopardy, and you have absolutely nothing to worry about." The last road sign Johnny and Billy passes has Louisville less than an hour away, they are headed for the Derby City Classic. They get there, and Johnny gets a suite. Billy returns to Lexington for business. He promises to return in time for Johnny's first match.

# CHAPTER 22

Johnny gets a call from Flo. "What's all the noise in the background?"

Flo tells Johnny, "It's Cindy, Marie, and your mother; we're all in the bar at the hotel having a victory drink. You never told me I'd be hanging around with a bunch of crazy women."

"What do you mean by crazy?"

"You do realize today was the opening round of the tournament in California, don't you? Cindy thought she was at a football game. She kept yelling out my name and cheering every time I made a nine-ball. Marie had to finally tell her she had to stop—"

"Who did you play?"

"I played the reigning state of California woman's nine-ball champion. She walked around the table like she had a dildo stuck up her ass. She had to have a pound of makeup on her face. She spoke with an accent I think she made up for herself." Flo starts laughing aloud over the phone. "Your mother is at the bar right now doing a perfect impersonation of her. Your mother and Cindy are wonderful people. I'm so glad you suggested we all get together. I'm having the time of my life hanging around with them. Marie won two hundred dollars. She's buying all the drinks."

"What was the score of the match?"

Flo giggles little before she says, "I played awful; I only beat her nine games to two."

"Don't try to drink with Cindy and my mother. You'll never make a ball in your next match."

"I'm not a drinker. Marie can join in with Cindy and your mom. I'm the designated driver. We're only having one drink here; your mother is taking us to a nice restaurant later on tonight."

Johnny makes small talk about his ups and downs on the road trip so far, and then ends with, "Well, I'll let you get back. Say hello to everyone for me."

The next night at eight is Johnny's first match against Randy LaBonte. Johnny promptly calls Billy, and he shares the news with him. Billy tells Johnny, "I'll leave here by six o'clock. The ride only takes an hour and twenty minutes. I'll be sitting in the stands by seven-thirty. Go spend some time on the tables. Get used to the lighting and the speed of the cloth."

Later, Johnny finds out there is also a room available to gamble. He is told that several money matches are going on. After practicing for half an hour, his curiosity gets the best of him. He goes to the action room to scope things out. Rico is playing a big-money match, and Johnny sits down to watch. Rico is giving up plenty of weight, yet he is still able to toy with his opponent. He's giving up three games on the wire, the wild seven-ball, and all the breaks in a race to eleven for a thousand dollars. He catches his opponent after five games. It's not enough for Rico to win the match and take the money. After he takes a nine to six lead, he starts to humiliate the man he's playing. The rest of the people gambling, start to get on Rico, to keep quiet, but he comes back saying. "If anyone of you think you're good enough to come over and shut me up, bring your money over here or shut the fuck up. I'm the king of this room, and I'll do whatever I please." Through all the nonsense, Johnny watches as Rico plays flawless pool. He is different than all the big mouth idiots Johnny has come across thus far: he has the game to backup all the bullshit. Johnny quietly removes himself from his seat and goes back to practice in the ballroom. He'll need the practice if he should encounter Rico anytime in the next few days. He plays until three-thirty, watches some early matches, then gets ready for his match.

Billy taps him on the shoulder and says, "I brought along Larry to root for you. I'd hate to be the only one clapping when you win a game."

LaBonte is introduced first, and Johnny finds out he's come down from Massachusetts to play in the tournament. Johnny remembers Billy talking about Nick Vlahos, and how he caught Billy by surprise the first time Billy was going to throw a match in the finals. Nick is also from Massachusetts. Johnny's sensors are even keener now. He's not about to let LaBonte catch him off balance. LaBonte gets a nice ovation from the crowd. Johnny's introduction is a little more than he's expecting. He's introduced as Johnny Jordan, a nephew of the great Mr. Billy Bates. The focus is directed towards Billy as he is asked to stand and be recognized by the crowd. While he's being recognized, the tournament director also tells everyone about Billy's up and coming tournament in December. When he tells everyone that it will be the largest payout of any nine-ball tournament in the history of the game, the arena explodes with enthusiasm. Luckily for Johnny, there are a few more matches to be introduced before he starts to play. He has time to collect himself and get his focus back on the game.

Diligent play by Randy leads to a two-to-two tie after four games. The race is only to seven games, and Johnny is at the table stuck behind the edge of a ball. He's too far away from the rail to elevate and jump over the object-ball. He elects to go with an elevated cue and masse around the object-ball. A beautiful stroke and follow through of the shot puts the three-ball cleanly into the corner pocket. The spin on the cue-ball catches the side and back rails, and Johnny ends up perfect on the four-ball. The next time Randy sees daylight, he's behind by three games. The spread of three games proves to be too much for Randy and Johnny goes on to win seven games to four. Randy shakes hands with Johnny. The crowd appreciates Johnny and Randy's play, and they get a nice ovation as they leave the playing area.

Turning his head to talk to a well-wisher, Johnny is bumped into by someone. His cue flies off his shoulder and lands on the floor. When Johnny gets it back together, he looks up to see Rico, who pretends it was all an accident, but Johnny knows better. Rico tries to stare down Johnny, but Johnny keeps his cool. He pretends it was his fault for not paying attention to where he was going. He gets Rico's ass a little when he says, "I'm sorry, all of these people clapping for me got me distracted." He hits Rico right between the eyes when he asks him, "Are you playing in the tournament?"

Rico boils over and says to Johnny, "Am I playing in the tournament? You know damn well I'm playing in the tournament. I'm Rico Sanchez, and I crushed your fuckin' uncle. And if you get in my way, I'll squish you like a little bug." Rico has caused a scene, and many of the spectators are booing his behavior. He turns and flips them the finger before going to his table to play his match.

Standing on the sidelines is Billy. He's ashamed Johnny has had to put up with all of Rico's bullshit because of him. He has a look of disgust on his face as he apologizes to Johnny. He also explains he had nothing to do with his introduction. He says to Johnny, "They got the nephew information through the grapevine. I guess our appearance in Providence a couple weeks ago is the talk of the pool community around the country."

Johnny puts his arm on Billy's shoulder and says, "All this was bound to happen. It's better we get it over with now."

"Didn't you just want to break his fuckin' head?"

"I was praying he'd try something stupid. I had my fist cocked and was ready to go."

"He's all mouth. I saw him go down like a lead balloon a couple of years ago in Kansas City. He ain't about to start a fight."

"That's too bad. I'd enjoy giving him a good beating."

Billy puts his arm around Johnny. "In due time, Rico will be yours."

Worrying about Rico is not the habit Billy wants Johnny to establish. Johnny has a lot more pool to play the next few days. Larry changes the subject to Billy's tournament, telling Johnny about all the new construction, the huge turnout, and how he won't recognize the place when he gets back to Lexington.

Billy tells them that he has to go back to Lexington tonight, but will be back tomorrow for Johnny's ten p.m. match. Johnny and Larry get the chance to spend time together. The next day they check out the horse races, and reminisce about their days in California. As it gets later in the day, they start back to the poolroom. On the way, Johnny asks Larry for some advice when he plays José Parica. Larry tells him, "Hang close and if you do, the pressure shifts to him. He's supposed to win."

Who's who in the world of pool are all lined up at different tables. Rico Sanchez is on table one playing Effern Reyes. Table two has Corey Duel playing Johnny Archer. Table three has Johnny playing José Parica. The introductions seem to take forever as each player has a long list of credentials. Johnny was more prepared for his introduction this time. José and Johnny do the customary handshakes before lagging for the break. Parica wins the lag, but Johnny pulls out the very close victory making the shot of the match in the final rack. The crowd responded to Johnny's great shot and the fact he's Billy's nephew.

Rico is upset that the crowd is concentrating its attention on Johnny. He had beaten Effern Reyes handily and no one seemed to notice. He starts walking over to where Billy, Larry, and Johnny are standing. Only Johnny can see him coming, he cautions Billy and Larry, "Rico's on his way." Billy says to let Rico make the first move. Five paces away Rico opens his big fucking mouth. The crowd opens a path as Rico spits out, in a high pitched voice, "Bill-y, Bill-y, Bill-y, I know you're packing plenty of molar, you always do. Do you have the guts to bet any of it on your nephew? I can get us a table in the action room. I'll give him plenty of weight if you're willing to bet say, twenty thousand."

Billy knows he could suck Rico into a bad game, but he also knows Rico is capable of winning no mater how foolish a game he makes, although Johnny is frothing at the mouth and Larry is signaling with his eyes he thinks Billy should jump all over Rico. Billy refuses to take the bait. He uses his room and the upcoming tournament as an excuse not to play. He tells Rico, "Not tonight. I've too many things going on. I might have to leave at a moment's notice."

Rico looks at Johnny and says, "You tell the world you're related to this fucking guy. I heard you and him cleaned up on the way here and now he won't bet on you with a chance to win twenty grand. The more you get to know him the more you'll understand why we parted ways years ago."

Rico turns and walks away cackling like a chicken as he walks towards the action room.

Although it's killing him and Johnny and Larry are pleading with him to go after Rico, Billy refuses to bend. Billy puts an end to it all when he says, "I have to be selfish. I want Rico to suffer the same humiliation as I had to endure."

Larry and Johnny back off after they hear Billy's request. They understand where he's coming from.

Johnny asks, "What's with him anyway/"

"Jealous," is the first word that comes from Billy's mouth. "He's jealous of anyone who gets more attention than he does. He wasn't a bad kid in the beginning. He was eager to learn, and we got along pretty well. Then, after he starts getting successful, he develops a huge ego. He insists on getting seventy-five percent of all the money we make, or as he put it, he made."

"Did he start taking drugs?"

"I wish it'd been drugs, then I could understand the way he was starting act. Rico has this ugly attitude. He thinks because he's a great pool player, the world owes him a living. It's a shame because he's missing out on any endorsements he might have had if he could only act civilized."

Lost in all the confusion is Johnny's fabulous shot on the six-ball to pull out his match with Parica. Billy and Larry both give Johnny high praise for the hanging in and having the guts to pull the trigger on such a tough shot. Johnny tells Larry, "I just tried to do what you told me earlier. Hang close and maybe he'll make a mistake. I think you were right. He did start to feel the pressure because he was the favorite; he was supposed to win."

Billy says to Larry, "You used my material on the boy."

"You weren't here. I had no other choice. The kid was acting like he could use some friendly advice. The only thing I did was give it to him."

"As long as he's getting the right advice, it really doesn't matter whose mouth it comes out of."

Johnny notices that his cell phone has a new voicemail. It's Flo telling him that she's won another match in California and she's been offered a modeling contract. Johnny calls her and tells her his great news that he beat one of the world's best, seven to six.

After telling Larry and Billy the news, the trio has a few drinks, then heads to bed.

The next day, Johnny must get focused for his match with Johnny Archer, who is already at the table when Johnny gets to where he has to go. Rico and Strickland are already on the table next to Johnny's warming up for their match. There is almost an hour to go before the match will start. The crowd grows every time Johnny looks around. Larry and Billy are sitting ringside. At two o'clock, the introductions begin. The opening lag hasn't even taken place and Rico and Earl are already in disagreement. Rico wants to lag from the side of the table from which Earl is lagging. The referee stands, rolling his eyes as two grown men argue such a stupid point. A flip of the coin to determine where each player will lag from, offered by the referee, doesn't satisfy either player. Finally, the ref tells Earl to lag, and he will mark his ball. Begrudgingly, Earl lags his ball, and, of course, he doesn't have a good lag. He bitches as Rico wins the lag and the opening break.

Torture has to be simpler than playing beside Earl and Rico. They manage, at three different points in their match, to shut down play on every table. The two Johnny's have to deal with constant bickering from both players. Hard to believe, but both Johnny and Archer are playing some pretty good pool despite what's going on around them. At five games apiece, Archer breaks and doesn't make a ball. Johnny comes to the table looking at a good chance to run out. He begins trudging his way through the rack. On the seven-ball, Johnny has a two-rail position shot into the right-and corner pocket. Rico comes right into his sights as he makes his commitment to the shot. Johnny's head comes off the shot, and he misses it. Rico is on the other table trying to get the cue-ball into a place it's never going to get. In the meantime, Johnny has sold out to

Archer. He comes out of his chair like a rocket. He knows he has gotten a chance he never expected. Archer not only makes the final three balls to win game six, he breaks and runs out the next rack to win the set. Furious and dejected, Johnny sits in his chair much the same way Billy did when Rico beat him on television. He gets a pat on the back from Billy consoling him and trying to lessen his agony of defeat.

Billy says to Johnny, "Let's get the fuck out of this place."

"I can buy back into the tournament for another hundred bucks."

"You want to pay another hundred bucks, so these fucking assholes can torture you again?" Johnny understands what Billy is saying to him; he breaks down his cue and puts it away. Billy, Larry, and Johnny walk away from the arena. A small amount of clapping can be heard as they're almost out of the ballroom. Johnny looks back, and Rico is parading around the table with his cue over his head. It's obvious to Johnny who has won the match on table one. Johnny makes a solemn vow to himself to someday get even.

Halfway back to Lexington, Billy breaks a long silence. "Do either one of you know what all the bullshit is about?"

Larry says, "You mean the bullshit between Earl and Rico was staged?"

"Naw," says Billy. "They're not that smart. It has to do with the fact that they're upset with the fact they are playing each other and either one of them could possibly lose. When a top player is playing a worthy adversary who may beat him, he gets insecure and starts acting like a little baby. What is also going on, they are pissing off the rest of the players. So whoever wins the match is going to be a big favorite to win the tournament. We have to eliminate any bullshit like that from my tournament. I won't tolerate it. I want it to be in print that actions like we witnessed today will not be tolerated. The player or players involved will be automatically disqualified. I want to be able to hear a pin drop when people are playing at my place. I want the best pool player to win my tournament, not the biggest fucking asshole." Billy looks back to Johnny. "Cat got your tongue back there?"

"I develop the problem, now and then. I've got this knot my stomach. I want to go back to Louisville and punch the shit out of Rico to get rid of it."

"You gotta let it go. If you walk around feeling that way, if you ever get on the table with him, that knot will be right back there, like it is now. Probably even bigger! You can't function with something like that eating at you."

"How do I get rid of it?"

"I used to scream at the top of my lungs, but this case is different. When you were playing, I was also watching Rico. He kept looking at you; that means you got his attention and respect. Take the positive things from the tournament. A great win over Parica, and you held your own against Archer. How's that knot feeling now?"

"It shrunk a bit." Johnny puts the window down and puts his head out the window and screams at the top of his lungs. "The lump is gone now."

The lump may be gone but deep in the crevices of Johnny's mind lying dormant is Johnny's desire to crucify Rico.

"I think your girlfriend could use some moral support in California. Why don't you head down there?"

Johnny is in shock, then comes to his senses and thanks Billy.

# CHAPTER 23

Johnny lands in Los Angeles, grabs some pizzas, and heads to his mother's house.

After catching up, Johnny and Flo decide to stay at Cindy's place since she has a guest house. They are finally able to get back in tune with each other after too much time apart. A night of passion ensues, then they fall asleep in each other's arms.

The next day, after Elaine tells Johnny numerous times how wonderful she thinks Flo is, they all make their way to the tournament.

Except for a few faces, many of the girls still playing are familiar to Johnny. Liz, Johnny, Elaine, Marie, and Cindy get seated to watch Flo's match. She's still undefeated and playing her third match of the tournament. Bets down, introductions made, Flo and Patty Baker lag for the opening break. Patty wins the lag and immediately starts to show why she's undefeated at this point in the tournament. Flo starts off shaky, but then gets into her zone and wins the last three games for a final score of nine to six. Patty's a gracious loser; she shakes Flo's hand and wishes her the best of luck the rest of the tournament.

Competition gets even stronger from here on for Flo. Johnny has talked to someone about the eight remaining women left, and they are all very well-respected players. Johnny's even happier he didn't bet the match when Flo's nemesis from Albuquerque shows up at her table for the next match. It's Becky Slater, and she looks awfully strong as she hits a few racks before the match starts. Flo doesn't seem too affected by Becky's presence. She goes about her business like she's the only one in the place.

Bracing himself for the worst, Johnny sits back in his chair to take in the match. Marie knows Flo has all she can handle playing Becky. She taps Johnny on the shoulder and shows him her fingers, which are crossed for good luck. Elaine senses both Johnny and Marie are nervous about the match.

Flo breaks out to an early lead and never looks back. She constantly frustrates Becky by doing all the little things that make or break you in a match. Whether it's playing great safeties or making tough shots when she needs too. Flo is playing a tune that Becky can't even hum. The frustration gets to Becky. She vents her anger by throwing the bridge on the floor after miscuing, attempting to make one of the few decent shots she gets in the race to nine. Flo wins the match by a final score of 9-3.

The next day, cameras are everywhere as television has shown up for the final day of the tournament. Flo is one of the final four undefeated players, so she has a short interview to which she's obligated to submit. She gets it out of the way as soon as possible, then hits the practice table and puts her nose to the grindstone. Not long after, her match starts against Christine Ly, who is regarded as one of the top Asian players on the tour.

After twelve games, they are tied six to six. Everyone is totally engulfed in Flo and Christine's match. They're the only two players who haven't finished their match. Christine has a big advantage. She has won the previous rack, which could have gone either way, and is breaking the final game. She makes a ball on the break. Her next move is playing a safety on the one-ball. She banks the one-ball back down table near the back rail for a possible combination of the one-nine and leaves Flo safe. If Flo fails to contact the one-ball she appears to be doomed. Flo hits the cue-ball, which contacts the side and back rails before contacting the one-ball; after it hits the one, the cue-ball slides along the back rail. It makes contact with the nine-ball, sending it into the corner pocket. The crowd erupts at the sight of the nine leaving the table. The celebration may be premature. The cue-ball is rolling towards the corner pocket. It runs out of energy just as it gets to the edge of the pocket. Flo has stood hovered over the cue-ball, holding her breath, hoping it would stay on the table. She gets her way. The crowd still stands applauding Flo's shot to win the match. Christine somehow staggers to the table to congratulate her.

Flo dodges the media and finds her way to Johnny and the others. Emotions are running high for Flo; she doesn't know whether to laugh or cry. Winning this match has guaranteed Flo a trip to Kentucky to play in Billy's tournament. Johnny pulls her back to earth when he reminds her she still has a lot of pool to play before the tournament is over. Flo plants a kiss on Johnny's lips, then reluctantly goes to do an interview.

Later that day, Flo is practicing for her next match, which is against Karen Black. Karen says, "I never dreamed I'd bump into you at this point of a major event. You had to have had an awfully easy draw."

Flo is not about to let Karen get the best of her at anything. "I used the thousand dollars I beat you out of in Albuquerque to bribe my opponents, and they let me win."

"Maybe you should have held on to the fuckin' money. I've got a thousand more that says I kick your ass."

"Oh, look," Flo points at Johnny, "There's my backer again. He's got two thousand that says you haven't got a fuckin' prayer to beat me. Are we on?"

"I can't afford to bet two thousand dollars; I have expenses to meet."

Flo politely says to Karen, "If you can't afford to make a bet, maybe you should learn to keep your mouth shut. Where

I come from, it's put up or shut up. So I guess you'll have nothing more to say to me during our match."

Karen grunts and groans a few things under her breath as the introductions of the players are about to begin. Karen wins the lag and breaks to start the match. The first rack starts out in the defensive mode for both players. A few balls are tied up, and the ladies jockey for position trying to gain an advantage. The rack lasts almost ten minutes before Flo manages to outmaneuver Karen and win the game. The purists of the game applaud Flo's ability to outthink Karen and win such a strategic rack.

Fueled by her victory in the first rack, Flo steps on the pedal the next few games. She manages to run-off four consecutive games before Karen is able to counterattack. One game hardly deters Flo's dominance of the match. She's back in control after she wins the next game. Karen sits in her chair slouched over. She's taking an awful beating. Karen manages to win two more games, but the final score of seven games to three leaves her shell-shocked. Karen never comes out of her chair to congratulate Flo. She extends a limp hand from her chair to Flo. Johnny leads a large group of fans giving Flo a standing ovation as she comes from the playing area. The announcer tells the crowd there will be a ten-minute break between the start of the next match, which is won by Becky Slater.

Build-up for the final match between Flo and Becky has the crowd buzzing. Flo has the first shot after breaking; she is jacked-up shooting over a ball. With very little hesitation, she fires the one-ball into the corner pocket. This sets the crowd off right from the start. It takes a while for them to settle down before Flo continues to shoot. She runs the table in convincing style. Any sign that she may be nervous never comes to light. Becky gets to the table and shows she's willing to fight back.

She makes a nice bank-shot off Flo's push-out and wins a game of her own. The crowd becomes the beneficiary of some of the finest play ever witnessed in a women's final. Ten games are played, and the score is even at five games apiece. Neither player has missed an attempted shot.

Grinding out shot after shot finally takes its toll on Becky. She over-cuts a tough six-ball shot at a side pocket. An unexpected chance has Flo suddenly in position to take the lead. The shot is simple, but Flo has to move the cue-ball back down table for position on the seven-ball. The nine-ball is in the natural path of the cue-ball, so Flo has to be creative. She makes a thin hit of the six using reverse English. The cue-ball hits the side and back rails, then goes back to the same side rail it had just left. There is enough spin on the cue-ball to propel it back down table. Flo ends up perfect on the seven and runs out the remaining balls.

Flo does what every great champion does when they get some one on the ropes. She delivers the knock-out punch, running out the final rack. The crowd noise is at a fever pitch. Flo's not sure how to act she's never done this before. Becky grabs her arm and raises it. She then proceeds to march Flo around the arena. Both ladies ham it up with the crowd The show they put on deserves all the accolades they receive from their adoring fans. Becky lets Flo stand alone in the middle of the arena to get the most of one final show of appreciation from the crowd. When everything finally gets quieted down, Flo unscrews her cue-stick and her break-stick and puts them into her case. She takes one final look around before walking over to her friends and Johnny.

Marie says to everyone, "Drinks are on me tonight."

After the celebration, Flo and Johnny are alone at last in Cindy's guesthouse. Until well after sunrise, Flo and Johnny continue the onslaught of sexual pleasure.

After getting up and getting ready, they head to the airport. On the way, Flo and Johnny's discuss their plans for Thanksgiving. They want everyone to meet in Albuquerque. At the airport, Johnny wishes Flo and Marie a safe trip back to New Mexico.

At dinner that night, Elaine tells Johnny what's going on with her divorce from Cliff. "He's fighting me all the way with this thing. He's not budging when it comes to giving up anything. The worst part is, if he finds out about Billy, things could get better for him and worse for me. My lawyer says I have to move fast before he finds out. I have to meet with him the day after tomorrow."

"Can't you just lie and tell the judge you had no idea I wasn't Cliff's son? He lied to you over and over all through the years you were married to him."

"A good lawyer will use his behavior as an excuse; he'll say Cliff behaved that way because he knew I had lied to him. It's so crazy." Elaine begins to break down. "I had no idea it could turn into something so big."

Johnny offers to stay home and forget about going back to Kentucky, but Elaine says, "It's my mess, and I'll clean it up." She gets up from the table and starts to clean it off. As she takes the dishes and everything else that goes with them, she says, "I wish the mess I made with my life was as easy to manage as cleaning up after a meal." Elaine and Johnny have little more to say to each other before they leave the kitchen and go to the den to watch television. Then Elaine goes to sleep.

# CHAPTER 24

The next day, Flo calls and says, "Liz called me today and said the shoe deal company wants to start out with two spokespeople, the winners of Billy's upcoming event. One woman and one man will have to tour the country putting on exhibitions in promoting the use of the shoes. The best news is, they're going to add two hundred thousand dollars to Billy's tournament."

"Exciting?" says Johnny. "It's absolutely fantastic! Just the fact that we got in the door of a major shoe company is exciting enough. The added money and the players touring the country is icing on the cake."

"Liz got me a cue company endorsement, and I have to go back to New York for a second look by the modeling agency. Liz is with Billy today, so I'm meeting her on Thursday. Liz told me that I should consider quitting my job. I'm going to be very busy flying around the country. What do you think I should do?"

"Talk it over with Giuseppe and let him make the decision. If it gets to be too much of a pain in the neck for him, I'm sure he'll let you know. I'm surprised you're able to talk this long. What's going on? Aren't you at work?"

"Oh, shit, I'm five minutes past my break time. Love you, goodbye."

Flo hangs up before Johnny can say anything.

Elaine comes in the room and says, "I talked to my lawyer this week and have a court date set up. The problem is, it's the second week in December. That's when you'll be playing in Kentucky. The good part is that it's on that Monday. I had hoped to come and watch you play. I asked my lawyer if he can get another date. He told me if we postpone it could be six months before I can get another date."

Johnny tells his mom to do what she has to do and not worry about whether she gets to watch him play in Kentucky.

The next day, Johnny and Elaine get tickets and fly to Albuquerque for Thanksgiving to be with Flo, Marie, and her husband Pedro.

Johnny goes out on the road for the next week. He drives up to Palo Alto and plays Dale Caldwell for a day and a half. He squeezes out four hundred dollars. Dale gives him names and rooms to play on his way back home. Johnny fattens his wallet, even more, and gets home the night before he and his mom leave for Albuquerque.

# CHAPTER 25

Elaine meets a nice man named David on the flight and tells him if she doesn't reconnect with Billy she'll give him a call. She's ready to move on from Cliff. Once on the ground, they head to see Flo at her work and have lunch. Flo tells Johnny, "The modeling agency has signed me to a two-year contract with a guarantee of at least forty thousand dollars work for the next two years."

Breaking the good news to everyone about Flo's two-year contract brings some mixed reviews. Marie fears Flo may have to move closer to New York to meet her modeling commitments and stay active on the women's professional tour. She says to Johnny and Elaine, "I finally got the daughter I wanted my whole life, and her success will probably force her away from here. I'm happy for her, but I'll miss her dearly."

Johnny tries to keep the day more upbeat. "Flo's not going anywhere right now, and if she does, she's only a phone call away."

Dessert consists of one strawberry shortcake and four spoons, so everyone can take a few bites. When the check comes, or fails to come in this case, Flo has already taken care of the bill. Johnny gives the waitress a substantial tip. Marie and Elaine decide to play some pool. Pedro is happy sitting around sipping a beer and watching the girls play. Johnny goes out to the car and gets his cue. He comes back inside, gets a rack of balls, and goes over in the far corner of the room to practice by himself.

A few hours go by and Elaine, Marie, and Pedro go back home and take a nap. The come back later on, and Flo and

Johnny play in a tournament. They are handicapped through the roof and finish third and fourth. Elaine is impressed watching her son play for the first time.

Line dancing, in the new wing of Giuseppe's restaurant, becomes the focus of the rest of the evening. Flo, Marie, Pedro, and Elaine join right in on all the fun. Johnny's a little reluctant at first so Flo takes him into the corner and gives him a few small pointers on how the dance steps go. Johnny's out there, in the middle of everything, after ten minutes of personal instruction from Flo. It's great for Elaine; she doesn't need a partner to participate in all the fun. When the music does change to a slow dance, Johnny and Pedro share their duties and dance with Elaine.

Last call comes in the middle of a slow song to which Johnny and his mom are dancing. Elaine says to Johnny, "You're going to think this is weird, but if I close my eyes, it's like I'm dancing with Billy."

Johnny asks his mom, "You danced with Billy?"

Elaine says to Johnny, "Didn't I tell you that part?"

"I'm not sure," says Johnny. "Can you refresh my memory?"

"We were in a club, and after Billy rescued me from this moron, we had a drink and then we danced."

"Now I remember, you did tell me that part of the story."

"I know what it is now. It's your hands and shoulders. That's where you two are very similar. Do you think I'm being weird?"

"I think it's great that after all these years you can still remember how it felt to be held by Billy."

"He was the one man who felt perfect in every way. How could I ever forget him?"

Everyone is stuffed to the gills after eating Thanksgiving dinner. Clean-up duties fall on Flo and Johnny. Marie and Elaine are worn out, and it's their turn to sit and relax. Pedro falls asleep, while Marie and Elaine shoot the breeze and sip on a glass of wine. Clean up takes a good half hour.

When Flo and Johnny are just about finished, the phone rings. It's Marie's son, and she lights up talking to him on the phone. The conversation lasts a long time as they cover everything from A to Z talking to her son, his wife, and their two children. Pedro even gets in a few minutes of airtime himself. That conversation leads to another conversation. Flo takes out her cell phone and calls her uncle and grandfather who practically raised her. After that, Johnny begins to call Billy on his cell phone. It's been awhile since they have spoken. Johnny asks his mom if she wants to say hello before he makes the call. Elaine's not sure whether or not she's ready to talk to Billy. She tells Johnny to ask Billy and see how he feels about talking to her. Johnny's isn't comfortable being put in the middle, but he goes along with his mom's request.

Three people talking on the phone, in the same room, doesn't add up for Johnny. He takes his phone into the kitchen before calling Billy. On the third ring, Billy answers the phone. "Hello," he says. Johnny returns his hello. They simultaneously say to each other, "Happy Thanksgiving." Billy takes over the first part of the conversation. He updates Johnny on all the great progress the tournament is making. He talks about his meeting with Liz and says to Johnny, "You might want to hook-up with that lady. She's got a lot on the ball and a bunch of great ideas." Billy asks Johnny, "Remember the girl in Maine I gave my card to?" Johnny remembers the girl and he tells Billy he does. "She's coming down here to work for me. She's going to start working here on Saturday. I think she's the last piece of the puzzle I need to organize the tournament. I'm putting her in charge of the housing at the university. She told me over the phone that she would have no problem taking care of that end of the business. Listen to me. I'm doing all the talking. I haven't even asked where you are."

"Albuquerque," says Johnny, "I'm with Flo, Marie, and her husband. My mom is also here. We flew from California the day before yesterday. My mom and Marie got friendly when Flo played in the tournament in Los Angeles. Marie invited us all to come here for the holiday."

Billy butts in, "That girl of yours is the talk of the pool world right now. I heard she's playing awfully good."

"You'll see for yourself in a few weeks time."

"The women won't start playing until a few days after the men because of the discrepancies in the sizes of the fields."

"Flo quit working full-time and plans on coming to Kentucky early to watch me play."

"That's great, I'm all for it. Have you played much pool since you left here?"

Describing all his exploits in California to Billy kicks up a bunch of old memories for Billy. When Johnny mentions the name Dale Cardwell, Billy can't believe his ears. "I played him years ago, and he was as tough as nails." Johnny tells Billy they played for a day and a half and he came out two sets ahead of Dale. Billy listens as Johnny tells them about the rest of the people he played and the rooms and towns they played in. Billy can envision most of the rooms and some of the players with whom Johnny bumped heads. Billy is happy with the work Johnny has done and tells him so. "Did you use the lure?"

"I sure did, and it worked to perfection."

"What's the grand total of winnings?"

Three thousand dollars after expenses sounds great to Billy. "I held back on the size of the lure I used because I was out on my own."

Billy commends Johnny for being smart. "You don't want to invite trouble by flashing too much money."

Arrangements are being discussed for when Johnny returns to Kentucky. Johnny will be back here on Monday. Billy tells him, "I've arranged a game for you in Cincinnati on Tuesday. Larry could use a break, so I'll have him make the trip with you. You might be gone a day or two. By the time you get back here there should be plenty of players filtering into town for some early action. I'm running tournaments all weekend long prior to the start of the tournament. I don't think you'll have any problem keeping busy."

Fresh coffee is starting to be brewed by Elaine in preparation for dessert. Marie has ended her conversation, and she starts taking desserts from the refrigerator. Billy and Johnny continue to talk and the conversation comes around to being with family. Johnny's senses Billy might like to say hello to Elaine. He works up the nerve to finally ask the question. Billy stalls for a few seconds, suggesting Elaine might be too busy to talk. Johnny puts Billy at ease when he says, "She's been dying to say hello. Why don't you two just take a minute and get reacquainted?" Johnny walks over to his mom and hands her the phone. Elaine's hand is shaking a little, she takes a deep breath, and says, hello to Billy.

Breaking the ice isn't easy. Billy takes the lead and says to Elaine, "Hello, Katie, it's been awhile."

Elaine feels like she's been stuck with a knife, she drops the phone and wraps her arms around herself. Her head falls down close to her lap and she is openly sobbing. She has to excuse herself and run into the bathroom. Johnny picks up the phone and tells Billy.

"My mom's a little upset."

He stalls long enough for Elaine to open the bathroom and signal to Johnny she's ready to talk again.

Alone in the bathroom Elaine, pulls herself together comes clean.

"I lied to you, my name isn't Katie Starr. It's Elaine Jordan, and when I met you my real name was Elaine Crawford. It's the last lie I ever told in my life."

"I wasn't exactly honest myself, and I wish that was the last time I ever told a lie. As you may remember I'm not the easiest person when it comes to opening up and expressing my feelings. But I have to tell you when Johnny hit me and threw your picture at me—when I saw you my body when numb. I couldn't feel anything but an aching in my heart. He also doesn't know, but one day I went into his place and found where he kept the picture. I had my own copy made and look at you often."

"I'm touched, and I must let you know I've watched the tape I made of you playing probably as often as you look at me."

"We can't change the past. Maybe deep down inside the reason I played on television was so that our lives could once again cross, I don't know. I'd love to see you again."

Elaine is more relaxed and she says, "I plan on coming to Kentucky, but I have to be in court on the Monday the tournament starts. I'll get there as soon as I can."

A light tap on the door leads to Johnny saying, "Deserts are on the table."

Elaine explains her situation, and Billy encourages her to go back and join everyone.

She says goodbye to Billy.

Billy tells her what a great job she did raising Johnny before he also says goodbye.

All eyes are on Elaine. She turns to her audience, lets out a big sigh of relief, and says, "That went pretty well." She's happy to tell everyone, "Billy wants me to come to Kentucky for the tournament." Marie tries to hand the Elaine a piece of apple pie and some ice cream. Elaine tells Marie, "I'll take half of what you put on my dish. When I go to Kentucky to see Billy I want to look my best." Elaine asks Marie, "Is there a spa or gym around here that I can go to the next two days?"

"I have a membership to a spa, and I can bring a guest." They make plans to go.

Early to rise the next day is Flo, and she suggests Johnny try Snooker's again for some action.

Meanwhile, Marie and Elaine have already made plans to go shopping. Johnny is off the hook as far as entertaining his mother is concerned. Marie tells him, "I promise that I'll keep her busy."

Forced to entertain himself for the day, Johnny gets cleaned up and heads out the door bound for Snooker's. He doesn't know it but a hotshot home from college had come in and challenged the whole place on Wednesday night. None of the better players were there, so he walked around like he was God offering anybody who wanted to play the wild eight-ball. Johnny soon finds out what went on from someone in the room who had watched him play the last time he was in town. Johnny asks the stranger who's telling the story to describe the person to him. The stranger tells Johnny, "I don't need to describe him. You'll know who he is five minutes after he comes in the door."

Mother Nature calls Johnny to the men's room. When he comes back into the room, he's called to from someone clear across the room. The words, "Hey you, you want to play some?" ring loud and clear. Johnny looks over, and here is a young man wearing a twisted baseball hat, flapping his mouth up and down chewing a wad of gum. He points his finger at Johnny and says, "I'm talking to you. You want to play some?" Johnny wants to punch the jerk right the mouth, but he'd rather punish him on the table first.

Johnny says to his challenger, "I was told you're giving the wild eight-ball to all comers." The trap is set, and Johnny has live meat for bait. The jerk is interested in getting to know Johnny.

He says to Johnny, "My name is Gary Dunn." Johnny introduces himself, but they never shake hands. Gary tells Johnny, "If you want the wild eight, it comes with a price. I like to play races to seven for a hundred dollars."

Johnny hems and haws for a while, and he makes a counter proposal to Gary. He says, "Why don't we play ten ahead for five hundred?"

Gary hasn't come equipped for this kind of action. He says to Johnny, "I'll have to run down the bank and get some money if were going to play for those kind of stakes."

Johnny tells Gary, "I'm not going anywhere. I can wait for you to go get the money."

Gary can't run out the door fast enough to get the money. He must think he has quite the fish dangling on his line. When Gary gets back to Snooker's, he and Johnny post five hundred apiece. Gary asks for a little practice time before they start. Johnny watches as Gary tries to impress him with flashy and less than intelligent play. Two racks of practice are all he needs to determine it's time to play.

Thirty games are all it takes for Johnny to rob Gary, and he's taking losing very badly. He says, "Nobody except for Bill and maybe Paco from this room is good enough to beat me with the wild eight." He screams at Johnny, "I played in this room all summer and never lost. Who the fuck are you, and where do come from?"

Johnny walks over to Gary and says, "Don't you think you should've found out before you played me for five hundred?"

Gary tries to appeal to Johnny human side. He's almost in tears when he says, "I just lost most of the money I had saved for school."

Johnny's unsympathetic. "Maybe you should consider finding a job when you go back to school."

Gary is desperate; he offers Johnny his cue in place of the money. Johnny tells Gary, "I don't need a cue, I have one." Johnny puts an end to the conversation. He tells Gary, "You came in here pointing your fingers acting like you were the greatest player in the world. You made an open challenge to me, and you lost your money. You made a bad game. I could've given you the wild eight, and you gave it to me. Maybe this little lesson today will help you grow up. Now, if you want to play for another five hundred, I'll play you even; if not, go bother someone else. I have nothing else to discuss with you."

Gary heads for the hills, slamming the door to Snooker's behind him. Johnny gets a couple of pats on the back from the local patrons. One of the patrons mocks Gary as he points his finger at Johnny and says, "Hey, you! Yeah, you! You want to play some?" Johnny can't help it, he sits down and laughs openly at what the patron has just said and done. Johnny calls the waitress over and orders a sandwich for himself. He also orders a cold beer and buys a drink for anyone in the room that wants one. Johnny spends the rest of the afternoon practicing and making new friends. He's had enough excitement for one afternoon.

Five o'clock rolls around and not much is happening at Snooker's. Johnny calls Marie to let her know that he will be having supper at the house. Marie tells Johnny that she had talked to Flo about twenty minutes ago. "Flo didn't want to call you in case you were in the middle of a game. We decided we'd go to a movie tonight after Flo gets out of work. I hope you don't mind."

"Sounds like a good idea to me."

They go to the movies and get back to Marie's after midnight.

Flo and Johnny lie awake in bed and talk privately about the events of the last few days. The highlight for both of them was Billy and Elaine's phone conversation.

"The call picked my mother's spirits up. I've been worried about her drinking so much wine. I was glad to see her have water at the restaurant."

"It's going to be exciting having everyone in Kentucky for the tournament." Flo does hesitate to ask, "What about Marie and Pedro?"

"Billy says he's gonna need a lot of help to pull this thing off. Maybe he can find a job for both of them. Who knows, Marie has made lot of money betting on you. She loves the action. Maybe they'll come just to enjoy the tournament."

After a small kiss, Flo turns on her side and says goodnight. Johnny rolls over and does the same.

Beehives can't get any more active than Flo when she's running late for work. Johnny smart enough to just stay out of the way and doesn't ask questions. When Flo leaves, Johnny starts to prepare for his grueling day at the poolroom, a little past eleven. He's out the door and driving to Snooker's shortly before noon. To his surprise, the room is fairly busy when he arrives.

Never noticing the hours were posted on the door at Snooker's, Johnny sees that it opens at ten o'clock on Saturday mornings. The houseman recognizes Johnny and greets him with a friendly hello. They talk about Johnny's demolition of Gary the day before. The houseman thanks Johnny for putting Gary in his place. "I was ready to bar the punk from this place. Most of the people who come in here want to relax and have fun. I don't need him coming in here and challenging the whole place. It makes people feel uncomfortable. I might start to lose some of my steady customers. I try to keep the social players and the gamblers away from each other in my room as much as possible." The houseman introduces himself to Johnny, he says, "I'm Jimmy Smith." He holds out his hand to shake hands with Johnny.

"Johnny Jordan, but you can call me J.J."

"Why can't more pool players act like you, quiet, confident, and less apt to make fools out of themselves?"

"Most pool players run with the assumption that the squeaky wheel gets the grease. If they don't create the action, it's never going to happen." Johnny tells Jimmy about Action Central in Billy's poolroom. Jimmy likes the idea and says he may try it.

"Are you interested in playing for twenty dollars?"

Johnny says to Jimmy, "I'd be willing to play for nothing. I just love the play the game."

Jimmy points over to a middle-aged man playing by himself on table three. He says to Johnny, "That guy over there will play all day for twenty dollars a set. He's quite a player, but he limits his betting to twenty dollars, hence the nickname, Twenty-Dollar Bill." Jimmy adds, "He's only betting twenty, but he plays like he's betting fifty thousand. He's a real grinder."

"I'll quietly go over and ask him to play."

Five sets later, Johnny tucks the toughest twenty dollars he's ever made in his pants pocket.

Space at tables is at Giuseppe's is at a premium. Flo manages to barter with a few of the regulars to carve out seating for five. Pedro tells Johnny he's willing to take on the responsibility of the designated driver. He tells Johnny to cut loose if he wants and have some fun. Elaine announces that she's off the wagon for the night. She's with good friends and wants to enjoy the evening. They order their first round of drinks and wait for the music to start at nine o'clock.

Like clockwork, the DJ starts playing on the dot of nine. The whole left side of the room shifts out onto the dance floor. For the next few hours, the DJ keeps the crowd pumped-up. He raises the volume of the music and plays it continually except for the karaoke breaks. It's a fun group, which makes it easy on the DJ. Not too many people sit around doing nothing. At twelve-thirty, last call is given, and the final opportunity to sing a song is also presented. Johnny picks a Kenny Roger's song, "She Believes in Me." When the song starts, Johnny changes the words to fit the life of a pool player. He sings:

While she lay sleeping, I stay out late at night and shoot some pool.

And sometimes, oh the nights can be so cruel.

It's good when I finally make it home, all alone, while she lays dreaming.

I try to get undressed without the light.

And quietly she says how was your night?

I come to her and say it was all right, and I hold her tight.

And she believes in me.

I'll never know just what she sees in me.

I told her someday, if I can get in stroke, and I don't choke.

I just might find a way.

But she has faith in me, and so I go on trying faithfully.

And who knows maybe on some special night, when the rolls are right.

I will find a way.

While she waits for me, while she waits for me.

While she lays waiting.

I stumble to the kitchen for a bite.

And see my little cue stick in the night.

Just waiting for me like a secret friend, there's no end.

I think about a shot I missed or two.

When I was torn between the things, I should do.

Then she says, for me to wake her up when I'm through.

God her love is true.

Many couples have come out onto the dance floor, when Johnny sings the final chorus of the song.

And she believes in me.

I'll never know just what she sees in me.

I told her someday, if my game is right.

I'll find a way, find a way.

While she waits, (big ending), for me.


A standing ovation is given to Johnny by many of the couples on the dance floor. A lot of the men and women are also involved in the game of pool.

When they get into the parking lot, Johnny tosses his keys to Pedro and tells him to drive home. Pedro says to Johnny, "You're not drunk."

"I want to sit in the back seat between my two favorite women in the world."

Nights like this don't come along every day of the week. Johnny and Flo know it, and they go inside and stay upstairs in Marie's house. They spend the next few hours talking about the past few weeks, and how much excitement Flo created for them in California. Johnny figures it's a good time to ask Marie and Pedro if they're coming to Kentucky. Marie's not sure if Pedro wants to go. She says to Johnny, "I'm not sure if we're going."

Pedro says to Marie, "I'm sure we're going, or at least I'm sure I'm going to go. I missed all the fun in California."

Marie looks at Johnny and says, "I guess were going."

Johnny tells Marie and Pedro he may be able to work something out with Billy to pay their expenses. "It may require working a few hours to help out with the tournament." Marie and Pedro had no qualms about earning their keep. With everything settled, good nights are said and Flo and Johnny go downstairs to be alone.

Any thoughts of a long, wild night of sex have been extinguished by too much alcohol and far too long of a day. Flo does manage to arouse Johnny's interests for one role in the hay. She comes out of the bathroom wearing a sailor's outfit. In this case, it's a half-drunken sailor.

Flo has a hat for Johnny, and as she puts it on his head. She laughs saying, "The captain of the ship has instructed me to do to you whatever floats your boat."

Floating his boat soon becomes rocking his world. Flo and Johnny are soon riding the waves of each other's body movements, swimming endlessly in a sea of love. The rush of the waves soon becomes too violent for their bodies to hold back their love, as their bodies erupt with pleasure, their love juices flow, cascading from their bodies. They hold each other for dear life as the feelings they have come to share drown them into a deep sleep.

The next day Johnny and Flo find out they're on their own until dinner time. Flo says, "I'd like to show you the place where I used to live. It's about an hour's ride out of town. It would mean a lot to me if you came and saw where I grew up as a child."

"I'd be glad to take a ride out there with you."

Soon, Johnny sees a sign for the reservation, then comes to a small run-down community. A swirling breeze blows tumbleweeds and debris into the air. Two small dogs run beside Johnny's car and bark as he drives. It's a far cry from his neighborhood. The houses border on being shacks. What signs of life there are consist of older men and women and very young parents with their children. Most people are smoking cigarettes. Johnny spots a few with bottles of alcohol. Flo stops Johnny on a corner lot. She gets out of the car and walks around for a while. Johnny has a feeling that Flo wants to be alone, so he leaves her that way. She drops to her knees and prays for a few minutes. She takes some dirt from the ground, tosses it the air, and watches as it disperses. She also says a few things in her native language looking into the sky. Johnny has come out of the car and comes up behind Flo, he places his hands lightly on here shoulders.

"Was it always like this?"

Flo stares straight ahead, "I never really noticed too much when I was living here. This was all I ever knew. The place we're standing is where my house used to be. My uncle fell asleep with a lit cigarette two years ago. He and my grandfather got out but they lost what little they had and since have moved away. The last I knew my uncle had a construction job in Phoenix and is supporting his father."

"Can't your people do anything to improve their situation?

"I'm a Pema, we're a small tribe, and most of us live in Arizona. We petitioned to build a casino. But another tribe with more influence was given the rights, and we were left out in the cold. To answer your question, it's getting worse every time I come back."

"The ritual you seemed to be going through. What was that all about?"

"I thanked my forefathers for sending me the person I feel has made me a complete woman and asked if they accept you as one of us. I asked if they could share part of their spirits with you. They asked if you were worthy of such a great gift from our people, and I told them you saved my soul and spirit and I feel a great need to share something this great with you."

Flo stands and faces Johnny, "My people have honored my request." She takes Johnny's hands in hers, "Can you feel the spirit?"

"Your hands are burning up."

"It's the spirits. Accept them into your soul. They will protect you from all that is evil." Johnny starts to relax his hands in Flo's grasp. The warmth of her hands is no longer there. "The spirits have entered your body. You will be protected from all evil the rest of your life if you fly straight and follow a righteous path."

Johnny squeezes Flo's hand, and it feels normal. "With you by my side, I have no cause to sway or drift from the good things in life."

They return to Marie's and eat dinner. Afterwards, Flo reaches into her bag and pulls out gifts for everyone. It's a little uncomfortable at first since Marie, Elaine, Pedro, and Johnny don't have a gift for Flo. Flo explains to them that she had gotten a healthy check from Liz and wanted to share her newfound wealth with her friends. Flo almost breaks down when she says, "I've waited a long time to have enough money to buy something nice for the people I love. Please accept these trinkets as a token of my love. It's a tradition for people of my tribe to offer up these tokens as a symbol of love to family members."

First to open their gifts are Marie and Elaine. They each get doves made from beautiful white porcelain. There not very big, but the detail put into the carving of them is exceptional. Pedro is next to open his gift. It's a beautiful golden hawk with a nice chain. Johnny is the last to open his gift. He receives a gold bald eagle about an inch and a half in size. It has two small diamonds placed in its eyes that seem to look right through a person. He also receives a magnificent chain. Over dessert and coffee, Flo receives high praise and is thanked for her very lovely gifts. Each person has Flo place their gifts around their necks. She does so with amazing pride knowing that she has moved into a position in life where she can share her wealth with people she loves. She wishes her uncle and grandfather were still around to share this day with her.

In the morning, Flo takes Elaine and Johnny to the airport. Elaine is heading back to California, and Johnny is flying to Lexington. They say their goodbyes, then head past security to their terminals.

# CHAPTER 26

Frankie picks Johnny up and takes him to Stripes and Solids. Frankie's a talker, so Johnny gets an earful. "Billy has been putting in some very long days. He's probably sleeping about four hours a day. He's had days that he's been very nasty to everyone. I came close to quitting a couple times. Since Thanksgiving, or should I say, the day after, he's been the nicest guy in the world. He gave everyone an increase in pay. Whatever was in the turkey he ate that day, I hope part of it gets stuck in him the rest of the time I'm working at his place." Johnny surmises Billy's change in personality has a lot to do with his mom coming to Kentucky. Johnny doesn't let Frankie know. He'll let Frankie believe what he wants to believe. Frankie tells Johnny, "The place looks great; you're probably going to have a hard time believing it's the same place."

Right away, as they pull into the parking lot, Johnny's sees the first change. The Stripes and Solids boast a marquee. It reads, "Come watch the greatest players in the world play in the biggest tournament ever, starting December 4th, until December 14." In smaller print, it says, "Five hundred and twelve men will be competing and sixty-four women." A nice new glass-enclosed window has pictures of many of the players signed-up to participate. Johnny notices a nice picture of Flo, portrayed as the hottest female player in the game today who will be making an appearance. The men's pictures displayed are a who's who in the game of pool from all over the world. Rico's picture is front and center. It's the largest of all the men's pictures.

Inside is still a work in progress. Both poolrooms are larger. Frankie starts telling Johnny, "Billy expanded the size of both rooms by ripping down walls to other rooms that were used for storage. Billy moved everything he was storing upstairs to the basement. He has put stadium seating in both poolrooms. He also figured out a way to take tables out of the poolrooms, as the field starts to dwindle in size, and add more seating. Every table is also equipped with a camera, so if there is a close match and people want to watch, it can be projected onto a big screen."

Sauntering around the place is Billy, looking around and admiring the work that has been completed in recent weeks. Johnny walks over and taps Billy lightly on the shoulder. He turns and says, "It's nice to have you back, even if it's only for a day." Johnny has a puzzled look on his face. "Did you forget about Cincinnati?"

"I guess I had forgotten about that trip." Johnny tries to give Billy back his share of the money he made in California, plus the lure.

"Use it when you go to Cincinnati. I heard the guy you're going to play likes to bet big."

Improvements in the room can be seen everywhere. Billy takes the next half hour showing Johnny all the changes he has made in the place. Johnny asks, "Did you know you have the skills of an architect when it comes to designing?"

"My carpenter, Scott, had a lot to do with the way things came out on paper. This guy is incredible; all I had to do was come up with a few ideas, and he ran with the rest. He's in the basement right now with Larry going over plans for the storage area." Billy gets summoned to another part of the building. Before he leaves, he asks, "How you like it?"

"I think it's fabulous."

"There's been a ring game the last two nights on table one. It starts around six o'clock and goes well past midnight. A bunch of Canadians are down for the tournament, and they've been playing amongst themselves." Billy advises Johnny to try to get into the game. "There's no playing safety; it will help your offense."

"I have some laundry to catch up on first." Johnny and Frankie go back outside to unload Johnny's luggage, then Johnny does his laundry. He takes a nap to have energy for the ring game, but as fast as he has fallen asleep, an hour and a half has passed. Johnny struggles to wake up. He hits the snooze alarm for an extra ten minutes before climbing out of bed. Once on his feet, he gets ready and heads to the poolroom.

Six o'clock comes, and Johnny starts feeling dejected. There's no sign of the Canadians. Larry comes by, and he and Johnny decide to leave at one o'clock tomorrow for Cincinnati. Johnny thinks the Canadians have just come through the door. Johnny says, "I'm going to try to get in the ring game with the Canadians. Do you have any suggestions on how to ask these guys if I can play with them?"

"Ask them if they want another player."

Johnny notices that one of the four men isn't taking part in the ring game. Johnny takes a simple approach that Larry had suggested, he asks, "Would you guys like another player?" The Canadians welcome Johnny into the game with open arms. Johnny has no clue that he's gotten involved with some of the most explosive players in the game. He ends up shooting third in the four-man rotation. The stakes are twenty dollars per man, per rack.

First names are all that Johnny can remember after the introductions. Luc is the first player at the table. He's a free-wheeling left-hander who has a hard time waiting for the cue-ball to stop before he shoots. He breaks and runs the first rack. Alien and Claude are the other two men Johnny will be playing with the rest of the evening. Struggling at first, Johnny finds himself down a few hundred dollars in the first two hours of play. Johnny is following Alien, and he's not missing much; when he does, he's not leaving much. Johnny catches a break when Alien scratches on a six-ball shot that looked virtually impossible to make. Johnny wins that rack, plus he strings together three more racks in a row to pull ahead money-wise.

Luc is starting to get impatient. He's the loser of the group thus far and wants to raise the stakes. All four men agree to raise the bet to thirty a game. Luc's night continues on a downward spiral. Johnny and Alien are the two winners at the end of the night. Claude comes out nearly even. Johnny makes about three hundred hard-earned dollars. Alien makes a little more than Johnny. As the game breaks up, Luc insists on playing the next night with the same group of players.

Luc says, "Same time same place tomorrow night. We start out playing for thirty a rack."

Johnny tells Luc, "I can't make it. I'm leaving town for a few days." Luc's not happy, but he respects the fact that Johnny has told the truth. Luc says to Johnny, "Maybe we can find someone who misses once in awhile to play with us tomorrow night."

Watching the game from a distance is Billy. When the game breaks up, he comes over to Johnny. "How'd ya make out?" Johnny takes his money out of his pocket and counts it.

"A little more than three hundred."

"How'd ya like playing with those guys?"

"There were a couple of times I didn't shoot for five racks. All three of them could make incredible shots."

"All the players who are coming here to play are capable of great things. This will be the finest field ever to play in a pool tournament. Every skill that you have in your body will have to be at its best to pull off winning this tournament. Tonight you took another big step in preparing to play the finest players in the world."

Over a bottle of beer, Johnny and Billy discuss future plans, and Johnny fills him in on Flo's status in the pool world. After the long day, Johnny finally gets to go to sleep.

Tuesday morning marks a week before the start of the tournament. Billy says, "I'm going to have all of the work taken care of by Saturday. I'll be damned if I can't get a little rest before the tournament starts. I'm putting everything into Barry's hands once the tournament starts. He's the professional tournament director." Larry guarantees Billy that Barry and his staff will be able to handle everything.

Ashley, the girl from Maine, had arrived at Billy's on Saturday. Billy says, "If Barry's crew can do as good a job as Ashley has done so far, I'll have nothing to worry about. She's broken everything down to which country or state these people come from. That's the way she plans on having them live." Billy also points out that Ashley has set up bus shuttles back and forth from the poolroom to the university every fifteen minutes. "I knew this girl was sharp."

Over breakfast, Larry and Johnny chat. Larry says, "Billy has gone through a sudden personality change."

Johnny informs Larry, "He talked to my mom over Thanksgiving, and my mom is coming to watch me play."

"That must have been some fling they had back in the day."

"It must have been something, because you're talking to the result of the fling." Larry tries to apologize, but Johnny stops him. He says, "I am what I am, and nothing can change it. I'm not ashamed of the way things worked out. I only wish I had come to know Billy sooner. My mom did what she had to do to protect me and provide me a good home. Cliff was not a good person, good husband, or father. My mom paid dearly for her life with him."

As Johnny and Larry start to walk back to get their luggage, Larry tells Johnny, "You have my word. I'll only tell people what you told me about Billy and your mom's relationship."

On the way to Cincinnati, Flo calls and says, "I'm not going be able to come to Kentucky on Thursday as I had originally planned. Liz called me today, and she wants me to come to New York again. It seems my winning the tournament has sped up a lot of things that were going on. Plus, it has also created a few more opportunities."

Johnny's happy for Flo, but a little disappointed that she won't be coming on Thursday. He asks her when she'll be able to get there.

"Probably Sunday night. Liz has set up a meeting with a new client Sunday afternoon. It's going to be a billiard parlor in New York City. Liz says if I can sell these people on using me to represent their product, it could be worth around one hundred thousand dollars. I'm nervous about this whole thing, Johnny; there's an awful lot of money riding on this deal."

"Relax and be yourself. You never falter at the table, and there's more pressure on you there than there is talking to a few people. Get them playing pool with you."

"The company makes tampons. I'd have to make a commercial straddling a table telling the entire world how much more comfortable I feel at the table wearing their product. I'm not sure I want the world examining my crotch. It may turn out to be a little humiliating."

"Insist on viewing the commercial before it airs to make sure it's done in good taste."

"Do you think I can get away with something like that?"

"If they want to use you in their ad bad enough, I'm sure they'll be willing to make some concessions. I wish you were coming down on Thursday, but I can live with the fact that you'll be there on Sunday." With Larry listening, Johnny whispers into the phone how much he loves and misses her, and then they hang up.

They make it to Cincinnati and pull into the parking lot of *Reds* pool hall to play Vinny "the weasel" Polombo.

Larry's the spokesperson. He asks the houseman, "Is Vinny 'the weasel' around?"

"Who wants to know?

'We're here from Lexington. The kid's suppose to play a money match with him.

"There are three men sitting at a table, drinking coffee." The houseman points and tells Larry, "Vinny's the one with his back to us."

Larry and Johnny make their way over to Vinny's table. He turns around.

"I guess you're Vinny. Billy sent us. Are you ready to play?"

"I'm ready, but my fuckin' asshole backer blew his brains out this week playing poker. I finally get someone to come into my room willing to play for big money, and I can't accommodate them. My reputation is this business is gone." Vinny crushes his empty coffee cup and flings it into a barrel as he stands and paces a small area blowing off steam. After he's through, he says, "I'm embarrassed to tell you I can't play but there is a guy over there that might play."

Johnny plays and salvages twelve hundred to make the trip worthwhile. The next morning they head back home.

"In your wildest dreams, did you ever picture you and I driving on a highway in Kentucky when you introduced yourself to me early last summer?"

"Nope! And I never dreamed you'd turn out to be such a great player in such a short time. You took that guy apart yesterday, except when you let up on him for one set."

"I never let up."

"You may think you never let up but I think you have Billy disease. You like to play too much. He used to let up the same way until I told him what I'm about to tell you. You have to be a prick! If you have somebody down in this game you have to smother them and take the life completely out of them." Larry raises his voice and says, "Kill the mother fuckers. If you don't they might turn the tide on you and by then your fuckin' head's spinning and all of a sudden they're holding your cash.. Be a fuckin' prick."

"I don't want to be like Rico Sanchez.

"Rico's a fuckin' asshole, he embarrasses and humiliates his opponents. Be a fuckin' prick."

Johnny thinks for a short time, and the things Larry said are right. He felt at any time he could have beaten his opponent yesterday. This is a bad habit to get into. He gets the message, and proclaims. "From now on, I'm a big prick, the biggest."

# CHAPTER 26

Back in Lexington, Larry and Johnny get Billy's attention and fill him in on what happened in Cincinnati.

Larry takes over the conversation and tells Billy how Johnny was able to grab twelve hundred off Rick, and turn a potential bust into a profitable trip. Larry also takes time to tell Billy, "Johnny was playing amazing nine-ball. Getting out from everywhere, it kinda reminded me of you in the old days."

Billy gets called away by Barry to handle a question by a player. Before he walks away, he gives Johnny instructions to be ready to play in a mini-tournament starting at six that evening. "Take a nap or use the private room and practice."

"I may do both."

"I like the way you're starting to think."

Hanging around with Larry the past few days has started paying dividends for Johnny. After practicing for an hour, he takes a nap.

Prepaid by Billy to play in the first mini-tournament, Johnny's name is called on the intercom. He gets to table for it just in the nick of time.

Johnny's opponent, Ned, is standing at the table ready to flip a coin as Johnny screws his cue together. He tells Johnny to call in the air as he flips a coin. Johnny chooses heads, and it comes up tails. His opponent waits to break the first rack. Johnny's opponent doesn't appear to be in a social mood, so Johnny doesn't ask his name. Johnny racks the balls in a hurry.

Ned shows why he's come to such a prestigious event. He breaks and easily runs out the rack. Johnny is already kicking himself in the ass for oversleeping.

Ned is on cruise control for the next few games. He runs out to leads of three to nothing and four to one. Ned makes his first major mistake. He over-strokes a two rail position shot and leaves himself safe on the five-ball. He had played flawless position up until this point in the match. He starts bitching about the speed of the new cloth. Johnny hadn't spent enough time on the table to even notice the new cloth. Ned bitches even more when he kicks and scratches off a five-ball in the corner pocket.

Something inside Johnny clicks after he runs-out the five remaining balls on the table. He manages to put a nice string of four racks together before Ned knows what's hit him. Ned still hasn't gotten over the fact that he played poor position a few racks ago.

Six to five isn't a very big lead in a race to nine. Somehow, some way, though, Ned's not the same player he was early in the match. He starts to make mental errors he wasn't making before, and Johnny wins the next game. When Ned finally wins a game to get back within a game of Johnny, his cue-ball flies the table on his next break. And if things weren't bad enough, Johnny has two easy shots to make before he pockets an easy three-nine combination. Ned has all but given up, at this point. His next trip to the table isn't a pleasant one. He manages to safe himself again. His emotions get the best of him. Ned fails to make legal hits on the object-ball. Johnny's seizes the opportunity; he runs-out the remaining balls and wins the game and the set. Ned's not offering any congratulations to Johnny. He sits in his chair talking to himself about how much he already hates the equipment. Johnny just gets away from Ned and reports the win to the tournament director. Johnny's right back in the room less than five minutes later. He's facing a brand new opponent. This time he's ready to play from the get-go.

Contrasts are something Johnny is starting to pick-up about personalities in the game of pool. Winston, Johnny's second opponent, is a far cry from Ned. He wants to talk for ten minutes before they start to play. Johnny's getting Winston's full background. The English accent and the dark skin start to make sense when Winston tells Johnny he's from Bermuda. Johnny lets his cue do the talking once the match starts; he disposes of Winston and moves to his next match.

Called to play another match, Johnny goes over to his assigned table. His opponent has been hitting balls, waiting for Johnny to finish up playing his last match. He lets his opponent know he needs to visit the men's room. He takes care of business and is ready to play in less than five minutes. When he comes back to the table, his opponent decides it's his turn to go to the men's room. Johnny tries to figure out what's going on, but he decides this is something Billy might be better off explaining. Johnny has learned to focus his attention and energy on playing the game. When it comes to trying to figure people out, he's learned to leave it for another time and place.

Toby, Johnny has learned his name from a player on the adjoining table, comes back in ten minutes. The first statement to Johnny by Toby is, "Are we ready to play now?" Toby takes a coin in his hand and flips it into the air. "Make the call." Johnny calls heads and wins. Johnny waits patiently as Toby takes his time racking the balls. The match finally gets underway.

Angered by stalling tactics by Toby, Johnny reaches back for a little extra on his break. The power is there, but Johnny loses some of his accuracy. The cue-ball bounces up into the air and heads towards the left-hand side rail. It bounces up onto the side rail before returning to the playing surface. Johnny makes a quick mental note as the balls traverse the table, *Don't do that again*. Fortunately, things work out well for Johnny. Toby gets left in the dust as Johnny puts a nine game to three games beating on him. Toby accuses Johnny of stalling at the start of the match. With time between his next match, he seeks out Billy to find the answer.

"Stalling," says Billy, "is that what Toby was mumbling to himself when he walked past me?" Billy asks Johnny for a recap of what led up to the start of the match. Johnny explains how he had finished playing Winston and took a bathroom break.

"Do you know how long Toby was waiting before you finished up playing with Winston?"

"I have no idea. Does it matter?"

"It does, and it doesn't; it's all in the player's head at this point. He might have waited a while for you to finish playing Winston and was tired of waiting. He figured you were stalling or making him wait a little longer before you played the match. It's a head game players play with each other, trying to gain a psychological advantage."

"I was holding a piss for the last three racks against Winston."

"Toby doesn't know what's going on with you. He's used to playing people trying to gain an advantage in any way they think they can. The fact that you were being honest and had to really go to the bathroom, never entered his mind. You might have the best psychological weapon of any of the players in the room."

"What's that?" asks Johnny.

"Honesty. Pool players are always trying to lie, cheat, and maybe even steal to gain an advantage. Your honesty may screw a lot of these guys up." Johnny's name is called for a match on table number one.

Johnny plays a tight match against undefeated tournament player Rudolpho and comes out the victor.

Canada has been well represented in the first mini-tournament. Alien and Claude are playing in the other semifinal match. Johnny gets to take a small break as Alien and Claude still have a few games to play before a winner will be determined. It's been a long grind up to this point and fatigue is starting to set in. Soon, applause can be heard behind Johnny; Alien has just defeated Claude. Barry announces, "The final match between Alien Martell and J.J. Jordan will be starting in five minutes."

Alien jumps all over Johnny right from the very start. His remarkable shooting skills are being displayed over and over. Before Johnny knows what's hit him, he's behind in the match six games to one. It's Johnny who sits in the chair slumped down feeling like a fighter who can't land a solid punch. Alien is strutting around the table knowing he has all facets of his game working to perfection. He lays the worst beating on Johnny he has yet to suffer. A final score of nine to two sucks the life from Johnny's body. He barely manages to come out of his chair to congratulate Alien for his victory. Barry announces the winner of the match to the entire room. Johnny's second-place finish never gets a mention.

Midnight is fast approaching. Johnny leaves the playing arena, walks past Billy, and never says a word.

Billy asks, "Wanna tell me where you're going?"

"To bed."

"You're not tired, you're beat. Alien gave you a beating, and all you want to do is run away and hide in your room. Is this the way you're going to react every time you lose? This could happen to you at any time in the upcoming tournament. Are you going to quit if you suffer a loss early in the tournament?"

"That's different. I'd never give up on myself in a tournament of that proportion."

Billy gets angry. "That's what all the front runners say after a loss, when they start running away from their problems. A man of character would've come up to Barry and asked if he could play in the next available tournament." Johnny wants nothing to do with what Billy is selling him right now; he starts to walk away. "You're entered in the last tournament of the night; it starts at midnight. The races have been shortened to races to seven. You can go to your room or you can stand and fight like a man; it's up to you."

Billy has had enough; he turns and walks away from Johnny before he starts to say a few things he might live to regret. Weighing all the things Billy has just said to him, Johnny decides to go back and play. He ends up playing a man named Bruno. Early in the match, Johnny is still carrying the chip on his shoulder from his loss against Alien and his talk with Billy. After four games, the score is tied at two games apiece. Johnny has made two mistakes in both racks Bruno has been able to win. Johnny watches as Bruno is playing the next rack. He has a shot, choppy stroke and limited playing skills. What he does have to make up for his limitations is desire. He's playing every shot like he's in the seventh game of the NBA Finals. Johnny starts to have a better understanding of what Billy was saying to him earlier. Here's a guy with limited talent who's putting everything he has into winning this match. Johnny gets back on the bike that he had fallen off earlier in the evening. He plays the rest of the match with Bruno, and the four more matches that follow, with a purpose. At three-thirty in the morning, Johnny is announced as the winner of the final mini-tournament of the evening. Twenty or so people are still hanging around at the time Johnny finishes playing. Some of them even applaud his efforts.

Billy comes to Johnny with his hand extended to congratulate him. It's Johnny's turn to do the talking. "You were right. I was so used to winning that I forgot how to deal with a loss. I wanted the glory of beating Alien in front of all those people who were watching us play. I had no idea how to handle myself after he gave me a beating."

"I used to run and hide in a bottle of something or even worse things I thought would help. The only thing that helps is facing the fact you just got beat by a better man, but it's not the end of the world. Maybe this will make it easier. Pretend you're in a fight, and you get knocked down. A man gets back on his feet and fights until the end. There's a big difference between getting knocked down and knocked out."

Johnny swallows his pride once again and says, "You were right."

"I don't want to be right. I want you to know how important it is to stay focused, even if all seems lost. Your determination and attitude may help you win a match you never thought possible. It may also keep you from losing a match you never thought you possibly could lose." With their relationship back on an even keel, Billy sends Johnny back to his room for a good night's rest. It's almost four in the morning when Billy says, "I entered you in another mini-tournament that starts at two in the afternoon. I held off on the one starting at noon and one o'clock. I figured you could use some extra rest."

Life for Johnny turns into one mini-tournament after another for the next two and one half days. Billy convinces him he needs to play as many different players as he can. If Johnny starts gambling, he could get locked-up playing the same person for a day or possibly the rest of the time before the tournament starts. Things go along smoothly for Johnny all day Friday and into the better part of Saturday. He wins two of the three minis he plays on Friday. His one loss is a hard-fought nine to eight match with a strong player.

Turmoil shows up in the form of Rico Sanchez shortly after seven o'clock on Saturday evening. Rico manages to get his hands on Barry's microphone. He openly challenges any and all players to play him for money. He's willing to spot any player the wild seven-ball. "That is, of course, if you're willing to bet at least five thousand dollars a set." Rico manages to fire off an insult to the players playing in the mini tournaments. He tells all of them, and maybe Johnny in particular, "You ladies down there playing in the mini-tournaments. If any of you are interested in playing me, I'll be in the other room where the *men* are playing." Barry, who had been in the men's room, comes back and takes the microphone away from Rico.

Scolding Rico, for less than his professional behavior, sets off an argument between Rico and Barry. Barry has had many dealings with Rico in the past and he's tired of his I'm-better-than-everyone-else-in-the-place attitude. What starts out as a reasonable conversation soon escalates into an out-of-control shouting match between them. Rico's bone of contention is he's the best player in the world, and he's willing to put his money where his mouth is. He just wants the rest of the people in the room to hear he's willing to play anyone.

Larry rushes to tell Billy what's going on. Billy comes out of his bed like a shot. He wastes no time at all getting to the poolroom. Rico and Barry are still going at it when he arrives. The sight of Billy standing behind Barry has an effect on Rico's attitude. When Billy calmly asks Rico what the argument is all about, his tone of voice changes dramatically. He says to Billy, "I was just trying to create a little action for myself. I picked up

Barry's microphone and used it to tell everyone I was willing to give anyone in the place the wild seven." Billy knows when Rico is lying. The large crowd that has gathered keeps Billy from losing his cool. He explains to Rico that they have what they call Action Central at the Stripes and Solids, and if he wants to announce any special games for gambling, they would be glad to do it for him.

Rico tries to get the last word when he says to Billy, "I've done this before at many tournaments. I like to give people my own personal touch when I issue a challenge."

As Rico starts to walk away, Billy says to him, "What you did in other places doesn't go in my place. It's my room and my tournament. As you will find out at the players meeting tomorrow night, I have a lot of rules and they will be strictly enforced. Any violation of these rules may lead to a loss of a match or being disqualified from the tournament completely."

Rico walks away. He childishly mimes some of the words Billy has said to him as he walks back through the crowd. Some find Rico amusing and laugh at what he's doing. Billy turns and apologizes to Barry for what has taken place. "We have to be on our toes when that son of a bitch is in the building. He'll do whatever it takes to draw attention to himself."

Later, Billy tells Johnny, "Rico's come to town with a stake horse. The guy's got a ton of money, and Rico is probably dead broke. If you play him and lose, all you'll be doing is adding fuel to his fire when he starts playing in the tournament. Any momentum he can build up by winning extra money will make him that much stronger later."

"I think I can beat him with that kind of spot."

Billy smiles and says, "I think you can beat him even. The secret is beating him at the right time and place. Let's see how things work out in the tournament before we think about gambling with him in the future. Now, get Rico out of your mind. I watched you play after the disruption, and you were lucky to win the match."

"I know."

Being champion of the next tournament plus another later that night carries Johnny into Sunday morning feeling great as he prepares to hit the sack. He figures out his record in the mini-tournaments since he started playing in them is thirty-one wins and only three losses. He has gotten over his loss to Alien Martell and his anger at Rico. He wakes up Sunday morning feeling great. He has one more mini-tournament to play before the players meeting at seven o'clock. This is also the day Flo will be back in his life. He has already gotten dinner reservations at Blair's. He takes his morning shower thinking of seeing Flo later that evening. He finishes up his personal hygiene, gets dressed, grabs his cue, and heads over to get some breakfast. Thoughts of Flo are still in his mind all through breakfast. He finishes eating his breakfast and has an hour to kill before his mini-tournament starts. He takes a walk over to the gambling room to see what's going on.

Smack dab in the middle of the room is a Rico Sanchez. Johnny keeps his distance and stays out of Rico's sight. He gets a full report of what's going on with Rico from someone who's been watching him play. It seems the person sweating Rico's action has a stake in who wins the match. He tells Johnny this is the third person who stepped up to play Rico since he arrived in town. So far, Rico has won over twenty-five thousand dollars from the first two players. The guy he's playing has already gone off for ten thousand. Rico is giving him the five-ball, plus they are alternating breaks. It's a race to eleven games, and Rico has a six to three lead. The consensus from the people watching the match is that Rico's opponent hasn't a chance to win. Johnny hears one of the sweaters of the match mumble, "This guy's a dog." He's referring to the person Rico is playing. It's not exactly a complement. Johnny has seen enough; he returns to the tournament area and waits for his match to be called.

Johnny goes on to the finals of his last mini-tournament, and he finds that he will go against Alien.

Billy tells Johnny, "There's a lot riding on this match."

"How much is a lot?"

"Fifteen thousand on the match."

He pretends to swallow something before telling Billy, "I'll be fine. Like I said, the money part doesn't bother me."

Redemption for his first loss to Alien provides Johnny with all the motivation he needs to slam the door in his face. The fact that Billy has so much money bet on the match also helps to keep Johnny heavily stimulated. It's not the same score as Alien had beaten him by, but the final score of nine games to three feels good enough to Johnny. Despite all the money won and lost on the match, Alien comes over to Johnny and raises Johnny's arm and salutes him as the winner of the match. The huge crowd and even Alien's fellow countrymen stand applauding Johnny as he comes from the playing area.

# CHAPTER 27

Starting the players meeting on time isn't going to happen. Pool players move at the speed of snails, especially when some are renewing friendships with people they haven't seen in years. Billy recognizes what's going on and instructs Barry to give everyone a little extra time to find a seat and get comfortable. Barry, his staff, and Billy are sitting down in the poolroom, and the players are sitting in the spectator seating area, looking down at them. A makeshift podium has been set up in the poolroom, which has a live microphone mounted on it. Billy makes an observation, and he is pleased: over five hundred people are seated in the main seating area, and there is still plenty of room for lots more people to be seated. Barry, with Billy's encouragement, gets up from his chair and walks up to the podium. After two tries, he gets everyone's attention, and he starts making his speech. He has in his hand a copy of all the rules by which the tournament will be governed. All of the rules are the standard rules, except for the final rule or what the copy of the rules lists as Billy's rule. Billy's rule states, "All matches are races to eleven except when a player is only ahead by one game. In this case, the match will be extended to as far as fifteen games or until either player goes ahead by two games. If the match goes to a score of fourteen to fourteen, the winner of the next game will win the match." The typical sounds of moans and groans can be heard. The true nature of the beast is exposed. Pool players have to find something to complain about.

Billy comes out of his chair as Barry leaves the podium. When Billy starts to talk about how much money the players will be playing for, the mood of the room changes. He tells everyone he has promised the largest pay-out in the history of the game. As he starts to talk figures, Rico makes his way into the spectator stands and creates a minor disturbance. Because Rico is being Rico, he has to come and sit right in the middle of everyone. Billy loses his train of thought and becomes upset at the fact Rico has walked into the meeting late. Billy looks up in Rico's direction and asks him, "Why are you late for the meeting? Everyone was told to be here at seven o'clock."

"I would have been here earlier, but the sucker I was playing insisted on losing another ten grand to me."

Billy doesn't want to get into anything else with Rico so he goes back to making his presentation to the players. "Everyone in the field that wins one match will get half of their entry fee back." The players like what they are hearing. Billy talks about how his partner had secured the free housing for everyone, and, once again, the players respond with another loud ovation. Building up everything, as he goes along, sets the audience up for the big announcement. "Now for the payout. How does one hundred thousand dollars sound?"

The crowd appreciates the amount of money, but it's kind of a letdown to what was anticipated. Billy waits a minute or so before he announces to the crowd, "For fourth place." The players go crazy. Billy can't hold back the suspense any longer. He announces to the players, "Third place will be two hundred thousand dollars; second place will be three hundred thousand dollars; and first place will be half a million dollars."

The players are hooting and hollering. Billy tries to restore order once, but he knows it's his crowning moment in his attempt to give back to the game, so he sits back and enjoys it. Ten minutes go by and Billy walks back to the podium. Chants of "Billy, Billy, Billy," rain down on him. He raises his hands and order is finally restored. At this time, he tells the players about the shoe manufacturer and the two hundred thousand dollar endorsement deal that also goes to the winner of the tournament. Billy explains how the male winner and the female winner will be asked to make periodic appearances around the country to endorse the shoes. The final eight players who appear on television will also be required to wear the shoes. The last thing Billy addresses is the behavior of the players. He promises each and every player that if they behave in a manner that he finds inappropriate, he will have them removed from the tournament and the building by a police escort. "The world will be watching what goes on here in the next eleven days. The future of the game is at stake. I cannot and will not have anyone jeopardize the future of the game." After a short pause, Billy asks, "Are there any questions?"

Questions come and are answered promptly. When everything starts to wind down, Rico raises his hand and asks, "Who do you think I'll beat in the finals, and how much tax will I have to pay on a half a million dollars?"

A chorus of boos can be heard from many of the players. Billy answers Rico's questions saying, "I'll let you know on the fourteenth of December, if you last that long."

Rico is angered by Billy's answer. "I'll be here, and I want my money in cash."

Billy ignores him and tells everyone that all matches will be posted on the large screen outside the playing area in one hour. The players have started to make their way out of the spectator area. Billy and Rico stand, staring at each other, until Barry pulls Billy away to ask him a question.

Johnny introduces Billy to Marie and Pedro. The introductions prove worthwhile. Marie speaks both fluent Portuguese and Spanish. Billy retains her in case they need an interpreter. Upgrades have been made in every part of Billy's room, but nothing compares to the ones made in the restaurant. The first thing that has changed is the location. Because so much room was needed to expand the poolroom, the dining area is located upstairs on the second and third floors. The room is split-level and wraps around the entire poolroom. No matter where you sit, you have a good view of the action going on in the room. If you happen to be unable to view a certain table as well as you would like to, every dining table has a monitor. You can select the table you wish to view, and it will come up on the monitor with a nice overhead shot of the action.

Everyone, except Billy, sits down and enjoys a delicious dinner. Billy is constantly interrupted trying to be a gracious host. Many people come over to his table to either congratulate him for putting on such an outstanding event or to renew old acquaintances. Billy eventually gives up trying to enjoy a quiet dinner. He pushes his plate aside. He starts telling Johnny, Pedro, and Marie he wishes he had told Barry to post the draw of the tournament as soon as the player's meeting was over. The suspense of waiting for an hour is killing him. Billy tries to excuse himself from the table. He wants to leave Johnny, Pedro, and Marie alone so they can enjoy each other's company and not have to deal with the distraction of sitting with him. Before leaving the table, Billy apologizes to Pedro and Marie for not being as sociable as he should be to Johnny's friends. He tells them he's nervous about the upcoming draw, and he still has a knot in his stomach from dealing with Rico.

Marie tells Billy, "You're letting Rico Sanchez ruin your day. I used to let my son do the same thing to me. Then I figured it all out one day. I couldn't control what he said to me or what he thought of me. I knew I had done a good job raising my son, but he was being influenced by people that grew up much differently than he did. He was envious of their position in life, and he resented to the fact that he didn't grow up with the advantages his friends had. He started to think and act like his new friends and forgot where he came from and what got him to where he was in his life. Forget about Rico Sanchez. I watched all the other people you have brought to this tournament. All I've seen so far are happy people who can't believe they're about to play in the biggest and best pool tournament ever held. You should be the happiest and proudest person in the place. You're letting one asshole ruin everything you've worked long and hard hours to accomplish. Rico is building himself up for the biggest letdown of his life."

Billy looks at Pedro and says, "You're a lucky man, Pedro. Your wife is a wise woman with exceptional insight. She should have been a pool player."

"I am one. The other night I ran my first rack of nine-ball. I wish I was twenty-five years younger. I might have had the ability to play with some of these ladies if I hadn't stopped playing the game for so many years." Billy stays seated in the booth with Marie, Pedro, and Johnny. He orders a fresh bottle of champagne. They all make small talk until the waitress returns with the champagne. He pours everyone a glass, then says "May Johnny and Flo play long and hard and make everyone at this table, plus a few of the missing people, glad they came so far to watch them play."

Johnny's asks, "Where is Larry tonight?"

"Larry met a lady at the bar last night, and he's gone out on a date. I haven't seen him as excited since the time he met his wife. They've gone to Blair's. Larry hopes it's more private than eating here."

"I took Flo to Blair's one night. It's a great place to take a lady if you're trying to impress her."

Johnny decides to call Flo.

Flo says, "They just got through putting the finishing touches on the commercial ten minutes ago. I've just gotten into a cab, and I'm headed towards the airport. I'm not sure what time I'll be able to get into Lexington tonight. I'm screwing everything up. Hopefully, I can get a non-stop flight and be there before midnight."

"There's no rush. I don't play until eight o'clock Monday evening." Johnny goes to tell her about his mini-tournaments that he won and fills her in on the tournament, then they say goodbye.

He then calls his mom, who says, "I think old Cliffy boy is starting to run scared. His lawyer called mine the other day, and he wants to make a few concessions on some of the things I asked for in our divorce. I'm feeling much better about my situation, and I'm not afraid of facing him in court. I got a brochure the other day from a local pool table distributor. I'm bringing it with me to Kentucky. I want you to help me pick out a table to put down in the basement. Either that or I add a room on upstairs big enough for a table and a big screen television. I'm sure Charlie would give me a fair price on an addition to the house. What's going on there? Has everyone else arrived?"

Johnny can tell his mom is nervous by the way her train of thought is jumping from one subject to another, but he doesn't say anything. He explains Flo's situation and tells her that Marie and Pedro are sitting with him at Billy's restaurant. After giving the flight information, they hang up.

Johnny meets Billy in his private practice room. Billy says, "I hate to tell you this, but the game has gotten into your blood.

You're a real pool player. I hope your mom doesn't hate me for the way you've turned out."

"What do I do now?"

"You do what everyone else has to do. Wait until it's your turn to play. Get yourself physically and mentally ready to play. If you do any practicing by yourself, play every shot like you're playing an opponent. After you break, if the best play you have is playing a safety, play the safety, and it better be a good one. Your opponent won't have any mercy on you. If you're kicking at the ball, try to leave yourself nothing to shoot at. These are the things you'll be facing in the tournament, so try to get used to it now. Use the same intensity and desire you would if you were playing an opponent. Some people think they have a switch they can throw and suddenly become a great pool player. They make a few mistakes, and before they know it, they are unscrewing their cues trying to figure out what the fuck just happened. Don't get caught up in that kind of thinking. Play every shot like your tournament life depends on it because that might be what's riding on it."

"Why didn't you tell me about how to practice until now?"

"I didn't think you were good enough to win at this big of an event. The last few weeks, I've changed mind." Billy winks at Johnny as he says, "Somewhere on Route 80 east in New Jersey I think I changed my opinion of your character and your game. Both of them are better than any other player in this tournament." Johnny has a broad smile on his face as Billy closes the door to the practice room.

After practicing a while, Johnny picks Flo up from the airport. Heads turn when Flo and Johnny walk into the poolroom. Flo's become a very recognizable figure in the pool world, and people are taking notice. A buzz is heard as Flo and

Johnny make their way through the crowded room. Johnny uses the same line he used in California. "I don't know what it is. Everywhere I go people start staring at me."

The last place Johnny saw Marie and Pedro was upstairs in the restaurant. He gives Flo the information, and they make their way upstairs. The table they were sitting at has a crowd of people standing around it, and Johnny can't tell who's sitting at the table until he gets close. Hard to believe, but it's not Pedro and Marie. Billy is up to his old tricks. He's holding court, telling stories of the past to entertain everybody while the DJ takes a break. Marie and Pedro are nowhere to be found but they have been replaced with some familiar faces, at least to Johnny anyway. Mike X. and Kerry Herbert have made the trip south and are sitting with Billy helping him recall some of the stories. When Billy sees Flo and Johnny, he finishes up his last story of the night and politely asks his audience for some privacy to talk to them. Reluctantly, the people disperse, but not before they get Billy to promise to tell more stories in the future.

Handing Flo a note from Marie, Billy moves over to make room. Billy introduces Flo to Mike and Kerry. The theme shifts quickly to money. Mike asks Billy why he didn't have a Calcutta for the tournament. Billy responds, "How could I have done that? It would take forever."

Johnny says to Billy, "I had an idea about doing one online, but I never brought it up."

Billy says to Johnny, "I want to hear every idea you or anyone else has on how we can bring more money into the game. It's too late now, but I want to hear all about it for my next event." Billy tells everyone at the table Johnny was the one who came up with the idea about raffling off the cars. Mike was unaware of the raffle, so he leaves the table for a few minutes to buy some tickets. Kerry, Mike, and Billy carry the load of the conversation. Johnny and Flo hold hands waiting for a good opportunity to go downstairs and be alone.

Last call comes in two forms. Larry and his date make an appearance as the waitress declares to everyone it's time to order their last drinks of the night. Johnny and Flo have a good excuse to leave the group. They relinquish their seats to Larry and Susan after an introduction. As they all say good night, Billy tells Johnny, "I put a new stairway in so we can get from here to our places without going back through the poolroom." Billy throws Johnny a set of keys. He points Johnny in the direction of a door and gives him directions.

When they get back to Johnny's room, they catch up on their between-the-sheets action, then go to sleep.

At one-thirty in the afternoon, Johnny's cell phone rings. It's Billy. "Play started an hour and a half ago. You're missing out on some great action already. Two big favorites to win their first round matches have already been upset. The second round matches are going to be starting in about a half an hour. Why don't you and Flo come join the rest of the party? Marie and Pedro got here bright and early."

"We'll be there as soon as we can." Johnny hangs up and fills Flo in on what's going on.

They sit at the restaurant and catch up on what has been going on in their lives outside of each other, then Johnny mentions how much of an asshole Rico has been. No sooner has Johnny gotten the words out of his mouth that someone walks by his table and announces he's on his way out to the spectator area to watch Rico play.

Flo says, "Why don't we go watch the match? Maybe you can pick up a weakness Rico might have watching him play."

Weaknesses are hard to locate in Rico's game. He wins the match eleven to one. The message has been sent to the rest of the field: Rico Sanchez has come to play and is one of the heavy favorites to win the tournament.

Johnny tells Flo, "I wish I never came over to watch. He's quite the player when he bears down and keeps his mouth shut. If we play and he shoots that well, I'm not so sure I can beat him. I'm not sure anybody can beat him."

Billy taps Johnny on the shoulder and says, "Are you conceding the tournament to him already? Should I have his name put on the trophy? Why did you watch him play?"

"I thought I might be able to find a weakness in his game."

"Great reason, great answer. Did you find anything?"

"He won eleven games to one and never missed an open shot. His break was rock solid, and his safety play was extremely good. No, I didn't find a weakness in him."

"Don't look at his game to find a weakness; look at his personality. He has to be the main focus of what's going on. When he was warming up to play, he looked up at the crowd to make sure the majority of people watching matches were focused on him. He's a person that loves to show off for everybody; it fuels his excitement for the game. It can also be his downfall. He can't handle anyone who may take the spotlight away from him. He's fired the first round of the tournament against a less-than-worthy opponent. The players who fire back are the ones he will notice. Eight o'clock tonight, your chance to fire back at him will arrive. He'll be watching. Leave a lasting impression on him, and your chances of beating him will increase. If I were you, I'd head for the practice room and start getting ready. The ball is in your court."

"That was incredibly deep," Flo says as he leaves. "Billy has amazing insight into people's personalities. Did he study all the same subjects you did in school?"

"Billy's classroom was a poolroom. That's why he's smarter than me. He just taught me another lesson in life. Let's do what he says. Let's go to the practice room."

They go and practice for a while, then separate. She chooses to stay in the practice room while Johnny goes to ready himself to play. Billy enters the practice room.

"Is he ready?" asks Billy.

"Johnny has a great teacher. He's as ready as any player in the field thanks to the way you have brought him along."

"I wish I could hand Johnny all my experience."

"Johnny has the spirit of my people; they will help to calm him."

This is a new one on Billy. He gives Flo a hug and tells her, "I hope you're right." Before he turns to leave, he says, "I'm sitting with Marie and Pedro. Johnny is playing on table four in the main poolroom. We'll hold a seat for you."

"I'll join you soon."

Overflowing crowds make it difficult for Flo to locate the gang, but she spots them. Marie is running around like a nut trying to find people willing to bet against Johnny. The word is out on Johnny, and action is hard to come by. Marie comes back to her seat and with two bets riding on Johnny. Billy has to bite his tongue when Marie tells him she gave up two games on the wire. They have made a partnership and are pooling their bets. Billy knows Marie is crazy when she tells him, "I bet the thousand dollars we are ahead so far today. It's all riding on Johnny's head. How can we lose?"

Billy turns to Flo and says, "I have a knot in my stomach as big as a grapefruit, and Marie isn't helping matters running around trying to give my money away."

Flo says, "You look calm."

"I have to look calm. Johnny doesn't need me or anyone else losing composure worrying about whether he wins or loses."

"We need to have the blind faith Marie has shown in Johnny. I'm going to see if anyone wants to take four games on the wire." Before she knows it, Flo is hit with a barrage of betters. The smallest offer to bet is a thousand dollars. She has a big problem on her hands. She never put a limit on how much she wanted to bet.

Billy knows Flo is in trouble. He stands and asks, "Who was the first to speak?" A man two rows back says he was. Billy tells him, "You're down for a G note." Billy sits down, and Flo thanks him for the help. "I can't believe all those people would take advantage of you like that. I'll take care of half your losses if you lose the bet." As the lights are flashed, the players take a seat.

Handshakes precede the opening lag. Johnny realizes who he is playing. It's the Canadian who was sick the night he took his place in the ring game. Johnny knows he's playing a quality opponent. The opening lag is a squeaker, but Johnny is nosed out. Marcel stays at the table to break while Johnny racks the balls and takes a seat. Any signs Marcel may still be sick aren't apparent after he runs the opening two racks. The knot in Billy's stomach can't be any better when Johnny finally gets a chance at the table. Johnny is facing a one or two rail kick to hit the two-ball; he hasn't decided yet. Two rails is the route Johnny takes, and it proves to be a wise decision. Johnny puts a few balls in motion beside the object-ball, and one of them finds a pocket. He is facing a reasonable two-nine combination when the balls come to rest. Johnny looks over the shot, goes in, and plays it. After the two-ball sends it in the desired direction, the nine splits the pocket. Johnny turns and puts his game on the wire as his opponent racks the balls. The next time Marcel comes to the table, he's kicking at a ball. The score is five games to two games, Johnny's favor. The hit is made, but the bleeding never stops. Johnny runs out the rack and continues on his way to run out the rest of the set. In the process, much of the spectator buzz has focused on Johnny's play. He receives a fine ovation from the audience when he finishes up playing. He and Marcel shake hands, and Johnny leaves the playing area to seek out Flo.

One by one, the matches finish up. A few minutes later, Johnny notices a voicemail from his mother: "My lawyer made the mistake of telling Cliff's lawyer I had booked a flight east at three o'clock today. I had a nine-thirty hearing time, so I figured I had plenty of time to catch my flight. Cliff was a no-show when the case is scheduled to be heard. His lawyer told the judge he had an emergency surgery to perform. He kept me waiting for four hours before he showed up. I missed my flight, and now I have to go to the airport to try to get on a plane heading in that direction. I'm so sorry. I may be another day trying to get there. I hope you played well and won your match. I miss you and love you. If you call my phone and I don't pick up, I'm probably on a plane headed east. I'll call you again if I see I missed your call."

Johnny calls her, and she now says, "I'm in St. Louis, and there aren't any more flights to Lexington until the morning."

"I play my next match at noon."

The first available flight to Lexington would land at 8 a.m., and Elaine doesn't want Johnny to lose sleep because of her. The next flight is even worse; it lands shortly after noon. Elaine is faced with little choice; she will take the late afternoon flight that will arrive in Lexington at 4:45. She lets Johnny in on her decision.

"I could get up early and get you at 8 o'clock."

"In order for me to make the early flight, I'm probably looking at waking up at 5 a.m. Is that something I really want to do? I don't think so. I expect a long night when I get to Lexington. I would like to have dinner with you, Billy, and Flo tomorrow night. If you could set it up, I would appreciate it. I hate to exclude Marie and Pedro, but I think the smaller number of people will help me relax. I'm starting to feel anxious. Oh, by the way, how did your match go?"

"I won, in a landslide."

"I'm sorry I had to miss such a great performance."

"There's plenty of pool still to be played."

"I want everyone to be in a good mood tomorrow night at dinner. I don't need to be looking at long faces when I sit down to dinner, so win your match." They wrap up the conversation.

Back at the empty table, Johnny finds out the party goes on without him. Marie, Pedro, Flo, Billy, Susan, and Larry have all found their way out on the dance floor. It's a line dance, so Johnny finds a nice comfortable spot next to Flo and joins in.

After dancing, dinner, and chatting, Flo and Johnny go to bed. Johnny is awakened by his phone. It's Billy wanting him to come to the practice room.

Upstairs in the practice room, renovations are taking place. Billy has decided he and Flo need their own practice tables and has moved things around to accommodate another table. He wants Johnny's opinion to make sure he likes the way he has rearranged the room. Johnny could care less, but he doesn't want Billy to think he doesn't appreciate what Billy has done for him and Flo. He tells Billy the room looks great and thanks him for the extra effort he has made. Billy takes a stroll around the room, and he's happy with the way things look.

Part two of the reason Billy wanted Johnny to come up to the practice room comes to light. Billy asks Johnny, "What's your mom's favorite meal? I want to make sure we have it."

"She usually orders chicken or veal parm depending on her mood." Billy is out to impress Elaine, so he asks Johnny more questions about the things she likes. "She's a woman of simple tastes. She'll be happy just to see you again. Don't drive me and yourself crazy trying to make tonight so perfect. I have a match to play in a few hours I have to get myself ready to play. My teacher once told me that the best prepared players usually come out on top. Flo tells me you were nervous about my match yesterday." Before Billy can rebut what Johnny has said, Johnny tells him, "Thanks for caring."

Segregating Johnny from the rest of what's going on around him seems to be part of Billy's plan. Johnny questions Billy on the very subject. Billy tells Johnny, "There are certain elements that go along with mixing it up with people around the game of pool. You need a clear head before you go out to play. Some people have a knack of saying dumb things to pool players right before they play a match. I want your head as clear as possible. That's why I'm getting out of here right now. I can say as many stupid things as the next guy. Get that girlfriend of yours up here; she knows what to say to you before play. If yesterday is any indication, she must have had some good things to say to you."

Johnny doesn't tell Billy, but his sex life was riding on his first match.

Billy leaves while Johnny starts to pour himself a cup of coffee. Flo comes in the other door and is happy that Billy has brought in another table. She tells Johnny, "I know I could use more time on the table the next two days. This is going to work out great for the both of us."

Johnny and his opponent get ten minutes to practice before they start to play. His opponent is a middle-aged man from Florida named Judd Foster. Judd appears nervous, and his opening lag reflects it. While Johnny prepares to break, he looks around the arena. The place is packed. He takes a walk around the table to refocus on his game and do some deep breathing.

When he is ready, Johnny goes to the table and places the cue-ball where he is going to break. A quick check of the rack to make sure it's tight gets him ready to go.

In dead silence, Johnny breaks. A ball finds it way into the pocket and Johnny plots his course of action while chalking his cue stick. Johnny never slows down, winning the match eleven to one.

Rico Sanchez must have watched Johnny's match on his monitor because he has words to say about Johnny's safety play as Johnny passes the booth he's sitting in. He tells Johnny, "You play me safe and I'll jump right over the ball. There is no escaping the great Rico Sanchez. I have every shot in the arsenal, and I will bury you if you try to run and hide from me." Johnny has no problem dealing with Rico's bullshit until he mentions Flo. "I'm rooting for your girlfriend to win the woman's event. I would love to travel around the country doing exhibitions with her. Maybe we could share a room to save on expenses."

Billy steps in front of Johnny and says, "This is one of the reasons I want to keep you away from the public as much as possible. Let what this asshole just said to you go." Johnny settles down, and Rico gets up from his booth to leave the dining area. Billy says to Rico before he leaves, "You're on a warning, Rico. Any more behavior like you just displayed, and I hold the right to disqualify you."

He politely says, "You can protect him out here, but sooner or later he will have to face me like a man in the arena. I will do to him what I did to you, maybe worse. Your little nephew will know what it's like to face the great Rico Sanchez. Watch me play at two o'clock. I will show you what I'm going to do to your little hero when and if we meet up in the future."

Protecting Johnny from Rico isn't going to help him in his future dealings with Rico, and Billy knows it and apologizes to Johnny for stepping in the middle. "I have to give up this personal vendetta I'm carrying for Rico. I let it effect me too much. I shouldn't have stepped in. I should have let you deal with him."

"Maybe it's best you stepped in. I might have popped him one in the face and gotten myself thrown out of the tournament."

"You were going to hit him?"

"I'm not sure. I guess we'll never know."

"This is exactly what Rico wants. He is trying to piss us off so all we do is talk about how much we want to beat him. It's a trap. Let's not fall in it. Let's try to use his actions against him."

"I said it before, and I'll say it again. I know he's afraid of me. I can see it in his face."

Between bites, Billy looks at his watch, and it's past two thirty. He puts the monitor on, to watch, Rico's match. Rico is ahead by a score of ten to nothing. He's in the process of making the last few balls on the table to win the final game. When he completes his mission, he looks up into the camera on the monitor and using his finger to indicate he wants something. He mimes the words *I want you, Johnny* several times. The group sitting at the table sit silent for awhile. Rico has made his point; he will be the one to beat the rest of the way.

Lunch ends, and things get back to normal. Johnny and Flo go into the practice room. Marie and Pedro and Larry and Susan decide to go to take a nap. Billy makes sure things are all set for dinner.

Later, Johnny picks his mom up from the airport. "Geez, Mom, you look great. Did you do something different with your hair?"

"The time I had to kill today in St. Louis really worked out great for me. I went to a hair dresser in the hotel; she showed me a new style and thought it would look great on me. I threw caution to the wind and told her to go for it. Do you think Billy will like it?"

"Billy has made all the arrangements for us to have dinner tonight. He's never been happier. Just the thought of seeing you again has him walking around on cloud nine. He's got a place for you to stay and everything. Your neighbors are Marie and Pedro."

They get to the room, and Johnny brings her luggage inside. It's almost quarter of six, and Johnny hits Elaine with the harsh reality that she and Billy will be having dinner in an hour. Twenty-three years of waiting for this moment takes its toll on Elaine; she breaks down and starts to cry. Johnny consoles her. The tears are happy tears, and Elaine is soon over her emotional ride. She urges Johnny get ready for dinner.

Back at the ranch, Billy is pacing the floor like an expectant father when Johnny makes his entrance to the dining room. Billy wants to know what kind of flowers Elaine likes so he can have them put into a vase placed on the dinner table.

"Carnations," says Johnny.

At dinner that night, Billy leads the way up the stairs and into the dining area. He looks across the room and sees Flo and Elaine sitting in the booth he has chosen. The closer he gets, the slower he starts to walk. Johnny is a step ahead of him when they are about twenty feet from the booth. That's when Billy draws a blank trying to remember Elaine's name. He prepared so much to make everything perfect, and he forgets her name. In desperation, he trips and falls to the floor on purpose, making plenty of noise so Johnny can hear him. Johnny rushes back to help Billy to his feet. Billy is gritting his teeth smiling at Johnny and telling him, "Your mom's first name; I can't remember her first name."

"Elaine."

The ladies are on their feet when Johnny and Billy finally reach the booth. Billy uses his fall to his advantage. He tells both of the ladies that his eyes were so fixed on the beauty they were seeing across the room, the rest of his body forgot how to function. Billy extends his hand to Elaine and says, "You're more beautiful today than the first time I saw you."

Billy takes Elaine's hand as she extends it to him and kisses it. Elaine loves Billy's grace and charm and tells him so. Champagne's at the table right after everyone gets comfortable, and Billy does the honors of opening and pouring. For the second time Billy shows Johnny he's human. Four toasts are raised and Billy's and Elaine's are shaking. "To the future." Glasses are all touched, and each person takes a sip.

Elaine asks "You didn't hurt yourself did you?

"I'm fine. Even if I wasn't nothing is about to break-up our getting reacquainted. I think and I hope we both have looked forward to this moment for far too long to let a little fall ruin the moment."

Johnny and Flo conveniently find a slow song as an excuse to leave the table. Billy moves closer to Elaine.

Elaine says, "My hand was shaking when I raised my toast glass and my stomach is turning over. I'm not ashamed to say, I'm really nervous, Billy."

Billy takes Elaine's hand and tells her, "I feel the same way. I don't think we'd be human if we didn't."

"Is this the right time and place to ask each other why we lied?"

"I have no problem with it, in fact if you want I'll go first. I wanted to ask at Thanksgiving. Its killing me."

"I wanted to do the same but I was afraid I might still be in Marie's bathroom."

"I hope I get it all straight I've been preparing this in my mind for a little while now." Billy takes a deep breathe, exhales slowly and begins to talk.

"You weren't the first woman I had met in the resorts of northern California, and you weren't the first I gave a fake name. I really thought it didn't matter who I was. Several women before you either took me to their place and asked me to leave when we finished or walked out of my place when we went there. I don't think they were too impressed with the fact I played pool for a living. I started feeling empty inside. I figured you were the same as all the other women I had met at the time until I realized you were different. But by then it was too late."

A small tear runs down the side of his face. He and Elaine hug for some time and tell each other how sorry they both are they had lied. Then Elaine gets her turn.

"As Cindy had told you, I was engaged to be married. I had built up relationships with every person I made love with and I had come to expect certain things even before I made love to them in my mind. They probably did the same thing. I guess deep down inside I didn't want that anymore. I wanted to experiment and find the real me. I thought being someone else might help bring out a different me. That night for whatever reason I did it, and the man of my dreams appeared before me. I lived a fairytale for that night and most of the following day. That's when I ran to seek advice."

Johnny and Flo return to the table as Billy and Elaine share another hug.

Dinner is ordered and served and the rest of the conversation focuses mainly on how successful Billy's first attempt at running a pool tournament has turned out. Elaine tells him she can't believe how many people have come to play. "The tournament in California was nice, but your tournament has that one beat by a mile from what I've seen so far."

Billy asks Elaine, "Do you enjoy watching the matches?"

"I'm starting to like the game. Didn't Johnny tell you I went out and bought a table for our home? I enjoy playing pool. It helps me relax. I'm looking forward to watching Johnny play tomorrow." Elaine asks Johnny, "What time is your match?"

"Eight o'clock tomorrow night."

"Are you nervous?"

"Up until now, I felt great. I like all the attention I've been getting from people; it stimulates me and makes me want to play my best."

"Do you get nervous, Flo?"

"Only when I have to sit and watch my opponent at the table. Once my feet hit the floor and it's my turn to shoot, I feel much better. If I do start to feel nervous, I take a few deep breaths to calm myself down. Johnny gave me that tip in Albuquerque, and it works."

"Billy was the one who told it me," adds Johnny.

After dinner, Billy asks Elaine to dance, but she prefers to take a short walk during which they can have another conversation.

California was a lot warmer the first time Elaine and Billy took their first walk together. By the time they get a block away from the poolroom, Billy breaks the ice and starts a conversation. "You've done a great job raising Johnny. He's a boy any parent would be proud to say was theirs."

"Johnny was always a pretty responsible child. He made my job a lot easier. He was also my link to you. I know it was crazy, but I named him after you, or as we have come to know the name you used the night we met."

Elaine stops walking and turns to Billy. They pull each other close and hug.

"I'm in the same position you were in when we talked at Thanksgiving. I've got a million things to tell you and I don't know where to start. In the next few days maybe we can catch up on what's taken place in our lives."

Billy isn't proud he lied to Elaine and neither is she, so they state the fact and the conversation moves ahead. They both reach the conclusion what happened in the past can't be changed, and the future, like Billy said when he proposed the toast, is all that matters now.

Walking back towards Billy's place, he asks Elaine if it would be all right if he held her hand. Elaine takes Billy's hand and says to him, "I would love to take this a lot further, but I think it would make more sense if we take things slower. I want you to know I've been consumed by you since that fateful day my son called me over to watch you play."

"I've been the same way. The only difference is my reintroduction to you happened a little different. Every night I lie awake and think, is she as beautiful as the first time I laid eyes on her? Earlier tonight, I got my answer. You're even more beautiful.

"I wouldn't mind if you kissed me."

Like two little kids, Billy and Elaine duck into a small alley, and twenty-four years later, the same passion and desire they felt for each other comes out. What starts out very innocent turns into a very passionate moment. The way they both feel about each other can't be held back. They want each other badly, but they know they have to wait for the right time and place. Billy comes to his senses and manages to pry himself away from Elaine. They both regain their composure and straighten themselves up before walking into Billy's place.

"I want Johnny to know we had a nice talk, and we both care for each other very much."

"I don't think telling him that would hurt his chances of winning the tournament."

"Good," says Elaine. "You tell him as soon as you get the chance."

At the table, Billy fills Johnny in on the details of his walk with Elaine. Johnny's pleased his mom's life is starting to turn around. When Flo returns, he grabs her hand and leads her out on to the dance floor. Billy and Elaine follow close behind. Johnny breaks away from Flo and asks the DJ to play the first song he and Flo ever danced to, and he kindly obliges.

He and Flo curl up in each others arms and move effortlessly around the dance floor. Elaine and Billy do the same thing. Elaine tells Billy, "I'm jealous of my son. He had the sense to know how much he was falling in love when the right woman came into his life." Billy reminds Elaine they felt the same way only their circumstances were different.

Billy puts his finger on Elaine's lips, "You need to stop punishing yourself."

Elaine manages to get a smile back on her face. The dancing portion of this session comes to an end and everyone returns to the booth.

Responsibility of refreshing everyone's glass with more champagne is given to Johnny. Elaine doesn't know what's going on and gets concerned about Billy's behavior. She gets up to go ask him what's going on as the DJ calls Billy to the microphone. Elaine sits back down.

Deep breaths are taken by Billy before he tells the audience what's going on in his life. He says, "Today, a woman I haven't seen in over twenty-three years has reentered my life. I'd like to dedicate this song to her." The introduction of the song starts and Billy starts to sing the words of the song looking directly into Elaine's eyes:

When somebody loves you
It's no good unless they love you
All the way
Happy to be near you
When you need someone to cheer you
Come what may
Taller than the tallest tree is
That's how good it's gotta feel
Deeper than the deep blue sea is
That's how good it feels, if it's real
So if you let me love you
It's for sure I'm going to love you
All the way, all the way

There's a short instrumental portion to the song. Billy comes across the dance floor and drops to his knees in front of Elaine. He doesn't need to see the words of the song to finish singing. He reenters the song perfectly. In a much louder voice, he proclaims to Elaine:

So if you let me love you
It's for sure I'm going to love you
All the way, all the way

Elaine comes to her feet and gives Billy a hug and a kiss. "If you keep this up, I'm going to have a harder time waiting until Johnny is out of the tournament," she whispers.

"Are you telling me in a nice way that you don't like my singing voice?"

"I love your voice, and I love the song you sang to me. If you keep impressing me the way you have tonight, I don't think

I'll last four days." Billy gives Elaine another short kiss before he returns the microphone to the DJ.

Afterwards, everyone heads to bed. Billy asks Elaine if he can drive her back to her place. Elaine tells Billy, "Between the long day I've had and the champagne, I should go back to my place and get some rest." Billy agrees with Elaine, and they leave the dance floor and walk outside to Billy's car.

Details of their time in California start to come back when Billy opens the car door.

"What ever happened to the GTO you were driving when I met you?"

"I went into a tail spin right after you and I got separated. I lost quite a bit of the money and had to sell it." Elaine tells Billy how sorry she is. Billy takes Elaine's hand and says, "We can't change the past. If we had stayed together, we might be the ones struggling in our relationship. Let's enjoy what we have instead of thinking about what happened to us so long ago."

Elaine moves close to Billy and rests her head on his shoulder. "Tonight was the second best night of my life. The song you sang to me was fantastic. I want this night to last a little longer. Could we take a short ride?"

Billy obliges. During the ride, Billy reminisces about some of the things they did in the short time that they knew each other, even plays a song they had listened to. She tells Billy, "I think we should head back to my place. I can see a lot of signs for motels, and I might get temped to tell you to pull into one if you pull another surprise for me."

"I have nothing more to offer; I've played all my cards."

Elaine is getting tired and asks Billy to take her back to her place. He pulls up in front of her place soon after. He opens Elaine's door, takes her into his arms, and kisses her passionately. Things get heated between them. Billy says, "I've kissed a lot of women, but I never felt the way I feel when I kiss you. You're a remarkable woman, Elaine. I love you. I have always loved you. I was a lonely, frustrated man when I lost you."

"I tried to get over you and love Cliff the way a wife should. I even managed to forget about you for many years, but when I saw you on television, everything changed. I started to get the feelings back for you I had for two days in the mountains. I loved you then and I know I could easily fall in love with you again. I'm willing to go inside with you right now and make love to you. I think we are both being foolish to think we can wait for four days to express the love we feel for one another." Elaine smiles, and with a giggle says, "I have a confession to make. I was yawning on purpose to get you to bring me back here."

Billy and Elaine enter her room.

Wine Elaine had bought and chilled is sitting in an ice bucket, and there is a corkscrew lying on the table. As Billy opens the wine bottle, he says, "Before today, I wasn't mentally ready to call him my son. I guess the closest I could muster was calling him my nephew."

"What about now? Could you call him your son?"

"Without a doubt, I could call him my son, but if I do it now it could have the wrong effect on him and cost him any chance of his winning the tournament. The extra attention that would be brought to him could prove to be fatal. I prefer to keep things the way they are. I hope you understand."

"Johnny knows the truth and so do I. The rest of the world will have to wait until you're ready to let them in on our little secret. I think I talk too much; let me get into the shower and get ready."

Billy pours the wine as Elaine gets ready. Candles are lit, and Elaine is lying on the bed wearing a bathrobe. As Billy comes closer to her, she sits up on the bed and opens the front of the bath robe. It is the night they have both been anticipating for over two decades, and neither is disappointed when the night of passion comes to an end.

Looking over at the clock, Elaine can't believe its two-thirty in the morning. "Are you staying the night?" she asks.

Billy wants to in the worst way, but he doesn't want Johnny to wake up and discover he has spent the night with his mom. Elaine agrees. As Billy starts to get dressed, Elaine tells him, "I'm not going to run away from you anymore. I love you too much to be foolish again."

"I love you, too."

He and Elaine kiss and hug one more time, then he heads back in his place.

The next day, Billy's day has started early as expected, but he's full of energy. Nothing is going to ruin his day. When Marie and Pedro show up, he asks them where Elaine is. Marie tells Billy, "Elaine needed a little more time to get ready, and she will be coming over in about an hour." Billy then goes to see Johnny in the practice room.

Before Johnny heads to the tournament, Billy extends his hand to Johnny and they shake. "You've come a long way, son." Johnny hugs Billy. Billy responds to Johnny's hug and says to him, "I'll be sitting with your mother. No matter what happens, we both love you very much." Billy has said his piece. He turns and walks slowly out of the practice room.

Johnny finds himself moving through a sea of people trying to make his way closer to the playing area. Flo comes over to Johnny and gives him a good luck kiss before going to find her seat. Elaine has showed up and is seated with Marie and Pedro.

All the ten o'clock matches are finished twenty minutes prior to the start of the next round. Johnny and the rest of his flight of players get some time on the tables before they begin to play.

Up in the stands there is plenty of interest in Johnny's match with Tony Robles. Marie gets up and leaves her seat, working the crowd to see if anyone wants to place a last minute wager on Tony. She has already booked another thousand dollars. Sitting right in front of Elaine is one of Tony's biggest fans, and he's not afraid to let everyone know he thinks Tony is going to beat Johnny easily because he was in New Jersey the last time they played. Marie is too far away from Elaine to hear what's going on. Elaine is tired of listening to the man in front of her so she taps him lightly on the shoulder. When he turns to face Elaine, she asks him, "Would you like to place a bet on the match between Tony and Johnny?"

The man is arrogant and treats Elaine with little respect. "What do you want to bet lady, twenty dollars? Don't bother me with small stuff. I'm looking to make bet with a man." Then the man turns around.

Elaine is boiling and sick of the arrogance this man is displaying. She taps him again and this time she asks. "Is five hundred dollars manly enough?"

The man figures he has all the best of the bet and he tells Elaine, "You got yourself a bet, lady."

The match begins. Solid as a rock, Johnny wins the lag. Tony racks the balls as Johnny seeks out his break cue. Johnny checks the rack as a formality. He knows Tony gave him good racks when they played in New Jersey, but he wants to walk around a little before he breaks to shake off his nervousness. He places the cue-ball on the table, and then lets it fly.

Johnny breaks two balls in and has a great shot at the one-ball to start playing the rest of the rack. Seven shots later, Johnny has won his first game of the match and is pushing the bead across the wire to indicate the score. Tony comes to the table to rack as Johnny prepares to break the next game.

Rack number two is far from what took place the previous rack. Johnny makes a ball on the break, but has nowhere to go with his first shot, so he elects to play a push-out. Tony plays a rail first shot and pockets the one-ball. His cue-ball comes off two rails and towards the center of the table. It ends up right in front of the six-ball. Tony has a shot at the two-ball, but he's jacked up high over the six-ball in his attempt to shoot. His body is stretched to the maximum trying to play the shot. Tony pays a huge price for an unfortunate roll. He miscues in his attempt at making the two-ball and fails to contact the object-ball. Taking ball-in-hand, Johnny lines up a two-nine combination and makes the shot to win his second game. The theme of the match continues for several games that follow. Johnny can do little wrong while Tony struggles to get something going. Johnny wins the match eleven games to four. Tony is a gracious loser and congratulates Johnny on his victory before the two players go their separate ways.

The money owed Elaine is being paid off, but this guy's not as gracious as Tony. He says Johnny was lucky, and Tony was a victim of many bad rolls. Elaine just nods her head; she has no idea what this guy is talking about. All she knows is she has five hundred dollars of his money, and she's keeping it.

The man wants a chance to bet against Johnny in the future and lets it be known to Elaine. He says, "The kid was fucking lucky to win."

Elaine says, "The kid is my son, and you were stupid enough to bet against him."

Flo congratulates Johnny with a kiss. If people in the crowd didn't know Flo and Johnny were an item, they certainly know now. They sit down with the others. The rest of the matches finish up by quarter of ten and the crowd disperses in all directions.

Billy and Elaine make plans to go to Blair's for their first official date. Elaine has gotten a room at a five-star-hotel downtown, and Billy meets her in her room. After relaxing for a minute, Elaine tells Billy, "I watched the tape of you playing Rico Sanchez so many times I almost wore it out. Ever since I saw your face again, I can't get you out of my mind. I've waited for this for a long time and I'm not going to jeopardize losing you again. I also love the way you make me feel as a woman. Is that wrong? I've never felt this way about any man before. The way you made me feel for two days in California was never duplicated again. I tried my best to feel the same way with Cliff, but it never happened. I lost all my inhibitions when I was with you. I never felt so free to express my love to anyone else the way I did with you. You brought out a different woman in me, and I like who I become when I am with you."

Billy comes to Elaine and tells her he feels the same way about her. He often compared other women, unfairly, to her and always left feeling empty.

Dimming the lights, Elaine reveals what she has on under her bathrobe, which puts an end to any more conversation. Elaine starts to remove his clothing. They let their passions take over, pushing everything out of their minds except each other.

Many of the people playing in the tournament and people who have just come to watch are in Blair's when Elaine and

Billy walk in. Elaine gets to experience what Johnny had to experience in Providence. Billy is a very popular guy, and people love to hear him tell stories of life on the road as a pool player. Elaine sits and listens while Billy entertains a small crowd of people sitting at the bar. She finds the stories entertaining and amusing. After the third time he promises one last story he turns his attentions back to Elaine and apologies for going on so long.

"Billy you're in your element, this is your time, I don't mind sharing you with your public. I'm right beside you and I'm enjoying the stories as much as anyone. Have you ever considered writing down some of his stories and getting them published?"

"Who would want to read about what I've done in my life? I'd bore people to death. Besides, I'm lucky if I can write my name, and my spelling is awful."

"I just witnessed a good half an hour of maybe thirty people sitting on the edge of their seats waiting for the next word that came from your mouth. They were spellbound. I would, and maybe I can help you write it all down some day and if you feel that wouldn't work how about a tape recorder."

"Um! Maybe you got something there."

They get to their table and order a bottle of wine and start talking.

Billy asks, "So where do we go after the tournament is over?"

"I haven't gotten that far yet. I know what I'm not going to be doing. I'm not going to run away looking for a second opinion. I called my aunt earlier and told her I had found you. She told me to hand cuff myself to you so I don't do something stupid again. My aunt has a bad habit of being brutally honest."

"What happened to us could have happened to a lot of people. Stop beating yourself up; we have the rest of our lives to make up for the mistakes we made in the past." Billy kisses Elaine lightly on the lips and tells her, "I only want to talk about good things the rest of the evening."

Billy asks Elaine if she would like to dance, and they move onto the dance floor. Holding each other in their arms brings them both back to the first time they met. They talk about the night like it was the day before. They both agree it was the best night of their lives. Before the dance ends, Elaine asks Billy, "Will you sing another song for me tonight?"

"Did you like the song I sang to you last night?"

"I never felt so special in my entire life. It gave me goose bumps. It's not every night a man gets up in front of a bunch of people and pours his heart out in a song dedicated to you."

Billy laughs and says, "Did you see the look on Johnny's face?"

"I never noticed; I was focused on you." The dance ends, and Elaine and Billy return to their booth. The main course arrives and they eat. Light conversation carries them through the rest of their meal. Another dance comes between coffee and them splitting a dessert. When they finish eating, Billy makes his move over to the DJ. He's to the microphone soon after, singing his heart out to Elaine. She sits there looking into his eyes, loving the way he is serenading her. Billy finishes up strong, and the audience lets him know they appreciate his efforts.

Elaine stands up as Billy comes back to the booth and takes her hand to lead her to the dance floor for a night with her sweetheart.

# CHAPTER 28

Ten o'clock rolls around, and sixty-four women are present and accounted for at the meeting. The top prize is four hundred and fifty thousand dollars. They go over the other rules, then draw for playing times.

Flo's phone rings and Liz tells her that she has cut Flo a separate deal with the shoe company, even if she loses the tournament. It's for one hundred thousand dollars.

She goes to the practice room and tells Johnny the good news. Then, Johnny must go play his match against Vinny "the weasel."

Vinny wins the opening lag and appears poised to win the first game after making two nice shots to start the first rack. He's facing a three-ball shot and needs to come off the back and side rails with the cue-ball to get position on the four-ball. Vinny pockets the three, but his position on the four-ball comes up short. He leaves the cue-ball behind the seven-ball and is forced to try and kick to make a legal hit on the four-ball. Vinny makes the required hit, but leaves Johnny a fairly easy shot to start running out the remaining balls on the table. Despite playing less than perfect position on the six- and seven-balls, Johnny manages to run out the balls remaining on the table to take a one-game lead. A pattern has been set in the early part of the match. Johnny wins eleven games to six.

Passing Flo on his way up to sit with the rest of the gang, Johnny and she only have time for a quick congratulations for Johnny and a quick kiss on the cheek and a wish of good luck for Flo.

Rico Sanchez is playing on the table next to Flo, and Johnny already knows what it's like trying to do anything when he's around. Johnny doesn't know it, but Rico is making comments to Flo every time she bends down to shoot. He's either commenting about her ass if he's behind her or when he's in front of her he's asking her to bend down lower so he can get a better view of her breasts. Rico is being discreet saying the things he's saying. He's saying them in Spanish, knowing Flo understands the language. What he doesn't know about Flo is she's willing to defend her honor. She finally takes a stand, walks over, and stands next to Rico. In a nice calm manner, she tells Rico in Spanish, "If you continue to talk to me the way you are talking to me, I will have to break a cue stick over your fucking head." Flo makes like her and Rico have just had a friendly conversation. She smiles at Rico and walks back to sit in her chair. It's the last she hears from Rico. Flo takes her frustrations and anger out on her opponent, winning the match nine to two.

Telling Johnny the story of what took place between her and Rico before she started playing brings tears to Flo's eyes. The more Johnny hears from Flo, the more he wants to go down into the playing area and punch the shit out of Rico.

Billy is listening to what's going on and puts his two cents into the conversation. He tells Flo and Johnny, "Rico is trying to get into Johnny's head through his actions with you." He also tells them Rico's stupidity might be having a reverse effect on him because he's involved in a tight match and has made a couple of dumb errors that have cost games. "As much as I'd like to see you punch the shit out of him, Johnny, why don't we ride this thing out and let Rico worry about our next move."

Unfortunately, Rico's opponent makes a couple of mistakes late in the match and Rico wins by a score of eleven to eight.

Later, Liz has shown up, and so have Cindy and her husband, Charlie.

Elaine fills Cindy in on her and Billy's relationship, and tells her to keep it a secret.

"You're secret is safe with me," she says.

Later, Johnny is getting ready for his next match. He's up against an old friend from the mini-tournament. Rudolpho and Johnny go as far as they can and Johnny pulls out the match after Rudolpho makes the nine on the break and scratches with the score tied at fourteen games apiece.

The next day, Flo and Johnny play and win their matches. In the shadows, Rico angrily watches his most formidable challenge move closer to him in the tournament.

The next morning, "I couldn't sleep," are the first words that come out of Elaine's mouth to Billy. "When I got back to my hotel room I had a voicemail message on my phone. It was my lawyer, and my husband and his lawyer want to meet with us on Thursday of next week. That's all he said to me. I tried calling him, but he's not answering his phone. My mind is running in circles; we weren't supposed to go back to court for more than a month. I know nothing good is going to happen if my husband and his lawyer want to meet before then. He's scheming something. I know the son-of-a-bitch too well to think he's not."

"Look at the bright side. You can stay here until Wednesday night before you have to return to California. Maybe we can go on another picnic together like we did when we met?"

"Can I be Piper Laurie this time? I've watched the movie so many times I'm sure I could play the part."

"You watched *The Hustler*?"

"I bought two copies of the movie shortly after I saw you play on television. I watched my copy probably fifty times in the past few months. I brought the other copy here and was going to surprise you with it if the right time presented itself. I love everything about the movie except the suicide. Couldn't they think of a better ending than that? I like happy endings. Are we going to have a happy ending?"

"I don't see any characters like Bert entering our lives."

"You haven't met my husband." Leaving it at that, the conversation switches to another subject.

"Scott's crew is rearranging the poolroom, and they are probably close to finishing. I wish I had one of the cooks come in early."

"I'll cook breakfast for everyone."

Billy takes her into the kitchen, and Elaine gets busy cooking breakfast for everyone. At this moment, she's very happy.

# CHAPTER 29

Right in the middle of Johnny and Flo, playing on table number three, it's none other than the great Rico Sanchez. Introductions of the player's don't take long because Barry only gives the name of the person and one major accomplishment. In Johnny's case, the best Barry can come up with is a second place finish in New Jersey. Of course, this plays right into Rico's hand. He casually mentions to Johnny, "You're just like your Uncle Billy; the best you'll ever do is finish second."

Johnny tries to brush off Rico's comment, but it's still in his head as he moves to the table to lag for break with Johnny Archer. The right Johnny plays superb pool, and jumps out to a big lead, despite the irritation. Archer does his best to try to get back in the match by winning three games in a row, but his fate is sealed when he scratches on the break. Johnny runs out that rack and the next one to put the match away.

Johnny notices that Flo wins her match, too. One by one, the rest of the matches finish up playing, except for Rico and Alien. Ten to ten is followed by Alien winning what would have been the deciding game of the match if Billy didn't change the rules. He seems to have it on his mind as he prepares to break the next game. Whether he does or not, the break turns into a disaster. He not only flies the table with the cue-ball, he leaves an easy combination for Rico to play and sink the nine-ball. Rico closes out the match by running two very impressive racks. He stands wallowing in his glory as the crowd gives him a fine ovation for his outstanding play. Billy, Flo, Johnny, and the rest of the crew sit watching as Rico is congratulated by his fans.

Billy does turn to Johnny and Flo and says, "You can't give a great player extra chances at the table. If you do, they will eventually eat you alive and spit you out."

Chanting of Rico's name starts like it did when Billy was humiliated by Rico, and it brings back to many bad memories for him. Any thoughts of him staying to watch the next round of matches go up in smoke. After collecting the bets he won on Johnny and Flo, he and Elaine take a break from the action to get a bite to eat. Everyone except Flo and Johnny remain in their seats to watch the action. They go off to the practice room. They have one more match to play the rest of the day, and it starts at 8 o'clock. The evening times have been changed because there are less matches being played and the room will undergo another change after the four o'clock matches. Eight more tables will be removed from the playing area. After hitting balls for twenty minutes, Johnny and Flo decide they could go for something to eat.

Sitting alone in the booth is Billy. Elaine is in the ladies' room, so Flo takes her bag and goes to the ladies' room to join her. Johnny sits down with the feeling Billy isn't in the best of moods.

Billy says, "I let the little bastard and his friends get to me, and I took my frustrations out on your mother. How big of a fucking asshole do I become when I let Rico get to me? I'm the biggest fucking asshole in the world."

Elaine and Flo are returning to the table to join the men. Billy apologizes to Elaine, and she lets him. When they finish eating, Flo and Johnny get back to their jobs while Billy and Elaine sit back enjoying each other's company. She asks Billy, "What's the real reason you get upset at Rico?"

"I don't get upset at Rico; I get upset at myself. I had every opportunity in the world to win a lot of tournaments and I sold out for the money. I guess I envy him. He's the one that cared enough about his reputation and his pride not to sell out. I'm sure he could have if he wanted to. That's why it hurt me so bad when he humiliated me. I was finally trying to win, and I couldn't."

Starting to work on removing the eight tables in the poolroom couldn't come at a better time. Elaine and Billy hug and kiss and go their separate ways.

For the next few days, Flo and Johnny play pool almost nonstop. When Flo's involved, Johnny and the rest of the gang are on the sidelines cheering her on. The same goes on when Johnny plays. They even manage to play at the same time on more than one occasion. They struggle the first time it happens but after that they feed off each other and when the final day arrives, they are still both undefeated.

Billy and Elaine are also in a feeding frenzy. They can't get enough of each other.

First to play on the final day is Flo and old friend Becky Slater. Flo quickly gives Becky possibly the biggest beating of her career. Johnny passes Flo on his way into the playing area. He offers her congratulations. She gives him a brief kiss on the cheek and offers him words of encouragement to defeat Rico.

Winning with such ease takes a lot less time than that what was anticipated to play Flo's match. The TV people are happy things are running ahead of schedule so they can allow extra time between Johnny and Rico's match. Flo's match ended at 12:20, and Barry comes over the intercom to inform everyone the next match will begin at 12:50. Half an hour can seem like forever when you're waiting to play the biggest match of your life. Johnny gets in a bad habit of looking at the clock while he's not at the table shooting an alternate rack with Rico.

Vultures are swarming down to the reserved seating area to talk to Marie and Billy. They want to bet on Rico to defeat Johnny. Billy has a short conference with his contingency to lay down the ground rules on the betting. He personally puts up thirty thousand dollars to cover bets on the match. He's ahead over twice that amount so far and he's willing to risk half of his winnings that Johnny will win the match. Marie, Mike X., Kerry, and even Charlie agree to do the same thing. When the money available is tallied up, they come up with over fifty thousand dollars. Billy tells them to get busy taking bets on the match, but only take bets from people who have lost money to them betting against Johnny in previous matches. He doesn't want someone sneaking in at the last moment and betting on Rico. The meeting breaks up, and the crew gets to work. Action comes fast and furious. When the dust settles, they have exceeded their agreed on total by two thousand dollars. Billy absorbs the overlay on the betting. As the lights are turned down to begin the introductions, Billy and the rest of the crowd return to their seats.

Elaine takes Billy's hand and squeezes it tightly as Johnny is introduced to the audience. He receives a fine ovation, then sits down while Rico is introduced. Mixed in with a fine ovation are a few boos. Rico takes offense to what's coming from the crowd, and he lets them know he doesn't like being booed. When he walks to the table to lag, he says to the crowd, "The great Rico Sanchez will show you why I'm the best player in the world today. You won't be booing me after I'm through playing." Rico and Johnny set their balls in motion for the lag.

Johnny wins the opening lag and appears to be on cruise control as he runs out the first game. The second rack appears to be his for the taking, but he misses position on the four-ball after his cue-ball travels three rails. He ends up safe behind the six-ball, and it seems to upset him. He kicks and hits the four, but Rico comes to the table with a good look at a shot to make the four-ball. He takes his time and pockets the ball. His position for the next shot is perfect, and he runs out the remaining balls on the table. Mistakes become prevalent by both players in the next two games. Rico misses an open shot at the three-ball in the next game, and Johnny returns the favor in the following game on the six-ball. They start the fifth rack tied at two games apiece and Rico is breaking to begin the game.

More of the same things continue to happen. Rico's cue-ball control on the break is poor, and he scratches in the right-hand side pocket. Johnny comes to the table and receives ball-in-hand from the referee to begin playing the rack. Unfortunately for Johnny, there is a lot of congestion on the table and the best he can do is run up to the three-ball and play safe. Remembering Rico had forewarned him he would jump over balls if Johnny played weak safeties against him, he locks up Rico close to the ball he is using to play safe. Johnny appears in good shape to come back to the table as Rico comes from his seat to the table. The object-ball Rico needs to hit is near the same side rail on the table as the cue-ball. It's a diamond away from the corner pocket. Rico is forced to kick off the opposite back rail and bring the cue-ball off the opposite side rail towards the object-ball. He takes his time and measures out where he wants to hit the first rail. When he's through calculating, he shoots the cue-ball at the spot on the back rail he has picked out. With the vantage point Johnny has, he gets to watch the flight of the cue-ball as it comes off the second rail and heads in the direction of the object-ball. He knows right away Rico is going to make a good hit on the object-ball. What happens after the cue-ball and the object-ball collide makes Rico and his supporters happy about his situation. The three-ball is sent up the remainder of the side rail and into the corner pocket. Johnny's supporters have a different perspective; they groan as Rico raises his cue above his head to celebrate his good fortune. The first big break of the match goes in Rico's favor, and Johnny pays a huge price. The next time he comes to the table, he's trailing by four games and kicking at a ball.

Effectively hitting the two-ball, Johnny leaves the table feeling good about the situation. The cue-ball is at one end of the table and the object-ball is at the other end, near the back rail. Leading by four games and facing a shot clock violation if he takes too much time to shoot, Rico makes a bold decision to cut the two-ball across the back rail and into the corner pocket. Like Johnny had done a couple of times in the past to his opponents, Rico cuts the edge of the two-ball razor thin. It starts on its flight to the pocket. The chanting Billy had come to despise starts as the two-ball drops into the corner pocket. "Rico, Rico" can be heard throughout the room as he takes a short stroll around the table to bask in his own glory. He pounds his chest a few times for good measure to acknowledge his own great shot. If the shot clock wasn't being enforced, this might have lasted longer. Rico calms himself down and goes back to his mission of destroying Johnny. He makes the remainder of the balls on the table to win another game.

Confident he has control of the match, Rico becomes the shooting machine he's capable of being. He dominates play for the remainder of the match and goes on to beat Johnny by a score of eleven games to four. When the match concludes, there is a less than meaningful handshake between Rico and Johnny. Rico's followers are chanting again, and he is playing along with them. He walks around the table a few times with his cue raised above his head. It's another moment of glory for him, and he's playing it to the hilt. Johnny gathers his things and gets out of the playing arena as fast as he can. He feels like a fool.

Elaine and Flo do their best to try to cheer up Johnny, but it's just not happening. Flo suggests that she and Johnny go to the practice room for a while. Johnny likes the idea of getting out of the public eye.

Counseling wasn't part of the deal Billy made with Johnny, but it's part of the learning process in the game of pool. When Billy enters the practice room, he gets exactly what he expects from Johnny. He's angry about the way he performed, and he's at the table whacking balls around without any purpose. Flo's sitting on the sidelines with a look of disgust on her face just watching what Johnny is doing. She tries to leave and let Billy and Johnny talk man to man. Billy tells Flo to sit down because what he has to say might help her some day. Until this moment, Billy had no idea what he would say to Johnny. He tells him to take a break from the table and sit down.

"Losing a pool match may be the most humiliating thing a person has to suffer through in life, especially when the person you lose to is someone you despise. It has a way of making you wish you were dead. But I think I mentioned this before, you're not dead. You're wounded and losing blood at a rapid rate, but you're going to live. The only way to mend your wounds and recover is to get back out there against Earl Strickland and show the world what you are made of. Earl's first loss was five matches ago; he's forgotten he even lost a match. If you go out there with the attitude you have right now, he's going to rip you apart at the seams." The intensity of Billy's voice grows, "Plus I blow the fifty grand I bet with Rico on the match before I came in here, and you lose out on a chance to play him again."

Johnny isn't about to listen to Billy yell at him. He starts screaming at the top of his lungs at Billy. After five minutes of yelling and screaming at each other, Billy and Johnny start laughing at each other. Billy has managed to get Johnny to release the anger. He asks Johnny, "Do you feel better now?" The knot Johnny had in his stomach is gone. He gets out of his seat and comes to the table. He starts to practice in a more productive manner. Billy leaves the practice room feeling better.

Johnny beats Earl with great ease and confidence.

It's Flo's turn. Liz reminds her, in a business way, how much is riding on the match. Flo walks out the door with Johnny. The rest of the crew gives Liz a funny look to let her know she could have let Flo go out the door without hearing what she had to say.

Billy finds Flo alone in the practice room when he arrives. She isn't running around the table as Billy might have thought she would be. Honest Indian Flo can't help spilling her guts to Billy. "I'm considering dumping this match because I can't stand the thought of going across the country and doing a bunch of exhibitions with Rico. Am I wrong thinking that way, Billy?"

"Go ahead! Why not? Maybe we can get some people to bet on you to win."

"That's cheating." After, she says she knows how foolish she sounds, but Billy doesn't remind her. He briefly tells her about what happened to him and how it affected him the rest of his life. Before Flo can say another word to Billy, Johnny comes back in the room. Billy and Flo's conversation is left hanging.

Johnny informs her, "The main arena is open, and you and Kathy are welcome to start practicing."

Dumping a match can be done in a lot of subtle ways, and if Flo is dumping, she's off to a good start. She over-hits the lag, and her ball comes back up table and bounces off the back rail a good ten inches. Kathy easily gets her ball inside of Flo's and wins the right to make the opening break. Kathy fails to pocket a ball on the break, and Flo comes to the table. She's facing a basic shot she has made a living on through the whole tournament, and she jaws the ball in the pocket and it spits back out. Billy gives Flo the benefit out the doubt on the shot because she is trying to draw back down table for position on her next shot. Kathy comes back to the table and starts to pocket the balls. Luckily or unluckily for Flo, Kathy is only able to run up to the six-ball. She manages to miss the seven-ball and leave it hanging in the right-hand corner pocket. Flo has three easy shots to finish the rack, and she does it to take a one game lead.

Flo goes on to win the match and the tournament.

Barry comes over the intercom and says, "Ladies and gentlemen, I give you the new queen of pocket billiards, Miss Flo Stevens." The crowd stands and cheers for Flo as long as time allows. Barry informs the crowd there will be a half-hour break, and the match to decide the king of pocket billiards will start then.

On Billy's way to his seat, he runs into Rico. Rico wants to bet fifty thousand dollars on himself. Billy had just won fifty thousand from Rico on Johnny's last match. After getting infuriated with Rico, Billy asks him, in front of several witnesses. "Why don't we bet the first and second place money on this match? Winner takes all."

Rico can't believe what he has just provoked Billy into saying. "You're fucking crazy! But, you got a fucking bet." He knows he got the best of Billy, and he runs to the arena to get ready to play Johnny. Elaine was tucked in behind some of the other people listening to Billy and Rico argue. She approaches Billy with a look of scorn on her face. She asks why he would do such a thing without consulting Johnny. Billy tells Elaine, "I can't stand the thought of Rico Sanchez walking around with money I had helped raise to better the game of pool. Whether he has two hundred and fifty thousand dollars or seven hundred and fifty thousand, it's still going to kill me. Maybe we can send him home broke this way. If Johnny does lose, I'll make good the money he's suppose to be getting. He shouldn't have to pay for my mistakes," Billy adds, "anymore."

Elaine's satisfied with Billy's explanation. She takes him by the arm and says, "Let's go root for our son. He needs us now more than ever."

Arm in arm, Billy and Elaine walk back to the arena and take their seats. Some small changes Billy wasn't aware of have been made for television purposes. Johnny and Rico are escorted from the arena five minutes before play is scheduled to start. Billy has no idea what's going on, and he really doesn't care. Marie fills him in on all the action she thinks he missed while he was gone. She and the boys booked close to sixty thousand more dollars in bets. She asks Billy if she can count on him for forty thousand. Elaine wants to tell Marie what happened out in the hallway but Billy stops her. He whispers to Elaine, "What's another forty thousand at this point?" He tells Marie to count him in. Billy's next move is to get to Barry and talk to him. He leaves the spectator area and seeks out Barry. He finds him and they have a conversation about changing the referee for the final match. Billy explains to Barry how much he has riding on the match and the fact Rico was able to make a ball on every break when he and Johnny played their first match. He feels the same referee may allow Rico the same comfort zone in his next match.

Barry tells Billy, "I know just the right guy for the job, Bob Harris. Almost every match he refereed, people bitched about making balls on the break."

Billy tells Barry, "I don't want to cheat."

"He racks 'em tight; they just have problems making balls."

"Go get him."

Showmanship is what people have come to expect at major sporting events, and this is provided to them as Johnny comes out with smoke all around him. He's carrying his cue-case on his shoulder. As he starts to be introduced to the crowd, he takes out his cue and puts it together. Rico comes out wearing opposite colors; he also receives a standing ovation from the crowd. The two men briefly shake hands, and the lights return to the room to signify the start of play. They approach the table and lag for break.

Rico wins a close call on the lag, and Mr. Harris fails in his first attempt to stop Rico. He breaks in two balls on the opening break and wastes little time collecting the rest of the rack to win the first game. His break is even better the next game as three balls go in the pockets. Rico faces a cross-side shot on the one-ball and easily sends it across table and into the pocket. Billy sits wondering if Johnny will ever see the table the way Rico is pocketing balls. Johnny makes a brief appearance in the next rack, but it's just to kick at the three-ball. He makes the hit, but it does little to slow Rico down. He's right back at the table, and he runs out the remainder of the rack. As if things can't get any worse, Rico breaks the nine in the next game. The rout appears to be on, and Rico loves every minute of it. The chants start again as Rico readies to break the next rack. He smashes another one and makes another ball. The good news is, he hasn't a good shot to pocket the one-ball. The bad news is, he has a great safety play, and he executes it perfectly. He has shot the one-ball close to the nine-ball on the back rail. The cue-ball is tucked in behind two balls on the same back rail.

When Johnny comes out of his seat, he wishes he weren't at the table. He has thirty seconds to make the biggest play of his pool career, and he doesn't know where to start. He takes an extension and tries to figure out his move. As the clock ticks, he remembers an old trick shot tape he watched where the person used the rail to jump the cue-ball over object-balls. As Mr. Harris counts down the seconds, Johnny lines up and elevates the back of his cue stick. On the count of two seconds, he shoots the cue-ball into the side rail, and it bounces up over the two object-balls he's trying to clear. On one bounce, it strikes the one-ball in mid-air sending it into the nine-ball. The nine-ball goes right into the corner pocket. The suspense builds as the cue-ball rolls along the top of the back rail and appears headed into the pocket. Just before the pocket, it makes a u-turn and comes back on the table. The crowd goes crazy as Johnny pushes the balls on the table forward for the referee to rack them. He pushes his first bead across the wire and breaks his first rack of the match.

The chanting of Johnny's name has started, and he likes the feeling it's giving him. He starts riding the emotional high he's getting, and it's strong enough to push him one game ahead of Rico on the wire before Rico is able to pocket another ball. Johnny has taken control of the match, and his faithful followers are letting him know how much they appreciate his fine play. The noise gets louder after every game he wins. Leading five games to four games, Johnny suffers his first bump in the road in a long time. He breaks and fails to pocket a ball on the break. Rico comes to the table, but it's not to play. He informs the referee he needs a five minute bathroom break and he is granted it by the referee. He places his cue on the table and walks out of the playing arena to the men's room. The crowd sits in silence waiting for his return.

Sitting just to the right of Billy is Flo, and he's dying to know what changed her mind when she was playing Kathy. He leans over and asks her the question whispering it in her ear. At first, Flo tries to deny the allegations, but one look from Billy and she knows she's not fooling him so she comes with the truth. She tells him, "I lost faith in the person who had all the faith in the world in me and holds the spirit of my people. Sitting in my seat, I came to realize it. I didn't have the right to do what I was about to do. If it weren't for Johnny, I wouldn't even be here. I also think, if I lost, he probably would have lost or maybe not given the same effort." Billy tells Flo she did the right thing as Rico makes his return to the playing arena. They both turn their attention back to the match as Rico picks up his cue.

Over five minutes of waiting and the crowd gets to witness the excitement of Rico playing a push-out when he returns to the table. Johnny comes out of his seat and examines the table. Rico has left him safe, and he would have to either kick at the one-ball or play a jump shot. Johnny sees very little reward for playing either shot so he gives it back to Rico. Jumping over balls is something Rico had promised he would do to Johnny if they ever played, and he keeps his word. He goes to the table and executes a perfect jump-shot to pocket the one-ball. The cue-ball draws back down table for position on the two-ball. Two shots later, Johnny is back at the table, but Rico has him locked up with a great safety play. He tries in vain to make a hit on the four-ball and Rico takes ball-in-hand and runs out the remaining balls on the table. The score is tied at five games apiece.

Finally, what Billy had hoped to happen starts to happen. Rico breaks the next rack and fails to pocket a ball. Johnny gets a great shot to start the rack and an added bonus three shots down the road. The four-ball is a half an inch away from the nine-ball which is two inches away from the left-hand side pocket. Johnny is in perfect line to play the shot after making the three-ball, and he easily makes the shot to win the game. Unfortunately for both players, the balls on the break that frequently found pockets earlier are now few and far between. Neither player is able to pull away by more than one game, and the score is knotted after eighteen games, nine to nine. The crowd is busy cheering for their favorite player, and thus far, it has been quite a show. Rico has won the previous game and his supporter's root heartily for him as he comes to the table to break the next rack. All Johnny can do is sit and wait for one more chance.

Elaine and Flo sit with a strangle hold on each of Billy's arms. They come to their feet after Rico has broken to start the next game. It appears he has failed to pocket a ball. That's when the last ball rolling wiggles its way through two balls and drops into the right-hand side pocket. Johnny's supporters groan as they sit back down. Rico's people are happy; they cheer his good fortune, and for good reason. He has a very good-looking rack of balls to negotiate. Wasting little time, Rico gets busy playing the rack. Despite a couple of small position errors, he gets the job done. He pushes his bead across the wire to the roar of support from his fans. He needs one more game, and he has the break to start the next game. He looks over at Billy as he comes to the table. He smiles because he knows he has a huge advantage. He waits for the referee to rack the balls and places the cue-ball on the table. His takes several long strokes of the cue and sends the cue-ball as fast as he can towards the face of the one-ball. His supporters yell and scream as the balls separate and look for places to go. Rico doesn't pocket a ball, but doesn't leave Johnny much to shoot at.

Tension can be felt throughout the room, but Johnny comes to the table like he's about to go for a walk in the park. He places his cue on the table and asks the referee if he can take a five-minute bathroom break. The referee grants his request and off he goes. The silence that was there earlier isn't there now. Every one is busy discussing Johnny's next move at the table. The Monday-morning quarterbacks are in their glory. The buzz continues until Johnny returns from the rest room. He takes his cue in his hand and gets busy trying to figure out what to do. At the ten second warning, he asks for and is granted an extension. He could push-out, but he knows what Rico is capable of doing. He decides to kick in behind the one-ball and play safe. He goes to the table and executes his shot as the referee counts him down to three seconds on the clock. His calculated risk turns out perfect. He sticks the cue-ball behind the seven-ball and the one-ball travels down to the other end of the table.

Rico comes to the table and is blocked by the seven-ball. He's also too close to the seven-ball to take the overland route. He is forced to use the rails and kick at the one-ball. He takes his extension and, when he shoots, he almost duplicates Johnny's effort. He leaves Johnny a very small piece of the one-ball to see and hit. With eight balls to help him, Johnny plays a safe on Rico. Rico comes to the table and tries to counter Johnny's move with one of his own. He makes a good play but not a great one. He leaves Johnny a bank-shot and a good place to duck the cue-ball in case he should miss the shot. Knowing he has insurance in case he doesn't make the bank, Johnny goes for the shot.

Sweet as it can get, the one-ball travels off the bank and splits the right-hand corner pocket. The cue-ball comes to rest in a perfect spot. Johnny has a shot at the two-ball and had he not made the one-ball Rico was going to be left safe. With this kind of confidence in his game, Johnny proceeds to play the rest of the rack flawlessly and tie the score of the match at ten games apiece.

Through a deafening crowd noise, Barry comes over the intercom and tells everyone the obvious. "Ladies and gentlemen, we have a hill, hill match. Billy's rule of winning by two games no longer applies. Good luck to both players."

As the referee racks the balls, Johnny keeps busy. He pushes his bead across the wire, and he also takes a nice big sip of his water. He places the cue-ball down on the table and takes several more deep breaths to help him relax. When he decides he's ready, he moves into place at the table and begins his pre-break routine. Several long practice strokes precede the inevitable; he contacts the cue-ball and sends it on its way. The entire crowd comes to its feet to watch the results.

Snakes sometimes bite the wrong people, and this appears to be one of those times. The rack and result Billy had hoped Rico would receive just jumped up to bite Johnny. All nine balls remain on the table, and the little church mouse that was sitting over in his seat explodes to the table. He just got one of the biggest breaks of his life. He knows Johnny crushed the rack, but he also knows nothing went in. When his heart rate finally settles down, he walks around to check out the rack. Not one ball is touching, and he has at least one pocket to shoot every ball into. The best part for Rico is, he has a perfect shot to start the run-out. After chalking his cue, he easily pockets the one-ball. A short roll forward of the cue-ball gives him a perfect spot to shoot the two-ball into the side pocket. He easily disposes of the two-ball and gets a little out of line to shoot the three-ball. A man of Rico's talents can make adjustments, and after pocketing the three-ball, he's right back in line to play the four-ball.

Elaine leans over and whispers to Billy, "This isn't good, is it?"

"No."

Rico is about to shoot the six-ball when Elaine refocuses on the match. Things get bleaker when the six- and seven-balls leave the table. Two more balls stand in the way of Rico and a lot of money, and he knows it. He has to cut the eight-ball into the side pocket and bring the cue-ball three rails around the table for position on the nine-ball. It's a thin cut to make the eight-ball, and Rico takes a good look at it before he shoots. He gets down, to shoot the shot, and sends the cue-ball in the direction of the eight-ball. True to form, Rico slices the eight thin, and it enters the side pocket. The cue-ball begins its three-rail trip around the table in the direction of the nine-ball.

As it comes off the third rail, Billy turns to Elaine and says quietly, "He hit it too hard." The crowd comes to its feet as the cue-ball inches its way closer to the nine-ball. There's a lot of gasping going on as the cue-ball rolls right up to the side of the nine-ball and freezes to its side. Rico turns several shades of different colors as he realizes what he has done. He examines his situation and sees he has absolutely no chance at pocketing the nine. As the shot clock winds down, he asks for an extension. He has one logical play: safety. He walks to the table and quickly takes a few practice strokes to determine his best play. It looks like he determines a masse of the cue-ball is required, and he takes several quick practice strokes, then he stops. He has another extension he can take because it's the last rack of the set, so he uses it. He backs away and walks to the corner pocket he will hopefully leave the cue-ball near when he plays his safety. He stands above the corner pocket chalking his cue and pondering his future. His extension time is starting to run out, so he moves quickly back to the table and gets ready to shoot. He elevates the back of his cue. After three strokes, Rico drops the tip of his cue on to the cue-ball. The cue-ball moves the nine-ball slightly sideways, then it starts to curve as it goes up table towards the corner pocket. It catches the side rail and appears to have enough speed to reach the pocket and possibly scratch. The crowd comes to its feet and watches as the cue-ball approaches the jaws of the pocket. It looks all but gone, but this is when they find out why Rico had gone and chalked his cue near the pocket. He had left some of the fragments of the chalk there in case he needed them. They prevent his cue-ball from scratching.

There's no mad dash to the table by Johnny. He knows Rico has played a great shot. When he arrives at the table, his first instincts are confirmed. He is facing one of the most difficult shots in the game of pool. The cue-ball is deep in the jaws of the corner pocket, and his first attempt at making a bridge to even shoot the shot has Johnny's hand shaking to a point he has to back off the shot. He takes an extension to try to steady his hand.

Rico sees Johnny is nervous, and he can't keep his big mouth shut. He says to Johnny and everyone else within an ear-shot of his voice, "The great Billy Bates would have trouble making this shot in the prime of his career. How is his puny little nephew, who hasn't won nothing, going to make this shot? Did Billy tell you? He bet the first and second place money on this match."

Johnny looks over at Billy, and he confirms what Rico has just said by nodding. Johnny's time is running out, and he has to go back to the table. As he does, Billy takes Elaine's hand, and the two of them stand up. Billy yells across the room for all to hear, "Our son would make this shot." The rest of the crowd also stands. Rico has the look of a man that just saw a million ghosts pass before his eyes. Johnny goes to the table with newfound confidence. Several strokes of his cue later, he sends the cue-ball in motion towards the nine-ball. The next sound heard tells the story. The nine-ball slaps the back side of the corner pocket as the crowd explodes in celebration of Johnny's effort.

Rico explodes from his seat and grabs his equipment. He runs out of the arena. Elaine thinks back to the very beginning and how Billy sat through his personal torture. She surmises Rico can't take the pain of the bull. Then she turns her focus to her son. He's not as blatant as Rico, but he is enjoying the glory of the matador as he parades around with his cue raised high above his head. His supporters are chanting his name. Johnny takes a quick victory lap around the arena to thank all his supporters as the chanting continues. Billy, Elaine, and Flo make their way through the bedlam down into the arena as Johnny finishes his victory walk. Johnny's not sure who to grab first. The group makes it easy for Johnny. They all grab him at once. It becomes a family celebration. Billy takes Johnny's arm and raises it in the air. It almost becomes a mob scene as the rest of Johnny's close supporters get into the act. Of course, Marie and Cindy are screaming the loudest.

When things settle down, the television people do their interview. Rico is long gone, and Johnny is the lone person interviewed. The announcer asks Johnny, "Is Billy really your father?"

Johnny's, jumping around from the excitement, he explains "We wanted to hold off telling everyone until after the tournament. They felt it may have been a big distraction if people found out earlier."

The announcer says to Johnny, "Billy came out with the truth at a time you seemed to need it the most."

Johnny is still being cheered by his loyal fans, and he raises his cue high in the air to recognize them. He then turns his attention back to the announcer's question. He tells him, just before he raises his cue for the final time, "Rico gave Billy the opening, and Billy's timing was perfect. You might say everything happened, right on cue!"

14911161R00214

Made in the USA
Lexington, KY
27 April 2012